THE SAILCLOTH SHRO

Stuart Rogers leaves Panan
One of them, Baxter, dies of
back to the States, and is buried at sea. Once they dock, the other man, Keefer, is fished out of the bay three days later after having been pistol-whipped to death. He had been seen flashing a lot of money around the night before. But as far as Rogers knew, Keefer was broke. Now the cops want to know where the money came from. They don't believe that Baxter really died at sea. Neither do the goons who pick up Rogers one night to beat the truth out of him. But if Baxter wasn't who he seemed to be, one thing Rogers knows for sure is that he's definitely dead—but who the hell was he?

ALL THE WAY

Marian Forsyth made Harris Chapman the prosperous man he is today. As his private secretary, she advised him on his acquisitions, and turned him into a very wealthy man. She assumed she would become his second wife. But Harris made a foolish mistake: he fell in love with a younger, prettier woman. And now Harris must pay. And to that end, Marian creates a brilliant and detailed plan to steal $175,000 from him. All she needs is someone who sounds enough like Harris that he can become Harris long enough to pull it off. That's where Jerry Forbes comes in—footloose, morally flexible, and completely obsessed with Marian. It's the perfect match.... for the perfect crime.

THE SAILCLOTH SHROUD

ALL THE WAY

CHARLES WILLIAMS

INTRODUCTION BY
NICHOLAS LITCHFIELD

Stark House Press • Eureka California

THE SAILCLOTH SHROUD / ALL THE WAY

Published by Stark House Press
1315 H Street
Eureka, CA 95501
griffinskye3@sbcglobal.net
www.starkhousepress.com

ISBN: 978-1-951473-35-8

Text design by Mark Shepard, shepgraphics.com
Cover design by Jeff Vorzimmer, ¡caliente!design, Austin, Texas
Proofreading by Bill Kelly
Cover art by Stanley Borack

First Stark House Press Edition: August 2021

7
Williams' Tales of Playing Dead and Fool-proof Murder
by Nicholas Litchfield

13
The Sailcloth Shroud
by Charles Williams

119
All the Way
by Charles Williams

240
Charles Williams
Bibliography

WILLIAMS' TALES OF PLAYING DEAD AND FOOL-PROOF MURDER

BY NICHOLAS LITCHFIELD

Distinguished British crime writer Julian Symons regarded Charles Williams (1909-1975) as "one of the best of the post-Chandler American crime-writers." He enjoyed the vigorous writing and lively pace of his novels, considering him as a specialist at action-filled thrillers. Fellow crime writer John D. MacDonald asserted: "No one can make violence seem more real." Other notable writers, such as book critic Anthony Boucher, proclaimed Williams as "just about as good as they come" (Boucher, 1953), deeming him and his Gold Medal contemporaries (John D. MacDonald, Donald Hamilton, and Vin Packer) "serious and substantial authors." These were the pioneers of the paperback mystery novel revolution—"the legitimate heirs to the dead pulps in which Hammett and Chandler flourished" (Boucher, 1964).

Williams is still revered to this day, with popular contemporary authors like Joe R. Lansdale and Ed Gorman singing his praises. Although, to be frank, many of his formidable, highly readable novels, which sold well when first released, have been overlooked for decades. In fact, the second novel in this noteworthy collection from Stark House hasn't been reprinted in English for close to forty years. Undeniably, Charles Williams is an author whose work should be front and center on the display case in any reputable bookstore, and the novels here—two of the author's finest—mark a welcome return to print.

The first tale, *The Sailcloth Shroud* (perhaps the more satisfying of the two novels), initially appeared in condensed form in *Cosmopolitan* magazine in September 1959. It was released in hardback by Viking Press in 1960 and the paperback issued by Dell in March 1961. A movie adaptation, filmed as *The Man Who Would Not Die*, appeared in 1975. Despite a strong cast that included Academy Award-winner Dorothy Malone, the film sank without a trace. The novel, reprinted by Harper Perennial in 1983, also seems to have faded from public consciousness.

Set mostly on land, though party at sea, it is an extraordinarily well-plotted, intensely gripping mystery that's full of explosive bursts of fight and flight drama and inspired plot twists. In contrast to the second novel in this collection, *All the Way*, where the lead protagonist, a besotted trickster, industriously commits fraud and becomes an accessory to murder, the narrator here, charter yacht captain Stuart Rogers, is a principled man, under a cloud of suspicion, who is continually striving to clear his name.

While sailing his newly purchased schooner back from Panama, his tight-lipped deckhand, Wendell Baxter, suffers a heart attack and dies on board. The subsequent burial at sea lands Rogers in very hot water. Although the port authorities clear him of any wrongdoing, his honesty is questioned when shocking revelations surface about the deceased man and Francis Keefer, the no-good merchant seaman Rogers hired in Panama. There is more than a hint that Rogers might have had a hand in Baxter's death and may be trying to cover up the theft of a substantial sum of money.

Breathless action ensues, with the police, the FBI, and hardened criminals hot on the trail of the unfortunate Rogers. As John D. MacDonald rightly noted, the pounding scenes of violence seem all too authentic, and the narrator's credibility is never in doubt. Honest and upright yet discomfited by his handling of his deckhand's watery burial, he feels compelled to play detective, expertly untangling the intriguing mystery surrounding the life and death of the curiously elusive Baxter.

Brilliant plotting, strong characterization, and excellent use of intermittent flashback make this thrilling crime story an absolute corker.

The book justly earned strong critical approval when it first came out. *The Baltimore Sun*, which highly recommended Williams' "skillful thriller" to readers with a taste for hard-edged suspense stories, drew attention to the "vivid descriptions, reasonably believable characters and dialogue, and a fast-moving plot." While insinuating that some plot elements may have been "slightly contrived," it was appreciative of the "carefully and cleverly constructed dénouement" that brought about a satisfying, atypical conclusion (Hyder, 1960). The Associated Press valued the tale's fast pace, its realistic and plausible action, and its "authoritative picture of the sea" (Standard-Speaker, 1960), echoing, practically word-for-word, the sentiments of the *Pottsville Republican* (Pottsville Republican, 1960). Elsewhere, Montreal's *The Gazette*, one of the foremost Canadian dailies, called it first-rate, describing it as "one of those 'up to 4 a.m. to finish' yarns" (Croll, 1960). Britain's major daily, *The Guardian*, considered it a familiar yet polished novel that decanted enlivening incidental information on small-boat sailing into its murky murder story (Iles, 1961).

Williams, who seemingly had a passion for sailing and diving, was a man with comprehensive knowledge of ships and seafaring life. Evidently, he gained invaluable know-how from his ten-year service as a radio operator on U.S. Merchant Marine vessels, as an ordinary seaman, and as a civilian doing radio communications and radar work for the U.S. Navy (Geller, 1955). A negligible criticism leveled at him concerns his excessive use of nautical terminology. Some are of the opinion that the "author's knowledge of small-boat seamanship occasionally becomes a little obtrusive" (Hyder, 1960). Arguably, his persistent use of nautical jargon and seafaring techniques add context and realism, lending authorial credibility and making his maritime stories shimmer with authenticity.

The second story, published as a paperback original by Dell in September 1958, bearing the title *All the Way*, is a tragic tale of obsession and heartache about a manipulative, spurned lover who seeks vengeance on the rich, hellishly handsome man who jilted her for a younger woman. Appealing, resourceful Marian Forsyth was the private secretary and mistress of Harris Chapman, a prosperous businessman in Thomaston in central Louisiana. Her expert business knowledge and sage assessment of the stock market enabled Chapman to acquire a cotton gin, a radio station, and a newspaper, helping launch him as an extremely wealthy entrepreneur. Having fallen in love with Chapman and assuming that they would one day become a happily married couple, she was crushed when he eventually dumped her for a prettier woman. In retaliation, she concocts a brilliant, deadly scheme to destroy Chapman and steal one-hundred and seventy-five thousand dollars in cash and stocks.

It's an intricate, meticulous plan that hinges on her finding someone as cunning, ruthless, and committed to success as Marian herself. Fortunately for her, Jerome Langston Forbes (Jerry), a young, broke drifter with a criminal past, fits the bill ideally. With a voice that is a carbon copy of Chapman's and a fondness for Marian that borders on addiction, he is the essential component to the operation. With coaching and sufficient encouragement, Jerry can execute the perfect crime, and the pair of them get away with it scot-free.

Jolts of violence punctuate Williams' absorbing, measured prose, and the author's consummate ability to breathe life into the central characters make this a truly memorable noir. More than sixty years after its release, the disquieting union between the pitiable, "unreachable" Marian and her besotted conspirator still has the power to shock and affect modern crime fiction connoisseurs.

Sufficiently different from other hardboiled stories of the era, this critically successful novel was adapted into a well-received movie, titled *The 3rd Voice*, released by 20th Century-Fox in 1960. Written and directed by Hubert Cornfield, regarded by *The Los Angeles Times* as having done "commendable work" in both capacities (Warren, 1960), *The Philadelphia Inquirer* thought it creditably directed, "well-acted and nearly always absorbing" (Martin, 1960). *The New York Times* considered it "properly taut, complex and eerily fascinating," despite its "telegraphed and contrived" dénouement (Weiler, 1960).

The ending remains a major talking point. Not just with the movie but the book itself. When it was released in the U.K., under the title *The Concrete Flamingo*, Francis Iles (pseudonym of crime writer Anthony Berkeley Cox) of *The Guardian* praised the "smooth operator" author for providing "a most intricately worked-out and almost fool-proof murder plot" that "holds the reader all the way" (Iles, 1960). His one objection was that Williams conformed to genre conventions, providing a rather inadequate, engineered resolution.

I'd argue that Williams' poignantly tender approach, sensitive handling of his central characters, and redemptive focus on atonement and remorse keep it from seeming conformist. The climax, far from being predictable or ineffective, offers powerful and affecting closure.

British author Andrew Cartmel once remarked: "A more prolific and longer lived Charles Williams would have left us with a greater bounty of superior fiction. But what we have remains invaluable."

From the fast-paced, seagoing opener to the slow-burning, hardboiled gem that follows it, the two exceptional, dissimilar tales contained in this volume are certainly something to treasure. Neither will easily be forgotten.

—May 2021
Rochester, NY

Nicholas Litchfield is the founding editor of the literary magazine *Lowestoft Chronicle*, author of the suspense novel *Swampjack Virus*, and editor of nine literary anthologies. His stories, essays, and book reviews appear in many magazines and newspapers, with work forthcoming in *BULL: Men's Fiction* and *The Virginian-Pilot*. Formerly a book critic for the *Lancashire Post*, syndicated to twenty-five newspapers across the U.K., he now writes for *Publishers Weekly* and regularly contributes to Colorado State University's literary journal *Colorado Review*. You can find him online at nicholaslitchfield.com.

Works cited:
Boucher, Anthony (Jan 5, 1964). "Adventures in Crime." *New York Times*, p.BRA8
Boucher, Anthony (Nov 29, 1953). "Report on Criminals at Large." *New York Times*, p.BR38
Cartmel, Andrew (Aug 7, 2020). "The Lost Classics of One of the 20th Century's Great Hard-Boiled Writers." CrimeReads https://crimereads.com/the-lost-classics-of-one-of-the-20th-centurys-great-hard-boiled-writers/
Croll, Bruce (Feb 6, 1960). "Crime Corner." The Gazette, p.19
Geller, Jonanna May (Nov 6, 1955). "Hi-Jinks On The High Seas." *Daily Press*, p.42
Hyder, William (Jan 24, 1960). "Thriller With A Novel Climax." The Baltimore Sun, p.45
Iles, Francis (Jan 20, 1961). "Criminal records." The Guardian, p.7
Iles, Francis (Mar 25, 1960). "Criminal records." *The Guardian*, p.9
Martin, Mildred (Apr 4, 1960). "At the Stanton: Fiendish Plot of 'Third Voice' Thrills, Chills." *The Philadelphia Inquirer*, p.15
Pottsville Republican (Mar 31, 1960). Pottsville Republican, p.20
Standard-Speaker (April 1, 1960). Standard-Speaker, p.11
Warren, Geoffrey (Jan 28, 1960). "'The Third Voice' Interesting Thriller". *The Los Angeles Times*, p.44
Weiler, A. H. (Mar 7, 1960). "Screen: Intricate Murder in Mexico: 'The Third Voice' Has Premiere at Victoria." http://www.nytimes.com/1960/03/07/archives/screen-intricate-murder-in-mexico-the-third-voice-has-premiere-at.html.

THE SAILCLOTH SHROUD

• • • • • • • • • • • • • • • • • • • •

CHARLES WILLIAMS

CHAPTER ONE

I was up the mainmast of the *Topaz* in a bosun's chair when the police car drove into the yard, around eleven o'clock Saturday morning. The yard doesn't work on Saturdays, so there was no one around except me, and the watchman out at the gate. The car stopped near the end of the pier at which the Topaz was moored, and two men got out. I glanced at them without much interest and went on with my work, hand-sanding the mast from which the old varnish had been removed. They were probably looking for some exuberant type off the shrimp boat, I thought. She was the *Leila M.,* the only other craft in the yard at the moment.

They came on out on the pier in the blazing sunlight, however, and halted opposite the mainmast to look up at me. They wore lightweight suits and soft straw hats, and their shirts were wilted with perspiration.

"Your name Rogers?" one of them asked. He was middle-aged, with a square, florid face and expressionless gray eyes. "Stuart Rogers?"

"That's right," I said. "What can I do for you?"

"Police. We want to talk to you."

"Go ahead."

"You come down."

I shrugged, and shoved the sandpaper into a pocket of my dungarees. Casting off the hitch, I paid out the line and dropped on deck. Dust from the sanding operation was plastered to the sweat on my face and torso. I mopped at it with a handkerchief and got a little of it off. I stepped onto the pier, stuck a cigarette in my mouth, and offered the pack to the two men. They shook their heads.

"My name's Willetts," the older one said. "This is my partner, Joe Ramirez."

Ramirez nodded. He was a young man with rather startling blue eyes in a good-looking Latin face. He appraised the *Topaz* with admiration. "Nice-looking schooner you got there."

"Ketch—" I started to say, but let it go. What was the use getting involved in that? "Thanks. What did you want to see me about?"

"You know a man named Keefer?" Willetts asked.

"Sure." I flicked the lighter and grinned. "Has he made the sneezer again?"

Willetts ignored the question. "How well do you know him?"

"About three weeks' worth," I replied. I nodded toward the ketch. "He helped me sail her up from Panama."

"Describe him."

"He's about thirty-eight. Black hair, blue eyes. Five-ten, maybe; a hundred and sixty to a hundred and seventy pounds. Has a chipped tooth in front. And a tattoo on his right arm. Heart, with a girl's name in it. Doreen, Charlene—one of those. Why?"

It was like pouring information into a hole in the ground. I got nothing back, not even a change of expression.

"When was the last time you saw him?"

"Couple of nights ago, I think."

"You think? Don't you know?"

I was beginning to care very little for his attitude, but I kept it to myself. Barking back at policemen is a sucker's game. "I didn't enter it in the log, if that's what you mean," I said. "But, let's see. This is Saturday—so it must have been Thursday night. Around midnight."

The detectives exchanged glances. "You better come along with us," Willetts said.

"What for?"

"Verify an identification, for one thing—"

"Identification?"

"Harbor Patrol fished a stiff out from under Pier Seven this morning. We think it may be your friend Keefer, but we haven't got much to go on."

I stared at him. "You mean he's drowned?"

"No," he said curtly. "Somebody killed him."

"Oh," I said. Beyond the boatyard the surface of the bay burned like molten glass in the sun, unbroken except for the bow wave of a loaded tanker headed seaward from one of the refineries above. Keefer was no prize, God knows, and I hadn't particularly liked him, but— It was hard to sort out.

"Let's go," Willetts said. "You want to change clothes?"

"Yeah." I flipped the cigarette outward into the water and stepped back aboard. The detectives followed me below. They stood watching while I took a change of clothing and a towel from the drawer under one of the bunks in the after cabin. When I started back up the companionway, Willetts asked, "Haven't you got a bathroom on here?"

"No water aboard at the moment," I replied. "I use the yard washroom."

"Oh." They went back on deck and accompanied me up the pier in the muggy Gulf Coast heat. "We'll wait for you in the car," Willetts said. The washroom was in a small building attached to one end of the machine shop, off to the right and beyond the marine ways. I stripped and showered. Could it be Keefer they were talking about? He was a drunk, and could have been rolled, but why killed and thrown in the bay? And by this time he couldn't have had more than a few dollars, anyway. The chances were it wasn't Keefer at all.

I toweled myself and dressed in faded washable slacks, sneakers, and a short-sleeved white shirt. After slipping the watch back on my wrist, I transferred wallet, cigarettes, and lighter, took the dungarees aboard the *Topaz,* and snapped the padlock on the companion hatch.

Ramirez drove. The old watchman looked up curiously from his magazine as we went out the gate. Willetts hitched around on the front seat. "You picked up this guy Keefer in Panama, is that it?"

I lighted a cigarette and nodded. "He'd missed his ship in Cristobal, and wanted a ride back to the States."

"Why didn't he fly back?"

"He was broke."

"What?"

"He didn't have plane fare."

"How much did you pay him?"

"Hundred dollars. Why?"

Willetts made no reply. The car shot across the railroad tracks and into the warehouse and industrial district bordering the waterfront.

"I don't get it," I said. "Wasn't there any identification on this body you found in the bay?"

"No."

"Then what makes you think it might be Keefer?"

"Couple of things," Willetts said shortly. "Was this his home port?"

"I don't think so," I said. "He told me he shipped out of Philadelphia."

"What else you know about him?"

"He's an A.B. His full name is Francis L. Keefer, but he was usually known as Blackie. Apparently something of a live-it-up type. Said he'd been in trouble with the union before, for missing ships. This time he was on an inter-coastal freighter, bound for San Pedro. Went ashore in Cristobal, got a heat on, and wound up in jail over in the Panamanian side, in Colon. The ship sailed without him."

"So he asked you for a job?"

"That's right."

"Kind of funny, wasn't it? I mean, merchant seamen don't usually ship out on puddle-jumpers like yours, do they?"

"No, but I don't think you get the picture. He was stranded. Flat broke. He had the clothes he was wearing, and the whisky shakes, and that was about it. I had to advance him twenty dollars to buy some dungarees and gear for the trip."

"And there were just the three of you? You and Keefer, and this other guy, that died at sea? What was his name?"

"Baxter," I said.

"Was he a merchant seaman too?"

"No. He was an office worker of some kind. Accountant, I think—though that's just a guess."

"Hell, didn't he say what he did?"

"He didn't talk much. As a matter of fact, he was twice the seamen Keefer was, but I don't think he'd ever been a pro."

"Did you and Keefer have any trouble?"

"No."

The pale eyes fixed on my face, as expressionless as marbles. "None at all? From the newspaper story, it was a pretty rugged trip."

"It was no picnic," I said.

"You didn't have a fight, or anything?"

"No. Oh, I chewed him out for splitting the mains'l, but you'd hardly call it a fight. He had it coming, and knew it."

The car paused briefly for a traffic light, and turned, weaving through the downtown traffic. "What's this about a sail?"

"It's technical. Just say he goofed, and wrecked it. It was right after Baxter died, and I was jumpy anyway, so I barked at him."

"You haven't kept in touch with him since you got in?"

"No. I haven't seen him since I paid him off, except for that few minutes night before last."

The car slowed, and turned down a ramp into a cavernous basement garage in which several patrol cars and an ambulance were parked. We slid into a numbered stall and got out. Across the garage was an elevator, and to the left of it a dingy corridor. Willetts led the way down the corridor to a doorway on the right.

Inside was a bleak room of concrete and calcimine and unshaded light. On either side were the vaults that were the grisly filing cabinets of a city's unclaimed and anonymous dead, and at the far end a stairway led up to the floor above. Near the stairway were two or three enameled metal tables on casters, and a desk at which sat an old man in a white coat. He got up and came toward us, carrying a clip board.

"Four," Willetts said.

The old man pulled the drawer out on its rollers. The body was covered with a sheet. Ramirez took a corner of it in his hand, and glanced at me. "If you had any breakfast, better hang onto it."

He pulled it back. In spite of myself, I sucked in my breath, the sound just audible in the stillness. He wasn't pretty. I fought the revulsion inside me, and forced myself to look again. It was Blackie, all right; there was little doubt of it, in spite of the wreckage of his face. There was no blood, of course—it had long since been washed away by the water—but the absence of it did nothing to lessen the horror of the beating he had taken before he died.

"Well?" Willetts asked in his flat, unemotional voice. "That Keefer?"

I nodded. "How about the tattoo?"

Ramirez pulled the sheet back farther, exposing the nude body. On one forearm was the blue outline of a valentine heart with the name Darlene written slantingly across it in red script. That settled it. I turned away, remembering a heaving deck and wind-hurled rain, and holding Keefer by the front of his sodden shirt while I cursed him. I'm sorry, Blackie. I wish I hadn't.

"There's no doubt of it?" Willetts asked. "That's the guy you brought up from Panama?"

"No doubt at all," I replied. "It's Keefer."

"Okay. Let's go upstairs."

The room was on the third floor, an airless cubicle with one dirty window looking out over the sun-blasted gravel roof of an adjoining building. The only furnishings were some steel lockers, a table scarred with old cigarette burns, and several straight-backed chairs.

Willetts nodded to Ramirez. "Joe, tell the lieutenant we're here."

Ramirez went out. Willetts dropped his hat on the table, took off his coat, and loosened the collar of his shirt. After removing a pack of cigarettes from the coat, he draped it across the back of one of the chairs. "Sit down."

I sat down at the table. The room was stifling, and I could feel sweat beading my face. I wished I could stop seeing Keefer. "Why in the name of God did they beat him that way? Is that what actually killed him?"

Willetts popped a match with his thumbnail, and exhaled smoke. "He was pistol-whipped. And killed by a blow on the back of his head. But suppose we ask the questions, huh? And don't try to hold out on me, Rogers; we can make you wish you'd never been born."

I felt a quick ruffling of anger, but kept it under control. "Why the hell would I hold out on you? If there's any way I can help, I'll be glad to. What do you want to know?"

"Who you are, to begin with. What you're doing here. And how you happened to be sailing that boat up from Panama."

"I bought her in the Canal Zone," I said. I took out my wallet and flipped identification onto the table—Florida driver's license, FCC license verification card, and memberships in a Miami Beach sportsman's club and the Miami Chamber of Commerce. Willetts made a note of the address. "I own the schooner *Orion*. She berths at the City Yacht Basin in Miami, and makes charter cruises through the Bahamas—"

"So why'd you buy another one?"

"I'm trying to tell you, if you'll give me a chance. Summer's the slow season, from now till the end of October, and the *Orion's* tied up. I heard about this deal on the *Topaz,* through a yacht broker who's a friend of mine. Some oil-rich kids from Oklahoma bought her a couple of months ago and took off for Tahiti without bothering to find out if they could sail a boat across Biscayne Bay. With a little luck, they managed to get as far as the Canal, but they'd had a belly-full of glamour and romance and being seasick twenty-four hours a day, so they left her there and flew back. I was familiar with her, and knew she'd bring twice the asking price back in the States, so I made arrangements with the bank for a loan, hopped the next Pan American flight down there, and looked her over and bought her."

"Why'd you bring her over here, instead of Florida?"

"Better chance of a quick sale. Miami's always flooded with boats."

"And you hired Keefer, and this man Baxter, to help you?"

"That's right. She's a little too much boat for single-handed operation, and sailing alone's just a stunt, anyway. But four days out of Cristobal, Baxter died of a heart attack—"

"I read the story in the paper," Willetts said. He sat down and leaned his forearms on the table. "All right, let's get to Keefer. And what I want to know is where he got all his money."

I looked at him. "Money? He didn't—"

"I know, I know!" Willetts cut me off. "That's what you keep telling me. You picked him up off the beach in Panama with his tail hanging out. He didn't have a nickel, no luggage, and no clothes except the ones he was wearing. And all you paid him was a hundred dollars. Right?"

"Yes."

Willetts gestured with his cigarette. "Well, you better look again. We happen to know that when he came ashore off that boat he had somewhere between three and four thousand dollars."

"Not a chance. We must be talking about two different people."

"Listen, Rogers. When they pulled Keefer out of the bay, he was wearing a new suit that cost a hundred and seventy-five dollars. For the past four days he's been driving a rented Thunderbird, and living at the Warwick Hotel, which is no skid-row flop, believe me. And he's still the richest stiff in the icebox. They're holding an envelope for him in the Warwick safe with twenty-eight hundred dollars in it. Now you tell me."

CHAPTER TWO

I shook my head in bewilderment. "I don't get it. Are you sure about all this?"

"Of course we're sure. Where you think we first got a lead on the identification? We got a body, with no name. Traffic's got a wrinkled Thunderbird with rental plates somebody walked off and abandoned after laying a block on a fire hydrant with it, and a complaint sworn out by the Willard Rental Agency. The Willard manager's got a description, and a local address at the Warwick Hotel, and a name. Only this Francis Keefer they're all trying to locate hasn't been in his room since Thursday, and he sounds a lot like the stiff we're trying to identify. He'd been tossing big tips around the Warwick, and told one of the bellhops he'd just sailed up from Panama in a private yacht, so then somebody remembered the story in Wednesday's *Telegram*. So we look you up, among other things, and you give us this song and dance that Keefer was just a merchant seaman, and broke. Now. Keefer lied to you, or you're trying to con me. And if you are, God help you."

The whole thing was crazy. "Why the hell would I lie about it?" I asked. "And I tell you he was a seaman. Look, weren't his papers in his gear at the hotel?"

"No. Just some new luggage, and new clothes. If he had any papers, they must have been on him when he was killed, and ditched along with the rest of his identification. We know he had a Pennsylvania driver's license. That's being checked out now. But let's get back to the money."

"Well, maybe he had a savings account somewhere. I'll admit it doesn't sound much like Keefer—"

"No. Listen. You docked here Monday afternoon. Tuesday morning you were both tied up in the US marshal's office on that Baxter business. So it was Tuesday afternoon before you paid Keefer off. What time did he finally leave the boat?"

"Three p.m. Maybe a little later."

"Well, there you are. If he sent somewhere for that much money, it'd have to come through a bank. And they were closed by then. But when he checked in at the Warwick, a little after four, he had the money with him. In cash."

"It throws me," I said. "I don't know where he could have got it. But I do know he was a seaman. You can verify that with the US marshal's office and the Coast Guard. He had to witness the log entries and sign the affidavits, so they've got a record of his papers."

"We're checking that," Willetts cut in brusquely. "Look—could he have had that money on the boat all the time without you knowing it?"

"Of course."

"How? It's not a very big boat, and you were out there over two weeks."

"Well, naturally I didn't prowl through his personal gear. It could have been in the drawer under his bunk. But I still say he didn't have it. I got to know him pretty well, and I don't think he had any money at all."

"Why?"

"Two reasons, at least. If he hadn't been on his uppers, he wouldn't even have considered working his way back to the States on a forty-foot ketch. Keefer was no small-boat man. He knew nothing about sail, and cared less. His idea of going to sea was eighteen knots, fresh-water showers, and overtime. So if he'd had any money he'd have bought a plane ticket—except that he'd have gone on another binge and spent it. When I met him, he didn't have the price of a drink. And he needed one."

"All right. So he left Panama flat broke, and got here with four thousand dollars. I can see I'm in the wrong racket. How much money did you have aboard?"

"About six hundred."

"Then he must have clouted it from Baxter."

I shook my head. "When Baxter died, I made an inventory of his personal effects, and entered it in the log. He had about a hundred and seventy dollars in his wallet. The marshal's office has it, along with the rest of his gear, to be turned over to his next of kin."

"Maybe Keefer beat you to it."

"Baxter couldn't have had that kind of money; it's out of the question. He was about as schooner-rigged as Keefer."

"Schooner-rigged?"

"Short of clothes and luggage. He didn't talk about it, any more than he did anything else, but you could see he was down on his luck. And he was sailing up because he wanted to save the plane fare. But why is the money so important, even if we don't know where Keefer got it? What's it got to do with his being butchered and dumped in the bay?"

Before Willetts could reply, Ramirez appeared in the doorway. He motioned, and Willetts got up and went out. I could hear the murmur of their voices in the hall. I walked over to the window. A fly was buzzing with futile monotony against one of the dirty panes, and heat shimmered above the gravel of the roof next door. They seemed to know what they were talking about, so it must be true. And if you knew Keefer, it was in character—the big splash, the free-wheeling binge, even the wrecked Thunderbird—a thirty-eight-year-old adolescent with an unexpected fortune. But where had he got it? That was as baffling as the senseless brutality with which he'd been killed.

The two detectives came back and motioned for me to sit down. "All right," Willetts said. "You saw him Thursday night. Where was this, and when?"

"Waterfront beer joint called the Domino," I said. "It's not far from the boatyard, up a couple of blocks and across the tracks. I think the time was around eleven-thirty. I'd been uptown to a movie, and was coming back to the yard. I stopped in for a beer before I went aboard. Keefer was there, with some girl he'd picked up."

"Was there anybody with him besides the girl?"

"No."

"Tell us just what happened."

"The place was fairly crowded, but I found a stool at the bar. Just as I got my beer I looked around, and saw Keefer and the girl in a booth behind me. I walked over and spoke to him. He was pretty drunk, and the girl was about half-crocked herself, and they were arguing."

"What was her name?"

"He didn't introduce us. I just stayed for a moment and went back to the bar."

"Describe her."

"Brassy type. Thin blonde, in her early twenties. Dangly earrings, plucked eyebrows, too much mascara. I think she said she was a cashier in a restaurant. The bartender seemed to know her."

"Did they leave first, or did you?"

"She left, alone. About ten minutes later. I don't know what they were fighting about, but all of a sudden she got up, bawled him out, and left. Keefer came over to the bar then. He seemed to be relieved to get rid of her. We talked for a while. I asked him if he'd registered at the hiring hall for a job yet, and he said he had but shipping was slow. He wanted to know if I'd had any offers for the *Topaz,* and when I thought the yard would be finished with her."

"Was he flashing money around?"

"Not unless it was before I got there. While we were sitting at the bar he ordered a round of drinks, but I wouldn't let him pay, thinking he was about broke. When we finished them, he wanted to order more, but he'd had way too much. I tried to get him to eat something, but didn't have much luck. This place is a sort of longshoremen's hangout, and in the rear of it there's a small lunch counter. I took him back and ordered him a hamburger and a cup of black coffee. He did drink the coffee—"

"Hold it a minute," Willetts broke in. "Did he eat any of the hamburger at all?"

"About two bites. Why?"

They looked at each other, ignoring me. Ramirez turned to go out, but Willetts shook his head. "Wait a minute, Joe. Let's get the rest of this story first, and you can ask the lieutenant for some help in checking it out."

He turned back to me. "Did you and Keefer leave the bar together?"

"No. He left first. Right after he drank the coffee. He was weaving pretty badly, and I was afraid he'd pass out somewhere, so I tried to get him to let me call a cab to take him back to wherever he was staying, but he didn't want one. When I insisted, he started to get nasty. Said he didn't need any frilling nurse; he was holding his liquor when I was in diapers. He staggered on out. I finished my beer, and left about ten minutes later. I didn't see him anywhere on the street."

"Did anybody follow him out?"

"No-o. Not that I noticed."

"And that would have been just a little before twelve?"

I thought about it. "Yes. As a matter of fact, the four-to-midnight watchman had just been relieved when I came in the gate at the boatyard, and was still there, talking to the other one."

"And they saw you, I suppose?"

"Sure. They checked me in."

"Did you go out again that night?"

I shook my head. "Not till about six-thirty the next morning, for breakfast."

Willetts turned to Ramirez. "Okay, Joe." The latter went out. "There's no way in and out of the yard except past the watchman?" Willetts asked.

"I don't think so," I replied.

Ramirez came back, carrying a sheet of paper. He handed it to Willetts. "That checks, all right."

Willetts glanced at it thoughtfully and nodded. He spoke to me. "That boat locked?"

"Yes," I said. "Why?"

"Give Joe the key. We want to look it over."

I stared at him coldly. "What for?"

"This is a murder investigation, friend. But if you insist, we'll get a warrant. And lock you up till we finish checking your story. Do it easy, do it hard—it's up to you."

I shrugged, and handed over the key. Ramirez nodded, pleasantly, nullifying some of the harshness of Willetts' manner. He went out. Willetts studied the paper again, drumming his fingers on the table. Then he refolded it. "Your story seems to tie in okay with this."

"What's that?" I asked.

"The autopsy report. I mean those two bites of hamburger he ate. It's always hard to place the time of death this long afterward, especially if the body's been in the water, so about all they had to go on was what was in his stomach. And that's no help if you can't find out when he ate last. But if that counterman at the Domino backs you up, we can peg it pretty well. Keefer was killed sometime between two and three a.m."

"It couldn't have been much later than that," I said. "They couldn't dump him off a pier in broad daylight, and it's dawn before five o'clock."

"There's no telling where he was thrown in," Willetts said. "It was around seven-thirty this morning when they found him, so he'd have been in the water over twenty-four hours."

I nodded. "With four changes of tide. As a matter of fact, you were probably lucky he came to the surface this soon."

"Propellers, the Harbor Patrol said. Some tugs were docking a ship at Pier Seven and washed him to the surface and somebody saw him and called them."

"Where did they find the car?"

"The three-hundred block on Armory. That's a good mile from the waterfront, and about the same distance from the area that beer joint's in. A patrol car spotted it at one-twenty-five Thursday morning. That'd be about an hour and a half after he left the joint, but there wasn't anybody in sight, so they don't know what time it happened. Could have been within a few minutes after you saw him. The car'd jumped the curb, sideswiped a fireplug, pulled back into the street again, and gone on another fifty yards before it jammed over against the curb once more and stopped. Might have been just a drunken accident, but I don't quite buy it. I think he was forced to the curb by another car."

"Teen-age hoodlums, maybe?"

Willetts shook his head. "Not that time of morning. Any ducktails blasting around in hot-rods after midnight get a fast shuffle around here. And there wasn't a mark on his hands; he didn't hit anybody. That sounds like professional muscle to me."

"But why would they kill him?"

"You tell me." Willetts stood up and reached for his hat "Let's go in the office. Lieutenant Boyd wants to see you after a while."

We went down the corridor to a doorway at the far end. Inside was a long room containing several desks and a battery of steel filing cabinets. The floor was of battered brown linoleum held down by strips of brass. Most of the rear wall was taken up with a duty roster and two bulletin boards festooned with typewritten notices and circulars. A pair of half-open windows on the right looked out over the street. At the far end of the room a frosted glass door apparently led to an inner office. One man in shirtsleeves was typing a report at a desk; he glanced up incuriously and went on with his work. Traffic noise filtered up from the street to mingle with the lifeless air and its stale smells of old dust and cigar smoke and sweaty authority accumulated over the years and a thousand past investigations. Willetts nodded to a chair before one of the vacant desks. I sat down, wondering impatiently how much longer it was going to take. I had plenty to do aboard the *Topaz*. Then I thought guiltily of Keefer's savagely mutilated face down there under the sheet. *You're* griping about your troubles?

Willetts lowered his bulk into a chair behind the desk, took some papers from a drawer, and studied them for a moment. "Did Keefer and Baxter know each other?" he asked. "I mean, before they shipped out with you?"

"No," I said.

"You sure of that?"

"I introduced them. So far as I know, they'd never seen each other before."

"Which one did you hire first?"

"Keefer. I didn't even meet Baxter until the night before we sailed. But what's that got to do with Keefer's being killed?"

"I don't know." Willetts returned to his study of the papers on his desk. Somewhere in the city a whistle sounded. It was noon. I lighted another cigarette, and resigned myself to waiting. Two detectives came in with a young girl who was crying. I could hear them questioning her at the other end of the room.

Willetts shoved the papers aside and leaned back in his chair. "I still don't get this deal you couldn't make it ashore with Baxter's body. You were only four days out of the Canal."

I sighed. Here was another Monday-morning quarterback. It wasn't enough to have the Coast Guard looking down your throat; you had to be second-guessed by jokers who wouldn't know a starboard tack from a reef point. It was simple, actually; all you had to be was a navigator, seaman, cardiologist, sailmaker, embalmer, and a magician's mate first class who could pull a breeze out of his hat. Then I realized, for perhaps the twentieth time, that I was being too defensive and antagonistic about it. The memory rankled because I was constitutionally unable to bear the sensation of helplessness. And I had been helpless.

"The whole thing's a matter of record," I said wearily. "There was a hearing—" I broke off as the phone rang on an adjoining desk. Willetts reached for it.

"Homicide, Willetts.... Yeah.... Nothing at all?... Yeah.... Yeah...." The conversation went on for two or three minutes. Then Willetts said, “Okay, Joe. You might as well come on in.”

He replaced the instrument, and swung back to me. “Before I forget it, the yard watchman’s got your key. Let’s go in and see Lieutenant Boyd.”

The room beyond the frosted glass door was smaller, and contained a single desk. The shirtsleeved man behind it was in his middle thirties, with massive shoulders, an air of tough assurance, and probing gray eyes that were neither friendly nor unfriendly.

“This is Rogers,” Willetts said.

Boyd stood up and held out his hand. “I’ve read about you,” he said briefly.

We sat down. Boyd lighted a cigarette and spoke to Willetts. “You come up with anything yet?”

“Positive identification by Rogers and the manager of the car-rental place. Also that bellhop from the Warwick. So Keefer’s all one man. But nobody’s got any idea where he found all that money. Rogers swears he couldn’t have had it when he left Panama.” He went on, repeating all I’d told him.

When he had finished, Boyd asked, “How does his story check out?”

“Seems to be okay. We haven’t located the girl yet, but the night bartender in that joint knows her, and remembers the three of ’em. He’s certain Keefer left there about the time Rogers gave us; says Keefer got pretty foul-mouthed about not wanting the taxi Rogers was going to call, so he told him to shut up or get out. The watchman at the boatyard says Rogers was back there at five minutes past twelve, and didn’t go out again. That piece of hamburger jibes with the autopsy report, and puts the time he was killed between two and three in the morning.”

Boyd nodded. “And you think Keefer had the Thunderbird parked outside the joint then?”

“Looks that way,” Willetts conceded.

“It would make sense, so Rogers must be leveling about the money. Keefer didn’t want him to see the car and start getting curious. Anything on the boat?”

“No. Joe says it’s clean. No gun, no money, nothing. Doesn’t prove anything, necessarily.”

“No. But we’ve got nothing to hold Rogers for.”

“How about till we can check him out with Miami? And get a report back from the Bureau on Keefer’s prints?”

“No,” Boyd said crisply.

Willitts savagely stubbed out his cigarette. “But, damn it, Jim, something stinks in this whole deal—”

"Save it! You can't book a smell."

"Take a look at it!" Willetts protested. "Three men leave Panama in a boat with about eight hundred dollars between 'em. One disappears in the middle of the ocean, and another one comes ashore with four thousand dollars, and four days later *he's* dead—"

"Hold it!" I said. "If you're accusing me of something, let's hear what it is. Nobody's 'disappeared,' as you call it. Baxter died of a heart attack. There was a hearing, with a doctor present, and it's been settled—"

"On your evidence. And one witness, who's just been murdered."

"Cut it out!" the lieutenant barked. He jerked an impatient hand at Willetts. "For Christ's sake, we've got no jurisdiction in the Caribbean Sea. Baxter's death was investigated by the proper authorities, and if they're satisfied, I am. And when I am, *you* are. Now get somebody to run Rogers back to his boat. If we need him again, we can pick him up."

I stood up. "Thanks," I said. "I'll be around for another week, at least. Maybe two."

"Right," Boyd said. The telephone rang on his desk, and he cut short the gesture of dismissal to reach for it. We went out, and started across the outer office. Just before we reached the corridor, we were halted by the lieutenant's voice behind us. "Wait a minute! Hold everything!"

We turned. Boyd had his head out the door of his office. "Bring Rogers back here a minute." We went back. Boyd was on the telephone. "Yeah.... He's still here.... In the office.... Right."

He replaced the instrument, and nodded to me. "You might as well park it again. That was the FBI."

I looked at him, puzzled. "What do they want?"

"You mean they ever tell anybody? They just said to hold you till they could get a man over here."

CHAPTER THREE

At least, I thought morosely as we stepped from the elevator, the Federal Building was air-conditioned. If you were going to spend the rest of your life being questioned about Keefer by all the law-enforcement agencies in the country, it helped a little if you were comfortable. Not that I had anything against heat as such; I liked hot countries, provided they were far enough away from civilization to do away with the wearing of shirts that did nothing but stick to you like some sort of soggy film. The whole day was shot to hell now, but this was an improvement over the police station.

I glanced sidewise in grudging admiration at Special Agent Soames—

cool, efficient, and faultlessly pressed. Sweat would never be any problem to this guy; if it bothered him he'd turn it off. In the ten minutes since I'd met him in Lieutenant Boyd's office, I'd learned exactly nothing about why they wanted to talk to me. I'd asked, when we were out on the street, and had been issued a friendly smile and one politely affable assurance that it was merely routine. We'd discuss it over in the office. Soames was thirty-ish and crew-cut, but anything boyish and ingenuous about him was strictly superficial; he had a cool and very deadly eye. We went down the corridor, with my crepe soles squeaking on waxed tile. Soames opened a frosted glass door and stood aside for me to enter. Inside was a small anteroom. A trim gray-haired woman in a linen suit was typing energetically at a desk that held a telephone and a switchbox for routing calls. Behind her was the closed door to an inner office, and to the left I could see down a hallway past a number of other doors. Soames looked at his watch and wrote something in the book that was on a small desk near the door. Then he nodded politely, and said, "This way, please."

I followed him down the hallway to the last door. The office inside was small, spotlessly neat, and cool, with light green walls, marbled gray linoleum, and one window, across which were tilted the white slats of a Venetian blind. There was a single desk, with a swivel chair in back of it. An armchair stood before it, near one corner, facing the light from the window. Soames nodded toward it, and held out cigarettes. "Sit down, please. I'll be right back."

I fired up the cigarette. As I dropped the lighter back in my pocket, I said curiously, "I don't get this. Why is the FBI interested in Keefer?"

"Keefer?" Soames had started out; he paused in the doorway. "Oh, that's a local police matter."

I stared blankly after him. If they weren't interested in Keefer, what *did* they want to know? Soames returned in moment carrying a Manila folder. He sat down and began emptying it of its contents: the log I had kept of the trip, the signed and notarized statement regarding Baxter's death and the inventory of his personal effects.

He glanced up briefly. "I suppose you're familiar with all this?"

"Yes, of course," I said. "But how'd it get over here? And just what is it you want?"

"We're interested in Wendell Baxter." Soames slid the notarized statement out of the pile, and studied it thoughtfully. "I haven't had much chance to digest this, or your log, so I'd like to check the facts with you just briefly, if you don't mind."

"Not at all," I replied. "But I thought the whole thing was closed. The marshal's office—"

"Oh, yes," Soames assured me. "It's just that they've run into a little difficulty in locating Baxter's next of kin, and they've asked us to help."

"I see."

He went on crisply. "You're owner and captain of the forty-foot ketch *Topaz,* which you bought in Cristobal, Panama Canal Zone, on May twenty-seven of this year, through Joseph Hillyer, Miami yacht broker who represented the sellers. That's correct?"

"Right."

"You sailed from Cristobal on June one, at ten-twenty a.m., bound for this port, accompanied by two other men you engaged as deckhands for the trip. One was Francis L. Keefer, a merchant seaman, possessing valid A.B. and Lifeboat certificates as per indicated numbers, American national, born in Buffalo, New York, September twelve, nineteen-twenty. The other was Wendell Baxter, occupation or profession unspecified but believed to be of a clerical nature, not possessed of seaman's papers of any kind but obviously familiar with the sea and well versed in the handling of small sailing craft such as yachts, home address San Francisco, California. Four days out of Cristobal, on June five, Baxter collapsed on deck at approximately three-thirty p.m. while trimming a jib sheet, and died about twenty minutes later. There was nothing you could do to help him, of course. You could find no medicine in his suitcase, the boat's medicine chest contained nothing but the usual first-aid supplies, and you were several hundred miles from the nearest doctor."

"That's right," I said. "If I never feel that helpless again, it'll be all right with me."

Soames nodded. "Your position at the time was 16.10 North, 81.40 West, some four hundred miles from the Canal, and approximately a hundred miles off the coast of Honduras. It was obvious you were at least another six days from the nearest Stateside port, so you put about immediately to return to the Canal Zone with his body, but in three days you saw you were never going to get there in time. That's essentially it?"

"In three days we made eighty-five miles," I said. "And the temperature down there in the cabin where his body was ran around ninety degrees."

"You couldn't have gone into some port in Honduras?"

I gestured impatiently. "This has all been threshed out with the Coast Guard. I could have tried for some port on the mainland of Honduras or Nicaragua, or gone on to Georgetown, Grand Cayman, which was less than two hundred miles to the north of us—except that I wasn't cleared for any of those places. Baxter was already dead, so it's doubtful the port authorities would have considered it a legitimate emergency. And just to come plowing in unauthorized, with no bill of health or anything, carrying the body of a man who'd died at sea of some unspecified ailment—we'd have been slapped in quarantine and tied up in red tape till we had beards down to our knees. Besides being fined. The only thing to do was go back."

"And you had nothing but bad luck, right from the beginning?"

"Look," I said hotly, "we tried. We tried till we couldn't stand it any longer. Believe me, I didn't want the responsibility of burying him at sea. In the first place, it wasn't going to be pleasant facing his family. And if we couldn't bring the body ashore for an autopsy, there'd have to be a hearing of some kind to find out what he died of. There's nothing new about burial at sea, of course, especially in the old days when ships were a lot slower than they are now, but a merchant or naval vessel with thirty to several hundred people aboard is—well, a form of community itself, with somebody in authority and dozens of witnesses. Three men alone in a small boat would be something else. When only two come back, you're going to have to have a little better explanation than just saying Bill dropped dead and we threw him overboard. That's the reason for all that detailed report on the symptoms of the attack. I wrote it out as soon as I saw we were probably going to have to do it."

Soames nodded. "It's quite thorough. Apparently the doctor who reviewed it had no difficulty in diagnosing the seizure as definitely some form of heart attack, and probably a coronary thrombosis. I wonder if you'd fill me in just briefly on what happened after you started back?"

"To begin with," I said, "we tore the mains'l all to hell. The weather had turned unsettled that morning, even before Baxter had the attack. Just before dusk I could see a squall making up to the eastward. It looked a little dirty, but I didn't want to shorten down any more than we had to considering the circumstances. So we left everything on and just turned in a couple of reefs in the main and mizzen. Or started to. We were finishing the main when it began to kick up a little and the rain hit us. I ran back to the wheel to keep her into the wind, while Keefer tied in the last few points and started to raise sail again. I suppose it's my fault for not checking, but I'd glanced off toward the squall line and when I looked back at the mains'l it was too late. He had the halyard taut and was throwing it on the winch. I yelled for him to slack off, but with all the rain he didn't hear me. What had happened was that he'd mixed up a pair of reef points—tied one from the second row to another on the opposite side in the third set. That pulls the sail out of shape and puts all the strain in one place. It was just a miracle it hadn't let go already. I screamed at him again, and he finally heard me this time and looked around, but all he did was shake his head that he couldn't understand what I was saying. Just as I jumped from behind the wheel and started to run forward he slipped the handle into the winch and took a turn, and that was the ball game. It split all the way across.

"We didn't have another one aboard. The previous owners had pretty well butched up the sail inventory on the way down to the Canal—blew out a mains'l and lost the genoa overboard. I managed to patch up this one after a fashion, using material out of an old stays'l, but it took two days. Maybe it wouldn't have made much difference anyway, because the weather went completely sour—dead calm about half the time, with occasional light airs that hauled all around the compass. But with just that handkerchief of a mizzen, and stays'l and working jib, we might as well have been trying to row her to the Canal. We ran on the auxiliary till we used up all the gasoline aboard, and then when there was no wind we just drifted. Keefer kept moaning and griping for us to get rid of him; said he couldn't sleep in the cabin with a dead man. And neither of us could face the thought of trying to prepare any food with him lying there just forward of the galley. We finally moved out on deck altogether.

"By Sunday morning—June eighth—I knew it had to be done. I sewed him in what was left of the old stays'l, with the sounding lead at his feet. It was probably an all-time low in funerals. I couldn't think of more than a half dozen words of the sea-burial service, and there was no Bible aboard. We did shave and put on shirts, and that was about it. We buried him at one p.m. The position's in the log, and I think it's fairly accurate. The weather improved that night, and we came on here and arrived on the sixteenth. Along with the report, I turned his personal belongings over to the marshal's office. But I don't understand why they couldn't locate some of his family; his address is right there—1426 Roland Avenue, San Francisco."

"Unfortunately," Soames replied, "there is no Roland Avenue in San Francisco."

"Oh," I said.

"So we hoped you might be able to help us."

I frowned, feeling vaguely uneasy. For some reason I was standing at the rail again on that day of oily calm and blistering tropic sun, watching the body in its Orlon shroud as it sank beneath the surface and began its long slide into the abyss. "That's just great," I said. "I don't know anything about him either."

"In four days, he must have told you *something* about himself."

"You could repeat it all in forty seconds. He told me he was an American citizen. His home was in California. He'd come down to the Canal Zone on some job that had folded up after a couple of months, and he'd like to save the plane fare back to the States by sailing up with me."

"He didn't mention the name of any firm, or government agency?"

"Not a word. I gathered it was a clerical or executive job of some kind, because he had the appearance. And his hands were soft."

"He never said anything about a wife? Children? Brothers?"

"Nothing."

"Did he say anything at all during the heart attack?"

"No. He seemed to be trying to, but he couldn't get his breath. And the pain was pretty terrible until he finally lost consciousness."

"I see." Soames' blue eyes were thoughtful. "Would you describe him?"

"I'd say he was around fifty. About my height, six-one, but very slender; I doubt he weighed over a hundred and seventy. Brown eyes, short brown hair with a good deal of gray in it, especially around the temples, but not thinning or receding to any extent. Thin face, rather high forehead, good nose and bone structure, very quiet, and soft-spoken—when he said anything at all. In a movie you'd cast him as a doctor or lawyer or the head of the English department. That's the thing, you see; he wasn't hard-nosed or rude about not talking about himself; he was just reserved. He minded his own business, and seemed to expect you to mind yours. And since he was apparently down on his luck, it seemed a little on the tasteless side to go prying into matters he didn't want to talk about."

"What about his speech?"

"Well, the outstanding thing about it was that there was damned little of it. But he was obviously well educated. And if there was any trace of a regional accent, I didn't hear it."

"Was there anything foreign about it at all? I don't mean low comedy or vaudeville, but any hesitancy, or awkwardness of phrasing?"

"No," I said. "It was American."

"I see." Soames tapped meditatively on the desk with the eraser end of a pencil. "Now, you say he was an experienced sailor. But he had no papers, and you don't think he'd ever been a merchant seaman, so you must have wondered about it. Could you make any guess as to where he'd picked up this knowledge of the sea?"

"Yes. I think definitely he'd owned and sailed boats of his own, probably boats in the offshore cruising and ocean-racing class. Actually, a merchant seaman wouldn't have known a lot of the things Baxter did, unless he was over seventy and had been to sea under sail. Keefer was a good example. He was a qualified A.B.; he knew routine seamanship and how to splice and handle line, and if you gave him a compass course he could steer it. But if you were going to windward and couldn't quite lay the course, half the time he'd be lying dead in the water and wouldn't know it. He had no feel. Baxter did. He was one of the best wind-ship helmsmen I've ever run into. Besides native talent, that takes a hell of a lot of experience you don't pick up on farms or by steering power boats or steamships."

"Did he know celestial navigation?"

"Yes," I said. "It's a funny thing, but I think he did. I mean, he never mentioned it, or asked if he could take a sight and work it out for practice, but somehow I got a hunch just from the way he watched me that he knew as much about it as I did. Or maybe more. I'm no whiz; there's not much occasion to use it in the Bahamas."

"Did he ever use a term that might indicate he could have been an ex-Navy officer? Service slang of any kind?"

"No-o. Not that I can recall at the moment. But now you've mentioned it, nearly everything about him would fit. And I'm pretty sure they teach midshipmen to sail at the Academy."

"Yes. I think so."

"He didn't have a class ring, though. No rings of any kind."

"You didn't have a camera aboard, I take it?"

"No," I said.

"That's too bad; a snapshot would have been a great help. What about fingerprints? Can you think of any place aboard we might raise a few? I realize it's been sixteen days—"

"No. I doubt there'd be a chance. She's been in the yard for the past four, and everything's been washed down."

"I see." Soames stood up. "Well, we'll just have to try to locate somebody in the Zone who knew him. Thank you for coming in, Mr. Rogers. We may be in touch with you later, and I'd appreciate it if you would think back over those four days when you have time, and make a note of anything else you recall. You're living aboard, aren't you?"

"Yes."

"Sometimes association helps. You might be reminded of some chance remark he let fall, the name of a city, or yacht club, or something like that. Call us if you think of anything that could help."

"Sure, I'll be glad to," I said. "I don't understand, though, why he would give me a fake address. Do you suppose the name was phony too?"

Soames' expression was polite, but it indicated the conversation was over. "We really have no reason to think so, that I can see."

I walked over and caught a cab in front of the Warwick Hotel. During the ten-minute ride across the city to the eastern end of the waterfront and Harley's boatyard, I tried to make some sense out of the whole affair. Maybe Willetts was right, after all; Keefer could have stolen that money from Baxter's suitcase. If you assumed Baxter had lied about where he was from, he could have been lying about everything. And he'd never actually said he didn't have any money; he'd merely implied it. That was the hell of it; he'd never actually said anything. He became more mysterious every time you looked at him, and when you tried to get hold of something concrete he was as insubstantial as mist.

But what about Keefer? Even if you could bring yourself to accept the premise that he was low enough to steal from a dead man—which was a little hard to swallow—how could he have been that stupid? Maybe he was no mental giant, but still it must have occurred to him that if Baxter was carrying that much money somebody must know about it, some friend or relative, and when the money turned up missing there'd be an investigation and charges of theft. Then a disquieting thought occurred to me. So far, nobody had claimed the money. What did you make of that? Had Keefer known, before he took it? But how could he? Then I shrugged, and gave up. Hell, there wasn't even any proof that Keefer had stolen anything.

The taxi bumped across the tracks. I got out at the boatyard entrance and paid off the driver. This end of the waterfront was quiet on Saturday afternoon. To the right was another small shipyard that was closed now, and a half mile beyond that the city yacht basin, and Quarantine, and then the long jetties running out into the open Gulf. To the left were the packing sheds and piers where the shrimp boats clustered in a jungle of masts and suspended nets. These gave way in the next block to the first of the steamship terminals, the big concrete piers and slips that extended along the principal waterfront of the port.

The old watchman swung back the gate. "Here's your key," he said. "They had me come with 'em while they searched the boat. Didn't bother anything."

"Thanks," I said.

"Didn't say what they was looking for," he went on tentatively.

"They didn't tell me either," I said. I went aboard the *Topaz* and changed clothes in the stifling cabin. Nothing was disturbed, as far as I could see. It was only three p.m.; maybe I could still get some work done. I loaded the pockets of my dungarees with sandpaper, went back up the mainmast, and resumed where I'd left off sanding, just below the spreaders. I sat in the bosun's chair, legs gripping the mast to hold myself in against it while I smoothed the surface of the spar with long strokes of the abrasive. For the moment I forgot Keefer, and Baxter, and the whole puzzling mess. This was more like it. If you couldn't be at sea, the next best thing was working about a boat, maintaining her, dressing her until she sparkled, and tuning her until she was like something alive. It seemed almost a shame to offer her for sale, the way she was shaping up. Money didn't mean much, except as it could be used for the maintenance and improvement of the *Orion*.

I looked forward and aft below me. Another three or four days should do it. She'd already been hauled, scraped, and painted with anti-fouling. Her topsides were a glistening white. The spars and other brightwork had been taken down to the wood, and when I finished sanding this one and the mizzen I could put on the first coat of varnish. Overhaul the tracks and slides, replace the lines in the outhauls, reeve new main and mizzen halyards, replace that frayed headstay with a piece of stainless steel, give the deck a coat of gray nonskid, and that would about do it The new mains'l should be here by Tuesday, and the yard ought to have the refrigerator overhauled and back aboard by then. Maybe I'd better jack them up about it again on Monday morning.

Probably start the newspaper ad next Wednesday, I thought. She shouldn't be around long at $15,000, not the way she was designed and built. If I still hadn't sold her in ten days, I'd turn her over to a yacht broker at an asking price of twenty, and go back to Miami. The new mains'l had hurt, and I hadn't counted on having to rebuild the refrigerator, but still I'd be home for less than nine thousand.

Six thousand profit wouldn't be bad for less than two months' work and a little calculated risk. It would mean new batteries and new generator for the *Orion*. A leather lounge and teak table in the saloon.... I was down on deck now. I stowed the bosun's chair and began sanding the boom.

"Mr. Rogers!"

I glanced up. It was the watchman, calling to me from the end of the pier, and I noted with surprise it was the four-to-midnight man, Otto Johns. I'd been oblivious of the passage of time.

"Telephone," he called. "Long distance from New York."

CHAPTER FOUR

New York? Must be a mistake, I thought as I went up the pier. I didn't know anybody there who would be trying to phone me. The watchman's shack was just inside the gate, with a door and a wide window facing the driveway. Johns set the instrument on the window counter. "Here you go."

I picked it up. "Hello. Rogers speaking."

It was a woman's voice. "Is this the Mr. Stuart Rogers who owns the yacht *Topaz?*"

"That's right."

"Good." There was evident relief in her voice. Then she went on softly, "Mr. Rogers, I'm worried. I haven't heard from him yet."

"From whom?" I asked blankly.

"Oh," she replied. "I *am* sorry. It's just that I'm so upset. This is Paula Stafford."

It was evident from the way she said it the name was supposed to explain everything. "I don't understand," I said. "What is it you want?"

"He *did* tell you about me, didn't he?"

I sighed. "Miss Stafford—or Mrs. Stafford—I don't know what you're talking about. *Who* told me about you?"

"You're being unnecessarily cautious, Mr. Rogers. I assure you I'm Paula Stafford. It must have been at least two weeks now, and I still have no word from him. I don't like it at all. Do you think something could have gone wrong?"

"Let's go back and start over," I suggested. "My name is Stuart Rogers, age thirty-two, male, single, charter yacht captain—"

"Will you please—" she snapped. Then she paused, apparently restraining herself, and went on more calmly. "All right, perhaps you're right not to take chances without some proof. Fortunately, I've already made plane reservations. I'll arrive at two-twenty a.m., and will be at the Warwick Hotel. Will you please meet me there as soon as I check in? It's vitally important." She hung up.

I shrugged, replaced the instrument, and lighted a cigarette. There was a weird one.

"Some nut?" Johns asked. He was a gaunt, white-haired man with ice-blue eyes. He leaned on the window shelf and began stoking a caked and smelly pipe. "I got a son-in-law that's a cop, and he says you get your name in the paper you're pestered with all kindsa screwballs."

"Probably a drunk," I replied.

"Too bad about that Keefer fella," Johns went on. "Did I tell you he was here Iookin' for you the other night?"

I glanced up quickly. "He was? When was this?"

"Hmmm. Same night they say he was killed. That'd be Thursday. I reckon I must have forgot to tell you because when you come in Ralph'd just relieved me and we was shootin' the breeze."

"What time was he here?"

"About seven, seven-thirty. Wasn't long after you went out."

I frowned. It was odd that Blackie hadn't mentioned it when I ran into him at the Domino. "You're sure it was Keefer?"

"That's the name he said. Dark-haired kind of fella. Said he was the one that sailed up from Panama with you. I told him you'd gone uptown to a movie and wouldn't be back till around eleven."

"Was he in a car?" I asked. "And was there a girl with him?"

Johns shook his head. "He was by hisself. And I didn't see no car; far as I know he was afoot. I reckon he'd had a couple snorts, because he got pretty hot under the collar when I wouldn't let him go aboard the boat. He told me again about bein' a friend of yours and comin' up from Panama on it, and I said it didn't make no difference to me if he'd helped you sail it here from Omaha, Nebraska. Long as he wasn't in the crew no more he wasn't goin' aboard without you was with him."

"What did he want?" I asked. "Did he say?"

"Said he forgot his razor when he was paid off. I told him he'd have to see you about that. He left, and didn't come back."

"Oh," I said. "The companion hatch was locked; he couldn't have got aboard anyway. He should have known that."

I went back aboard the *Topaz*. It was after six now; I might as well knock off for the day. I walked over to the washroom, showered, shaved, and dressed in clean slacks and a fresh sport shirt. Back in the cabin, as I was putting away my shaving gear, I thought of Keefer. Odd, with all that money he had, that he would come clear back out here just to pick up the cheap shaving kit he'd bought in Panama. I paused. Now that I thought about it, I hadn't even seen it since Keefer had left. Was it just an excuse to get aboard? Maybe the man *was* a thief. I pulled open the drawer under the bunk Keefer had occupied. There was no razor in it. Why, the dirty ... Well, don't go off half-cocked, I thought; make sure it's not aboard. I stepped into the head and pulled open the tiny medicine cabinet above the basin. There it was, the styrene case containing a safety razor and a pack of blades. My apologies, Blackie.

I went up the companion ladder. The deck now lay in the lengthening shadows of the buildings ashore, and with a slight breeze blowing up bay from the Gulf it was a little cooler. I sat down in the cockpit, took out a cigarette, and then paused just as I started to flip the lighter.

Paula.

Paula Stafford.

Was there something familiar about the name? Hadn't I heard it before, somewhere? Oh, it was probably just imagination. I dropped the lighter back in my pocket, and inhaled deeply of the smoke, but the nagging idea persisted. Maybe Keefer had mentioned her sometime during the trip. Or Baxter.

Baxter ... For some reason I was conscious again of that strange sensation of unease I had felt there in the office of the FBI. Merely by turning my head I could look along the port side of the deck, between mizzen and main, where I had stood that day with head bared to the brazen heat of the sun and watched the body as it faded slowly and disappeared, falling silently into the depths and the crushing pressures and eternal darkness two miles below. It was the awful finality of it—the fact that if the FBI couldn't find out something about him, pick up his trail somewhere, they might never know who he was. There'd never be a second chance. No fingerprints, no photograph, no possibility of a better description, nothing. He was gone, forever, without leaving a trace. Was that it? Was it going to bother me the rest of my life—the fact that I had failed to bring the body ashore where it might have been identified?

Oh, hell, I thought angrily, you're just being morbid. You did everything humanly possible. Except remove the stomach; that would have helped, but you chickened out. So you did like the man; that's no excuse. It's done. But it wouldn't have changed anything in the long run. You were still three hundred miles from the Canal. And in that heat, trying to stretch it any longer would have been more than just unpleasant; it could have become dangerous. Burial was a practical necessity long before it became a ritual.

But there must be some clue. We'd been together for four days, and in that length of time even a man as uncommunicative as Baxter would have said *something* that would provide a lead as to where he was from. Think back. What was it Soames had said about association? Right here within this span of forty feet was where it had all taken place. Start at the beginning, with the first time you ever saw Baxter, and go over every minute.

I stopped. Just why was it necessary? Or rather, why did I feel it was? Why this subconscious fear that they weren't going to find anybody in Panama who knew Baxter? The man said he'd worked there. If he had, the FBI would run him down in a day. Was it merely because the San Francisco address had proved a dead end? No, there must be more....

It had rained during the afternoon, a slashing tropical downpour that drummed along the deck and pocked the surface of the water like hail, but it was clear now, and the hot stars of the southern latitudes were ablaze across the sky. The *Topaz* was moored stern-to at a low wooden wharf with her anchor out ahead, shadowy in the faint illumination from a lamp a half block away where the row of palms along the street stirred and rustled in the breeze blowing in from the Caribbean.

It was eight p.m. Keefer had gone off to the nearest bar with two or three dollars he had left from the twenty I'd advanced him. I went below to catalogue and stow the charts I had bought. I switched on the overhead light and stood for a moment at the foot of the companion ladder, looking forward. She was all right. She had a good interior layout, and the six-foot-two-inch headroom was adequate.

The small bottled-gas stove and stainless-steel sink of the galley were on the port side aft, with the wooden refrigerator below and stowage above. To starboard was a settee. Above it was the RDF and radiotelephone, and a chart table that folded back when not in use. Just forward of this area were two permanent bunks, and beyond them a locker to port and the small enclosed head to starboard. These, and the curtain between them, formed a passage going into the forward compartment, which was narrower and contained two additional bunks.

The charts were in a roll on the settee. I cut the cord binding them, and pulled down the chart table. Switching on the light above it, I began checking them off against my list, rolling them individually, and stowing them in the rack overhead. It was hot and very still here below, and sweat dripped off my face. I mopped at it, thinking gratefully that tomorrow we would be at sea.

I had a Hydrographic Office general chart of the Caribbean spread out on the table and was lighting a cigarette when a voice called out quietly from ashore, "Ahoy, aboard the *Topaz.*"

I stuck my head out the companion hatch. The shadowy figure on the wharf was tall but indistinct in the faint light, and I couldn't see the face. But he sounded American, and judging from the way he'd hailed he could be off one of the other yachts. "Come on aboard," I invited.

I stepped back, and the man came into view down the companion ladder—heavy brogues first, and then long legs in gray flannel slacks, and at last a brown tweed jacket. It was an odd way to be dressed in Panama, I thought, where everybody wore white and nothing heavier than linen. The man's face appeared, and he stood at the foot of the ladder with his head inclined slightly because of his height. It was a slender, well-made face, middle-aged but not sagging or deeply lined, with the stamp of quietness and intelligence and good manners on it. The eyes were brown. He was bareheaded, and the short-cropped brown hair was graying.

"Mr. Rogers?" he asked politely.

"That's right," I said.

"My name is Baxter. Wendell Baxter."

We shook hands. "Welcome aboard," I said. "How about some coffee?"

"Thank you, no." Baxter moved slightly to one side of the companion ladder, but remained standing. "I'll get right to the point, Mr. Rogers. I heard you were looking for a hand to take her north."

I was surprised, but concealed it. Baxter had neither the appearance nor the bearing of one who would be looking for a job as a paid deckhand. College students, yes; but this man must be around fifty.

"Well, I've already got one man," I said.

"I see. Then you didn't consider taking two? I mean, to cut the watches."

"Watch-and-watch does get pretty old," I agreed. "And I certainly wouldn't mind having two. You've had experience?"

"Yes."

"Offshore? The Caribbean can get pretty lumpy for a forty-foot yawl."

Baxter had been looking at the chart. He glanced up quickly, but the brown eyes were merely polite. "Yawl?"

I grinned. "I've had two applicants who called her a schooner, and one who wanted to know if I planned to anchor every night."

A faint smile touched Baxter's lips. "I see."

"Have you had a chance to look her over?" I asked.

"Yes. I saw her this morning."

"What do you make of her?"

"This is just a guess, of course, but I'd say she was probably an Alden design, and New England built, possibly less than ten years ago. She seems to have been hauled recently, probably within two months, unless she's been lying in fresh water. The rigging is in beautiful shape, except that the lower shroud on the port side of the main has some broken strands."

I nodded. I already had the wire aboard to replace that shroud in the morning before sailing. Baxter was no farmer. I nodded toward the chart. "What do you think of the course, the way I've laid it out?"

He studied it for a moment. "If the Trades hold, it should be a broad reach most of the way. Once you're far enough to the north'ard to weather Gracias a Dios, you can probably lay the Yucatán Channel on one course. Do you carry genoa and spinnaker?"

"No," I said. "Nothing but the working sails. We'll probably be twelve days or longer to Southport, and all I can offer you is a hundred for the passage. Are you sure you want to go?"

"The pay isn't important," he replied. "Primarily, I wanted to save the plane fare."

"You're an American citizen, I suppose."

"Yes. My home's in San Francisco. I came down here on a job that didn't work out, and I'd like to get back as cheaply as possible."

"I see," I said. I had the feeling somehow that behind the quiet demeanor and well-bred reserve Baxter was tense with anxiety, wanting to hear me say yes. Well, why not? The man was obviously experienced, and it would be well worth the extra hundred not to have to stand six-and-six. "It's a deal, then. Can you be aboard early in the morning? I'd like to get away before ten."

He nodded. "I'll have my gear aboard in less than an hour."

He left, and returned in forty-five minutes carrying a single leather suitcase of the two-suiter variety. "Keefer and I are in these bunks," I said. "Take either of those in the forward compartment. You can stow your bag in the other one."

"Thank you. That will do nicely," he replied. He stowed his gear, removed the tweed jacket, and opened the mushroom ventilator overhead. He came out after a while and sat silently smoking a cigarette while I rated the chronometer with a time signal from WWV.

"I gather you've cruised quite a bit," I said tentatively.

"I used to," he replied.

"In the Caribbean, and West Indies?"

"No. I've never been down here before."

"My normal stamping ground is the Bahamas," I went on. "That's wonderful country."

"Yes. I understand it is." The words were uttered with the same grave courtesy, but from the fact that he said nothing further it was obvious he didn't wish to pursue the discussion.

Okay, I thought, a little hacked about it; you don't have to talk if you don't want to. I didn't like being placed in the position of a gossipy old woman who had to be rebuffed for prying. A moment later, however, I thought better of it and decided I was being unfair. A man who was down on his luck at fifty could quite justifiably not wish to discuss his life story with strangers. Baxter, for all his aloofness, struck me as a man you could like.

Keefer returned about an hour later. I introduced them. Baxter was polite and reserved. Keefer, cocky with the beer he'd drunk and full of the merchant seaman's conviction that anybody who normally lived ashore was a farmer, was inclined to be condescending. I said nothing. Blackie was probably in for a few surprises; I had a hunch that Baxter was a better sailor than he ever would be. We all turned in shortly after ten. When I awoke just at dawn, Baxter was already up and dressed. He was standing beside his bunk, just visible past the edge of the curtain, using the side of his suitcase as a desk while he wrote something on a pad of airmail stationery.

"Why don't you use the chart table?" I asked.

He looked around. "Oh. This is all right. I didn't want to wake you."

I threw the third cigarette over the side, and stood up and stretched. There was nothing in any of that except the fact that Baxter's flannels and tweeds were a little out of place in Panama. But maybe he merely hadn't wanted to spend money for tropical clothes, especially if the job had looked none too permanent.

It was dusk now, and the glow over the city was hot against the sky. I snapped the padlock on the hatch, and walked up to the gate. Johns looked up from his magazine. "Goin' out for supper?"

"Yes. What's a good air-conditioned restaurant that has a bar?"

"Try the Golden Pheasant, on Third and San Benito. You want me to call you a cab?"

I shook my head. "Thanks. I'll walk over and catch the bus."

I crossed the railroad tracks in the gathering darkness and entered the street. The bus stop was one block up and two blocks to the right. It was a district of large warehouses and heavy industry, the streets deserted now and poorly lighted. I turned right at the corner and was halfway up the next block, before a shadowy junkyard piled high with wrecked automobiles, when a car turned into the street behind me, splashing me for an instant with its lights. It swerved to the curb and stopped. "Hey, you," a voice growled.

I turned, and looked into the shadowy muzzle of an automatic projecting from the front window. Above it was an impression of a hat brim and a brutal outcropping or jaw. "Get in," the voice commanded.

The street was deserted for blocks in each direction. Behind me was the high, impassable fence of the junkyard. I looked at the miles of utter nothing between me and the corner. "All right. The wallet's in my hip pocket—"

"We don't want your wallet. I said get in!" The muzzle of the gun moved almost imperceptibly, and the rear door opened. I stepped toward it. As I leaned down, hands reached out of the darkness inside and yanked. I fell inward. Something slashed down on my left shoulder. My arm went numb to the fingertips. I tried to get up. Light exploded just back of my eyes.

My head was filled with a running groundswell of pain. It rose and fell, and rose again, pressing against my skull in hot waves of orange, and when I opened my eyes the orange gave way to a searing white that made me shudder and close them again. Muscles tightened spasmodically across my abdomen as nausea uncoiled inside me. I was conscious of a retching sound and of the sensation of strangling.

"Prop him up," a bored voice said. "You want him to drown in it?"

I felt myself hauled upward and pushed against something behind me. I retched and heaved again. "Throw some water on him," the voice commanded. "He stinks."

Footsteps went away and came back. Water caught me in the face, forcing my head back and running up my nostrils. I choked. The rest of it splashed onto the front of my shirt. I opened my eyes again. The light burned into them. I reached for it to push it away, but found it was apparently glaring at me from some incalculable distance, because my fingertips could not reach it. Maybe it was the sun. Maybe, on the other hand, I was in hell.

Somewhere in the darkness beyond my own little cosmos of light and pain and the smell of vomit, a voice asked, "Can you hear me, Rogers?"

I tried to say something, but only retched again. More water slapped me in the face. When it had run out of my nose and mouth I tried again. This time I was able to form words. They were short words, and very old ones.

"Rogers, I'm talking to you," the voice said. "Where did you put him ashore?"

I groped numbly around in my mind for some meaning to that, but gave up. "Who? What are you talking about?"

"Wendell Baxter. Where did you put him ashore?"

CHAPTER FIVE

"Baxter?" I put a hand up over my eyes to shield them I from the light. "Ashore?"

"He couldn't be that stupid." This seemed to be a different voice. Tough, with a rasping inflection. "Let me belt him one."

"Not yet." This was the first one again—incisive, commanding, a voice with four stripes.

A random phrase, torn from some lost context, boiled up through the pain and the jumbled confusion of my thoughts ... Professional muscle ... That policeman had said it. Willard? Willetts? That was it. *Sounds like professional muscle to me....*

"We're going to have to soften him up a little."

"Shut up. Rogers, where did you land him? Mexico? Honduras? Cuba?"

"I don't know what you're talking about," I said.

"We're talking about Wendell Baxter."

"Baxter is dead," I said. "He died of a heart attack—"

"And you buried him at sea. Save it, Rogers; we read the papers. Where is he?"

My head was clearing a little now. I had no idea where I was but I could make out that I was sitting on a rough wooden floor with my back propped against a wall and that the light glaring in my face was a powerful flashlight held by someone just in front of and above me. Now that I looked under it I could see gray-trousered legs and a pair of expensive-looking brogues. To my right was another pair of shoes, enormous ones, size twelve at least. I looked to the left and saw one more pair. These were black, and almost as large, and the right one had a slit along the welt about where the little toe would be, as if the wearer had a corn. In my groggy state I fastened onto details like that like a baby seeing the world for the first time. Water ran out of my clothing; I was sitting in a puddle of it. My hair and face were still dripping, and when I licked my lips I realized it was salt. We must be on a pier, or aboard a boat.

"Where was Baxter headed?"

Maybe they were insane. "He's dead," I repeated patiently. "We buried him at sea. For God's sake, why would I lie about it?"

"Because he paid you."

I opened my mouth to say something, but closed it. A little chill ran down my spine as I began to understand.

"Let me work him over."

"Not yet, I tell you. You want to scramble his brains again and have to wait another hour? He'll talk. All right, Rogers, do you want me to spell it out for you?"

"I don't care what you spell out. Baxter is dead."

"Listen. Baxter came aboard the *Topaz* on the night of May thirty-first in Cristobal. The three of you sailed the next morning, June first, and you and Keefer arrived here on the sixteenth. Baxter paid you ten thousand dollars to land him somewhere on the coast of Central America, Mexico, or Cuba, and cook up that story about the heart attack and having to bury him at sea—"

"I tell you he died!"

"Shut up till I'm finished. Baxter should have had better sense than to trust a stupid meathead like Keefer. We know all about him. The night before you sailed from Panama he was down to his last dollar, mooching drinks in a waterfront bar. When you arrived here sixteen days later he moved into the most expensive hotel in town and started throwing money around like a drunk with an expense account. They're holding twenty-eight hundred for him in the hotel safe, and he had over six hundred in his wallet when his luck ran out. That figures out to somewhere around four grand altogether, so you must have got more. It was your boat. Where's Baxter now?"

"Lying on the bottom, in about two thousand fathoms," I said hopelessly. What was the use? They'd never believe me; Keefer had fixed that, for all time. I thought of the pulpy mess the gun barrels had made of his face, and shuddered. These were the men who'd done it, and they'd do the same thing to me.

"Okay," the voice said in the darkness beyond the flashlight. "Maybe you'd better prime him a little."

A big arm swung down and the open hand rocked my face around. I tried to climb to my feet; another hand grabbed the front of my shirt and hauled. I swayed weakly, trying to swing at the shadowy bulk in front of me. My arms were caught from behind. A fist like a concrete block slugged me in the stomach. I bent forward and fell, writhing in agony, when the man behind turned me loose.

"Where's Baxter?"

I was unable to speak. One of them hauled me to a sitting position again and slammed me against the wall. I sobbed for breath while the light fixed me like some huge and malevolent eye.

"Why be stupid?" the voice asked. "All we want to know is where you put him ashore. You don't owe him anything; you carried out your end of the bargain. He's making a sucker of you, anyway; he knew he was letting you in for this, but he didn't tell you that, did he?"

"Then why would I lie about it?" I gasped. "If I'd put him ashore, I'd tell you. But I didn't."

"He promised you more money later? Is that it?"

"He didn't promise me anything, or give me anything. I don't know where Keefer got that money, unless he stole it out of Baxter's suitcase. But I do know Baxter's dead. I sewed him in canvas myself, and buried him."

The rasping voice broke in. "Cut out the crap, Rogers! We're not asking *if* you put him ashore. We know that already, from Keefer. But he didn't know where, because you did all the navigation. It was the mouth of some river, but he didn't know which one, or what country it was in."

"Was this *after* you'd broken all the bones in his face?" I asked. "Or while you were still breaking them? Look, you knew Baxter, presumably. Didn't he ever have a heart attack before?"

"No."

"Is Baxter his right name?"

"Never mind what his name is."

"I take it that it's not. Then why are you so sure the man who was with me is the one you're looking for?"

"He was seen in Panama."

"It could still be a mistake."

"Take a look." A hand extended into the cone of light, holding out a photograph.

I took it. It was a four-by-five snapshot of a man at the topside controls of a sport fisherman, a tall and very slender man wearing khaki shorts and a long-visored fishing cap. It was Baxter; there was no doubt of it. But it was the rest of the photo that caught my attention—the boat itself, and the background. There was something very familiar about the latter.

"Well?" the voice asked coldly.

I held it out. "It's Baxter." Lying was futile.

"Smart boy. Of course it is. You ready to tell us now?"

"I've already told you. He's dead."

"I don't get you, Rogers. I know you couldn't be stupid enough to think we're bluffing. You saw Keefer."

"Yes, I saw him. And what did it buy you? A poor devil out of his mind with pain trying to figure out what you wanted him to say so he could say it. Is that what you want? I'm no braver with a broken face than the next guy, so I'll probably do the same thing."

"We've wasted enough time with him!" This was the tough voice again. "Grab his arms!"

I tried to estimate the distance to the flashlight, and gathered myself. It was hopeless, but I had to do something. I came up with a rush just before the hands reached me pushing myself off the wall and lunging toward the light. A hand caught my shirt. It tore. The light swung back, but I was on it; it fell to the floor and rolled, but didn't go out. The beam sprayed along the opposite wall. There was an open doorway, and beyond it a pair of mooring bitts, and the dark outline of a barge. A blow knocked me off balance; a hand groped, trying to hold me. I spun away from it, driving toward the door. Shoes scraped behind me, and I heard a grunt and curses as two of them collided in the darkness. Something smashed against the side of my head, and I started to fall. I hit the door frame, pushed off it, and wheeled, somehow still on my feet, and I was in the open. Stars shone overhead, and I could see the dark gleam of water beyond the end of the barge.

I tried to turn, to run along the pier. One of them crashed into me from behind, and tackled me around the waist. Our momentum carried us outward toward the edge. My legs struck one of the mooring lines of the barge, and I shot outward and down, falling between it and the pier.

Water closed over me. I tried to swim laterally before I surfaced, and came up against solid steel. I was against the side of the barge. I kicked off it and brushed against barnacles that sliced into my arm. It was one of the pilings. I grabbed it, pulled around to the other side, and came up.

"Bring the light! Somebody bring the light!" a man was yelling just above me. Apparently he'd caught the mooring line and saved himself from falling. I heard footsteps pounding on the wooden planking overhead. They'd be able to see me, unless I got back farther under the pier, but the tide was pushing me out, against the barge. I tried to hold onto the piling and see if there was another one farther in that I could reach, but the darkness in that direction was impenetrable. The current was too strong to swim against.

Light burst on the water around me. "There he is! There's the creep!" somebody yelled. "There's his hand!" I took a deep breath and went under, and immediately I was against the side of the barge again. I might swim alongside it for some distance, but when I surfaced I'd still be within range of that light. I did the only thing left. I swam straight down against the side of the barge. My ears began to hurt a little, so I knew I was below twelve feet when the plates bent inward around the turn of the bilge and there was only emptiness below me. It was frightening there in the pitch darkness, not knowing how wide she was or how much water there was under the flat bottom, but it wasn't half as deadly as the three goons back there on the wharf. There was no turning back, anyway; the current was already carrying me under. I kicked hard, and felt the back of my head scrape along the bottom plates.

Then there was mud under my hands. For a moment I almost panicked; then I regained presence of mind enough to know that the only chance I had was to keep on going straight ahead. If I turned now I'd never get out. Even if I didn't lose all sense of direction and get lost completely, I'd never be able to swim back up against the current. I kicked ahead. The water shoaled a little more; my knees were in mud now, with my back scraping along the bottom of the barge.

Suddenly there was only water below me and I was going faster. My lungs began to hurt. I passed the turn of the bilge and shot upward. My head broke surface at last, and I inhaled deeply—once, twice, and then I went under again just as the light burst across the water not ten feet off to my left. They had run across the barge and were searching this side. I stayed under, kicking hard and letting the tide carry me. When I surfaced again I was some fifty yards away. They were still throwing the light around and cursing. I began swimming across the current toward the dark line of the beach. In a little while I felt bottom beneath my hands and stood up. I turned and looked back.

I was a good two hundred yards from the pier and the barge now. The flashlight was coming along the shore in my direction. I eased back out until just my head was above water, and waited. I could hear them talking. When they were almost opposite me, they turned and went back. A few minutes later a car started up, near the landward end of the pier. The twin beams swung in an arc, and I watched the red taillights fade and disappear. I waded ashore in the dark. The reaction hit me all of a sudden, and I was weak and very shaky in the knees, and I had to sit down.

After a while I took off my clothes and squeezed some of the water out of them. I still had my wallet and watch and cigarette lighter. I pressed as much water as I could out of the soggy papers and the money in the wallet and threw away the mushy cigarettes. It was hard getting the wet clothes back on in the darkness. There was no wind, and mosquitoes made thin whining sounds around my ears. Far off to my right I could see the glow of Southport's lights reflected against the sky. I stood up, located Solaris to orient myself, and started walking.

"Where is it?" Willetts asked. "Can you describe the place?"

"Yes," I said. "It must be eight or ten miles west of town. I walked about three before I could flag a patrol car. It's a single wooden pier with a shed on it. There's a steel barge moored to the west side of it. The buildings ashore apparently burned down a long time ago; there's nothing left but foundations and rubble."

He exchanged a glance with Ramirez, and they nodded. "Sounds like the old Bowen sugar mill. It's outside the city limits, but we can go take a look. You better come along and see if you can identify it. You sure you're all right now?"

"Sure," I said.

It was after ten p.m. We were in Emergency Receiving at County Hospital, where the men in the patrol car had brought me. They had radioed in as soon as I gave them the story, and received word back to hold me until it could be investigated. A bored intern checked me over, said I had a bad bruise on the back of my head but no fracture, cleaned the barnacle cuts on my arms, stuck on a few Band-Aids, and gave me a cigarette and two aspirins.

"You'll live," he said, with the medic's vast non-interest in the healthy.

I wondered how long. They'd given up for the moment, but when they found out I hadn't drowned they'd be back. What should I do? Ask for police protection for the rest of my life? That would be a laugh. A grown man asking protection from three pairs of shoes.

Who was Baxter? Why did they want him? And what in the name of God had given them the idea we had put him ashore? I was still butting my head against the same blank wall twenty minutes later when Willetts and Ramirez showed up. They'd been off duty, of course, but were called in because Keefer was their case. I repeated the story.

"All right, let's go," Willetts said.

We went out and got in the cruiser. Ramirez drove—quite fast, but without using the siren. My clothes were merely damp now, and the cool air was pleasant; the headache had subsided to a dull throbbing. We rode a freeway for a good part of the distance, and the trip took less than fifteen minutes. As soon as we came out to the end of the bumpy and neglected shell-surfaced road and stopped, I recognized it. Willetts and Ramirez took out flashlights and we walked down through the blackened rubble to the pier.

We found the doorway into the shed, opposite the barge. Inside it was black and empty. The floor against the opposite wall was still wet where I'd vomited and they'd thrown water on me, and nearby was the fire bucket they'd used. It had a piece of line made fast to the handle. Willetts took it along to be checked for fingerprints. There was nothing else, no trace of blood or anything to indicate Keefer had been killed there. We went out on the pier. Ramirez shot his light down into the water between the piling and the side of the barge. "And you swam under it? Brother."

"There wasn't much choice at the time," I said.

We went back to the police station, to the office I'd been in that morning. They took down my statement.

"You never did see their faces?" Willetts asked.

"No. They kept that light in my eyes all the time. But there were three of them, and at least two were big and plenty rough."

"And they admitted they killed Keefer?"

"You've got their exact words," I said. "I wouldn't say there was much doubt of it."

"Have you got any idea at all why they're after Baxter?"

"No."

"Or who Baxter really is?"

"Who Baxter really *was*," I said. "And the answer is no."

"But you think now he might be from Miami?"

"At some time in his life, anyway. I don't know how long ago it was, but that picture they showed me was taken on Biscayne Bay. I'm almost positive of it."

"And they didn't give any reason for that idea you'd put him ashore? I mean, except that Keefer turned up with all that money?"

"No."

He lighted a cigarette and leaned across the desk. "Look, Rogers. This is just a piece of advice from somebody who's in the business. Whatever happened in Panama, or out in the middle of the ocean, is out of our jurisdiction and no skin off our tail, but you're in trouble. If you know anything about this you're not telling, you'd better start spilling it before you wind up in an alley with the cats looking at you."

"I don't know a thing about it I haven't told you," I said.

"All right. We have to take your word for it; you're the only one left, and we've got no real evidence to the contrary. But I can smell these goons. They're pros, and I don't think they're local. I've put the screws on every source I've got around town, and nobody knows anything about 'em at all. Our only chance to get a lead on 'em would be to find out who Baxter was, and what he was up to."

"That's great," I said. "With Baxter buried at the bottom of the Caribbean Sea."

"The thing that puzzles me the most is what the hell he was doing on that boat of yours in the first place. The only way you can account for that money of Keefer's is that he stole it from Baxter. So if Baxter was running from a bunch of hoodlums and had four thousand in cash, why would he try to get away on a boat that probably makes five miles an hour downhill? Me, I'd take something faster."

"I don't know," I said. "It gets crazier every time I look at it. The only thing I'm sure of any more is that I wish to Christ I'd never heard of Baxter or Keefer."

"Okay. There's nothing more we can do now. I've got a hunch the FBI is going to want to take a long, slow look at this, but they can pick you up in the morning. We'll send you back to your boat in a squad car. And if you have to go chasing around town at night, for God's sake take a taxi."

"Sure," I said. "They struck me as being scared to death of taxi drivers."

"They're scared of witnesses, wise guy. They all are. And you've always got a better chance where they can't get a good look at you."

It was 12:20 a.m. when the squad car dropped me off before the boatyard gate and drove away. I glanced nervously up and down the waterfront with its shadows and gloomy piers and tried to shrug off the feeling of being watched. It was as peaceful as the open sea, with nobody in sight anywhere except old Ralph, the twelve-to-eight watchman, tilted back in a chair just inside the gate reading a magazine in his hot pool of light. He glanced curiously at the police car and at my muddy shoes, but said nothing. I said good night, and went on down through the yard. As I stepped aboard the *Topaz* and walked aft to the cockpit, I reached in my pocket for the key. Then I saw I wasn't going to need it.

The hatch was open and the padlock was gone, the hasp neatly cut through, apparently with bolt cutters. I looked down into the dark interior of the cabin, and felt the hair raise along the back of my neck. I listened intently, standing perfectly still, but knew that was futile. If he was still down there, he'd heard me already. Well, I could find out.

The light switch was right beside the ladder, accessible from here. I stepped to one side of the hatch, reached down silently, and flipped it on. Nothing happened. I peered in. He was gone. But he'd been there. The whole cabin looked as if it had been stirred with a giant spoon.

CHAPTER SIX

The bunks had been torn apart. The bedding was piled on the settee and in the sink. My suitcase and duffel bag were emptied into the bunks, the drawers beneath them dumped upside down on the deck. Food lockers were emptied and ransacked. Charts, nautical almanacs, azimuth tables, magazines, and books were scattered everywhere. I stared at it in mounting rage. A hell of a security force they had here, one creaky old pensioner sitting up there calmly reading a magazine while thieves tore your boat apart. Then I realized it wasn't his fault, nor Otto's. Whoever had done this hadn't come in the gate, and was no ordinary sneak thief. The watchmen made the round of the yard once every hour with a clock, but there was no station out here on the pier. I grabbed a flashlight and ran back on deck.

The *Topaz* lay near the outer end of the pier, bow in and starboard side to. There was a light at the shoreward end of the pier, but out here it was somewhat shadowy, especially aft. The marine railway and the shrimp boat that was on it blocked the view from the gate. There was a high wire fence, topped with barbed wire, on each side of the yard, so no one could go in or out afoot except through the gate, but the bayfront was wide open, of course, to anyone with a boat.

I threw the beam of the flashlight over the port side, and found it almost immediately. Freshly painted white topsides are both the joy and the curse of a yachtsman's life; they're beautiful and dazzling as a fresh snowfall, and just as easily marred. Right under the cockpit coaming was a slight dent, with green paint in it. Skiff, I thought, or a small outboard; it had bumped as it came alongside. If they had a motor, they had probably cut it some distance out and sculled in. Probably happened on Otto's watch, right after I left. That meant, then, that there were at least four of them. But what were they looking for?

I was just straightening up when I saw something else. I stopped the light and looked again to make sure. There was another dent, about ten feet forward of this one. What the hell, had they come alongside at twenty knots and ricocheted? I stepped forward and knelt to have a closer look. There was a smear of yellow paint in this one. *Two boats?* That made no sense at all. One of the dents must have been made before, I thought. But it couldn't have been very long ago, because it was only Thursday I'd painted the topsides.

Well, it didn't make any difference. The point was that they'd been here, and they could come back. If I wanted to get any sleep I'd better move to a hotel; this place was too easy to get into. I went below and straightened up the mess. So far as I could tell, nothing was missing. I changed into a lightweight suit—the only one I had with me—put on some more shoes, and packed a bag with the rest of my gear. I gathered up the sextant and chronometer, the only valuable items aboard, and went up to the gate.

The old man was shocked and apologetic and a little frightened when I told him about it. "Why, I didn't hear a thing, Mr. Rogers," he said.

"It probably happened on Otto's shift," I said. "But it doesn't matter; nobody would have heard them, anyway. Just keep this chronometer and sextant in your shack till Froelich gets here in the morning." Froelich was the yard foreman. "Turn them over to him, and tell him to put a new hasp and padlock on that hatch. At yard expense, incidentally. And tell him not to let anybody down in the cabin until the police have a chance to check it for fingerprints. I'll be back around nine o'clock."

"Yes, sir," he said. "I'll sure do that. And I'm awful sorry about it, Mr. Rogers."

"Forget it," I told him. I called the police and reported it, with a request that they notify Willetts when he came on shift again. This had to be explained, because Willetts was in Homicide and had nothing to do with burglary. We got it straightened out at last, and I called a cab. The driver recommended the Bolton as a good commercial hotel.

I watched the empty streets as we drove through the warehouse and industrial district. No one followed us. Even the thought of violence seemed unreal. The Bolton was in the heart of the downtown business district, about three blocks from the Warwick. It was air-conditioned.

I registered, and followed the boy through the deserted corridors of two a.m., reminded of the description of a hotel in one of Faulkner's novels. *Tiered cubicles of sleep*. The room was a cubicle, all right, but it had a night latch and a chain on the door. When the boy had gone I slipped the chain in place, took a shower, and lay down on the bed with a cigarette.

Who was Baxter?

He's a legacy, I thought. An incubus I inherited, with an assist from Keefer. Baxter to Keefer to Rogers—it sounded like the infield of a sandlot baseball team. Why had he come aboard the *Topaz?* He'd obviously lied about the job and about wanting to save plane fare home. He hadn't struck me as a liar, either; aloof, maybe, and close-mouthed, but not a liar. And certainly not a criminal. I'd liked him.

Who were the men after him? And why wouldn't they believe he had died of a heart attack? And just what did I do now? Spend the rest of my life looking under the bed, sleeping behind locked doors on the upper floors of hotels? It was chilling when you thought of it, how little the police could actually do about a thing like this, unless I wanted to go down there and live in the squad room and never go out at all. And trying to convince myself that I was any match for professional hoodlums was farcical. Violence was their business. It wasn't a sport, like football, with rules, and time out when you got hurt. Even if I had a gun and a permit to carry it, it would be useless; I was no gunman, and didn't want to be one.

I lighted another cigarette, and looked at my watch. It was almost three a.m.

The only way to get a line on them, Willetts had said, was to find out who Baxter was. And since the physical remains of Baxter were buried beyond the reach of the human race for eternity, the only thing left was trailing him backward in search of some clue. That, obviously, was a job for the FBI. But so far the FBI didn't even have a place to start. I had four days.

Take it from where you left off, I thought: the morning we sailed. After breakfast the three of us had turned to, replacing the stainless-steel lower shroud on the port side of the mainmast. Baxter was a willing worker and he was good with wire, but his hands were soft and he apparently had no gloves. I noted also that he was working in the pair of gray flannel slacks. While we were still at it, the stores came down. We carried them aboard and stowed them. There was a discrepancy in the bill that I wanted to take up with the ship chandler, so I asked the driver for a ride back to town in the truck. Just as I was going ashore, Baxter came up from below and called to me.

He handed me twenty dollars. "I wonder if you'd mind getting me two pairs of dungarees while you're uptown? The stores were closed last night."

"Sure," I said. "What size?"

"Thirty-two waist, and the longest they have."

"Right. But why not come along yourself? We're in no bind."

He declined apologetically. "Thanks, but I'd just as soon stay and finish that wire. That is, if you don't mind getting the dungarees."

I told him I didn't. He took an airmail letter from his pocket and asked if I'd drop it in the box for him—

Paula Stafford!

I sat up in bed so suddenly I dropped my cigarette and had to retrieve it from the floor. That's where I'd heard the name. Or had seen it, rather. When I was mailing the letter I'd noticed idly that it was addressed to somebody at a hotel in New York. I wasn't prying; it was merely that the New York address had struck me, since he was from San Francisco, and I'd glanced at the name. *Stanford? Sanford? Stafford?* That was it; I was positive of it.

God, what a dope! I'd forgotten all about her call. She was probably over at the Warwick Hotel right now, and could clear up the whole mystery in five minutes. I grabbed the telephone.

I waited impatiently while the operator dialed. "Good morning," a musical voice said. "Hotel Warwick."

"Do you have a Paula Stafford registered?" I asked.

"One moment, please.... Yes, sir...."

"Would you ring her, please?"

"I'm sorry, sir. Her line is busy."

Probably trying to get me at the boatyard, I thought. I sprang up and began throwing on my clothes. It was only three blocks to the Warwick. The traffic lights were blinking amber, and the streets were empty except for a late bus or two and a Sanitation Department truck. I made it to the Warwick in three minutes. The big ornate lobby was at the bottom of its day's cycle; all the shops were closed, and some of the lights were turned off around the outlying areas with only the desk and switchboard and one elevator still functioning, like the nerve centers of some complex animal asleep. I headed for the house phones, over to the right of the desk.

She answered almost immediately, as if she had been standing beside the instrument. "Yes?"

"Miss Stafford?" I asked.

"Yes," she said eagerly. "Who is it?"

"Stuart Rogers. I'm down in the lobby—"

"Oh, thank Heavens!" She sounded slightly hysterical. "I've been trying to get you at that shipyard, but the man said you were gone, he didn't know where. But never mind. Where are you?"

"Down in the lobby," I repeated.

"Come on up! Room 1508."

It was to the right, the boy said. I stepped out of the elevator and went along a hushed and deep-carpeted corridor. When I knocked, she opened the door immediately. The first thing that struck me about her were her eyes. They were large and deeply blue, with long dark lashes, but they were smudged with sleeplessness and jittery with some intense emotion too long sustained.

"Come in, Mr. Rogers!" She stepped back, gave me a nervous but friendly smile that was gone almost before it landed, and shook a pill out of the bottle she was holding in her left hand. She was about thirty-five, I thought. She had dark hair that was a little mussed, as if she'd been running her hands through it, and was wearing a blue dressing gown, belted tightly about her waist. Paula Stafford was a very attractive woman, aside from an impression that if you dropped something or made a sudden move she might jump into the overhead light fixture.

I came on into the room and closed the door while she grabbed up a tumbler of water from the table on her left and swallowed the pill. Also on the table was a burning cigarette in a long holder, balanced precariously on the edge, another bottle of pills of a different color, and an unopened pint bottle of Jack Daniel's. To my left was the partly opened door of the bathroom. Beyond her was a large double bed with a persimmon-colored spread. The far wall was almost all window, covered with a drawn Venetian blind and persimmon drapes. Light came from the bathroom door and from the floor lamp beside the dresser, which was beyond the foot of the bed, to my left. A dress, apparently the one she'd been wearing, was thrown across the bed, along with a half slip, her handbag, and a pair of sun glasses, while her suitcase was open and spilling lingerie and stockings on the luggage stand at the foot of it. It was hard to tell whether she'd taken up residence in the room or had been lobbed into it just before she went off.

"Tell me about him!" she demanded. "Do you think he's all right?" Then, before I could open my mouth, she broke off with another nervous smile and indicated the armchair near the foot of the bed, at the same time grabbing up the bottle of Jack Daniel's and starting to fumble with the seal. "Forgive me. Won't you sit down? And let me pour you a drink."

I lifted the bottle of whisky out of her hands before she could drop it, and placed it on the table. "Thanks, I don't want a drink. But I would like some information."

She didn't even hear me, apparently, or notice that I'd taken the whisky away. She went right on talking. "… half out of my mind, even though I know there must be some perfectly good reason he hasn't got in touch with me yet."

"Who?" I asked.

This got through to her. She stopped, looked at me in surprise, and said, "Why, Brian—I mean, Wendell Baxter."

It was my turn this time. It seemed incredible she didn't know. I felt rotten about having to break it to her this way. "I'm sorry, Miss Stafford, but I took it for granted you'd read about it in the papers. Wendell Baxter is dead."

She smiled. "Oh, of course! How stupid of me." She turned away, and began to rummage through her handbag on the bed. "I must say he made no mistake in trusting you, Mr. Rogers."

I stared blankly at the back of her head, and took out a cigarette and lighted it. There was a vague impression somewhere in my mind that her conversation—if that was what it was—would make sense if only you had the key to it.

"Oh, here it is," she said, and turned back with a blue airmail envelope in her hand. I felt a little thrill as I saw the Canal Zone postmark; it was the one I'd mailed for him. At last I might find out something. "This should clear up your doubts as to who I am. Go ahead and read it."

I slid out the letter.

Cristobal, C.Z.
June 1st

Dearest Paula:

There is time for just the briefest of notes. Slidell is here in the Zone and has seen me. He has the airport covered, but I have found a way to slip out.

I am writing this aboard the ketch *Topaz,* which is sailing shortly for Southport, Texas. I have engaged to go along as deckhand, using the name of Wendell Baxter. They may find out, of course, but I might not be aboard when she arrives. As soon as we are safely at sea I am going to approach Captain Rogers about putting me ashore somewhere farther up the Central American coast. Of course it is possible he won't do it, but I hope to convince him. The price may be high, but fortunately I still have something over $23,000 in cash with me. I shall write again the moment I am ashore, either in Southport or somewhere in Central America. Until then, remember I am safe, no matter what you might hear, and that I love you.

Brian

Twenty-three thousand dollars … I stood there dumbly while she took the letter from my fingers, folded it, and slid it back into the envelope.

She looked up at me. "Now," she cried out eagerly, "where is he, Mr. Rogers?"

I had to say something. She was waiting for an answer. "He's dead. He died of a heart attack—"

She cut me short with a gesture of exasperation, tinged with contempt. "Aren't you being a little ridiculous? You've read the letter; you know who I am. Where did you put him ashore? Where was he going?"

I think that was the moment I began to lose my head. It was the utter futility of it. I caught her arms. "Listen! Was Baxter insane?"

"Insane? What are you talking about?"

"Who is Slidell? What does he want?"

"I don't know," she said.

"You don't know?"

She jerked her arms free and moved back from me. "He never told me. Slidell was only one of them, but I don't know what he wanted."

"Has anybody read this letter except me?"

"Mr. Rogers, are *you* crazy? Of course nobody else has seen it."

"Well, look," I went on, "do you think he had twenty-three thousand dollars with him?"

"Yes. Of course he did. But why are you asking all these questions? And why don't you answer mine? Where is he?"

"I keep trying to tell you," I said. "He died of a heart attack four days after we left Cristobal. And in those four days he never said anything at all about wanting to be put ashore. I made an inventory of his personal effects, and he didn't have any twenty-three thousand dollars. He had about a hundred and seventy-five. Either Baxter was insane, or we're not even talking about the same man."

Her face became completely still then. She stared at me, her eyes growing wider and wider. "You killed him," she whispered. "That's why I've never heard from him."

"Stop it!" I commanded. "There has to be some answer—"

"You killed him!" She put her hands up alongside her temples and screamed, with the cords standing out in her throat. "You killed him! *You killed him!"*

"Listen!"

She went on screaming. Her eyes were completely mad. I ran.

CHAPTER SEVEN

Doors were opening along the corridor and faces were peering out. When I reached the elevator it was on its way up. That would be the hotel detective. I plunged down the stairs with the screams still ringing in my ears. When I reached the lobby at last, it was quiet. Hotels in the Warwick's class don't like police milling around in the lobby if they can help it. I crossed the deserted acres, feeling the eyes of the clerk on my back. In less than five minutes I was back in my own room at the Bolton. I hooked the chain on the door and collapsed on the side of the bed. I reached for a cigarette and got it going somehow.

Now what? There was no use trying to talk to her again; she was on the ragged edge of a crackup. Even if they got her calmed down, seeing me would only set her off again. The thing to do was call the FBI. Then I thought of the letter. If they ever saw that …

It was absolutely deadly; the more I looked at it, the worse it became. How could anybody ever believe me now? Baxter had sailed on the *Topaz* with $23,000 and had never been seen again. I swore he'd died of a heart attack and that all the money he'd had was $175. Then Keefer was discovered to have $4000 nobody could explain, and he was killed. I was the only survivor. There was only my unsupported word that Baxter had even had a heart attack, and $19,000 was still missing.

The least I would be suspected of would be stealing from a dead man and then burying him at sea and destroying his identification to cover up the theft. Or landing him on the coast of Central America as he'd asked, and swearing to a false report that he was dead. The third was even worse. Keefer and I could have killed him. Maybe they couldn't convict me of any of it—they wouldn't have any more actual proof on their side than I had on mine—but even the suspicion would ruin me. I was in the charter business. *Cruise the exotic Bahamas with Captain Rogers, and disappear.* They'd take away my license. Except of course that the hoodlums who were after Baxter might kill me before any of these other things could happen. I sat on the side of the bed with my head in my hands.

Then I was struck by an odd thought. What had given them the idea I'd put Baxter ashore? It seemed now there was some basis for their insane theory, but how had they known it? So far as I knew he'd written only that one letter, and she swore nobody else had seen it.

I closed my eyes, and I could see Baxter. Baxter at the wheel, watching the compass, looking aloft for the flutter at the luff of the mains'l, Baxter trimming and starting the sheets, Baxter washing dishes, Baxter quietly smoking a cigarette and looking out across the darkening sea at dusk. He haunted me. He was becoming an obsession. If he'd meant what he had written to Paula Stafford, why had he never once, in all those four days, brought up the subject of being put ashore? I wouldn't have done it, of course, but there was no way he could have been sure of that until he'd dangled the proposition and the money in front of me. Why had he changed his mind? If he'd had $23,000, where was it? Maybe Keefer had stolen $4000 of it, but why stop there?

He'd had four whole days in which to bring up the subject, but he never had. Why? Something must have changed his mind, but what? For one agonizing instant I had the feeling that I knew the answer to that, and that I should know who Baxter really was. Then the whole thing was gone. I wanted to beat my fists against my head.

All right, I thought angrily, what did I know about him? Add it all up. He was from Miami, or had been in Miami at some time. I was from Miami myself, and knew a lot of people there, especially around the waterfront. His first name was Brian. The photograph had showed him at the topside controls of a sport fisherman, which was definitely a clue because I had an idea of the type and had seen the last two letters of the name. Maybe I'd seen him somewhere before, or had heard of him. Why not go back to Miami now, instead of sitting here like a duck in a shooting gallery? I reached for the phone.

There were two airlines with service from here to Florida. The first had nothing available before 12:30 p.m. I called the other.

"Yes, sir," the girl at the reservations desk said, "we still have space on flight 302. That departs Southport five-fifty-five a.m., and arrives Miami at one-forty-five p.m., with stops at New Orleans and Tampa."

I looked at my watch. It was twenty minutes of five. "Right," I said. "The name is Stuart Rogers. I'll pick up the ticket at the airport as soon as I can get there."

I broke the connection and got the hotel operator again. "Give me long distance, please."

When the long-distance operator came on, I said, "I'd like to put in a call to Miami." I gave her the number.

"Thank you. Will you hold on, please?"

I waited, listening to the chatter of the operators. Bill Redmond would love being hauled out of bed this time of morning. He was an old friend—we'd been classmates at the University of Miami—but he was a reporter on the *Herald,* and had probably just got to sleep. The *Herald* is a morning paper.

"Hello." It was a girl's voice. A very sleepy girl.

"I have a long distance call from Southport, Texas—" the operator began.

"I don't know any Texans—"

"Lorraine," I broke in, "this is Stuart."

"Oh, good God. Bachelors! There ought to be a law."

"Will you put Bill on? It's important."

"I'll bet. Well, stand back, and I'll poke him with something."

I heard him mutter drowsily. Then, "Look, pal, you got any idea what time it is?"

"Never mind," I said. "You can sleep when you get old. I need some help. It's about that trip up from Cristobal with that ketch I went down there to buy."

He interrupted, fully awake now. "I know about it. AP carried a few lines, and we ran it on account of the local angle. Guy died of a heart attack, what was his name?"

"That's it exactly," I said. "What was his name? It was supposed to be Baxter, but it turns out that was phony. There was something wrong about him, and I'm in a hell of a jam I'll tell you about as soon as I can get there. I've got to find out who he was. I think he was from Miami, and there's some sort of screwy impression I've heard of him before. Are you still with me?"

"Keep firing. What did he look like?"

I gave him a short description, and went on. "The Miami hunch comes from a photograph of him that was shown me. I'm pretty sure what I saw in the background was part of the MacArthur Causeway and some of those islands along Government Cut. He was on the flying bridge of a sport fisherman. It was a big one and expensive looking, and I think it was one of those Rybovich jobs. If he owned it, he was probably well-heeled when he was around there because they're not exactly the playthings of the Social Security set. One of the life rings was just behind him, and I could see the last two letters of the name. They were 'a-t.' From the size of the letters, it could be a long name. His first name was Brian. B-r-i-a-n. Got all that?"

"Yeah. And I'm like you. I think I hear a bell trying to ring."

"There was also mention of another man I don't know anything about at all. Slidell. Maybe somebody's heard of him. I'll be in Miami as soon as I can get there. See if you can find out anything at all."

"Right. Take it easy, sailor."

Packing was no problem; I hadn't unpacked. I called the desk to get my bill ready and send for a cab. The lobby was empty except for the clerk. I settled the bill and was putting away my change when the taxi driver came in and got the bag. We went out. It was growing light now. The street had been washed, and for this brief moment just at dawn the city was almost cool and fresh. I looked up and down the street; there were no pedestrians in sight, and only an occasional car. "Airport," I told the driver, and we pulled out.

I watched out the rear window, and just before we reached the end of the block I saw a car pull out from the curb behind us. It had its lights on, so it was impossible to get an idea of what make it was, or what color. Two blocks ahead we turned to the left. The car—or another one—was still behind us. I kept watching. For a time there were two, and then three, and then we were back to one again. There was no way to tell if it was the same one, but it always stayed the same distance back, about a full city block. We made another turn, picking up the highway leading out of town, and it was still there.

I began to worry. The airport was pretty far out, and there were no doubt plenty of deserted stretches of road where they could force us off if they were after me. My only chance—if I had any—would be to jump and run for it. I'd have to warn the driver, though. If he tried to outrun them, they'd probably kill him. The minute I saw them start to close in, I'd tell him to stop.

Then, suddenly, they turned off and we were alone. After another mile with the pavement completely empty behind us I heaved a sigh of relief. False alarm. I was too jittery.

Hell, they didn't even know I was at the hotel; nobody had followed us when I came uptown from the boatyard.

Then I realized I was a baby at this sort of thing and that I was up against professionals. Maybe they had been following us. By the time we'd reached the place where they had turned off it was obvious where I was headed so they no longer had to stay in sight. It could have been the same thing when I came up from the yard. They'd merely called the hotels until they located me; there probably weren't over half a dozen. I felt ridiculous and stupid, and a little scared.

If they were after me, what was the best plan? I remembered what Willetts had said—they're all afraid of witnesses. Then stay in the open, surrounded by plenty of people, I thought. We left the city behind, rolling through the outlying housing developments, and crossed a bayou overhung with dark liveoaks and dangling pennants of Spanish moss. The sun was just rising when we pulled up in front of the airport passenger terminal. I paid off the driver and went inside with my bag.

It was a good-sized terminal, busy even at this hour in the morning. Long windows in front looked out toward the runways, and at either end were the concourses leading to the gates. To the left were some shops and the newsstand and restaurant, while all the airline counters were strung out along the right. I went over, checked in, and paid for my ticket.

"Thank you, Mr. Rogers," the girl said. She clipped my luggage check to the boarding pass and gave me my change. "Concourse B, Gate Seven. The flight will be called in approximately ten minutes."

I bought a newspaper, moved back to a leather-cushioned bench, and sat down to sweat out the ten minutes. If they were following me, they'd try to get on this flight, or at least get one man on it. I was just in back of the two lines checking in. I looked them over cautiously while pretending to read the paper. There was a slight, graying man with a flyrod case. Two young girls, who might be teachers on vacation. An elderly woman. A fat man carrying a briefcase. A Marine. Two sailors in whites. A squat, heavy-shouldered man carrying his coat over his arm. My eyes stopped, and came back to him.

He was at the head of the line now, in the row in which I'd checked in. He would have been about two places behind me, I thought. The girl was shaking her head at him. I strained to hear what she was saying.

"... sold out. We'd be glad to put you on stand-by, though; there are still about four who haven't checked in."

He nodded. I could see nothing but his back.

"Your name, please?" the girl asked.

"J. R. Bonner."

The voice was a gravelly baritone, but there was none of the rasp and menace there'd been in the other. Well, why should there be, under the circumstances? You couldn't tell much about a voice from one or two words, anyway. I glanced down at his shoes. They were black, size ten or eleven, but I was a little to the left and couldn't see the outside of the right one. I returned to my paper, pretending to read. In a moment he turned away from the counter. I looked at him in the unseeing, incurious way your eyes go across anyone in a crowd.

Aside from an impression of almost brutal strength about the shoulders and arms, he could have been anybody—line coach of a professional football team, or the boss of a heavy construction outfit. He wore a soft straw hat, white shirt, and blue tie, and the coat he carried over his arm and the trousers were the matching components of a conservative blue suit. He was somewhere around forty, about five-nine, and well over two hundred pounds, but he walked as lightly as a big cat. His eyes met mine for an instant with the chill, impersonal blankness of outer space, and moved on. He sat down on the bench over to my left. I looked back at my paper. How did you know? What did appearances mean? He could be a goon with the accomplished deadliness of a cobra, or he might be wondering at the moment whether to buy his five-year-old daughter a stuffed bear or one of the Dr. Seuss books for a coming-home present. I glanced at his feet again, and this time I could see it. The right shoe had been slit along the welt for about an inch just under the little toe.

I folded the paper, slapped it idly against my hand, and got up and walked past him. He paid no attention. I strolled over and looked out the long glass wall in front at the runways and dead grass and the bright metal skin of a DC-7 shattering the rays of morning sunlight. It was a weird sensation, and a scary one, being hunted. And in broad daylight, in a busy, peaceful airport. It was unreal. But what was even more unreal was the fact that there was nothing I could do about it. Suppose I called the police. Arrest that man; he's got a cut place in his shoe.

I wondered if he had a gun. There didn't seem to be any place he could be carrying one unless he had it in the pocket of the coat slung over his arm. If he held it just right, nobody could tell. He had no luggage. And the chances were he was alone. With the flight sold out there wasn't much percentage in more than one of them bucking the stand-by list. If he got aboard, he could keep me in sight until the others caught up. Well, he wasn't aboard yet. Maybe he wouldn't make it. They announced the flight. I walked out Concourse B, feeling his eyes in the middle of my back in spite of the fact that I knew he probably wasn't even looking at me. Why should he? He knew where I was going.

Number 302 was a continuing flight, so there were only nine or ten people at Gate 7 waiting to go aboard. Some through passengers who had deplaned to stretch their legs were allowed to go through first. Boarding passengers went through single file while the gate attendant checked our tickets. I was last. As I went up the steps I resisted an impulse to look back. He would be watching from somewhere to be sure I went aboard. There were still four or five empty seats, but that meant nothing. Two would be for the stewardesses, and some of the through passengers might still be in the terminal. I took one on the aisle, aft of the door. There might even be people ahead of him on stand-by. I waited. I was on the wrong side to see the gate, even if I'd had a window seat. It was stifling with the plane on the ground. Sweat gathered on my face. Another passenger came aboard, a woman. Then one in uniform, an Air Force major. I began to hope. The captain and first officer came through the doorway and went forward. The door to the flight compartment closed. Then two minutes before they took away the ramp Bonner came through the door. He took the last empty seat.

We were down in the steamy heat of New Orleans at 8:05 for a twenty-minute stop. Bonner played it very cagey; I remained in my seat while the first wave deplaned, but he went out with them. I could see the beauty of that. He could watch the ramp from inside the terminal to see if I got off or not, so he had me bottled up without being in evidence himself. But if he stayed and I got off, five minutes later he would have to follow me. Smart, I thought. I left the plane. As soon as I was inside the terminal I saw him. He was reading a newspaper, paying no attention to me. I sauntered out front to the limousines and taxis. There he was, still paying no attention.

There was no longer any doubt. Maybe I could call the police and have him picked up. No, that wouldn't work. I had no proof whatever. He would have identification, a good story, an alibi—they couldn't hold him ten minutes. I had to escape from him some way. But how? He was a professional and knew all the tricks; I was an amateur. Then I began to have an idea. Make it novice against novice, and I might have a chance.

We landed at Tampa at 11:40 a.m. As soon as the door was open I arose and stretched and followed the crowd into the terminal. I stood for a moment looking idly at the paperback books in the rack at the newsstand, and then drifted outside. I'd had a forlorn hope that I might catch the taxi stand with only one cab on station, but there was no such luck. There were four. The driver of the lead-off hack, however, was behind the wheel and ready to go. Bonner was just coming through the door about twenty feet to my left, lighting a cigarette and looking at everything except me. I strolled on past the line until I was abreast the lead one.

Turning quickly, I opened the door and slid in. "Downtown. Tampa," I told the driver.

"Yes, sir." He punched the starter. We pulled away from the loading zone. As we headed for the street I looked back. Bonner was climbing into the second cab. We had a lead of about a block. I took a twenty from my wallet and dropped it on the front seat beside the driver.

"There's a cab following us," I said. "Can you lose him?"

His eyes flicked downward at the money and then straight ahead. "Not if he's a cop."

"He's not."

"That's what you say."

"Why would he take a cab?" I asked. "There's a sheriffs car right there at the terminal."

He nodded. Swinging into the street, he bore down on the accelerator. "Mister, consider him lost."

I looked back. The other cab was weaving through traffic slightly less than a block behind us now. We wouldn't have a chance, I thought, if he had one of his fellow professionals at the wheel, but now the odds were even. No, they were a little better than even. We knew what we were going to do, but he had to wait till we'd done it to find out. It took less than ten minutes. The second time we ran a light on the amber and he tried to follow us through on the red, he locked fenders with a panel truck in the middle of the intersection.

"Nice going," I said. "Now the Greyhound Bus terminal."

I got out there and paid him for the meter in addition to the twenty. As soon as he was out of sight, I walked through the station and over to a taxi stand in front of a hotel, and took another cab to a Hertz agency. Thirty minutes later I was headed south on US 41 in a rented Chevrolet. There was no telling how long my luck would last, but for the moment I'd lost them.

My head began to ache again and I was having trouble staying awake. I suddenly realized it was Sunday afternoon now and I hadn't been to bed since Friday night. When I reached Punta Gorda I pulled into a motel and slept for six hours. I rolled into Miami shortly after 2 a.m. Going out to the airport to claim my bag would be too dangerous, even if I got a porter to pick it up. Bonner would be there, or he'd have somebody watching it. I turned the car in, and took a cab to a hotel on Biscayne Boulevard, explained that my bag had got separated from me when I changed planes in Chicago, and registered as Howard Summers from Portland, Oregon. They wouldn't locate me this time merely by calling the hotels. I asked for a room overlooking Bayfront Park, bought a *Herald,* and followed the boy into the elevator. The room was on the twelfth floor. As soon as he left I went over to the window and parted the slats of the Venetian blind. Just visible around to the left was City Yacht Basin. Sticking up out of the cluster of sightseeing and charter fishing boats were the tall sticks of the *Orion*. It made me sick to be this near and not be able to go aboard.

I turned away and reached for the telephone. Bill Redmond should be home by now. He answered on the first ring.

"Stuart—" I began.

He cut me off. "Good God, where are you?"

I told him the hotel. "Room 1208."

"You're in Miami? Don't you ever read the papers?"

"I've got a *Herald,* but I haven't looked at—"

"Read it. I'm on my way over there now." He hung up.

The paper was lying on the bed, where I'd tossed it when I came in. I spread it open, put a cigarette in my mouth, and started to flick the lighter. Then I saw it.

LOCAL YACHT CAPTAIN
SOUGHT IN SEA MYSTERY

The police had Baxter's letter.

CHAPTER EIGHT

It was datelined Southport.

> The aura of mystery surrounding the voyage of the ill-fated yacht *Topaz* deepened today in a strange new development that very nearly claimed the life of another victim.

> Still in critical condition in a local hospital this afternoon following an overdose of sleeping pills was an attractive brunette tentatively identified as Miss Paula Stafford of New York, believed by police to have been close to Wendell Baxter, mysterious figure whose death or disappearance while en route from Panama to Southport on the *Topaz* has turned into one of the most baffling puzzles of recent years....

I plunged ahead, skipping the parts of it I knew. It was continued in a back section. I riffled through it, scattering the pages, and went on. Then I sat down and read the whole thing through again.

It was all there. The hotel detective had gone up to her room shortly after 3:30 a.m. when guests in adjoining rooms reported a disturbance. He found her wildly upset and crying out almost incoherently that somebody had been killed. Since there were no evidences of violence and it was obvious no one else was there, dead or otherwise, he had got her calmed down and left her after she'd taken one of her sleeping pills. At 10 a.m., however, when they tried to call her and could get no response, they entered the room with a pass key and found her unconscious. A doctor was called. He found the remaining pills on the table beside the bed, and had her taken to a hospital. It wasn't known whether the overdose was accidental or a suicide attempt, since no note could be found, but when police came to investigate they found the letter from Baxter. Then everything hit the fan.

My visit came out. The elevator boy and night clerk gave the police my description. They went looking for me, and I'd disappeared from the boatyard. The letter from Baxter was printed in full. There was a rehash of the whole story up to that time, including Keefer's death and the unexplained $4000.

Now apparently $19,000 more was missing, I was missing, and nobody had an idea at all as to what had really happened to Baxter.

> . . . in light of this new development, the true identity of Wendell Baxter is more deeply shrouded in mystery than ever. Police refused to speculate as to whether or not Baxter might even still be alive. Lieutenant Boyd parried the question by saying, "There is obviously only one person who knows the answer to that, and we're looking for him."
>
> Local agents of the Federal Bureau of Investigation had no comment other than a statement that Captain Rogers was being sought for further questioning.

I pushed the paper aside and tried the cigarette again. This time I got it going. The letter itself wasn't bad enough I thought; I had to make it worse by running. That's the way it would look; the minute I read it I took off like a goosed gazelle. By this time they would have traced me to the Bolton and then to the airport. And I'd rented the car in Tampa under my own name, and then turned it in here. As soon as the man in the Hertz agency read the paper he'd call them; the taxi driver would remember bringing me to the hotel. Then it occurred to me I was already thinking like a fugitive. Well, I was one, wasn't I? There was a light knock on the door.

I went over. "Who is it?"

"Bill."

I let him in and closed the door. He sighed and shook his head. "Pal, when you get in a jam, you're no shoestring operator."

We're the same age and about the same height, and we've known each other since we were in the third grade. He's thin, restless, blazingly intelligent, somewhat cynical, and one of the world's worst hypochondriacs. Women consider him handsome, and he probably is. He has a slender reckless face, ironic blue eyes, and dark hair that's prematurely graying. He smokes three packs of cigarettes a day, and quits every other week. He never drinks. He's an AA.

"All right," he said, "let's have it."

I told him.

He whistled softly. Then he said, "Well, the first thing is to get you out of here before they pick you up."

"Why?" I asked. "If the FBI is looking for me, maybe I'd better turn myself in. At least they won't kill me. The others will."

"It can wait till morning, if that's what you decide. In the meantime I've got to talk to you. About Baxter."

"Have you got any lead on him at all?" I asked.

"I'm not sure," he said. "That's the reason I've got to talk to you. What I've come up with is so goofy if I tried to tell the police they might have me committed. Let's go."

"Where?" I asked.

"Home, you goof. Lorraine's scrambling some eggs and making coffee."

"Sure. Harboring a fugitive's just a harmless prank. Be our guest in charming, gracious Atlanta."

"Oh, cut it out, Scarface. How would I know you're a fugitive? I never read anything but the *Wall Street Journal.*"

I gave in, but insisted we leave the hotel separately. He told me where the car was, and left. I waited five minutes before following. The streets were deserted. I climbed in, and he swung onto Biscayne

Boulevard, headed south. They lived close to downtown, in a small apartment house on Brickell Avenue. From habit, I looked out the rear window. As far as I could tell, nobody was following us.

"The Stafford woman's still alive, the last we got," he said, "but they haven't been able to question her yet."

"I've got a sad hunch she doesn't know too much about him, anyway," I said. "She told me she didn't know who those men were, or what they wanted, and I think she was telling the truth. I'm beginning to doubt Baxter even existed; I think he's an hallucination people start seeing just before they crack up."

"You haven't heard anything yet," he said. "When I tell you what I've come up with you'll think we're both around the bend."

"Well, be mysterious about it," I said sourly. "That's just what I need."

"Wait'll we get inside." He swung into a driveway between shadowy palms and parked beside the building. It had only four apartments, each with its own entrance. Theirs was the lower left. We came back around the hibiscus-bordered walk, and went in the front. The living room was dim and quiet, and cool from the air-conditioner. There were no lights on, but there was enough illumination from the kitchen to find our way past the hi-fi and record albums and rows and stacks of books, and the lamps and statuary Lorraine had made. She does ceramics.

At the moment she was scrambling eggs, a long-legged brunette with a velvety tan, rumpled dark brown hair, and wide, humorous, gray eyes. She was wearing Bermuda shorts and sandals, and a white shirt that was pulled together and knotted around her waist. Beyond the stove was a counter with a yellow formica top and tall yellow stools, a small breakfast nook, and a window hung with yellow curtains.

She stopped stirring the eggs long enough to kiss me and wave a hand toward the counter. "Park it, Killer. What's this rumble you're hot?"

"Broads," Bill said. "Always nosy." He set a bottle of bourbon and a glass on the counter in front of me. His theory was that nobody could be sure he didn't drink if there was none around. I poured a big slug and downed it, had a sip of scalding black coffee, and began to feel better. Lorraine put the eggs on the table and sat down across from me, rested her elbows on the counter, and grinned.

"Let's face it, Rogers. Civilization just isn't your environment. I mean land-based civilization. Any time you come above high tide you ought to carry a tag, the way sandhogs do. Something like "This man is not completely amphibious, and may get into trouble ashore. Rush to nearest salt water and immerse."

"I'll buy it," I said. "Only the whole thing started at sea. That can scare you."

"Have you told him yet?" she asked Bill.

"I'm going to right now." He pushed the untouched eggs off his plate onto mine and lighted a cigarette. "Try this on for size—your man was forty-eight to fifty, six feet, a hundred and seventy pounds, brown hair with a little gray in it, brown eyes, mustache, quiet, gentlemanly, close-mouthed, and boat-crazy."

"Right," I said. "Except for the mustache."

"Somebody may have told him about razors. He came here about two and a half years ago—February of nineteen-fifty-six, to be exact—and he seemed to have plenty of money. He rented a house on one of the islands—a big, elaborate one with private dock—and bought that sport fisherman, a thirty-foot sloop, and a smaller sailboat of some kind. He was a bachelor, widower, or divorced. He had a Cuban couple who took care of the house and garden, and a man named Charley Grimes to skipper the fishing boat. Apparently didn't work at anything, and spent nearly all his time fishing and sailing. Had several girl friends around town, most of whom would have probably married him if he'd ever asked them, but it appears he never told them any more about himself than he told anybody else. His name was Brian Hardy, and the name of the fishing boat was the *Princess Pat*. You begin to get it now?"

"It's all fits," I said excitedly. "Every bit of it. That was Baxter, beyond a doubt."

"That's what I'm afraid of," Bill replied. "Brian Hardy's been dead for over two months. And this is the part you're going to love. He was lost at sea."

It began to come back then. "No!" I said. "No—"

Lorraine patted my hand. "Poor old Rogers. Why don't you get married, so you can stay out of trouble? Or be in it all the time and get used to it."

"Understand," I said, "I'm not prejudiced. Some of my best friends are married. It's just that I wouldn't want my sister to marry a married couple."

"It happened in April, and I think you were somewhere in the out islands," Bill went on. "But you probably heard about it."

"Yeah," I said. "Explosion and fire, wasn't it? Somewhere in the Stream."

"That's right. He was alone. He'd had a fight with Grimes that morning and fired him, and was taking the *Princess Pat* across to Bimini himself. He'd told somebody he planned to hire a native skipper and mate for a couple of weeks' marlin fishing. It was good weather with hardly any wind, and the Stream was as flat as Biscayne Bay. He left around noon, and should have been over there in three or four hours.

Afterward, there were two boats that reported seeing him drifting around, but he didn't ask for help so they didn't go over. Some time after dark he called the Coast Guard—"

"Sure," I broke in. "That was it. I remember now. He was talking to them right at the moment she blew up."

Bill nodded. "It was easy enough to figure out what happened. When he got hold of them, he said he'd been having engine trouble all afternoon. Dirt or rust in the fuel tanks. He'd been blowing out fuel lines and cleaning strainers and settling bowls and probably had the bilges full of gasoline by that time. He'd know enough not to smoke, of course, so it must have been the radio itself that set it off. Maybe a sparking brush on the converter, or a relay contact. That was the Coast Guard theory. Anyway, he went dead right in the middle of a sentence. Then about fifteen minutes later a northbound tanker pretty well out in the Stream off Fort Lauderdale reported what looked like a boat afire over to the eastward of them. They changed course and went over, and got there before the Coast Guard, but there wasn't anything they could do. She was a mass of flame by then and in a matter of minutes she burned to the waterline and sank. The Coast Guard cruised around for several hours, hoping he'd been able to jump, but if he had he'd already drowned. They never found any trace of him. There wasn't any doubt, of course, as to what boat it was. That was just about the position he'd reported. He'd been drifting north in the Stream all the time his engines were conked out."

"Did they ever recover his body?" I asked.

"No."

"Did his life-insurance companies pay off?"

"As far as anybody could ever find out, he didn't carry any life insurance."

We looked at each other in silence. We both nodded.

"When they come after you," Lorraine said, "tell them to wait for me. I think so too."

"Sure," I said excitedly. "Look—that's the very thing that's been puzzling me all the time. I mean, why those three goons were so sure I'd put him ashore somewhere, without even knowing about the letter. It's simply because he'd done it to 'em once before."

"Not so fast," Bill cautioned. "Remember, this happened at least twenty miles offshore. And on his way out that day he stopped at a marine service station in Government Cut and gassed up. They were positive he didn't have a dinghy. Sport fishermen seldom or never do, of course, so they'd have noticed if he had."

"That doesn't prove a thing," I said, "except that we're right. He *wanted* it known he didn't have another boat with him. Somebody else took him off, and five will get you ten it was a girl named Paula Stafford. The Stream was flat; she could have come out from Fort Lauderdale in any kind of power cruiser, or even one of those big, fast outboard jobs. Finding him in the dark might be a tough job for a landlubber, unless he gave her a portable RDF and a signal from the *Princess Pat* to home on, but actually she wouldn't have to do it in the dark. She could have been already out there before sundown, lying a mile or so away where she wouldn't have any trouble picking up his lights. Or if there were no other boats around, she could have gone alongside before it got dark."

"But neither the tanker nor the Coast Guard saw any other boat when they got there."

"They wouldn't," I said. "Look. They took it for granted the explosion occurred while he was talking to them, because his radio went dead. Well, his radio went dead simply because he turned it off. Then he threw several gallons of gasoline around the cabin and cockpit, rigged a fuse of some kind that would take a few minutes to set it off, got in the other boat, and shoved. It would have taken the tanker possibly ten minutes to get there, even after they spotted the fire. So with a fast boat, Baxter was probably five to seven miles away and running without lights when it showed up, and by the time the Coast Guard arrived he was ashore having a drink in some cocktail lounge in Fort Lauderdale. It would be easy. That's the reason I asked about the insurance. It would be so simple to fake that if he had a really big policy they probably wouldn't pay off until after seven years, or whatever it is."

"Well, he didn't have any," Bill replied, "so that was no strain. He also had no heirs that anybody has been able to locate, and the only estate besides the other boats seems to be a checking account with about eleven thousand in it."

"What else did you find out?" I asked.

"I pulled his package in the morgue, but there wasn't a great deal in it after the clippings for those first few days. So I started calling people. The police are still trying to locate some of his family. The house is sitting there vacant; he had a lease, and paid the rent on a yearly basis, so it has until next February to run. Nobody can understand his financial setup. The way he lived was geared to a hell of a big income, but they don't know where it came from. They couldn't find any investments of any kind, no stocks, bonds, real estate, savings, or anything. Just the checking account."

"Well, the bank must know how the checking account was maintained."

"Yes. Mostly by big cashiers' checks, ten thousand or more at a time, from out-of-town banks. He could have bought them himself."

"That sounds as if he were on the run, and hiding from somebody, even then. If he had a lot of money it was in cash, and he kept it that way so he could take it with him if he had to disappear."

"The police figure it about the same way. After all, he wouldn't be exactly unique. We get our share of lamsters, absconding bank types, and Latin American statesmen who got out just ahead of the firing squad with a trunk full of loot."

I lighted a cigarette. "I want to get in that house. Do you know the address?"

He nodded. "I know the address, but you couldn't get in. It'd be tough, even for a pro. That's about seventy thousand dollars' worth of house, and in that class they don't make it easy for burglars."

"I've got to! Look—Baxter's going to drive me insane, get me killed, or land me in jail. There must be an explanation for him. If I could only find out who the hell he really was, I'd at least have a place to start."

He shook his head. "You wouldn't find it there. The police have been over every inch of it, and they found absolutely nothing that would give them a lead, not a letter or a clipping or a scrap of paper, or even anything he'd bought before he came to Miami. They even checked the labels and laundry marks in his clothes, and they're all local. He apparently moved in exactly the way a baby is born—naked, and with no past life whatever."

I nodded. "That's the impression you begin to get after a while. He came aboard the *Topaz* the same way. He just appears, like a revelation."

"But about the house," Bill went on, "I haven't told you everything yet. I was in it this afternoon, and there's just a chance I stumbled onto something. I don't know."

I looked up quickly. "What?"

"Don't get your hopes up. The chances are a thousand to one it's nothing at all. It's only an autographed book and a letter."

"How'd you get in?" I demanded. "What book is it, and who's the letter from?"

He lighted another cigarette. "The police let me in. I went to a lieutenant I know and made him a proposition. I wanted to do a Sunday-supplement sort of piece on Hardy, and if they'd cooperate it might help both of us. Any newspaper publicity is always helpful when you're trying to locate friends or relatives of somebody who's dead. You know." He made an impatient gesture, and went on.

"Anyway, they were agreeable. They had a key to the place, and sent a man with me. We spent about an hour in the house, prowling through all the desks and table drawers and his clothes and leafing through books and so on—all the stuff that had been sifted before. We didn't find anything, of course. But when we were leaving, I noticed some mail on a small table in the front hall. The table was under the mail slot, but we hadn't seen it when we came in because it's behind the door when it's open.

"Apparently what had happened was that this stuff had been delivered between the time the police were there last—shortly after the accident—and the time somebody finally got around to notifying the Post Office he was dead. Anyway, it was all postmarked in April. The detective opened it, but none of it amounted to anything. There were two or three bills and some circulars, and this letter and the book. They were both postmarked Santa Barbara, California, and the letter was from the author of the book. It was just a routine sort of thing, saying the book was being returned, autographed, as he'd requested, and thanking him for his interest. The detective kept them both, of course, but he let me read the letter, and I got another copy of the book out of the public library. Just a minute."

He went into the living room and came back with it. I recognized it immediately; in fact, I had a copy of it aboard the *Orion*. It was an arty and rather expensive job, a collection of some of the most beautiful photographs of sailing craft I'd ever seen. Most of them were racing yachts under full sail, and the title of it was *Music in the Wind*. A good many of the photographs had been taken by the girl who'd collected and edited the job and written the descriptive material. Her name was Patricia Reagan.

"I'm familiar with it," I said, looking at him a little blankly. I couldn't see what he had in mind. "They're beautiful photographs. Hey, you don't mean—"

He shook his head. "No. There's no picture of anyone in here who resembles the description of Brian Hardy. I've already looked."

"Then what is it?" I asked.

"A couple of things," he replied. "And both pretty far out. The first is that he had hundreds of books, but this is the only one that was autographed. The other thing is the name."

"Patricia!" I said.

He nodded. "I checked on it. When he bought that fishing boat its name was *Dolphin III,* or something like that. He was the one who changed it to *Princess Pat.*"

CHAPTER NINE

"You both have a boarding-house reach," Lorraine said.

"Where I'm sitting, I need one," I replied. "How was the letter worded? Any indication at all that she knew him?"

"No. Polite, but completely impersonal. Apparently he'd written her, praising the book and sending a copy to be autographed. She signed it and sent it back. Thank you, over, and out. The only possibility is that she might have known him by some other name."

"You don't remember the address?"

He looked pained. "That's a hell of a question to ask a reporter. Here." He fished in his wallet and handed me a slip of paper. On it was scrawled, *"Patricia Reagan, 16 Belvedere Pl., Sta. Brba., Calif."*

I looked at my watch and saw that even with the time difference it would be almost one a.m. in California. "Hell, call her now," Bill said. I went out in the living room, dialed the operator, gave her the name and address, and held on. While she was getting Information in Santa Barbara I wondered what I'd do if somebody woke me up out of a sound sleep from three thousand miles away to ask me if I'd ever heard of Joe Blow the Third. Well, the worst she could do was hang up.

The phone rang three times. Then a girl said sleepily, "Hello?"

"Miss Patricia Reagan?" the operator asked. "Miami is calling."

"Pat, is that you?" the girl said. "What on earth—"

"No," the operator explained. "The call is for Miss—"

I broke in. "Never mind, Operator. I'll talk to anyone there."

"Thank you. Go ahead, please."

"Hello," I said. "I'm trying to locate Miss Reagan."

"Oh, I'm sorry," the girl replied. "She's not here; I'm her roommate. The operator said Miami, so I thought it was Pat that was calling."

"You mean she's in Miami?"

"Yes. That is, Florida. Near Miami."

"Do you know the address?"

"Yes. I had a letter from her yesterday. Just a moment."

I waited. Then she said, "Hello? Here it is. The nearest town seems to be a place called Marathon. Do you know where that is?"

"Yes," I said. "It's down the Keys."

"She's on Spanish Key, and the mailing address is care of W. R. Holland, RFD One."

"Does she have a telephone?"

"I think so. But I don't know the number."

"Is she a guest there?" I didn't like the idea of waking up an entire household with a stupid question.

"She's staying in the house while the owners are in Europe. While she works on some magazine articles. I don't know how well you know her, but I wouldn't advise interrupting her when she's working."

"No," I said. "Only while she's sleeping. And thanks a million."

I hung up. Bill and Lorraine had come into the living room. I told them, and put in the call to the Marathon exchange. The phone rang, and went on ringing. *Five. Six. Seven*. It was a very big house, or she was a sound sleeper.

"Hello." She had a nice voice, but she sounded cross. Well, I thought, who wouldn't?

"Miss Reagan?" I asked.

"Yes. What is it?"

"I want to apologize for waking you up this time of morning, but this is vitally important. It's about a man named Brian Hardy. Did you ever know him?"

"No. I've never heard of him."

"Please think carefully. He used to live in Miami, and he asked you to autograph a copy of *Music in the Wind*. Which, incidentally, is a very beautiful book. I have a copy of it myself."

"Thank you," she said, a little more pleasantly. "Now that you mention it, I do seem to have a hazy recollection of the name. Frankly, I'm not flooded with requests for autographs, and as I recall he mailed the book to me."

"That's right. But as far as you know, you've never met him?"

"No. I'm positive of that. And his letter said nothing about knowing me."

"Was the letter handwritten or typed?"

"Typed, I think. Yes, I'm sure of that."

"I see. Well, did you ever know a man named Wendell Baxter?"

"No. And would you mind telling me just who you are and what this is all about? Are you drunk?"

"I'm not drunk," I said. "I'm in trouble up to my neck, and I'm trying to find somebody who knew this man. I've got a wild hunch that he knew you. Let me describe him."

"All right," she said wearily. "Which shall we take first? Mr. Hardy, or the other one?"

"They're the same man," I said. "He would be about fifty years old, slender, maybe a little over six feet tall, brown eyes, graying brown hair, distinguished looking, and well educated. Have you ever known anybody who would fit that?"

"No." I thought I detected just the slightest hesitancy, but decided I was reaching for it. "Not that I recall. Though it's rather general."

"Try!" I urged her. "Listen. He was a quiet man, very reserved, and courteous. He didn't use glasses, even for reading. He was a heavy smoker. Chesterfields, two or three packs a day. Not particularly dark-complexioned, but he took a good tan. He was a superb small-boat sailor, a natural helmsman, and I would guess he'd done quite a bit of ocean racing. Does any of that remind you of anyone you've ever known?"

"No," she said coldly. "It doesn't."

"Are you sure? No one at all?"

"Well, it does happen to be an excellent description of my father. But if this is a joke of some kind, I must say it's in very poor taste."

"What?"

"My father is dead." The receiver banged in my ear as she hung up.

I dropped the instrument back on the cradle and reached dejectedly for a cigarette. Then I stopped, and stared at Bill. How stupid could I get? Of course he was. That was the one thing in common in all the successive manifestations of Wendell Baxter; each time you finally ran him down, he was certain to be dead.

I grabbed up the phone and put in the call again. After it had rung for three minutes with no answer I gave up.

"Here's your ticket," Bill said. "But I still think you ought to take the car. Or let me drive you down there."

"If they picked me up, you'd be in a jam too. I'll be safe enough on the bus, this far from the Miami terminal."

It was after sunrise now, and we were parked near the bus station in Homestead, about thirty miles south of Miami. I'd shaved and changed into a pair of Bill's slacks and a sport shirt, and was wearing sun glasses.

"Don't get your hopes too high," Bill cautioned. He was worried about me. "It's flimsy as hell. She'd know whether her own father was dead or not."

"I know," I said. "But I've got to talk to her."

"Suppose it's nothing, then what? Call me, and let me come after you."

"No," I said. "I'll call the FBI. I'm not doing myself any good, running like this, and if I keep it up too long Bonner and those other goons may catch up with me."

The bus pulled in. Bill made a gesture with his thumb and forefinger. "Luck, pal."

"Thanks," I said. I slid out of the car, and climbed aboard. The bus was about two-thirds filled, and several passengers were reading copies of the *Herald* with my description on the front page, but no one paid any attention to me. There was no picture, thank God. I found a seat in the rear beside a sailor who'd fallen asleep, and watched Bill drive away.

In a little over an hour we were on Key Largo and beginning the long run down the Overseas Highway. It was a hot June morning with brilliant sunlight and a gentle breeze out of the southeast. I stared out at the water with its hundred gradations of color from bottle green to indigo and wished I could wake up from this dream to find myself back aboard the *Orion* somewhere in the out islands of the Bahamas. How long had it been going on now? This was—what? Monday? Only forty-eight hours. It seemed a month. And all it ever did was get worse. I'd started out with one dead Baxter, and now I had three.

And what would I prove, actually, if I did find out who he was? That wouldn't change anything. It would still be my unsupported word against the rest of the world as to what had become of him and that money he'd said he had. I was beating my brains out for nothing. No matter how you sliced it, there was only one living witness, I was it, and there'd never be any more.

We passed Islamorada and Marathon. It was shortly after eleven when we rolled onto Spanish Key and pulled to a stop in front of the filling station and general store. I got down, feeling the sudden impact of the heat after the air-conditioning, and the bus went on. I could see the secondary road where it emerged from the pines about a quarter of a mile ahead, but I didn't know which branch I wanted. A gaunt, leathery-faced man in overalls and a railroad cap was cleaning the windshield of a car in the station driveway. I called over to him.

"Holland?" He pointed. "Take the road to the left. It's about a mile and a half."

"Thanks," I said.

For the first half mile there were no houses at all. The unsurfaced marl road wound through low pine and palmetto slash that was more like the interior of Florida than the Keys. From time to time I caught glimpses of water off to my right. Then the road swung in that direction and I passed near some beach houses and could see out across the half-mile channel separating Spanish Key from the next one to the westward. The houses were boarded up with hurricane shutters as if their owners were gone for the summer. I stopped to light a cigarette and mop the sweat from my face. All sound of cars passing on the Overseas Highway had died out behind me now. If she wanted an isolated place to work, I thought, she'd found it.

The pine began to thin out a little and the road swung eastward now, paralleling the beach along the south side of the Key. The next mailbox was Holland's. The house was on the beach, about a hundred yards back from the road, with a curving drive and a patch of green lawn in front. It was large for a beach house, solidly constructed of concrete block and stucco, and dazzling white in the sun, with a red tile roof and bright aluminum awnings over the windows and the door. In the carport on the right was an MG with California license plates. She was home.

I went up the short concrete walk and rang the bell. Nothing happened. I pushed the button again, and waited. There was no sound except the lapping of water on the beach around in back, and somewhere farther offshore an outboard motor. About two hundred yards up the beach was another house somewhat similar to this one, but there was no car in evidence and it appeared to be unoccupied. There was still no sound from inside. The drapes were drawn behind the jalousie windows on either side of the door. The outboard motor sounded nearer. I stepped around the corner and saw it. It was coming this way, a twelve- or fourteen-foot runabout planing along at a good clip. At the wheel was a girl in a brief splash of yellow bathing suit.

There was a long low porch back here, another narrow strip of lawn, a few coconut palms leaning seaward, and a glaring expanse of white coral sand along the shore. There were several pieces of brightly colored lawn furniture on the porch and under the palms, and a striped umbrella and some beach pads out on the sand. The water was very shoal, and there was no surf because of the reefs offshore and the fact that the breeze had almost died out now. Far out I could see a westbound tanker skirting the inshore edge of the Stream. A wooden pier ran out into the water about fifty feet, and the girl was coming alongside it now.

I started out to take a line for her, but she beat me there. She lifted out a mask and snorkel and an under-water camera in a clear plastic housing, and stepped onto the pier.

She was slender and rather tall, a girl with a deep tan and dark wine-red hair. Her back was toward me momentarily as she made the painter fast. She straightened and turned then, and I saw her eyes were brown. The face was slender, with a very nice mouth and a stubborn chin, and was as smoothly tanned as the rest of her. There was no really striking resemblance to Baxter, but she could very well be his daughter.

"Good morning," I said. "Miss Reagan?"

She nodded coolly. "Yes. What is it?"

"My name is Stuart Rogers. I'd like to talk to you for a minute."

"You're the man who called me this morning." It was a statement, rather than a question.

"Yes," I said, just as bluntly. "I want to ask you about your father."

"Why?"

"Why don't we go over in the shade and sit down?" I suggested.

"All right." She reached for the camera. I picked it up and followed her. She was about five feet eight inches tall, I thought. Her hair was wet at the ends, as if the bathing cap hadn't covered it completely, and tendrils of it stuck to the nape of her neck. It was a little cooler on the porch. She sat down on a chaise with one long smooth leg doubled under her, and looked up questioningly at me. I held out cigarettes, and she thanked me and took one. I lighted it for her.

I sat down across from her. "This won't take long. I'm not prying into your personal affairs just because I haven't got anything better to do. You said your father was dead. Could you tell me when he died?"

"In nineteen-fifty-six," she replied.

Hardy had showed up in Miami in February of 1956. That didn't allow much leeway. "What month?" I asked.

"January," she said.

I sighed. We were over that one.

The brown eyes began to burn. "Unless you have some good explanation for this, Mr. Rogers—"

"I do. I have a very good one. However, you can get rid of me once and for all by answering just one more question. Were you present at his funeral?"

She gasped. "Why did you ask that?"

"I think you know by now," I said. "There wasn't any funeral, was there?"

"No." She leaned forward tensely. "What are you trying to say? That you think he's still alive?"

"No," I said. "I'm sorry. He is dead now. He died of a heart attack on the fifth of this month aboard my boat in the Caribbean."

Her face was pale under the tan, and I was afraid she was going to faint. She didn't, however. She shook her head. "No. It's impossible. It was somebody else—"

"What happened in nineteen-fifty-six?" I asked. "And where?"

"It was in Arizona. He went off into the desert on a hunting trip, and got lost."

"Arizona? What was he doing there?"

"He lived there," she replied. "In Phoenix."

I wondered if I'd missed, after all, when I'd been so near. That couldn't be Baxter. He was a yachtsman, a seaman; you couldn't even imagine him in a desert environment. Then I remembered *Music in the Wind*. She hadn't acquired that intense feeling for the beauty of sail by watching somebody's colored slides. "He wasn't a native?" I said.

"No. We're from Massachusetts. He moved to Phoenix in nineteen-fifty."

Now we were getting somewhere. "Look, Miss Reagan," I said, "you admitted the description I gave you over the phone could be that of your father. You also admit you have no definite proof he's dead; he merely disappeared. Then why do you refuse to believe he could be the man I'm talking about?"

"I should think it would be obvious," she replied curtly. "My father's name was Clifford Reagan. Not Hardy—or whatever it was you said."

"He could have changed it."

"And why would he?" The brown eyes blazed again, but I had a feeling there was something defensive about her anger.

"I don't know," I said.

"There are several other reasons," she went on. "He couldn't have lived in that desert more than two days without water. The search wasn't called off until long after everybody had given up all hope he could still be alive. It's been two and a half years. If he'd found his way out, don't you consider it at least a possibility he might have let me know? Or do you think the man who died on your boat was suffering from amnesia and didn't know who he was?"

"No," I said. "He knew who he was, all right."

"Then I believe we've settled the matter," she said, starting to get up. "It wasn't my father. So if you'll excuse me—"

"Not so fast," I snapped. "I'm already in about all the trouble one man can get in, and you can't make it any worse by calling the police and having me thrown in jail. So don't try to brush me off till we're finished, because that's the only way you're going to do it. I think you'd better tell me how he got lost."

For a moment I wouldn't have offered much in the way of odds that she wasn't going to slap me across the face. She was a very proud girl with a lot of spirit. Then she appeared to get her temper in hand. "All right," she said.

"He was hunting quail," she went on. "In some very hilly and inaccessible desert country ninety or a hundred miles southwest of Tucson. He'd gone alone. That was Saturday morning, and he wasn't really missed until he failed to show up at the bank on Monday."

"Didn't you or your mother know where he was?" I asked.

"He and my mother were divorced in nineteen-fifty," she replied. "At the same time he moved to Phoenix. We were living in Massachusetts. He had remarried, but was separated from his second wife."

"Oh," I said. "I'm sorry. Go on."

"The bank called his apartment, thinking he might be ill. When they could get no answer, they called the apartment-house manager. He said he'd seen my father leave on Saturday with his gun and hunting clothes, but he wasn't sure where he'd planned to hunt or how long he intended to stay. The sheriff's office was notified, and they located the sporting-goods store where he'd bought some shells Friday afternoon. He'd told the clerk the general locality he was going to hunt in. They organized a search party, but it was such an immense area and so rough and remote that it was Wednesday before they even found the car. It was near an old trace of a road at least twenty miles from the nearest ranch house. He'd apparently got lost while he was hunting and couldn't find his way back to it. They went on searching with jeeps and horses and even planes until the following Sunday, but they never did find him. Almost a year later some uranium prospectors found his hunting coat; it was six or seven miles from where the car had been. Are you satisfied now?"

"Yes," I said. "But not quite the way you think. Have you read the paper this morning?"

She shook her head. "It's still in the mailbox. I haven't gone after it yet."

"I'll bring it," I said. "I want you to read something."

I went and got it. "I'm the Captain Rogers referred to," I said as I handed it to her. "The man who signed himself Brian in the letter is the same one who told me his name was Wendell Baxter."

She read it through. Then she folded the paper and put it aside defiantly. "It's absurd," she said. "It's been two and a half years. And my father never had twenty-three thousand dollars. Nor any reason for calling himself Brian."

"Listen," I told her. "One month after your father disappeared in that desert a man who could be his double arrived in Miami, rented a big home on an island in Biscayne Bay, bought a forty-thousand-dollar sport fisherman he renamed the *Princess Pat*—"

She gasped.

I went on relentlessly. "—and lived there like an Indian prince with no apparent source of income until the night of April seventh of this year, when *he* disappeared. He was lost at sea when the *Princess Pat* exploded, burned to the waterline, and sank, twenty miles off the Florida coast at port Lauderdale. And again, no body was ever found. His name was Brian Hardy, and he was the one who sent you that book to be autographed. Slightly less than two months later, on May thirty-first, Brian Hardy came aboard my ketch in Cristobal, using the name of Wendell Baxter. I'm not guessing here, or using descriptions, because I saw a photograph of Hardy, and this was the same man. And I say Hardy was your father. Do you have any kind of photograph or snapshot?"

She gave a dazed shake of the head. "Not here. I have some in the apartment in Santa Barbara."

"Do you agree now it was your father?"

"I don't know. The whole thing is so utterly pointless. Why would he do it?"

"He was running from somebody," I said. "In Arizona, and then in Miami, and again in Panama."

"But from whom?"

"I don't know," I said. "I was hoping you might. But the thing I really want to know is this—did your father ever have a heart attack?"

"No," she said. "Not that I ever heard."

"Is there any history of heart or coronary disease in the family at all?"

She shook her head. "I don't think so."

I lighted a cigarette and stared out across the sun-drenched blues and greens over the reefs. I was doing just beautifully. Apparently all I'd accomplished so far was to establish that aboard the *Topaz* Baxter had died for the third time with great finality and dramatic effect without leaving a body around to prove it. So all I had to do was convince everybody that this time it was for real. If he died of bubonic plague on the speaker's platform at an AMA convention, I thought bitterly, and was cremated in Macy's window, nobody would take it seriously. He'll turn up fellas; just you wait.

"Does the name Slidell mean anything to you?" I asked.

"No," she said. I was convinced she was telling the truth. "I've never heard it before."

"Do you know where he could have got that money?"

She ran despairing hands through her hair, and stood up. "No. Mr. Rogers, none of this makes the slightest sense to me. It *couldn't* have been my father."

"But you know it was, don't you?" I said.

She nodded. "I'm afraid so."

"Did you say he worked for a bank?"

"Yes. In the Trust Department of the Drovers National."

"There was no shortage in his accounts?"

For an instant I thought the anger was going to flare again. Then she said wearily, "No. Not this time."

"This time?"

She made a little gesture of resignation. "Since he may be the one who got you into this trouble, I suppose you have a right to know. He did take some money once, from another bank. I don't see how it could have any bearing on this, but maybe it has. If you'll wait while I shower and change, I'll tell you about it."

CHAPTER TEN

She brushed sand from her bare feet and opened the door at the left end of the porch. The kitchen was bright with colored tile and white enamel. I followed her through an arched doorway into a large dining and living room. "Please sit down," she said. "I won't be long." She disappeared down a hallway to the right.

I lighted a cigarette and looked around at the room. It was comfortable, and the light pleasantly subdued after the glare of the white coral sand outside. The drapes over the front window were of some loosely woven dark green material, and the lighter green walls and bare terrazzo floor added to the impression of coolness. Set in the wall to the left, next to the carport, was an air-conditioner unit whose faint humming made the only sound. Above it was a mounted permit, a very large one. Between it and the front window on that side was a hi-fi set in a blond cabinet. At the rear of the room was a sideboard, and a dining table made of bamboo and heavy glass. A long couch and two armchairs with a teak coffee table between them formed a conversational group near the center of the room. The couch and chairs were bamboo with brightly colored cushions. On the other side of the room, between the hallway and the front, were stacks of loaded book shelves. Just to the right of the hallway was a massive desk on which were a telephone, a portable typewriter, several boxes of paper, and two more cameras, a Rollieflex and a 35-mm job. I walked over to the desk and saw that it also held several trays of colored slides and a pile of photographs of Keys scenes, mostly eight-by-ten blowups in both black-and-white and color. I wondered if she'd done them, and then remembered *Music in the Wind*. She was an artist with a camera. Somewhere down the hall was the muted sound of a shower running.

In a few minutes she came back. She had changed to a crisp summery dress of some pale blue material, and was bare-legged and wearing sandals. Her hair, cut rather short in a careless, pixie effect, seemed a little darker than it had in the sun. Patricia Reagan was a very attractive girl. She had regained her composure somewhat, and managed a smile. "I'm sorry to keep you waiting."

"Not at all," I said. We sat down and lighted cigarettes.

"How did you locate me?" she asked.

I told her. "Your roommate in Santa Barbara said you were doing some magazine articles."

She made a deprecating gesture. "Not on assignment, I'm afraid. I'm not a professional yet. An editor has promised to look at an article on the Keys, and I had a chance to stay in this house while Mr. and Mrs. Holland are in Europe. They were neighbors of ours in Massachusetts. And in the meantime I'm doing some colored slides, under-water shots along the reefs."

"Skin-diving alone's not a very good practice," I said.

"Oh, I'm just working in shallow water. But the whole area's fascinating, and the water's beautiful."

I grinned. "I'm a Floridian, and I don't like to sound unpatriotic, but you ought to try the Bahamas. The colors of the water under the right light conditions almost make you hurt."

She nodded somberly. "I was there once, when I was twelve. My mother and father and I cruised in the Exumas and around Eleuthera for about a month in a shallow-draft yawl."

"A charter?" I asked.

"No. It was ours. He and I brought it down, and Mother flew to Nassau to join us. She always got sick offshore."

"What was the name of the yawl?"

The brown eyes met mine in a quick glance. Then she shook her head, a little embarrassed. "*Enchantress*. Princess Pat was a pet name, one of those top-secret jokes between fathers and very young daughters. He was the only one who ever used it."

"I'm sorry about all this," I said. "But how did he get to Phoenix?"

Downhill, as it turned out. She told me, and even after all this time there was hurt and bewilderment in it. The Reagans were from a small town named Elliston on the coast of Massachusetts near Lynn. They'd always been sailors, either professional or amateur, several having been mates and shipmasters during the clipper-ship era in the 40s and 50s and another a privateer during the Revolution. Clifford Reagan belonged to the yacht club and had sailed in a number of ocean races, though not in his own boat.

I gathered his father was fairly well-to-do, though she made as little of this as possible. He'd been in the foundry business and in real estate, and owned considerable stock in the town's leading bank and was on its board of directors. Clifford Reagan went to work in the bank when he finished college. He married a local girl, and Patricia was their only child. You could tell she and her father were very close when she was small. Then when she was sixteen the whole thing went on the rocks.

Her mother and father were divorced, but that was only the beginning. When her mother's attorneys wanted an accounting of the community property the rest of it was discovered; he'd lost not only everything they owned gambling on Canadian mining stocks, but also $17,000 he'd taken from the bank.

"Nobody ever knew about it except the president of the bank and the family," she said, staring down at her hands in her lap. "My grandfather made the shortage good, so he wasn't prosecuted. The only stipulation was that he resign, and never work in a bank again."

"But he was working in one in Phoenix," I said.

She nodded. "Actually, there was no way anyone could stop him. It had all been so hushed up before that even the bonding company didn't know about it. Grandfather was afraid it would happen again, but what could he do? Tell the bank out there that his own son had stolen money? And perhaps ruin the last chance he'd ever have to live it down and redeem himself?"

"But how did a man who was already past forty get a job in a bank without references?" I asked.

"A woman," she said. "His second wife."

Reagan had probably settled on Arizona as being about as remote from any connection with his past life as it would be possible to get and still stay on the same planet. He'd worked for a while as an account representative in a brokerage office, and soon came to know a great many people in some of the high-bracket suburbs of Phoenix. He met Mrs. Canning about that time, and married her in 1951. She was the widow of a Columbus, Ohio, real-estate developer who had bought a big ranch near Phoenix and raised quarter horses. She also owned a big block of stock in the Drovers National, so nothing could be simpler than Reagan's going to work there if that was what he wanted to do.

The marriage didn't last—they were separated in 1954—but oddly enough the job did. They liked him at the bank, and he worked at the job and was good at it. The distinguished appearance, quiet, well-bred manner, and the fact that he was on good terms with lots of wealthy potential customers did him no harm either. He was promoted several times, and by 1956 was in charge of the trust department.

"He was unhappy, though," she went on. "I think desperately unhappy. I could sense it, even though we couldn't talk to each other the way we used to. I saw him only once a year, when I went out there for two weeks after school was out. We both tried very hard, but I guess it's a special kind of country that fathers and very young daughters live in, and once you leave it you can never go back. We'd play golf, and go riding, and skeet shooting, and he'd take me to parties, but the real lines of communication were down."

She realized that he hated the desert. He was in the wrong world, and he was too old now to go somewhere else and start over. She didn't think he drank much; he simply wasn't the type for it. But she thought there were lots of girls, each one probably progressively younger, and trips to Las Vegas, even though he would have to be careful about that in the banking business.

She was a senior in college that January in 1956 when the call came from the sheriff's office. She flew out to Phoenix. "I was afraid," she went on, "and so was Grandfather. Neither of us believed they'd ever find him alive. Suicide was in our minds, though for different reasons. Grandfather was afraid he'd got in trouble again. That he'd taken money from the bank."

"But he hadn't?" I asked.

"No," she said. "Naturally, it would have been discovered if he had. He even had several hundred dollars in his own account, and almost a month's salary due him."

There you are, I thought; it was an absolutely blank wall. He hadn't stolen from the bank, but he'd deliberately disappeared. And when he showed up a month later as Brian Hardy he was rich.

She had fallen silent. I lighted a cigarette. Well, this must be the end of the line; I might as well call the FBI. Then she said quietly, "Would you tell me about it?"

I told her, playing down the pain of the heart attack and making it as easy for her as I could. I explained about the split mains'l and being becalmed, and the fact that I had no choice but to bury him at sea. Without actually lying about it I managed to gloss over the sketchy aspect of the funeral and the fact that I hadn't known all the sea-burial service. I told her it was Sunday, and gave the position, and tried to tell her what kind of day it was. She gave a little choked cry and turned her face away, and I looked down at my cigarette when she got up abruptly and went out in the kitchen. I sat there feeling rotten. Even with all the trouble he'd got me into, I'd liked him, and I was beginning to like her.

Well, I'd known all along it wasn't going to be easy when I had to face his family and tell them about it. And it was even worse now because, while she knew in her heart that it was her father, there could never be any final proof. That little residue of doubt would always remain, along with all the unanswerable questions. Was he lying somewhere out in the desert, or under two miles of water in the Caribbean Sea? And wherever he was, why was he there? What had happened? What was he running from?

Then suddenly it was back again, that strange feeling of uneasiness that always came over me when I remembered the moment of his burial, that exact instant in which I'd stood at the rail and watched his body slide into the depths. There was no explanation for it. I didn't even know what it was. When I reached for it, it was gone, like a bad dream only partly remembered, and all that was left was this formless dread that something terrible was going to happen, or already had. I tried to shrug it off. Maybe it *had* been a premonition. Why keep worrying about it now? I'd already got all the bad news.

She came back in a minute, and if she'd been crying she had carefully erased the evidence. She was carrying two bottles of Coke from the refrigerator. "What are you going to do now?" she asked.

"I don't know," I said. "Call the FBI, I suppose. I'd rather try convincing them than those gorillas. Oh, I suppose this is pretty hopeless, but did you ever hear of a man called Bonner? J. R. Bonner?" The name would be phony, of course. I described him.

She shook her head. "No. I'm sorry."

"I hate to drag you into this," I said, "but I'll have to tell them. There'll probably be an investigation of your father."

"It can't be helped," she said.

I lighted a cigarette. "You're the only one so far who hasn't accused me of killing him, stealing his money, or putting him ashore and lying about his death. Don't you think I did, or are you just being polite?"

She gave me a brief smile. "I don't believe you did. It's just occurred to me that I know you—at least by reputation. Some friends of mine in Lynn speak very highly of you."

"Who?" I asked.

"Ted and Frances Holt. They've sailed with you two or three times."

"For the past three years," I said. "They've shot some terrific underwater movies around the Exumas."

"I suppose one of us really ought to say it's a small world," she mused. "Mr. Rogers—"

"Stuart," I said.

"Stuart. Why doesn't anybody seem to think this man Keefer could have taken all that money—assuming it was even aboard? He seems to have had a sizable amount nobody can explain."

"They'd have found it," I said. "When they add up what was in the hotel safe and what he conceivably spent, it still comes out to less than four thousand, and not even a drunk could throw away nineteen thousand dollars in three days. But the big factor is that he couldn't have had it with him when he left the boat. I was right there. He didn't have any luggage, you see, because all his gear was still on that ship he'd missed in Panama. He'd bought a couple of pairs of dungarees for the trip, but I was standing right beside him when he rolled those up, and he didn't put anything in them. And he didn't have a coat. He might have stowed four thousand dollars in his wallet and in the pockets of his slacks, but not twenty-three thousand, unless it was in very large bills. Which I doubt. A man running and trying to hide out would attract a lot of attention trying to break anything larger than hundreds."

"Maybe he took it ashore when you first docked."

"No. I was with him then too."

She frowned. "Then it must still be aboard the *Topaz."*

"No," I said. "It's been searched twice. By experts."

"Then that seems to leave only one other possibility," she said. She paused, and then went on unhappily. "This isn't easy to say, under the circumstances, but do you suppose he could have been—unbalanced?"

"I don't think so," I said. "I did when I first read the letter, of course. I mean, he said he had twenty-three thousand with him, but nobody else ever saw it. He said he was going to ask me to put him ashore, but he never did. And the fact that he was going to wait and put a wild proposition like that to me *after* we got to sea didn't sound very logical, either. A rational man would have realized how slim the chances were that anybody would go for it, and would have sounded me out before we sailed. But if you look at all these things again, you're not so sure.

"He apparently did have some money with him. Four thousand, anyway. So if he had that much, maybe he had it all. And waiting till we got to sea to proposition me makes sense if you look at it correctly. If he brought it up before we sailed, I might refuse to take him at all. Getting out of the Canal Zone before this Slidell caught up with him was the number-one item. If he brought up the other thing later and I turned him down, at least he was out of Panama and safe for the moment."

"So we wind up right where we started."

"That's right," I said. "With the same two questions. What became of the rest of the money? And why did he change his mind?"

The doorbell chimed.

We exchanged a quick glance, and got to our feet. There'd been no sound of a car outside, nor of footsteps on the walk. She motioned me toward the hallway and started to the door, but before she got there it swung open and a tall man in a gray suit and dark green glasses stepped inside and curtly motioned her back. At the same instant I heard the back door open. I whirled. Standing in the arched doorway to the kitchen was a heavy-shouldered tourist wearing a loud sport shirt, straw cap, and an identical pair of green sunglasses. He removed the glasses and grinned coldly at me. It was Bonner.

Escape was impossible. The first man had a gun; I could see the sagging weight of it in his coat pocket. Patricia gasped, and retreated from him, her eyes wide with alarm. She came back against the desk beside the entrance to the hall. Bonner and the other man came toward me. The latter took out a pack of cigarettes. "We've been waiting for you,

Rogers," he said, and held them out toward me. "Smoke?"

For an instant all three of us seemed frozen there, the two of them in an attitude almost of amusement while I looked futilely around for a weapon of some kind and waited dry-mouthed for one of them to move. Then I saw what she was doing, and was more scared than ever. She couldn't get away with it, not with these people, but there was no way I could stop her. The telephone was directly behind her. She had reached back, lifted off the receiver, set it gently on the desk top, and was trying to dial Operator. I picked up one of the Coke bottles. That kept their eyes on me for another second or two. Then the dial clicked.

Bonner swung around, casually replaced the receiver, and chopped his open right hand against the side of her face. It made a sharp, cracking sound in the stillness, like a rifle shot, and she spun around and sprawled on the floor in a confused welter of skirt and slip and long bare legs. I was on him by then, swinging the Coke bottle. It hit him a glancing blow and knocked the straw cap off. He straightened, and I swung it again. He took this one on his forearm and smashed a fist into my stomach.

It tore the breath out of me, but I managed to stay on my feet. I lashed out at his face with the bottle. He drew back his head just enough to let it slide harmlessly past his jaw, grinned contemptuously, and slipped a blackjack from his pocket. He was an artist with it, like a good surgeon with a scalpel. Three swings of it reduced my left arm to a numb and dangling weight; another tore loose a flap of skin on my forehead, filling my eyes with blood. I tried to clinch with him. He pushed me back, dropped the sap, and slammed a short brutal right against my jaw. I fell back against the controls of the air-conditioner unit and slid to the floor. Patricia Reagan screamed. I brushed blood from my face and tried to get up, and for an instant I saw the other man. He didn't even bother to watch. He was half-sitting on the corner of the desk, idly swinging his sunglasses by one curved frame while he looked at some of her photographs.

I made it to my feet and hit Bonner once. That was the last time I was in the fight. He knocked me back against the wall and I fell again. He hauled me up and held me against it with his left while he smashed the right into my face. It was like being pounded with a concrete block. I felt teeth loosen. The room began to wheel before my eyes. Just before it turned black altogether, he dropped me. I tried to get up, and made it as far as my knees. He put his shoe in my face and pushed. I fell back on the floor, gasping for breath, with blood in my mouth and eyes. He looked down at me. "That's for Tampa, sucker."

The other man tossed the photographs back on the desk and stood up.

"That'll do," he said crisply. "Put him in that chair."

Bonner hauled me across the floor by one arm and heaved me up into one of the bamboo armchairs in the center of the room. Somebody threw a towel that hit me in the face. I mopped at the blood, trying not to be sick.

"All right," the other man said, "go back to the motel and get Flowers. Then get the car out of sight. Over there in the trees somewhere."

Patricia Reagan was sitting up. Bonner jerked his head toward her. "What about the girl?"

"She stays till we get through."

"Why? She'll just be in the way."

"Use your head. Rogers has friends in Miami, and some of them may know where he is. When he doesn't come back they may call up here looking for him. Put her on the sofa."

Bonner jerked a thumb. "Park it, kid."

She stared at him with contempt.

He shrugged, hauled her up by one arm, and shoved. She shot backward past the end of the coffee table and fell on the sofa across from me. Bonner went out.

"I'm sorry," I said. "It's my fault. But I thought I'd lost them."

"You did, temporarily," the man put in. "But we didn't follow you here. We were waiting for you."

I stared at him blankly.

He pulled the other chair around to the end of the coffee table and sat down where he could watch us both. If Bonner was a journeyman in the field of professional deadliness, this one was a top-drawer executive. It was too evident in the crisp, incisive manner, the stamp of intelligence on the face, and the pitiless, unwavering stare. He could have been anywhere between forty and fifty, and had short, wiry red hair, steel-gray eyes, and a lean face that was coppery with fresh sunburn.

"She doesn't know anything about this," I said.

"We're aware of that, but we weren't sure you were. When we lost you in Tampa we watched for you here among other places."

Blood continued to drip off my face onto my shirt. I mopped at it with the towel. My eyes were beginning to close and my whole face felt swollen. Talking was difficult through the cut and puffy lips. I wondered how long Bonner would be gone. At the moment I was badly beaten, too weak and sick to get out of the chair, but with a few minutes' rest I might be able to take this one, or at least hold him long enough for her to get away. Then, as if he'd read my thoughts, he lifted the gun from his pocket and shook his head.

"Don't move, Rogers," he said. "You're too valuable to kill, but you wouldn't get far without a knee."

The room fell silent except for the humming of the air-conditioner. Patricia's face was pale, but she forced herself to reach out on the coffee table for a cigarette and light it, and look at him without wavering.

"You can't get away with this," she said.

"Don't be stupid, Miss Reagan," he replied. "We know all about your working habits; nobody comes out here to bother you. You won't even have any telephone calls unless it's somebody looking for Rogers. In which case you'll say he's been here and gone."

She glared defiantly. "And if I don't?"

"You will. Believe me."

"You're Slidell?" I said.

He nodded. "You can call me that."

"Why were you after Reagan?"

"We're still after him," he corrected. "Reagan stole a half million dollars in bonds from me and some other men. We want it back, or what's left of it."

"And I suppose you stole them in the first place?"

He shrugged. "You might say they were a little hot. They were negotiable, of course, but an amount that size is unwieldy; fencing them through the usual channels would entail either a lot of time or a large discount. I met Reagan in Las Vegas, and when I found out what he did I sounded him out; he was just the connection we needed. He didn't want to do it at first, but I found out he owed money to some gamblers in Phoenix and arranged for a little pressure. He came through then. He disposed of a hundred thousand dollars' worth for the commission we agreed on, and we turned the rest of them over to him. I suppose she's told you what happened?"

I nodded.

He went on. "We were keeping a close watch on him, of course, and even when he started out on the hunting trip that Saturday morning we followed him long enough to be sure he wasn't trying to skip out. But he was smarter than we thought. He either had another car hidden out there somewhere, or somebody picked him up. It took us two years to run him down, even with private detectives watching for him in all the likely spots. He was in Miami, but staying out of the night clubs and the big flashy places on the Beach. It was just luck we located him at all. Somebody spotted a picture in a hunting and fishing magazine that seemed to resemble him, and when we ran down the photographer and had a blowup made from the original negative, there was Reagan.

"But he beat us again. He apparently saw the picture too, and when we got to Miami and tracked him down we found he'd been killed two weeks before when his boat exploded and burned between Florida and the Bahamas. At first we weren't too sure this was a fake, but when we searched the house and grounds and couldn't turn up even a safe-deposit key, we began checking his girl friends and found one who'd left for Switzerland the very same day. Or so she'd told everybody. But she was careless. When we searched her apartment we found a travel-agency slip in her wastebasket confirming reservations for a Mr. and Mrs. Charles Wayne on a flight to San Juan. He must have seen us there, because by the time we located him he was gone again. We trailed him to New York. By this time they'd separated and he'd hidden her somewhere because he knew we were closing in on him. He flew to Panama. I was one day behind him then, and missed him by only twelve hours in Cristobal when he left with you."

"And now he's dead," I said.

He smiled coldly. "For the third time."

"I tell you—" I broke off. What was the use? Then I thought of something. "Look, he must have cached the money somewhere."

"Obviously. All except the twenty-three thousand he was using to get away."

"Then you're out of luck. Don't you see that? You know where she is; she's in the hospital in Southport, and if she lives, the police are going to get the whole story out of her. She'll have to tell them where it is."

"She may not know."

"Do you know why she came to Southport?" I said. "She wanted to see me, because she hadn't heard from him. Don't you see I'm telling the truth? If he were still alive he'd have written her."

"Yes. Unless he was running out on her too."

I slumped back in the chair. It was hopeless. And even if I could convince them I was telling the truth, what good was it now? They'd kill us anyway.

"However," he went on, "there is one serious flaw in that surmise. If he'd intended to run out on her, there would have been no point in writing her that letter from Cristobal."

"Then you'll admit he might be dead?"

"That's right. There are a number of very strange angles to this thing, Rogers, but we're going to get to the bottom of them in the next few hours. He could be dead for any one of a number of reasons. You and Keefer could have killed him."

"Oh, for God's sake—"

"You're a dead duck. Your story smelled to begin with, and it gets worse every time you turn it over. Let's take that beautiful report you turned in to the US marshal's office, describing the heart attack. That fooled everybody at first, but if I've found out how you did it, don't you suppose the FBI will too? They may not pay as much for information as I do, but they've got more personnel. You made it sound so convincing. I mean, the average layman trying to make up a heart attack on paper would have been inclined to hoke it up and overplay it a little and say Reagan was doing something very strenuous when it happened, because everybody knows that's always what kills the man with coronary trouble. Everybody, that is, except the medics. They know you can also die of an attack while you're lying in bed waiting for somebody to peel you a grape. And it turns out you know that too. One of your uncles died of a coronary thrombosis when you were about fifteen—"

"I wasn't even present," I said. "It happened in his office in Norfolk, Virginia."

"I know. But you *were* present when he had a previous attack. About a year before, when you and he and your father were fishing on a charter boat off Miami Beach. And he wasn't fighting a fish when it happened. He was just sitting in the fishing chair drinking a bottle of beer. It all adds up, Rogers. It all adds up."

It was the first time I'd even thought of it for years. I started to say so, but I happened to turn then and glance at Patricia Reagan. Her eyes were on my face, and there was doubt in them, and something else that was very close to horror. Under the circumstances, I thought, who could blame her? Then the front door opened. Bonner came in, followed by a popeyed little man carrying a black metal case about the size of a portable tape recorder.

CHAPTER ELEVEN

"Both of you stay where you are," Slidell ordered. He stood up and turned to Bonner. "Bring Flowers a table and a chair."

Bonner went down the hall and came back with a small night table. He set it and one of the dining chairs near the chair I was in, and swung me around so I was facing the front window with the table on my right. Then he lighted a cigarette and leaned against the front door, boredly watching.

"This jazz is a waste of time, if you ask me," he remarked.

"I didn't," Slidell said shortly.

Bonner shrugged. I glanced around at Patricia Reagan, but she avoided my eyes and was staring past me at Flowers, as mystified as I was. He was a slightly built little man in his thirties with a bald spot and a sour, pinched face that was made almost grotesque by the slightly bulging eyes. He set the black case on the table and removed the lid. The top panel held a number of controls and switches, but a good part of it was taken up by a window under which was a sheet of graph paper and three styli mounted on little arms.

I glanced up to find Slidell's eyes on me in chill amusement. "We are about to arrive at that universal goal of all the great philosophers, Rogers. Truth."

"What do you mean?"

"That's a lie-detector."

"Cut it out. Where the hell would you get one?"

"There is nothing esoteric about a lie-detector. Almost anybody could make one. Operating it, however, is something else, and that's where we're very fortunate. Flowers is a genius. It talks to him."

Flowers paid no attention. He ran a long cord over to an electrical outlet, and turned the machine on. Then he began connecting it to me as calmly and methodically as if this were a police station. If it occurred to him at all that there was any quality of madness in the situation, he apparently dismissed it as irrelevant. The whole thing was merely a technical problem. He wrapped a blood-pressure cuff about my right arm above the elbow and pumped it up. Then a tube went about my chest. He threw another switch, and the paper began to move. The styli made little jagged lines as they registered my pulse, blood pressure, and respiration. The room became very quiet. He made minor adjustments to the controls, pulled up the chair and sat down, hunched over the thing with the dedicated expression of a priest. He nodded to Slidell.

"All right, Rogers," Slidell said. "All you have to do is answer the questions I put to you. Answer any way you like, but answer. Refuse, and you get the gun barrel across your face."

"Go ahead," I said. It did no good now to think how stupid I'd been not to think of this myself. I could have asked the FBI to give me a lie-detector test.

"It won't work," Bonner said disgustedly. "Everybody knows how they operate. The blood pressure and pulse change when you're upset or scared. So how're you going to tell anything with a meatball that's scared stiff to begin with?"

"There will still be a deviation from the norm," Flowers said contemptuously.

"To translate," Slidell said, "what Flowers means is that if Rogers is scared stiff as a normal condition, the instrument will tell us when he's scared rigid. Now shut up."

Bonner subsided.

"What is your name?" Slidell asked.

"Stuart Rogers."

"Where were you born?"

"Coral Gables, Florida."

"Where did you go to school?"

"The University of Miami."

"What business is your father in?"

"He was an attorney."

"You mean he's dead?"

"Yes," I said.

"What did he die of?"

"He was killed in an automobile accident."

There were fifteen or twenty more of these establishing questions while Flowers intently studied his graphs. Then Slidell said, "Did you know a man who told you his name was Wendell Baxter?"

"Yes," I said.

"And he sailed with you from Cristobal on June first aboard your boat?"

"Yes."

"And you put him ashore somewhere in Central America or Mexico?"

"No," I said.

Slidell was leaning over Flowers' shoulder, watching the styli. Flowers gave a faint shake of the head. Slidell frowned at me.

"Where *did* you put him ashore?"

"I didn't," I said.

"Where is he?"

"He's dead."

Flowers looked up at Slidell and spread his hands.

"You don't see any change in pattern at all?" Slidell asked.

"No. Of course, it's impossible to tell much with one short record—"

Bonner came over. "I told you it wouldn't work. Let me show you how to get the truth." His hand exploded against the side of my face and rocked me back in the chair. I tasted blood.

"You'll have to keep this fool away from him," Flowers said bitterly. "Look what he's done."

The styli were swinging violently.

"Hate," Flowers explained.

I rubbed my face and stared at Bonner. "Tell your machine it can say that again."

"Get away from him," Slidell ordered.

"Let me have that gun, and give me five minutes—"

"Certainly," Slidell said coldly. "So you can kill him before we find out anything, the way you did Keefer. Can't you get it through your head that Rogers is the last? He's the only person on earth who can answer these questions."

"Well, what good is that if he keeps lying?"

"I'm not sure he is. Reagan could be dead this time. I've told you that before. Now get back."

Bonner moved back to the door. Slidell and Flowers watched while the styli settled down. Patricia Reagan had turned away with her face down on her arms across the back of the couch. I couldn't tell whether she was crying.

"Listen, Rogers," Slidell said, "we're going to get the truth of what happened out there on that boat if it takes a week, and you have to account for every hour of the trip, minute by minute, and we repeat these questions until you crack up and start screaming. The police will never find you, and you can't get away. Do you understand?"

"Yes," I said wearily.

"Good. Is Reagan dead?"

"Yes."

"When did he die?"

"Four days out of Cristobal. On June fifth, at about three-thirty p.m."

"Did you and Keefer kill him?"

"No."

"How did he die?"

"Of an attack of some kind. The doctor who reviewed the report said it was probably a coronary thrombosis."

"Did you make up the report?"

"I wrote it."

"You know what I mean. Was it the truth?"

"It was the truth. It was exactly as it happened."

Slidell turned to Flowers. "Anything yet?"

Flowers shook his head. "No change at all."

"All right, Rogers. You read the letter Reagan wrote to Paula Stafford. He said he had twenty-three thousand dollars with him, and that he was going to ask you to put him ashore somewhere. Nineteen thousand dollars of that money is missing. Keefer didn't have it, and it's not on your boat. If Reagan is dead, where is it?"

"I don't know," I said.

"You stole it."

"I've never even seen it."

"Did Regan ask you to put him ashore?"

"No."

"In four days he didn't even mention it?"

"No."

"Why didn't he?"

"How do I know?" I said.

Flowers held up a hand. "Run through that sequence again. There's something funny here."

I stared at him. One of us must be mad already.

"You're lying, Rogers," Slidell said. "You have to be. Reagan sailed on that boat for the purpose of having you slip him ashore. He even told Paula Stafford that. You read the letter."

"Yes."

"And you mean to say he didn't even ask you?"

"He never said anything about it at all."

"Why didn't he?"

"I don't know," I said.

"There it is again," Flowers interrupted. "A definite change in emotional response. I think he does know."

"You killed him, didn't you?" Slidell barked.

"No!" I said.

Then I was standing at the rail again on that Sunday afternoon watching the shrouded body fade into the depths below me, and the strange feeling of dread began to come back. I looked at the machine. The styli jerked erratically, making frenzied swings across the paper.

Slidell shoved his face close to mine. *"You and Keefer killed him!"*

"No!" I shouted.

Flowers nodded. "He's lying."

My hands were tightly clenched. I closed my eyes and tried to find the answer in the dark confusion of my thoughts. It was there somewhere, just beyond my reach. In God's name, what was it? The water closed over him and a few bubbles drifted upward with the release of air trapped within the shroud, and he began to fall, sliding deeper and fading from view, and I began to be afraid of something I couldn't even name, and I wanted to bring him back. I heard Patricia Reagan cry out. A hand caught the front of my shirt and I was half lifted from the chair, and Bonner was shouting in my face. I lost it completely then; everything was gone. Slidell's voice cut through the uproar like a knife, and Bonner dropped me, and the room was silent.

"When did you kill him?" Slidell barked.

"I didn't!"

He sighed. "All right. Begin with the first day."

We ran out of the harbor on the auxiliary, between the big stone breakwaters where the surf was booming. Baxter took the wheel while Keefer and I got sail on her. It was past midmorning now and the Trade was picking up, a spanking full-sail breeze out of the northeast with a moderate sea in which she pitched a little and shipped a few dollops of spray that spatted against the canvas and wet the cushions of the cockpit. She was close-hauled on the starboard tack as we began to beat our way offshore.

"How does she handle?" I asked Baxter.

He was bareheaded and shirtless, as we all were, and his eyes were happier than they had been. "Very nicely," he said. "Takes just a little weather helm."

I peered into the binnacle. "Any chance of laying the course?"

He let her come up a little, and slides began to rattle along the luff of the mains'l. The course was still half a point to windward. "It may haul a little more to the easterly as we get offshore," he said.

I took her for a few minutes to see how she felt, and called to Blackie. "If you want to learn to be a helmsman, here's a good time to start."

He grinned cockily, and took the wheel. "This bedpan? I could steer it with a canoe paddle. What's the course?"

"Full-and-by," I told him.

"What's that?"

"It's a term seamen use," I said. "Mr. Baxter'll explain it to you while I make some coffee."

I made sandwiches at noon and took the helm. The breeze freshened and hauled almost a point to the eastward. Baxter relieved me at four with the mountains of Panama growing hazier and beginning to slide into the sea astern. She was heeled over sharply with all sail set, lifting to the sea with a long, easy corkscrew motion as water hissed and gurgled along the lee rail with that satisfying sound that meant she was correctly trimmed and happy and running down the miles. Spray flew aft and felt cool against our faces. When he took the wheel I looked aloft again and then eyed the main sheet with speculation. He smiled, and shook his head, and I agreed with him. You couldn't improve on it.

"What's her waterline length?" he asked.

"Thirty-four," I said.

There is a formula for calculating the absolute maximum speed of a displacement hull, regardless of the type or amount of power applied. It's a function of the trochoidal wave system set up by the boat and is 1.34 times the square root of the waterline length. I could see Baxter working this out now.

"On paper," I said, "she should do a little better than seven and a half knots."

He nodded. "I'd say she was logging close to six."

As I went below to start supper I saw him turn once and look astern at the fading coastline of Panama. When he swung back to face the binnacle, there was an expression of relief or satisfaction in the normally grave brown eyes.

The breeze went down a little with the sun, but she still sang her way along. Keefer took the eight-to-twelve watch and I slept for a few hours. When I came on deck at midnight there was only a light breeze and the sea was going down....

"What the hell is this?" Bonner demanded. He came over in front of us. "Are we going to sail that lousy boat up from Panama mile by mile?"

"Foot by foot, if we have to," Slidell said crisply, "till we find out what happened."

"You'll never do it this way. The machine's no good. He fooled it the first time."

Flowers stared at him with frigid dislike. "Nobody beats this machine. When he starts to lie, it'll tell us."

"Yeah. Sure. Like it did when he said Baxter died of a heart attack."

"Shut up!" Slidell snapped. "Get back out of the way. Take the girl to the kitchen and tell her to make some coffee. And keep your hands off her."

"Why?"

"It would be obvious to anybody but an idiot. I don't want her screaming and upsetting Rogers' emotional response."

We're all crazy, I thought. Maybe everybody who had any contact with Baxter eventually went mad. No, not Baxter. His name was Reagan. I was sitting here hooked up to a shiny electronic gadget like a cow to a milking machine while an acidulous gnome with popeyes extracted the truth from me—truth that I apparently no longer even knew myself. I hadn't killed Reagan. Even if I were mad now, I hadn't been then. Every detail of the trip was clear in my mind. But how could it be? The machine said I was trying to hide something. What? And when had it happened? I put my hands up to my face, and it hurt everywhere I touched it. My eyes were swollen almost shut. I was dead tired. I looked at my watch, and saw it was nearly two p.m. Then it occurred to me that if they had arrived five minutes later I would already have called the FBI. That was nice to think about now.

Bonner jerked his head, and Patricia Reagan arose from the couch and followed him into the kitchen like a sleepwalker, or some long-legged mechanical toy.

"You still have plenty of paper?" Slidell asked Flowers. The latter nodded.

"All right, Rogers," Slidell said. He sat down again, facing me. "Reagan was still alive the morning of the second day—"

"He was alive until after three-thirty p.m., of the fourth day."

He cut me off. "Stop interrupting. He was alive the morning of the second day, and he still hadn't said anything about putting him ashore?"

"Not a word," I said.

He nodded to Flowers to start the paper again. "Go on."

We went on. The room was silent except for the sound of my voice and the faint humming of the air-conditioner. Graph paper crawled slowly across the face of the instrument from one roll to another while the styli kept up their jagged but unvarying scrawls.

Dawn came with light airs and a gently heaving sea, and we were alone with no land visible anywhere. As soon as I could see the horizon, Baxter relieved me so I could take a series of star sights. I worked them out under the hooded light of the chart table while Keefer snored gently in the bunk just forward of me. Two of them appeared to be good. We were eighty-four miles from Cristobal, and had averaged a little better than four and a half knots. We'd made slightly more leeway than I'd expected, however, and I corrected the course.

At seven I called Keefer and began frying eggs and bacon. When I was getting them out of the refrigerator, I noticed it was scarcely more than cool inside and apparently hadn't been running the way it should. After breakfast I checked the batteries of the lighting system, added some distilled water, and ran the generator for a while. We were shaking down to the routine of sea watches now, and Baxter and I were able to get a couple of hours' sleep while Keefer took the morning watch from eight to twelve. He called me at eleven-thirty.

I got a good fix at noon that put us a little over a hundred miles out from Cristobal. Baxter took the wheel while I worked it out, and Keefer made a platter of thick sandwiches with canned corned beef and slices of onion. I ate mine at the wheel after I took over for the twelve-to-four trick. I threw the empty milk carton overboard, watched it fall astern as I tried to estimate our speed, and lighted a cigarette. I was content; this was the way to live.

It was a magnificent day. The wind had freshened a little since early morning and was a moderate easterly breeze now, directly abeam as she ran lightfooted across the miles on the long reach to the northward, heeled down with water creaming along the rail. The sun shone hotly, drying the spray on my face and arms, and sparkling on the face of the sea as the long rollers advanced, lifted us, and went on. I started the main sheet a little, decided it had been right before, and trimmed it again. Baxter came on deck just as I finished. He smiled. "No good sailor is ever satisfied, I suppose."

I grinned. "I expect not. But I thought you'd turned in. Couldn't you sleep?"

"A day like this is too beautiful to waste," he replied. "And I thought I'd get a little sun."

He was wearing a white bathrobe with his cigarettes and lighter in one of the pockets. He lighted a cigarette, slipped off the robe, rolled it into a pillow, and stretched out in the sun along the cushions in the starboard side of the cockpit, wearing only a pair of boxer shorts. He lay feet forward, with his head about even with the wheel. He closed his eyes.

"I was just looking at the chart," he said. "If we keep on logging four to five knots we should be up in the Yucatan Channel by Sunday."

"There's a chance," I said idly. Sunday or Monday, it didn't really matter. I was in no hurry. You trimmed and started the sheets and steered and kept one eye forever on the wind as if that last fraction of a knot were a matter of life or death, but it had nothing to do with saving time. It was simply a matter of craftsmanship, of sailing a boat rather than merely riding on it.

He was silent for a few minutes. Then he asked, "What kind of boat is the *Orion?*"

"Fifty-foot schooner. Gaff-rigged on the fore and jib-headed on the main, and carries a fore-tops'l, stays'l, and working jib. She accommodates a party of six besides the two of us in the crew."

"Is she very old?"

"Yes. Over twenty years now. But sound."

"Upkeep gets to be a problem, though," he said thoughtfully. "I mean, as they get progressively older. What is your basic charter price?"

"Five hundred a week, plus expenses."

"I see," he said. "It seems to me, though, you could do better with something a little larger. Say a good shallow-draft ketch or yawl, about sixty feet. With the right interior layout, it would probably handle more people, so you could raise your charter price. Wouldn't take any larger crew, and if it were still fairly new your maintenance costs might be less."

"Yes, I know," I said. "I've been on the lookout for something like that for a long time, but I've never been able to swing it. It'd take fifteen thousand to twenty thousand more than I could get for the *Orion.*"

"Yes," he agreed, "it would be pretty expensive."

We fell silent. He sat up to get another cigarette from the pocket of his robe. I thought I heard him say something, and glanced up from the compass card. "I beg your pardon?"

He made no reply. He was turned slightly away from me, facing forward, so I saw only the back of his head. He had the lighter in his hand as if he'd started to light the cigarette and then had forgotten it. He tilted his head back, stretching his neck, and put a hand up to the base of his throat.

"Something wrong?" I asked.

It was almost a full minute before he answered. I glanced at the compass card, and brought the wheel up a spoke. "Oh," he said quietly. "No. Just a touch of indigestion."

I grinned. "That's not much of a recommendation for Blackie's sandwiches." Then I thought uneasily of the refrigerator; food poisoning could be a very dangerous thing at sea. But the corned beef was canned; it couldn't have been spoiled. And the milk had tasted all right.

"It was the onions," he said. "I should never eat them."

"There's some bicarbonate in one of the lockers above the sink," I told him.

"I have something here," he said. He carefully dropped the lighter back in the pocket of his robe and took out a small bottle of pills. He shook one out and put it in his mouth.

"Hold the wheel," I said, "and I'll get you some water."

"Thanks," he said. "I don't need it."

He lay back with his head pillowed on the robe and his eyes closed. Once or twice he shifted a little and drew his knees up as if he were uncomfortable, but he said nothing further about it except to reply with a brief "Yes" when I asked if he felt better. After a while he groped for the bottle and took another of the pills, and then lay quietly for a half hour, apparently asleep. His face and body were shiny with sweat as the sun beat down on him, and I began to be afraid he'd get a bad burn. I touched him on the shoulder to wake him up.

"Don't overdo it the first day," I said.

He wasn't asleep, however. "Yes, I expect you're right," he replied. "I think I'll turn in." He got up a little unsteadily and made his way down the companion ladder. After he was gone I noticed he'd forgotten to take the robe. I rolled it tightly and wedged it in back of a cushion so it wouldn't blow overboard.

A school of porpoises picked us up and escorted us for a while, leaping playfully about the bow. I watched them, enjoying their company as I always did at sea. In about a half hour Keefer came up from below carrying a mug of coffee. He sat down in the cockpit.

"You want a cup?" he asked.

I looked at my watch. It was three now. "No, thanks. I'll get one after Baxter takes over."

"We ought to have our tails kicked," he said, "for not thinking to buy a fish line. At this speed we could pick up a dolphin or barracuda."

"I intended to," I said, "but forgot it."

We talked for a while about trolling. Nowadays, when practically all ships made sixteen knots or better, it was out of the question, but when he'd first started going to sea just before the Second World War he'd been on a few of the old eight- and ten-knot tankers on the coastwise run from Texas to the East Coast, and sometimes in the Stream they'd rig a trolling line of heavy sashcord with an inner tube for a snubber. Usually the fish tore off or straightened the hook, but occasionally they'd manage to land one.

He stood up and stretched. "Well, I think I'll flake out again."

He started below. Just as his shoulders were disappearing down the companion hatch my eyes fell on Baxter's robe, which was getting wet with spray. "Here," I called out, "take this down, will you?"

I rolled it tightly and tossed it. The distance wasn't more than eight feet, but just before it reached his outstretched hand a freakish gust of wind found an opening and it ballooned suddenly and was snatched to leeward. I sprang from the wheel and lunged for it, but it sailed under the mizzen boom, landed in the water a good ten feet away, and began to fall astern. I looked out at it and cursed myself for an idiot.

"Stand by the backstay!" I called out to Keefer. "We'll go about and pick it up."

Then I remembered we hadn't tacked once since our departure from Cristobal. By the time I'd explained to him about casting off the weather backstay and setting it up on the other side as we came about, the robe was a good hundred and fifty yards astern. "Hard a-lee!" I shouted, and put the helm down. We came up into the wind with the sails slatting. I cast off the port jib sheet and trimmed the starboard one. They ran aft through fairleads to winches at the forward end of the cockpit. Blackie set up the runner. We filled away, and I put the wheel hard over to bring her back across our wake. I steadied her up just to leeward of it.

"Can you see it?" I yelled to Keefer.

"Dead ahead, about a hundred yards," he called back. "But it's beginning to sink."

"Take the wheel!" I ordered. I slid a boathook from under its lashing atop the doghouse and ran forward. I could see it. It was about fifty yards ahead, but only a small part of it still showed above the surface. "Left just a little!" I sang out. "Steady, right there!"

It disappeared. I marked the spot, and as we bore down on it I knelt at the rail just forward of the mainmast and peered down with the boathook poised. We came over the spot. Then I saw it directly below me, three or four feet under the surface now, a white shape drifting slowly downward through the translucent blue of the water....

"Look!" Flowers cried out.

CHAPTER TWELVE

They crowded around the table, staring down at the instrument and the sudden, spasmodic jerking of its styli.

I gripped the arms of the chair as it all began falling into place—the nameless fear, and what had actually caused it, and the apparently insignificant thing that had lodged in my subconscious mind on an afternoon sixteen years ago aboard another boat, a chartered sport fisherman off Miami Beach. I *had* killed Baxter. Or at least I was responsible for his death.

Bonner growled, and swung around to grab me by the shirt. "You're lying! So now let's hear what really happened—"

I tried to swing at his face, but Slidell grabbed my arm before I could pull the instrument off the table by its connecting wires. "Shut up!" I roared. "Get off my back, you stupid ape! I'm trying to understand it myself!"

Slidell waved him off. "Get away!" Bonner stepped back, and Slidell spoke to me. "You didn't get the bathrobe?"

"No," I said. All the rage went out of me suddenly, and I leaned back in the chair with my eyes closed. "I touched it with the end of the boathook, but I couldn't get hold of it."

That was what I'd seen, but hadn't wanted to see, the afternoon we buried him. It wasn't his body, sewn in white Orlon, that was fading away below me, disappearing forever into two miles of water; it was that damned white bathrobe. And all the time I was trying to bury it in my subconscious, the other thing—already buried there—was trying to dig it up.

"And they were the only ones he had?" Slidell asked.

"I guess so," I said dully. I could hear Patricia Reagan crying softly over to my left.

Bonner's rasping voice cut in. "What the hell are you talking about?"

Slidell paid no attention. Or maybe he gestured for him to shut up. My eyes were still closed.

"And he still didn't tell you what they were?" Slidell went on. "You didn't realize it until he had the second one, the one that killed him—"

"Look!" I cried out angrily. "I didn't even realize it then! Why should

I? He said it was indigestion, and he took a pill for it, and then he took another one, and he lay there resting and getting a suntan for about a half hour and then went below and turned in. He didn't groan, or cry out. It wasn't anything like the other one; the pain probably wasn't anywhere near as bad, or he wouldn't have been able to cover it up that way.

"I had no reason to connect the two. I understand now why he didn't say anything about it, even when I told him about the bathrobe. He knew I'd take him back to Panama, and he'd rather risk another ten days at sea without the medicine than do that. But why would I have any reason to suspect it? All I knew about him was what he'd told me. His name was Wendell Baxter, and he got indigestion when he ate onions."

No, I thought; that wasn't completely true. Then, before I could correct myself, Flowers' voice broke in. "Wait a minute—"

He'd never even looked up, I thought; people as such didn't really exist for him; they were just some sort of stimulating devices or power supplies he hooked onto his damned machine so he could sit there and stare enraptured into its changing expressions. Maybe this was what they meant about the one-sided development of genius.

"All right," I said. "I'm lying. Or I was. I was lying to myself. There was a reason I should have known it was a heart attack, but I didn't understand what it was until today, when I thought about the one my uncle had."

"What was that?" Slidell asked.

"He didn't swallow those pills," I said.

"Why?" Bonner asked. "What's that got to do with it?"

"They were nitroglycerin," Slidell told him impatiently. I straightened up in the chair and groped mechanically for a cigarette.

"I think it must have stuck in my mind all those years," I went on. "I mean, it was the first time I'd ever heard of pills you took but didn't swallow. You dissolved them under your tongue. Reagan was doing the same thing, but it didn't quite click until just now. I merely thought he was swallowing them without water."

Slidell sat down again, lighted a cigarette, and regarded me with a bleak smile. "It's regrettable your medical knowledge isn't as comprehensive as that stupid conscience of yours and its defense mechanisms, Rogers. It would have saved us a lot of time."

I frowned. "What do you mean?"

"That it probably wouldn't have made the slightest difference if he'd had a tubful of those nitroglycerin pills. They're a treatment for angina, which is essentially just the warning. The danger signal. Reagan, from your report, was killed by a really massive coronary, and you could just as well have given him aspirin or a Bromo-Seltzer."

"How do you know so much about it?" I asked.

"I went to a doctor and asked," he said. "When you're dealing with sums in the order of a half million dollars you cover all bases. But never mind. Let's get on with it."

I wondered what he hoped to find out now, but I didn't say it aloud. With Reagan admittedly dead and lying on the bottom of the Caribbean with his secret the show was over, but as long as he refused to accept it and kept me tied to this machine answering questions Patricia Reagan and I would stay alive. When he gave up, Bonner would get rid of us. It was as simple as that.

"We can assume," he went on, "that we know now why Reagan didn't ask you to put him ashore. That first heart attack—and losing his medicine—scared him off. There's no doubt he'd already been suffering from angina, or he wouldn't have had the nitroglycerin, but this was more than that—or he thought it was, which amounts to the same thing. Of course, he still might die before he reached Southport, but even at that he'd have a better chance staying with the boat than he would landing on a deserted stretch of beach and having to fight his way through a bunch of jungle alone. So he played the percentages."

"Yes," I said. That seemed more or less obvious now.

"What was he wearing when he died?"

"Dungarees," I said, "and a pair of sneakers."

"If he'd had a money belt around him, you would have seen it?"

"Yes. But he didn't have one."

Flowers and Bonner were silently watching the machine. I turned and shot a glance at Patricia Reagan. Her face was pale, but she didn't avoid my eyes now. That was something, anyway. Maybe she didn't blame me for his death.

"Did you put any more clothes on him when you buried him?"

"No," I said.

"And everything he owned was turned over to the US marshal?"

"That's right."

He exhaled smoke and stared up at the ceiling. "Now I think we're getting somewhere, wouldn't you say? Somewhere around nineteen thousand dollars of that money is still missing. It didn't go ashore with his things, it wasn't buried with him, Keefer didn't have it, you haven't got it, and I don't think there's a chance it's on your boat. What does that leave?"

"Nothing," I said. "Unless he just didn't have it with him."

He smiled coldly. "But I think he did."

I began to get it then. You had to remember two things. The first was that he wasn't even remotely interested in $19,000 worth of chickenfeed; from his point of view the fact that it was missing was the only good news he had left. And the other thing you had to keep in mind was that Reagan had been warned. He knew there was at least a chance he wouldn't reach the States alive.

Excitement quickened along my nerves. All the pieces were beginning to make sense now, and I should know where that money was. And not only the money. The same thing he was looking for—a letter. I could have done it long ago, I thought, if I hadn't subconsciously tried to reject the idea that I was to blame for Reagan's death.

"Here's something," Flowers called out softly.

I glanced up then, and finally realized the real beauty of the trap they had me in. Even thinking of the answer would get me killed. Bonner's hard eyes were on my face, and Slidell was watching me with the poised deadliness of a stalking cat.

"Have you thought of something?" he asked.

The telephone rang.

The unexpected sound of it seemed to explode in the silence, and everybody turned to look at it except Slidell. He stood up and nodded curtly to Patricia Reagan. "Answer it, and get rid of whoever it is. If it's somebody looking for Rogers, he left. You don't know where he went. Understand?"

She faced him for a moment, and then nodded, and crossed unsteadily to the desk. He was beside her as she picked up the receiver, and motioned for her to tilt it so he could hear too. Bonner turned and watched me. "Hello," she said. Then, "Yes. That's right."

There was a longer pause. Then she said, "Yes. He was here. But he left.... No, he didn't say...."

So it was Bill. She was listening. She looked helplessly at Slidell. He pulled the receiver down, put his hand over it, and said, "Tell him no. It couldn't have been. And hang up."

She repeated it. "You're welcome," she said, and replaced the instrument.

What would he do now? There was no doubt as to what he'd asked. And I'd told him if the Reagan lead proved a dead end I was going to call the FBI. As a reporter he could conceivably find out whether I had or not. How much time would go by before he decided something was wrong? It was only a very slight one, and there was no way he could have known, but Slidell had finally made a mistake.

He motioned for her to go back, and picked up the phone himself. "Southport, Texas," he said. "The Randall Hotel, and I want to speak to

Mr. Shaw."

He held on. Patricia sat down on the couch, and when I turned toward her she made a helpless, almost apologetic sort of gesture, and tried to smile. I nodded and tried it myself, but it wasn't much more successful.

"Hello?" Slidell said. "Yes. Some progress here. We ran into an old friend, and we're having quite a discussion. Anything new there? ... I see ... But they still haven't been able to talk to her? ... Good.... What about the other one? ... That's fine.... Sounds just about right. Well, stand by. I'll call you when we get something." He hung up.

There were only parts of it I understood. One man was still in Southport, covering that end of it. Paula Stafford was alive, but the police hadn't been able to question her yet, as far as he knew. But I couldn't guess what he meant by the "other one."

He came back and sat down. I wondered what Bill would do, and how much longer we had.

"Let's consider what Reagan would do," he said. "He knew he could die before he reached the States. You would turn his suitcase over to the US marshal or the police, and the money would be discovered. At first glance, that would seem to be no great hardship, since he wouldn't need it any longer, but it's not quite that simple. I've made a rather thorough study of Reagan—anybody who steals a half million dollars from me is almost certain to arouse my interest—and he was quite a complex man. He was a thief, but an uncomfortable thief, if you follow me. It was gambling that always got him into trouble. But all that's beside the point. What I'm getting at is that he loved his daughter very much. He'd made a mess of his life—that is, from his viewpoint—and while he was willing to take the consequences himself, he'd do almost anything to keep from hurting her again."

Patricia made a little outcry. Slidell glanced at her indifferently and went on.

"I'm fairly certain the real reason, or at least one reason, he agreed to go along with us is that he'd been dipping into the till at the Drovers National, as he had at the other bank, and he saw a way to put the money back before they caught up with him. But there was risk in this too, so he decided to take it all and fade.

"At any rate, if you're still following me, he was dead, buried, and honest, as far as his daughter was concerned. But if all that money came to light there'd be an investigation, eventually they'd find out who he really was, and she'd have to bury him all over again, this time as one of the most publicized thieves since Dillinger.

"So he had to do something with it? But what? Throw it overboard? That might seem just a little extreme later on when he arrived in

Southport still in good health. Hide it somewhere on the boat? That would be more like it, because then if he arrived all right he merely pulled it out of the hiding place and went on his way. But there are two difficulties; it'd be pretty hard, if not downright impossible, to hide anything permanently on a forty-foot boat, to begin with, and then there was Paula Stafford. She knew he had it, of course, so when it turned up missing she might come out of hiding and jump you about it, which could lead to an investigation, the very thing he was trying to avoid. And there's no doubt he would much rather she had it anyway. *Along with the rest of it*. So the chances are he'd try to arrange for her to get it, in case he died, without anyone's ever knowing he had it aboard. But how? And what went wrong?"

He was approaching it from a different direction, but he was leading me toward it as inevitably as I'd been headed for it myself. I wondered how near we would get before the machine betrayed me, or before the conscious effort of my holding back was written there in its jagged scrawls for Flowers to see. The things it measured were outside voluntary control.

His eyes shifted from the machine to my face like those of a big cat, just waiting. "We don't know how he tried to do it. But what went wrong, obviously, was Keefer. When he had the big one, how long was it from the time it struck until he died?"

"I guessed it at about twenty minutes," I said. "Naturally, I wasn't watching a clock. And it's not an easy thing to tell, anyway, in spite of the offhand way they do it on television. He could have been dead five or ten minutes before we were sure." Add all the details possible, I thought, as long as they're true and don't really matter.

"Thank you, Doctor," he said, with a bleak smile. "Approximately how long was he conscious?"

"Just the first few minutes. Five at the most."

"He didn't say anything?"

"No." Nothing coherent, I started to add, but thought better of it. She was having a bad enough time of it as it was without being told the kind of sounds he made.

"Was Keefer alone with him at any time?"

"No," I said.

"So he was the one who went to look in the suitcase for medicine?"

"Yes."

Flowers was watching the scrawls with rapt attention, but he had said nothing yet. As long as I concentrated on one question at a time I was all right. But each one was a step, leading up to where the noose was waiting.

"When did you inventory his things?"

"The next morning."

"And at least half of that time you would have been on deck, at the wheel, while he was below alone?"

"If you mean could he have gone through Reagan's suitcase," I said coldly, "of course he could. And he probably did, since he had four thousand dollars when we arrived in Southport. But he couldn't have carried twenty-three thousand ashore with him unless it was in five hundred-or thousand-dollar bills. He didn't have it, anyway, or the police would have found it."

"I know that," he broke in. "But let's plug all the holes as we go. You docked in Southport Monday afternoon, the sixteenth. Was that at the boatyard?"

"No," I said. "We didn't go alongside a pier at all that day. We anchored at the City Yacht Basin."

"Did you go ashore?"

"I didn't. Keefer did. He put the bite on me for another twenty-dollar advance and went uptown."

"Then he wasn't entirely stupid. You knew he was broke, so he had sense enough to ask you for money. Could he have been carrying any of it then?"

"Not much," I said. "I was below when he washed up and dressed, so he didn't have it tied around his body anywhere. I saw his wallet when he put the twenty in it. It was empty. He couldn't have carried much just in his pockets."

"You didn't leave the boat at all?"

"Only when I rowed him over to the pier in the dinghy. I went over to the phone in the yacht club and called the estimators in a couple of boatyards to have them come look the job over."

"What time did Keefer come back?"

"The next morning, around eight. About half drunk."

"He must have had some of the money, then, unless he set a world's record for milking a twenty. What about that morning?"

"He shaved and had a cup of coffee, and we went up to the US marshal's office. He couldn't have picked up anything aboard the boat because it was only about ten minutes and I was right there all the time. We spent the morning with the marshal and the Coast Guard, and went back to the Yacht Basin about two-thirty p.m. I paid him the rest of his money, he rolled up the two pairs of dungarees, the only clothes he had to carry, and I rowed him over to the pier. He couldn't have put anything in the dungarees. I wasn't watching him deliberately, of course; I just happened to be standing there talking to him. He rode off with the truck from Harley's boatyard. They'd brought me some gasoline so I could get over to the yard; the tanks were dry because we'd used it all trying to get back to Cristobal when we were becalmed. The police say he definitely had three to four thousand with him a half hour later when he checked in at the hotel, so he must have had it in his wallet."

"You moved the boat to Harley's boatyard that afternoon, then? Did you go ashore that night?"

"No."

"Wednesday night?"

"No," I said. "Both nights I went up to that Domino place for a bite to eat and was gone a half hour or forty-five minutes at the most, and that was before dark. I had too much work to do for any night life."

"You didn't see Keefer at all during that time?"

"No," I said.

"But you did go ashore Thursday night, and didn't get back till twelve. Keefer could have gone aboard then."

"Past the watchman at the gate?" I said, wondering if would get by with it. "The cabin of the boat was locked, anyway."

"With a padlock anybody could open with one rap of stale doughnut."

"Not without making enough noise to be heard out at the gate," I said. "That's the reason your man used bolt-cutters on the hasp."

We were skirting dangerously close now, and I had to decide in the next minute or so what I was going to do. Sweat it out, and hope they would hold off until that man in Southport could go check? It would be another seven or eight hours before he'd be able to, because he'd have to wait at least until after it was dark, and even as isolated as this place was they couldn't hang around forever. And as he had said, we were closing the holes as we went; when we got to the last one, what was left?

"How many keys were there to that padlock?" he asked.

"Only one," I said, "as far as I know."

"But there could have been another one around. Padlocks always come with two, and the lock must have been aboard when you bought the boat. Where was the key kept when you were at sea?"

"In a drawer in the galley. Along with the lock."

"So if Keefer wanted to be sure of getting back in later on, he had ten days to practice picking that lock. Or to make an impression of the key so he could have a duplicate made. It wouldn't take much more than a hundred-and-forty IQ to work that out, would it?"

"No," I said.

"All right. He had the rest of that money hidden somewhere in the cabin so he could pick it up when you weren't around. You and the yard people were working on the boat during the day, and you didn't go ashore at night, so he was out of luck for the next two days. Then Thursday night you went uptown to a movie. You'd hardly got out of sight when he showed up at the gate and tried to con the watchman into letting him go aboard. The watchman wouldn't let him in. So he did the same thing we did, picked up a skiff over at that next dock where all the fishing boats were, and went in the back way."

"It's possible," I said. "But you're only guessing."

"No. Shaw talked to that girl he was with in the Domino. She said Keefer was supposed to pick her up at eight-thirty. He called and said he might be a little late, and it was almost ten when he finally showed. Now guess where he'd been."

"Okay," I said. "But if he came aboard and got it, what became of it? He picked the girl up at ten, he was with her until I ran into them a little before midnight, and you know what happened to him after that."

He smiled coldly. "Those were the last two holes. He didn't give it to the girl, and we know he didn't throw it out of the car when Bonner and Shaw ran him to the curb about twenty minutes later and picked him up to ask him about Reagan. Therefore, he never did get it. When he got aboard, it was gone."

"Gone?" I asked. "You mean you think I found it?"

He shook his head. "What equipment was removed from that boat for repairs?"

"The refrigerator," I said, and dived for him.

He'd been watching Flowers, and was already reaching for the gun.

CHAPTER THIRTEEN

I was on him before it came clear. His chair went over backward under the two of us. I felt the tug of the wires connecting me to the lie-detector as I came out to the end of their slack, and I heard it crash to the floor behind us, bringing the table with it. Flowers gave a shrill cry, whether of outrage or terror I couldn't tell, and ran past us toward the door.

Slidell and I were in a hopeless tangle, still propped against the upended chair as we fought for the gun. He had it out of his pocket now. I grabbed it by the cylinder and barrel with my left hand, forcing it away from me, and tried to hit him with a right, but the wire connected to my arm was fouled somewhere in the mess now and it brought me up short. Then Bonner was standing over us. The blackjack sliced down, missing my head and cutting across my shoulder. I heaved, rolling Slidell over on top of me. For an instant I could see the couch where she had been sitting. She was gone. Thank God, she'd run the second I'd lunged at him. If she had enough lead, she might get away.

We heaved over once more, with Bonner cutting at me again with the blackjack, and then I saw her. She hadn't run. She'd just reached the telephone and was lifting it off the cradle and starting to dial. I heard Bonner snarl. Slidell and I rolled again, and I couldn't see her, but then I heard the sound of the blow and her cry as she fell.

My arm was free now. I hit Slidell in the face. He grunted, but still held onto the gun, trying to swing it around to get the muzzle against me. I hit him again. His hold on it was weakening. I beat at him with rage and frustration. Wouldn't he ever let go? Then Bonner was leaning over us, taking the gun out of both our hands. Beyond him I saw Patricia Reagan getting up from the floor, beside the telephone where Bonner had tossed it after he'd pulled the cord out of the wall. She grasped the corner of the desk and reached for something on it. I wanted to scream for her to get out. If she could only understand that if one of us got away they might give it up and run …

Just as he got the gun away from us she came up behind him swinging the 35-mm camera by its strap. It caught him just above the ear and he grunted and fell to his knees. The gun slid out of his fingers. I grabbed it, and then Slidell had it by the muzzle.

"Run!" I yelled at her. "Get away! The police!"

She understood then. She wheeled and ran out the front door.

Slidell raged at Bonner. "Go get her!"

Bonner shook his head like a fighter who's just taken a nine count, pushed to his feet, and looked about the room. He rubbed a hand across his face and ran toward the back door.

"The front!" Slidell screamed. He tore at the gun and tried to knee me in the groin. I slid sidewise away from him, avoiding it, and hit him high on the side of the face. Jagged slivers of pain went up my arm. Bonner turned and ran out the front door. I jerked on the gun, and this time I broke Slidell's grip. I rolled away from him and climbed to my feet. My knees trembled. I was sobbing for breath, and the whole room was turning. When the front door came by I lunged for it. But the wreckage of the lie-detector was still fast to my right arm; it spun me around and threw me off balance just as Slidell scrambled up and hit me at the waist with a hard-driving tackle. We fell across the edge of the table the instrument had been on. Pain sliced its way through my left side and made me cry out, and I heard the ribs go like the snapping of half-green sticks. The table gave way under us, and when we landed the gun was under me. I pulled it free, shifted it from my left hand to the right, and hit him across the left temple with it just as he was pushing up to his knees. He grunted and fell face down in what was left of the table.

I made it to my feet, and this time I remembered Flowers' beloved machine. I tried to unwrap the pressure cuff from around my arm, but my fingers were trembling and I couldn't half see, so I stepped on the machine and pulled upward against the wire. It broke. The one to the tube around my chest had already parted. I ran to the front door. A steel trap of pain clamped shut around my left side. I bent over with my hand against it and kept going.

The sunlight was blinding after the dimness inside. I saw Bonner. He was a good hundred yards away, near the mailbox, running very fast for a man with his squat, heavy build. I started after him. She wasn't in sight from here, but he turned left, toward the highway, when he reached the road.

My torso felt as if it had been emptied and then stuffed with broken glass or eggshells. Every breath was agony, and I ran awkwardly, with a feeling that I had been cut in two and the upper half of my body was merely riding, none too well balanced, on the lower. Then I saw her. She was running along the marl road less than fifty yards ahead of him. He was gaining rapidly. Just as I came out onto the road she looked back and saw him. She plunged off to the right, running through the palmetto and stunted pine to try to hide. I would never get there in time. I raised the gun and shot, knowing I couldn't hit him at that distance but hoping the sound would stop him. He paid no attention. Then he was off the road, closing in on her.

I plunged after him. For a moment I lost them and was terrified. It wouldn't take him more than a minute to kill her. Why didn't she scream? I tore through a screen of brush then and saw them in an open area surrounding a small salt pond. She ran out into it, trying to get across. The water was a little more than knee-deep. She stumbled and fell, and he was on her before she could get up. He bent down, caught her by the hair, and held her head under.

I tried to yell, but the last of my breath was gone. My foot caught in a mangrove root and I fell into the mud just at the edge of the water. He heard me. He straightened, and looked around. She threshed feebly, tried to get up, but fell back with her face under water.

"Pick—pick—" I gasped. "Lift her—"

He faced me contemptuously. "You come and get her."

I cocked the gun, rested it across my left forearm, and shot him through the chest. His knees folded and he collapsed face down. When I got to her the water around him was growing red, and he jerked convulsively and drew his legs up and kicked, driving his head against my legs as I put my arms around her shoulders and lifted. I got her out somehow, up beyond the slimy mud, and when she choked a few times and began to breathe I walked another few steps and fell on my knees and was sick.

After a while we started out to the highway and a phone. When the police got back to the house they picked up Slidell over in the pines trying to bridge the switch on their rented car. The keys were in Bonner's pocket.

A doctor in Marathon taped my side, and by that time the FBI men were there. They took me to a hospital in Miami for X-rays and more tape and a private room that seemed to be full of people asking questions. They said Patricia Reagan had been examined and found to be all right, and she had gone to a hotel. I finally fell asleep, and when I awoke in the morning with a steel-rigid side and a battered face through which I could see just faintly, there were some more FBI men, and after they were gone Bill came in.

"Brother, what a face," he said. "If that's the only way to become a celebrity, include me out."

Soames, the FBI agent in Southport, had found the letter. It was in the door of the *Topaz'* refrigerator, in the electrical shop at the Harley boatyard, along with a large Manila envelope containing $19,000. It was a thick door, wood on the outside and enameled steel inside, and packed with insulation. Keefer had taken out some screws, pulled away the steel enough to remove some of the insulation, and put in the envelope. That wasn't what caused it to need repairs, of course; the trouble was in the refrigeration unit itself and had begun the first day out of Panama. If Keefer hadn't been an indifferent sailor who never paid any attention to what went on aboard a boat he might have known I'd have it overhauled when we got to the yard.

Reagan had worked it out very cleverly. The letter was in a separate airmail envelope, stamped, addressed to Paula Stafford, but not sealed. The money was in this large Manila deal he'd found on the boat; it had originally held some Hydrographic Office bulletins. But he hadn't merely stuffed the money in, by single bills or bundles; he had packed it in a dozen or more individual letter-sized envelopes and sealed them, so that when the big one was closed it felt like a bunch of letters. It was sealed—or had been until Keefer tore it open.

The letter read:

Yacht *Topaz*
At Sea, June 3rd

My Darling Paula:

I don't really know how to start this—I write it with a heavy heart, for if you read it at all it will only be because I am dead. The truth is that I have been troubled by angina for some time, and yesterday I suffered what I think was a coronary attack. And while there is no reason to think I might have another before we reach port, I felt I should write this just in case one did cause my death before I had a chance to say my last good-by to you.

I am afraid this has changed my plans for the future that I wrote you about, but if I arrive safely in Southport we can discuss new ones when we are together. I still have all your precious letters that have meant so much to me. They are in an envelope in my bag, which will be sent to you in case I have a fatal attack before we reach port.

My darling, I hope you never receive this letter. But if you do, remember that I love you and that my last thoughts were of you.

Forever,
Wendell

"Very neat," Bill said. "This one would have been open in the suitcase, so you'd read it to find out whom to notify and where to ship his stuff. And naturally you wouldn't open a sealed package of old love letters. Inside the sealed envelope with the money there was another note to her, this one signed Brian, saying he'd put the other suitcase in a bonded warehouse of the Rainey Transfer and Storage Company in New York. Enclosed was the storage receipt and a letter signed Charles Wayne authorizing the Rainey people to turn the bag over to her. He told her to get it, but if Slidell caught up with her to turn it over to him rather than try to run any longer."

I nodded. It made my face hurt. "Apparently we were wrong, though, about Keefer's first seeing the money when he went to search the bag for medicine. The big envelope was already sealed then. So he must have seen Reagan when he was fixing it up."

Bill grinned. "Well, it's lucky old Nosy Keefer smelled even more and bigger money in the letter and decided to hang onto it too. If he'd thrown it overboard, you might have been an old man before it was settled to everybody's satisfaction that Reagan did have a bad heart. Think of trying to run down the doctor who wrote the prescription for those nitro pills, with the places Reagan had been and the names he'd used the past two months."

"Lay off," I said. "It still scares me. Have they found out yet who Slidell is?"

He lighted a cigarette and gestured toward the paper. "Big-shot hoodlum from Los Angeles. Several arrests for extortion and a couple for murder, but no convictions. The bonds came from three or four big bank robberies in Texas and Oklahoma. They're not sure yet whether Slidell actually took part, or just planned them. Ran with the café-society set quite a bit, or what passes for it in Southern California, and owned a home in Phoenix. Funny part is he came from about the same kind of family background Reagan did, and was well educated, even a couple of years in medical school. Bonner was his bodyguard and hunker and general muscle man. The FBI was able to talk to the Stafford woman last night, and they got the suitcase out of the warehouse in New York, but they're still buttoned up as to how much it was. They're pretty sure she didn't know anything about where it had come from, or that her boy friend's real name was Clifford Reagan. When he closed the book, pal, he closed it."

I looked out the window. "What about Bonner? Nobody's said anything yet."

"Justifiable homicide, what else? They took her statement this morning. Were you supposed to stand there and watch him kill her?"

I didn't say anything. In the movies and on television, I thought, you point the gun and everybody obeys, but maybe they didn't run into Bonners very often. There hadn't been any choice. But it would be a long time before I forgot the horror of that moment when he kicked out with his legs and nudged his head against me in the reddening water. If I ever forgot it.

I was waiting impatiently when Patricia Reagan finally came to see me that afternoon. She'd gone back to close the house and get her things. She was fully recovered, and looked lovely except for a little puffiness on one side of her face. I wanted to pay for the damage to the furnishings and having the phone reinstalled. We argued amicably about it and finally decided we'd share the responsibility. We talked for a while, sticking pretty closely to boats and sailing, the things we both knew and loved, but it trailed off and she left.

She came back again, the following afternoon, and it was the same thing. I was waiting eagerly for her, she seemed prettier each time, and apparently was glad to see me, she smiled, we talked happily about the Bahamas and about her future in photo journalism, and how we'd go out to the Islands where she could shoot some really terrific pictures, and then it began to trail off and we grew polite and formal with each other.

Just before she left, Bill and Lorraine showed up. Bill had already met her, but I introduced her to Lorraine.

After she'd gone, Lorraine looked at me with that old matchmaker's gleam in her eye. "There's a really stunning girl, Rogers, old boy. What's between you two?"

"Her father," I said.

I had a card from her after she'd gone back to Santa Barbara, but I never saw her again.

THE END

ALL THE WAY

CHARLES WILLIAMS

CHAPTER ONE

I was talking sailfish with some man from Ohio when I noticed her. She was off to the right and a little behind us, sitting cross-legged on a large beach towel with her face lowered slightly over the book spread open between her knees. At the moment she registered merely as a pair of nice legs and a sleek dark head, but after I'd looked away something about her began to bother me.

"I thought I'd go nuts," the Ohio man was saying. "This damn sail kept trailing the bait like a kitten after a ball of yarn—"

"They'll do that sometimes," I said. I shot another glance at the girl. Somehow she seemed vaguely familiar, but that still wasn't it exactly. Then I began to catch on. The pose was phony. She wasn't reading that book; she was listening.

To us? What woman would waste her time eavesdropping on a pair of filberts second-guessing a sailfish? But there was no doubt of it. There were a few sunbathers sprawled around in the vicinity, but ours was the only conversation near enough to be heard. And she was listening. Her eyes didn't move when she turned a page.

Well, maybe she was a screwball, or a fisherman herself. But she didn't appear to fit either category—if they were two categories. I tried to tag her, but the only thing I could come up with was clothes horse, which was a little on the bizarre side in view of the fact she was about seventy per cent naked at the time. I wondered how a woman could look smart, patrician, and faintly elegant while wearing a bathing suit, and decided it must be the chignon and the beautifully tapered hands.

It was a still and muggy afternoon in early November. The place was Key West, and we were lying on the narrow strip of sand before the private beach club to which I'd been given a guest card by the motel where I was staying.

"You going out again tomorrow?" I asked the Ohio man.

"No," he replied. "We've got to leave for home. How about you?"

"I don't know," I said. "I was hoping to find somebody to split a charter with."

"I know what you mean," he replied. "It's a shame to have to charter the whole boat when you're alone. And damned expensive."

I glanced around at the girl, and a slight movement of her face told me I'd almost caught her looking at us. I was conscious again of the impression that I'd seen her before. But where? I'd been so many places the past two weeks they were hard to sort out. It couldn't have been here. This was only the third day I'd been in Key West, and the other two I'd spent out in the Stream, fishing. Miami Beach? Chicago? Las Vegas?

The Ohio man looked at his watch and stood up, brushing sand from his thick-set body. "I've got to get back and start packing. Take it easy, pal."

He departed. The girl went on staring at the pages of her book. Far out, a westbound tanker hugged the edge of the reef to avoid the current of the Stream. I'd better start packing myself, I thought, and get out of Key West. I had to come up with something pretty soon; in another ten days I'd be broke. Sooner, if I spent any more on fishing trips.

I wondered about the girl again. Propping myself on an elbow, I glanced around at her. "What's the world record for dolphin?"

I expected a blank stare, of course, or one right out of the deep freeze, but instead she said calmly, without even looking up, "Hmmm. Just a moment." She leafed back through the book. "Seventy-five and a half pounds."

It caught me completely off balance. She glanced up finally. Her eyes were very dark blue, almost violet, in a thin but fine-boned face. They regarded me with urbane coolness, but then amusement got the upper hand. "All right. I *was* listening."

I sat up and slid over by her. Picking up the book, I glanced at the jacket. It was a volume on salt water fishing. "I wouldn't have said you were a fisherman."

She reached for the pack of cigarettes at her side. When I held the lighter, she smiled at me over the flame. "I'm not, as a matter of fact. I just thought I'd try it."

"Why?" I asked. She still didn't look like an outdoor type.

"A man I used to work for. He talked so much about marlin and sailfish I decided if I ever had a chance I'd see what the attraction was. Perhaps you could tell me what the boats cost."

"Mostly sixty a day," I said. "A few are sixty-five."

"They're rather expensive, aren't they?"

"Nothing's ever cheap about boats," I said. "And don't forget you're hiring two men all day, plus bait, tackle, and gasoline. Are you alone?"

While I was speaking I noticed the same intent expression on her face I'd seen when she was listening to us. It puzzled me. "Oh," she said abruptly, as if she'd been thinking of something else. "I—yes, I'm alone."

"Well, if you'd like to try it tomorrow we could split a charter. It's cheaper."

She appeared to think about it. "We-ell—"

"Come on, I'll buy you a drink," I told her. "We can talk it over."

She smiled. "All right." I helped her up, and gathered up her towel and my robe. She was a little over average height, I noted, and very slender. Too slender, I thought, to attract much attention among all the stacked and sun-gilded flesh lying around on Florida beaches, but she was smart looking and exquisitely feminine and she moved nicely. She appeared to be around thirty.

The bar was located on a screened porch at one end of the dining room. It was empty at the moment except for the white-jacketed barman. We sat down at one of the small tables along the screened side facing the beach. The barman came over. She ordered a screwdriver, and I asked for a martini. A big fan in the corner blew humid air across us.

"My name's George Hamilton," I said.

She dropped the book on a chair beside her. "Forsyth. Marian Forsyth. How do you do, Mr. Hamilton."

"Have you been here very long?"

"Just two days," she replied.

"You know, I keep thinking I've seen you somewhere before."

Again I was conscious of the urbane amusement in her eyes. "Really? I thought we had by-passed that one."

"No," I said. "I mean it. There is something familiar about you. Where are you staying?"

"The Hibiscus Motel, just up the street."

"Then we're neighbors. I'm there too."

"That must have been where you saw me. In the lobby, perhaps."

"I suppose so," I said. "But I don't see why I'd be so hazy about it. You're quite striking, you know. I mean, the Black Irish coloring, and the classic line of that hairdo. It sings."

She propped her elbows on the table, with her chin on her laced fingers, and smiled. "And what other personality problems do you have, Mr. Hamilton, besides shyness?"

I grinned. "I'm sorry. But that chignon is beautiful."

"Thank you." Then she added, "Incidentally, I'm not Irish. I'm Scotch. My maiden name was Burns."

"Oh?" I said. "I didn't know you were married." She wore no ring.

"I'm divorced," she said. "Where are you from, Mr. Hamilton?"

The barman brought our drinks. "Texas," I told her.

She took a sip of the screwdriver and looked at me thoughtfully. "I'd never have known it. You don't sound a bit like a Texan."

"I'm not a professional," I said. "It's a fallacy, anyway. All Texans don't go around saying, 'Howdy, pardner.'"

"Yes, I know. I'm from Louisiana, myself. But I do have a pretty fair ear for accents. You've lost yours entirely."

"I never really had one," I said. "But while we're on this Professor 'Iggins kick, you can spot it if you listen closely. I still boot one occasionally. *Thanks*giving, for instance. And *after*noon. That over-stressed first syllable is pure Texican."

She nodded. "And Southern. You must have a good ear yourself."

I shrugged. "I had a little speech training. At one time I was going to be an actor."

She regarded me with interest. "But you're not in show business?"

"No," I said. "Advertising. But how about the fishing?"

"I'd like very much to try it. But I'm not sure yet I can make it tomorrow. Could I let you know tonight?"

"Sure," I said. "Why don't we have dinner together?"

She smiled. "I'm afraid I couldn't, tonight. But thanks, anyway. Suppose I call you around ten or eleven. Will you be in then?"

I said yes. She asked several more questions about fishing, refused the offer of another drink, and left to go back to the motel. I swam for a while, wondering about her. Somehow her interest in fishing didn't ring true. I wondered if she had money. A bathing suit revealed a lot of interesting statistical data, but it didn't say a damn thing when it came to financial status.

I was lying in bed around eleven reading *The Hidden Persuaders* when the phone rang. "Well, I can go," she said eagerly.

"That's great. Here's hoping you land a sail."

"Can we still get a boat, do you think?"

"Yes," I said. "I've already talked to Captain Holt. He's the one I've been fishing with. I'll call now and confirm."

"I hate to keep bothering you with questions," she apologized, "but what shall I take? What time do we leave, and how long are we out?"

"What room are you in?" I asked. "I could come over—" The brush was polite, but firm. She was about to go to bed. She repeated the questions.

"Hat, or fishing cap," I said. "Long sleeves, dark glasses, suntan lotion. That sun is murder. We'll leave the dock at eight, and come in around four-thirty or five. They furnish the tackle; all we have to bring is our lunch. There's a restaurant on Roosevelt Boulevard. I don't have a car, but I'll call a cab—"

"I have one," she interrupted. "I'll meet you in the parking area behind the motel at seven-thirty. Will that be all right?"

"Fine," I said.

"Just one other thing," she said. "Could you tell me what the outriggers are for?"

I wondered why she wanted to go into that in the middle of the night over the phone. She seemed to have an insatiable curiosity about the mechanics of big-game fishing. I explained why the lines were trolled clipped to the ends of the outriggers to give an automatic drop-back when a billfish struck. "He raps it with his bill," I finished. "It stops dead in the water when it snaps off the rigger, so he thinks he's killed it. He takes it in his mouth then."

"I see," she said thoughtfully. "Well, thank you very much, Mr. Hamilton. I'll see you in the morning."

After she'd hung up I lay there thinking about her, studying the whole thing a little warily. Then I dismissed the worry. Hell, she couldn't possibly know me, and I was three thousand miles from Las Vegas. The prospect of another fishing trip was irresistible, and she might turn out to be a very interesting deal. I don't dig you at all, Mrs. Forsyth, but you're beginning to intrigue me. We'll see what we can find out tomorrow.

It wasn't much—at least, not to begin with. And then when I finally did figure out what she was doing, she puzzled me even more.

It was a beautiful day with a light breeze out of the southeast. When I'd shaved and showered, and emerged from the room with the beach bag containing glasses, fishing cap, tanning lotion and cigarettes, she was just coming out of No. 17, diagonally across from me. She had on a conical straw hat, blue Bermuda shorts, and a long-sleeved blouse, and was carrying a big purse. She waved and smiled. "Good morning, Mr. Hamilton."

I learned nothing from the car. As the great American status symbol it was useless, because it wasn't hers; it was an Avis rental job she'd picked up at the airport in Miami. She was wearing a watch, however, that had cost at least five hundred. She didn't have much to say while we were eating breakfast; and afterward, while we were running out to the Stream with the engines hooked up, talking was difficult because of their noise.

It was a few minutes before nine and Key West was down on the horizon when we crossed the edge of the Stream shortly to the south and east of Sand Key light. It was beautiful, running dark as indigo in a ragged line beyond the reefs with just enough breeze to riffle the light groundswell rolling up from the southeast. The *Blue Runner* slowed, and Sam the Mate came down from topside. He swung out the outriggers, nodded for Mrs. Forsyth to take the port chair, and put out her line, baited with balao. She watched as he clipped it to the outrigger halyard and ran it out to the end. He fitted the butt of the rod into the gimbal in her chair.

She took it and looked around at me. "Now what do I do?"

Normally I detest people who want to talk when I'm fishing, but this was different. I was curious about her, and becoming more so all the time. "Just watch your bait," I said. "You see it? A little to your right, and about seventy feet back."

She looked. It skipped across the surface momentarily, and slid under again, fluttering. "Yes. I can see it now."

"Keep your eye on it," I said. "Watch it every minute."

She nodded. "That's so I'll know when I get a bite?"

I restrained an impulse to wince. "Strike," I said. "These fish out here don't nibble; they hit. But that's not the reason, anyway. You'll know when you get a strike, but if you don't actually see the fish hit it you're missing half the fun of this kind of fishing."

I glanced at her. She was wearing dark glasses now, so I couldn't see her eyes, but I had that feeling I'd had the other times, that she was hanging onto every word with rapt attention. Sam handed me the other rod. For the time I forgot her, watching my own bait with the old eager anticipation while we trolled quietly. The sun was hot. Flying fish skittered out of the blue side of a swell. A tanker in ballast went past to seaward, rocking us in its wake. Water boiled under my bait, and there was a slight click as the line snapped off the outrigger.

"Mackerel," Holt said laconically.

I lowered the rod tip, and then struck. It was a small one. "Good marlin bait," Sam said, as he grasped the leader and dropped it in the box. I glanced at Mrs. Forsyth. She was lighting a cigarette. The fish appeared to bore her. Well, it wasn't much of a fish.

An hour went by. I landed a bonito that came in badly slashed by barracuda. She had no action at all, but didn't appear to mind. She seemed to be lost in thought.

"Bird," Sam said behind us.

"I see him," Holt replied. The beat of the engine picked up, and we swung in a sharp turn.

Mrs. Forsyth glanced around at me. "We aren't going to chase birds, are we?"

"Man-o'-war," I said. "A frigate bird." I stood up and looked forward, and spotted him. He was about half a mile ahead, off the starboard bow. She stuck her rod in the holder on the rail and came over to look too.

"When you see one hovering like that," I told her, "he's usually following a fish."

"Why?" she asked.

"Table scraps," I explained. "When the fish locates a school of bait and starts to feed, he drives them to the surface. That gives the bird a chance at 'em."

Captain Holt was staring forward. "Probably dolphin," he said. "I see some dunnage."

"How about taking it on the port side?" I asked.

"Sure."

"Get set," I told Mrs. Forsyth. She sat down in the chair and I fitted the rod into the gimbal for her. I told her how to strike.

"How do they know it's a dolphin?" she asked, watching me with that intent expression on her face.

"They don't actually," I said. "It's just an educated guess. Dolphin like to lie under anything floating on the surface." We came abeam of the plank, and then it began to drop astern. I stood up to watch. Her bait fluttered past it, started to draw away.

"Here he comes!" Holt said tersely.

It was one of those moments that'd still give you a thrill if you fished for a hundred years. I saw the blue bolt of flame under the surface, and then he came clear, quartering and behind the bait. It was a bull of eighteen or twenty pounds flashing green and gold and blue in the sunlight, and he took the bait going down. Her line snapped off the outrigger.

She forgot to strike him, but he set the hook himself, leaped, made one fast, slashing run, leaped three more times, and was gone. She reeled in. Sam looked at the leader. "Kink," he said.

"What did I do wrong?" she asked, casually taking cigarettes from the pocket of her blouse.

"Nothing," I said.

"But he got away."

I was beginning to get it now, though it made no sense at all. The whole thing had bored her profoundly and she didn't mind in the slightest that she'd lost the fish, but she wanted me to explain why.

I explained. "When he was jumping, he threw a kink in the leader. Wire'll always break if it kinks. It happens to everybody."

"Oh," she said thoughtfully.

She wasn't interested in fishing, and never had been. She was listening to my voice.

There was no possible explanation for it, but I knew I was right. I watched her closely the rest of the day, checking it, and found that whenever I was talking, no matter what the subject, she listened in that same way. She said nothing about herself except that she was the private secretary to a businessman in a small town named Thomaston in central Louisiana. There was no longer any doubt that fishing bored her. She raised a sail, and lost it, with no more interest than she'd shown in the dolphin. I landed a small sail and asked Holt to release it. We were back at the dock at four forty-five.

We paid Holt, and I drove her rental Ford back to the motel. Outside No. 17, she held out her hand and smiled.

"It's been wonderful. I enjoyed every minute of it."

"Would you like to go out again tomorrow?" I asked.

"I'd rather not take that much sun again so soon."

"How about dinner tonight?"

I got the same cool, polite brush. "Really, I couldn't. But thank you just the same."

I went on to my own room. After I'd showered and changed into gray flannel slacks and a light sport shirt, I sat down in front of the air-conditioner with a cigarette and went back over the whole thing from the time I'd noticed she was eavesdropping. She'd looked me over and dropped me. Why? And what had she really wanted? An adventure, an interlude, a station-break? Whatever it was, I'd failed to measure up somewhere. Well, you couldn't win 'em all. The phone rang.

"I'm just stirring some martinis," she said warmly. "Why don't you come over, Mr. Hamilton, and have one with me to celebrate your sailfish?"

You never know, I thought; maybe that's why they're so fascinating. "Love to," I said. I dropped the phone back in the cradle and was out the door in two strides.

I knocked on No. 17, and stepped inside. She'd changed into a pleated black skirt and white blouse, and was very smart, and very, very attractive from the sling pumps to the sleek dark head. There was a bucket of ice on the glass top of the dresser, and she was stirring martinis in a pitcher.

She turned and smiled. "Do sit down, Mr. Forbes."

CHAPTER TWO

The way she said it told me there was no point in trying to bluff. I stepped inside and closed the door. Her room was exactly the same as mine, furnished with a brown carpet and drapes, twin beds with yellow spreads, a dresser, and a glass-covered desk at the right of the door. The telephone was located on the desk, and beside it—almost under my hand—were two sheets of motel stationery covered with the slashes and pot-hooks of shorthand. Two names were spelled out in the message; one of them was Murray, and the other Forbes.

I glanced up at her. "You just got this?"

She nodded coolly, and poured the martinis. "Just a few minutes ago."

"Are you from the police?"

"Of course not," she said. She handed me the martini, and picked up her own. "Here's to your sailfish. Or should we drink to Mr. Murray's durability, or the high cost of extradition?"

"What about Murray?" I demanded.

"Haven't you heard?"

"How could I? I was afraid to call anybody on the Coast. And there was no mention of it in the papers I could get."

"Then you were still afraid you'd killed him?"

I took a sip of the drink; I needed it. "No. I assumed he was tougher than that. But felonious assault is pretty damn serious itself. What do you know about it?"

"Would you hand me those notes, please?"

I passed them to her, so completely at sea now I didn't feel anything. She walked around between the beds and sat down on the farther one with a leg doubled under her and the pleated skirt spread carefully over her knees. She put her drink on the night table and groped for a cigarette. I held the lighter for her. She smiled, and nodded to the armchair. "Please sit down."

"What about Murray?" I said impatiently.

"Broken jaw," she said, consulting the notes. "Mild concussion. Scalp lacerations. Various minor injuries. A hundred and fifty dollars damage to his camera, and possibly two hundred to the furnishings of a motel room. He's recovering, and the woman's husband appears to have used a little influence to smooth it over and keep it hushed up. There's no felony charge. Nothing they would extradite you for."

I sighed with relief.

"You apparently don't care much for private detectives."

"I can contain my enthusiasm for 'em," I said. "Snoopy bastards."

"You're lucky it was no worse."

I lighted a cigarette. "Would you mind telling me who you are, and just what this is all about?"

"I've already told you who I am," she replied, taking a sip of her drink. "Mrs. Marian Forsyth."

"And you're a private secretary to some businessman in Louisiana," I said. "Don't give me that."

"I am," she said. "Or was, rather. However, let me finish this dossier. Correct me if there are any errors. Your full name is Jerome Lawrence Forbes, you're usually called Jerry, you're twenty-eight, and you *are* from Texas—at least, originally. You're single. You drink moderately, but you gamble too much, and at least twice you've been involved in a messy affair with a married woman. You attended Rice Institute and the University of Texas, but didn't graduate from either. I believe it was some trouble over a crap game at Rice, and you left the University of Texas to go into the Navy during the Korean War. You don't appear to be the plodding type of wage-earner, to say the least. Since your discharge from the service in 1953 you've owned a bar in Panama, written advertising copy for two or three San Francisco ad agencies, been a race-track tout, and at the time you got into this brawl in Las Vegas you were doing publicity for some exhibitionist used-car dealer in Los Angeles. Is that fairly accurate?"

"Except for a minor point," I said. "I wasn't the racetrack tout; I was the man behind him. It was a public-relations deal. But never mind that. How'd you find out all this?"

She smiled. "You'll love this. From a private detective."

"But for God's sake *why?* And where was it I saw you before?"

"Miami Beach," she said. "Six days ago."

"Oh. Then you were staying—"

She nodded. "At that same Byzantine confection you were. The Golden Horn."

The Golden Horn was one of those chi-chi motels in the north end of Miami Beach that really aren't motels at all except that you can park your own car if you want. I didn't have a car, of course; I'd stayed out there merely because it was less expensive than the big places.

"It was by the pool," she went on. "You were trying to pick up some girl from—Richmond, I believe."

I frowned. "I remember the girl, all right. Silver blonde with a seven-word vocabulary. Priceless, hilarious, hysterical—I can't remember the other four. But I don't know why I'm so vague about seeing you. As attractive—"

"Competition, perhaps," she said. "The pool-side is not my terrain. Nor the beach. I'm too thin."

"You're entitled to your own opinions," I said. "Don't try to brainwash me. I still say I'd have noticed you. I could spot the line of that head a hundred yards—"

"I had my hair up, and I was wearing a swimming cap," she said crisply. "Now, if we're through discussing my visibility, or lack of it, would you care to know what I was doing?"

"That I've already figured out. You were listening."

She gave me an approving glance. "Right."

"But why? What was it about my voice?"

"For the moment, let's just say your voice has a certain unique quality that interests me. And it might make you a lot of money."

"How?" I asked.

"I'd rather not say yet. But that's why I started investigating you—especially after I began to suspect your name wasn't really George Hamilton."

"What tipped you off about that?" I asked. "I thought I was pretty careful."

"Pure chance," she replied. "It just happened there was a man named Forbes registered there at the same time—"

"Oh," I said. "Sure. I remember now. And he was paged, there by the pool. Was it that obvious?"

"No," she replied. "In fact, you recovered beautifully. It just happened I was looking right at you. Naturally, it made me wonder, since I'd just heard you tell the girl your name was Hamilton. I don't remember whether that was before or after you told her your father was Chairman of the Board of Inland Steel."

"It was a waste of breath," I said. "But what did you do then?"

"I went up to my room," she said. "It was on the second floor, overlooking the patio and the pool, and I could watch you from the window. I called the desk and asked them to page Mr. Hamilton."

"Oh. I remember that call. So you were the mixed-up type from Eastern Airlines that kept insisting she'd found the luggage I hadn't even lost?"

She nodded coolly. "That's right."

"Why?"

"Several reasons. I had to find out if you really were registered under that name, or just lying to the girl on the premise that you should always lie to girls. And I wanted to hear your voice on the telephone—"

"Oh," I interrupted. "And that was the reason for all those questions about fishing last night, over the phone?"

"Of course." She gestured impatiently with a slim hand. "But to get back—I also wanted to watch you while you were paged."

"I see." This girl was clever. "And I flunked?"

"You flunked. The boy practically had to shake you before you remembered you were Mr. Hamilton."

I nodded. "So then you put the private snoops on me? But how did they find out where to dig? I've been running scared, believe me. I've used three different names from Las Vegas to Los Angeles to Chicago to Miami, and I registered from San Antonio."

"It was quite simple," she said. "I got your correct name and your Los Angeles address off an old credit card."

"*What?*"

"When you try to change your identity, you should clean out your wallet. And when you're swimming in the ocean, you shouldn't leave your room key in your bathrobe on the beach."

I stared at her, beginning to feel like an absolute chump. This girl had picked me to pieces like a rube at a county fair.

"The detective agency put their Los Angeles office on it," she went on coolly. "And when you checked out of the Golden Horn they told me where you were staying down here. I came down. I wanted to keep in contact, and perhaps meet you, but not commit myself until I received the report from California and learned a little about you. When we came in a while ago, I called Miami. They'd heard from the West Coast at last, and gave me the report over the phone. I liked what I heard, so I called you to come over."

"What do you want?" I asked.

"First, to know quite a bit more about you. What are your plans?"

"I don't know," I said. "If your information's accurate, I suppose I can go back to my right name and start looking for a job. Probably in New York."

"Would you consider putting it off for a few days? I have a proposition in mind, but I can't tell you what it is until I'm sure of several things."

"What kind of proposition?" I asked.

"A very unusual one, and highly profitable. But how would you like to go back to Miami Beach?"

"When?" I asked.

She stood up. "Right now. I'm expecting some very important mail, and I have to do some shopping in the morning."

I arose. "Sounds fine to me." Then I took hold of her arms, and said, "In fact, I've just had a wonderful idea—"

The blue eyes were coolly satirical. "That I don't doubt in the slightest. No."

"But you haven't even heard it."

"I don't have to. But it just happens I still have my room at the Golden Horn, and that I'm expecting the mail there, under my own name. I suggest you re-register as George Hamilton; after all, they'll probably remember you."

"But—"

"I'll drop you in downtown Miami Beach, and you can take a cab. I'd rather no one knew of our relationship."

"Relationship," I said. "Hah!"

We'd stopped for dinner in Marathon, so it was shortly after eleven when she let me off in Miami Beach. "I'll see you in the morning," she said. "Call me in room 316."

"Sure," I replied. I carried the bag into a bar and killed about ten minutes over a drink before I called a cab and went out to the Golden Horn. After I'd signed the registry card I followed the boy across the corner of the patio court, past the illuminated pool and palms bearing clusters of colored lights. We entered a corridor in the left wing and took an elevator to the third floor. 312 was just around the corner from her room. It was identical with the one I'd had before, done in turquoise and persimmon, with an oversized double bed and a picture window overlooking the ocean. The boy put the bag on the luggage stand, adjusted the air-conditioner thermostat, thanked me for the tip, and left. I waited three minutes before I stepped down the corridor and knocked on 316. The door opened slightly and she looked out around the edge of it.

"I might have known," she said.

"I just thought of several more things I should tell you about myself," I replied. "It was in Panama I first became interested in big-game fishing—"

"I see. And you're afraid you might forget them before morning?"

"They might be lost forever. But I don't have to come in; I can tell you from out here in the hall. Or through the door."

She sighed. I couldn't tell whether she was really angry or not. "Just a moment." She disappeared. I heard a rustling sound, and then she pulled the door open and I stepped inside. She closed it. Her room was the same layout and color scheme. She'd scrubbed off what makeup she'd been wearing, even the lipstick, and had on a rather conservative nightgown under the negligee she was struggling with, but she was unbelievably exciting. I didn't know why.

"Mostly trivia," I said. "But revealing. For instance, when I was a kid, all the other slobs put their money in the Christmas Club, but I kept mine in a regular account. Got two per cent."

"You don't have to hit me over the head," she replied. I kissed her. This was even more exciting, in spite of the fact she obviously didn't care whether it was or not. She finally broke it up, but she said, "All right." It was rather the way you'd buy a potato peeler from a salesman to get rid of him, but by this time I didn't even care what the terms were.

She was smooth, deft, experienced, and agreeably cooperative about the whole thing. I lay there afterward in the annealed and quiescent dark trying to pin down her exact attitude, and decided the word I was looking for was pleasant. That was it. She was quite pleasant about it—the perfect hostess, in fact.

"You mentioned acting," she said. "Was that by any chance true?"

"Yes. But just amateur. In college."

"Were you a fast study?"

"Fairly so," I said. "I usually had my lines by the time we finished blocking. For some reason I learned fast. Luck, I suppose."

"Tell me about your family."

"I'm it, except for my stepfather. My mother and father were divorced when I was about five. He was a geologist; spent most of his time in South America, usually in the high Andes. My mother wouldn't live up there. He was killed the summer after the divorce; a station wagon he was riding in went off the road into a gorge. My mother remarried a couple of years later. A widower several years older than she was, partner in a Houston brokerage firm. She died while I was at sea, during the Korean thing. She left me a little money; that's when I bought the bar in Panama."

"What happened to the bar?"

"It was put off-limits for military personnel because of a couple of bad fights, so I sold it. Then lost most of the money in Las Vegas."

"Tell me about the tout business."

I reached over and turned on the reading lamp. She looked at me questioningly. "What's that for?"

"I don't know," I said. "I just wanted to look at you."

"Why?"

"Tell me," I said. I raised myself on an elbow and ran a fingertip along the line of her cheek. "You're beautiful. Is that it?"

"Don't be silly."

"I was never less silly. How about striking? Exciting? It's a quality of some kind—fragile, elegant, cool, hard-boiled, and sexy, all at the same time. There's no such combination? I was afraid not."

She shook her head with exasperation, but she did smile. "Turn out the light."

I turned it out, and took her in my arms and kissed her. She came to me quite readily, and was as deftly and pleasantly co-operative as before.

"What about the tout business?" she asked after a while.

"It was nothing," I said. "You know how they operate. You've seen 'em by the dozens passing out their sheets at the entrances to race tracks—Clocker Joe, Stablehand Maguire, Exercise Boy—no imagination, working for buttons. So I made a deal with this one; I'd put him in the big time for half the take. We set it up as a telegraphic service and I bought time on a Tijuana radio station to sell him—a real saturation build-up about the time Santa Anita was opening. Lot of spot announcements and a half hour of hillbilly junk with a plug every minute or two. That's about all there was to it, except convincing him he had to raise his prices. Obviously, nobody has any confidence in a cheap tip on a horse race; you've got to charge plenty to be good. We were splitting two thousand a week for a while."

"What happened?"

"He couldn't stand prosperity; turned out to be a lush. Kept getting his records fouled up so he couldn't remember who got the winners yesterday. And you're dead without records."

"I see," she said thoughtfully.

I woke once during the night. She was lying quite still beside me, but after a while I began to suspect she was awake. I put my hand on her thigh. It was tense and rigid. Her arm felt the same way, and when I slid my hand down to hers, lying at her side, I found it was clenched into a fist.

"What's the matter?" I asked.

She made no reply. I asked again. She still said nothing, so I left her alone. I'm a casual type, and I operate off the top of my head most of the time, but it was beginning to sink in that this girl was from another league. I'd been able to blackmail my way in here because she wanted something from me, and she had submitted with grace, but there wasn't anything casual about it at all. It was just beautifully controlled.

CHAPTER THREE

When I awoke it was after eight. I groped for a cigarette, lighted it, and turned to look at her. She was sleeping quietly with the dark hair like spilled ink across the pillow. She had the flat stomach and narrow hips of a fashion model and rather small breasts that were spread out and flattened as she lay on her back. I looked at the slender patrician face with the long lashes like soot against her skin; it was a willful face, I thought, and it just escaped being bony, but the bones were good. She was no pinup, but she reminded me of something very thin and expensive that was made before good workmanship went out of style. I wondered what she wanted.

Her purse was on the dresser; it might tell me something. I went over and opened it. A thin folder held eleven $100 Express checks. I pulled out the wallet and checked her driver's license. The little she'd told me about herself appeared to be true. *Mrs. Marian Forsyth,* it said, *714 Beauregard Drive, Thomaston, La. Hair, black. Eyes, blue. 5'-7". 112 pounds. Born Nov. 8, 1923*. She'd be thirty-four in a few days. This surprised me; I wouldn't have thought she was over twenty-nine or thirty. The wallet held about six hundred dollars. I dropped it back in the purse.

I dressed, and looked out in the corridor. It was clear. I went back to my room, called down for orange juice and coffee and the *Miami Herald,* and had a quick shower and shave. It was 9:25 and I was just finishing the coffee when she called. She was going over to Miami, and would be back at noon. I killed a couple of hours swimming off the beach and came in and changed to slacks and a white cotton T-shirt. Shortly after twelve the phone rang. When I answered there was a hint of suppressed excitement in her voice. "I've got something to show you," she said.

I knocked lightly on 316, and she opened almost immediately. Her hair was up in the chignon, of course, softly clubbed and worn low on the nape of the neck, and she looked as slender and smart as a fashion show. I kissed her. She submitted, but I could sense impatience. Pulling away from me, she nodded toward the dresser.

There were two things on it that hadn't been there this morning. One was a small tape recorder, and the other was an old briefcase plastered all over with tags and waybills. It had come air express, and I could see the return address on one of the tags. It was the same as that on her driver's license.

"That's the mail you were waiting for?" I asked.

She nodded. "It just came. And the tape recorder is what I went to Miami for. Have you ever heard your voice on one?"

"I don't think so," I said.

She unstrapped the briefcase. I could see excitement growing in her face as she began removing its contents. They appeared to me to be largely rubbish. There were a dozen or more thin pamphlets I recognized as the annual statements of corporations, some old fire insurance policies, and a couple of stenographer's notebooks. She casually tossed all this in the wastebasket.

"I didn't want my housekeeper to know what I was really after," she explained. "So I told her to ship the briefcase intact. Oh— Here we are."

There were two of them: flat cardboard boxes about seven inches square. They held full reels of tape. She selected one and put it on the machine, and stuck an empty reel on the other spindle. When the tape was connected, she ran several feet of it onto the empty reel with a control on the front panel, and pressed the *PLAY* switch. A man's voice issued from the speaker. She adjusted the gain.

"... take a chance and hold the Lukens Steel for another five points. I think it'll go, but the minute it does, sell. It's too volatile for my blood pressure. How'd Gulf Oil close, Chris?"

"Let's see." This was also a man's voice. *"Here we are. Gulf was up three quarters."*

"Good. Buy me another hundred shares in the morning."

"Right. One hundred Gulf at the market. Anything else, Mr. Chapman?"

"Just one more thing. Will you ask the Research Department to send me everything they've got on an outfit called Trinity Natural Gas? It's a pipeline company that was formed about two years ago. The stock sold over-the-counter until last month, but now it's listed on the American Exchange. Marian has a hunch about it. She went to college with the man who's head of it, and says he's a ball of fire."

She stopped the machine and glanced at me. "Do you know what it is?"

I lighted a cigarette. "Sure. A man talking to his broker on the phone." I couldn't see what the excitement was.

"Right," she said. She ran the tape back, watching the mechanical counter on the panel. "Now listen closely. I'm going to play that last speech again, and I want you to repeat it."

"Okay," I said.

She pressed the *PLAY* switch again. Chapman's voice began. *"Just one more thing. Will you ask the Research Department ...?"* I listened, noting at the same time that she was taking it down in shorthand. It was only five or six sentences. She stopped the machine at the end of it, and transcribed her notes and handed them to me.

"I don't need them," I said. "I've heard it twice."

"Read it anyway," she said. "So you won't pause or stumble." Plugging in the microphone, she handed it to me. She put the machine on *RECORD*, and I read the speech into it. She stopped the machine, and ran the tape back, still watching the counter. I could sense she was keyed up. I knew what she was doing now, of course, but it struck me as absurd. She pressed the *PLAY* switch, and sat down near me on the end of the bed. I started to say something, but she cut me off with an imperious gesture of her hand.

"Just one more thing," Chapman's voice said. *"Will you ask the Research Department ...?"* Chapman's voice went on through the speech. At the end there was a little whrrp where she'd put it on *RECORD* and I'd started speaking.

"Just one more thing. Will you ask the Research Department to send me everything they've got..."

I sat bolt upright. "Hey!" She clamped a hand over my mouth. We both sat perfectly still until it was finished.

She got up and turned it off. Then she turned to me with a faint smile. "Now you know what I was listening to all the time."

I stared at her. "It's incredible. They're almost identical."

She nodded. "That's the reason I wanted to do it this way, with the two voices end-to-end. As a comparison check, it's absolutely conclusive. It's not only the timbre—plenty of male voices are down in that low end of the baritone range —but you both have the same quick, alert, self-assured way of speaking. Clipped, and rather aggressive."

"But are we really that much alike?" I asked. "Or is it just the recording?"

She took a cigarette from a pack on the dresser, and leaned down. I held the lighter for her. She sat in the armchair, facing me with her knees crossed. "I could tell you apart, in person. And on hi-fi equipment. I might even, in fact, on the telephone—because I'm aware there are two of you."

"What do you mean by that?" I asked.

She gestured with the cigarette. "It's obvious, isn't it? If you were speaking over the telephone to anybody who knew Harris Chapman but didn't know you, you'd be Chapman."

"I'm not so sure—"

"Let me explain," she interrupted. "If you said you were Harris Chapman, why should anyone doubt it? Your voices are almost identical, and they're not there side-by-side for comparison. Add to that the way you both speak—which is almost exactly alike, and very much *unlike* Southern speech in general. He lives in Thomaston, Louisiana. You follow me, don't you?"

"Yes," I said. "In other words, he's unique—at least, in his manner of speech. They hear it—it's Chapman."

"Exactly. You could fool anybody who knows him."

"For just about five seconds," I said.

She smiled. "No. You're wrong."

"If you're speaking of impersonation, it takes one other thing. Information."

"I was coming to that," she said. "It happens I know more about Harris Chapman than anybody else in the world."

"What are you driving at?"

"This. In ten days of intensive study, you could *become* Harris Chapman—that is, to the extent that Harris Chapman as a personality or an individual is projected over a telephone circuit."

I stood up and crushed out my cigarette. "And why should I?"

"Would you consider $75,000 a good reason?"

I paused, still holding the mangled cigarette stub. "Where would you get that much money?"

"From him, naturally."

"You mean steal it?"

She nodded coolly. "I suppose you would call it stealing. A rather unusual type of theft, and one that's absolutely foolproof."

"There is no such animal."

"In this particular case, there is. It's unique. You've no doubt heard of the 'perfect crime.' This is it."

I lighted another cigarette, still looking at her. She had me badly confused now. I sat down on the corner of the bed near her. "I'll admit I don't know as much about girls as I did when I was nineteen," I said. "But, even so, your picture and sound track don't match. Perfect crime—I'd say the worst crime you've ever committed was taking advantage of a stuck parking meter."

She shrugged. "I didn't say I'd ever stolen anything before."

"But you're going to now. Why?"

"We can go into the reasons later. Are you interested?"

"I'm always interested in money."

"Have you ever stolen anything?"

"No. But I doubt that's highly significant. Nobody's ever tried me with $75,000 before."

"Then you *could?*"

"Probably. But it couldn't be as foolproof as you say."

"It is," she said definitely. "In fact, nobody will ever know it was stolen."

"Why? Money doesn't evaporate. And just where is it?"

She studied me thoughtfully. "Your stepfather was a broker, I believe you said. So you know what a trading account is?"

"Sure."

"All right. Harris Chapman has a trading account with a New Orleans brokerage firm. The man called Chris you just heard is the registered representative who handles it for him. And at the present moment the stocks and cash in the account add up to a little over $180,000."

I whistled. Then I glanced sharply at her. "So?"

"Well, you know how a trading account like that is handled."

"Sure. The stocks he buys are credited to his account, but they're kept there at the brokerage house in the vault, so he doesn't have to go through all the rigmarole of endorsing them and sending them back when he wants to sell. He buys and sells all the time, just by picking up the phone—" I got it then, and she was crazy.

"You see?" she said.

"I see nothing," I replied. "Money in a brokerage account is just as safe as money in a bank account. It takes a signature to get it; you ought to know that. Two signatures, as a matter of fact. You have to sign a receipt for the transaction, and then endorse the check to cash it."

She interrupted. "Will you listen just a minute? The idea is nothing like as simple as that. Of course it wouldn't work in any other set of circumstances, but as I told you before, this is unique. All it'll require is the most elemental sort of forgery because nobody'll ever look at the signatures anyway."

"Why?"

"Because there'll never be the slightest doubt but that Harris Chapman drew the money out himself. I'll take care of that."

"You'd better fill me in a little," I said. "Just who is Chapman, and what's your connection with him?"

She leaned over to tap ash off her cigarette. "He's a businessman, and for a small town a fairly wealthy one. He owns Chapman Enterprises, which consists of a newspaper, a radio station, cotton gin, and a warehouse, among other things."

"And you worked for him?"

Her eyes met mine without any expression at all. "I worked for him. I was his private secretary, mistress, executive officer, fiancée—you name it. I went to work for him eight years ago, and for the past six I've been a sort of combination of executive vice-president and full-time wife. Except that I wasn't married to him."

"Why not?"

"For the tired old reason that he already had a wife."

"You don't look like the type that'd dangle that long."

"Shall we drop that part of it for the moment?"

"Sorry," I said. "But I still don't see how you think you're going to get away with it. What's Chapman going to be doing all the time you're looting his trading account?"

"Nothing," she said. "He'll be dead."

"How do you know?"

"Because I'm going to kill him."

I caught a no-show out of the Miami airport at 4:15, and was at Idlewild a little after eight. I took the limousine over to town. It was a blustery November night, not really wet but with scattered shot-charges of rain hurled on a cold north wind. I didn't have a topcoat. People stared at me as if I were crazy as I came out of the terminal and caught a cab. The small hotel where I'd stayed once before was all right, but the room faced an airwell and was small and cheerless.

I sat down on the bed and counted my money. I had three hundred and sixty left. Three hundred, I thought, after I buy a coat. No, I had to have a hat, too. This was New York. I couldn't go job-hunting along Madison Avenue looking like a refugee from Muscle Beach. It was going to be tough enough as it was; the last reference I could give was two years old. I went up the street to a bar, but the drink only made me feel worse. After a while I went back to the room and tried to read, but it was futile. I kept thinking about $75,000 and blue water and sunlight and a sleek dark head. I threw the magazine on the floor and lay on the side of the bed staring down at it.

What did I care what happened to some man who was nothing to me but a name? If I were so concerned over his safety, why didn't I call him and tell him she was going to kill him? That was it; she was anyway. My walking out hadn't changed anything, except that I'd thrown away $75,000. I remembered the way she'd lain there in the darkness, rigid and wide awake and staring, with her hands clenched, and wondered what he'd done to her. Well, I'd never know; but the chances were excellent he'd never do it to anybody else.

All she'd wanted me to do was get that money for her—from a man who would already be dead. Wasn't it?

How would I know? I thought bitterly. I'd run off before she could tell me.

The next morning I bought a topcoat and hat and started out. I filled out forms. I left my name and telephone number. I talked to supercilious personnel men. My feet grew tired. The weather was still blustery and cold, with a lowering sky like dirty metal. If this were the movies, I thought, I'd pass a travel agency window and there'd be a big sun-drenched picture of a brunette in a bathing suit sitting on the beach in front of a white hotel with the caption *Come to Miami*. She was a blonde, as it turned out, and the invitation was *Come to Kingston*. A man was landing a marlin off the end of a pier. With a fly rod, as nearly as I could tell. You could see Jamaica was a fisherman's paradise.

I came back to the bar across the street from the hotel around 2 p.m. and had a Scotch while I wondered what she was doing. And how a girl managed to look elegant in a bathing suit. Not lifted-pinkie elegant, but eighteenth century elegant. I went up to my room and lay down on the bed. It was raining now; I could see it falling into the airwell. I picked up the phone and asked for long distance.

"Miami Beach," I said. "The Golden Horn Motel. Person-to-person to Mrs. Marian Forsyth." At least I could talk to her.

"Hold the line, please."

I waited. I could hear the operators.

"Golden Horn," a girl's voice said. "Who? Mrs. Forsyth? Just a moment, please ... I'm sorry; she's checked out."

I dropped the phone back on the cradle. Well, it wasn't everybody who was smart enough to turn down a $75,000 proposition before he'd even heard it. And then in a moment I realized it wasn't the money I was thinking about at all. It was her. I'd never see her again. I lighted a cigarette and watched the rain fall into the airwell.

Thirty minutes later the phone rang. It was Miami Beach. Her voice was exactly as cool, urbane, and pleasant as ever. "I finally decided you were never going to call, so—"

I suppose I could ask, I thought. But why bother? There was something inevitable about her; if I'd been holed up in a lamasery in Tibet it wouldn't have made the slightest difference.

"You win," I said. "I'll be there sometime tonight."

"That's wonderful, Jerry."

"Where?" I asked.

"You're sweet. Then you did try to call me?"

"You know damn well I did. Where?"

"206 Dover Way," she replied.

I caught a flight out of Idlewild at five forty-five. The rain had stopped, but it was colder. As I was going up the loading ramp of the DC-7, a boy from the catering department was coming down. I dropped the topcoat on his arm. "Have a good Christmas," I said.

When we were airborne and the *No Smoking* sign went off, I lighted a cigarette. She'd known where I was all the time. All her detectives had to do was notify their New York office what flight I'd taken out of Miami, and have me picked up at Idlewild again and tailed to the hotel. The rest of it, however, was considerably more subtle—waiting me out till I called first and learned she'd checked out of the motel without a forwarding address. And then giving me a long half hour to think about what I'd thrown away forever. That was a nice touch.

We were down at Miami shortly after nine p.m. I took a cab. It seemed to take forever through the evening traffic of the city and across the North Bay Causeway. Dover Way was a quiet side street only three or four blocks long. 206 was half a side-by-side duplex set back off the street with a hedge in front and shadowy, bougainvillea-covered walls on both sides. I paid off the cab and went up the walk. Lights were on behind the curtained front window, and a small porch light was burning beside the door, but the adjoining apartment appeared to be dark. I pressed the button.

She was wearing a dark skirt and severe white blouse. I kicked the door shut, dropped the bag, and took her in my arms. She submitted to being kissed in the same cool way—quite gracious about it, but uncommitted. She smiled. "How do you like our place?"

It was small, well-furnished, air-conditioned, and very quiet. The living room was carpeted in gray, and the floor-length drapes were dark green. The sofa and three chairs were Danish modern, and there was a long coffee table made of teak and covered with plate glass. There were three hassocks covered with corduroy in explosive colors. Straight back, an open doorway led into the bedroom. Just to the right of it another opened into a small dining area and kitchen. A radio-phonograph console in limed oak stood in the corner near the bedroom door, and near it was a table on which was the telephone.

The tape recorder was set up on one end of the coffee table. There were several boxes of tape beside it, and some stenographer's notebooks and pencils.

"I was working," she explained. She sat down on one of the hassocks beside the coffee table and reached for a cigarette. I lighted it for her, and one for myself, and sat cross-legged on the floor.

I looked around at the apartment. "You were pretty sure I'd come back, weren't you?"

"Yes," she said. "I've been studying you for a week."

"And $75,000 would do it? All it took was a little time?"

She nodded. "Actually, I don't think you care a great deal for money as such, but you have some very expensive tastes. And you're quite cynical."

She was probably right, I thought. I looked at the classic line of the head and the brilliant coloring and the severe formality of the blouse that ended in a plain band collar around the softness of her throat, and wondered if she'd considered the possibility I might have come back because of her. I asked her.

"No," she said. "Why should I?"

"Because maybe I did, in part."

"That sounds rather unlikely."

"Why?" I asked.

"You're quite an attractive young man. I doubt you have any great problem with girls; and the country's full of them."

"Don't overdo the modesty. And why did you call me a young man?"

Her eyebrows raised. "Twenty-eight?"

"And what's thirty-four? Incidentally, you don't look thirty."

"You're quite flattering," she said. "And now if we're through assessing my drawing power, shall we get down to business?"

This was beginning to bug me. No woman had any right to be as attractive as she was and at the same time as contemptuous of the fact and of its effect on somebody else. I pulled her down on the floor beside me and held her in my arms and kissed her. Instead of objecting, however, she put her arms around my neck. In a moment her eyes opened, very large and dreamy, just under mine. I kissed her again, feeling tremendous excitement in just touching her.

After a while I picked her up and carried her into the bedroom and turned off the light and undressed her very slowly, and she was as beautifully adept and as pleasant and as far away and unreachable as ever. Clearly, the simplest way to rid the agenda of distracting minor issues like sex was to get them over with.

I thought about it for a while. "Gee, thanks," I said.

"What?" she asked ominously.

"If there's anything I love it's a gracious hostess. By God, if one of the guests wants to play croquet in the rain—"

"What do you want from me?" she lashed out. "What do you expect?"

"I don't know," I said. "I'm just curious, I guess, as to what's on the other side of the wall." I touched her, and she was trembling. Gathering her up in my arms, I held her tightly with my face pressed against the top of her head.

"I'm sorry," she said after a while. "And there's nothing on the other side of the wall. Leave it alone."

CHAPTER FOUR

I could see the glowing tip of her cigarette beside me in the darkness. "All right," I said. "Tell me the whole thing."

"I'm going to destroy him."

"Why?"

"Try a wild guess as to why a woman might hate a man after she'd wrecked her own marriage for him and thrown away her reputation and helped him make a fortune, and lived for him twenty-four hours a day for six of the last few years she'd ever have to give anybody—"

"Take it easy," I said. "I just asked. So he left you?"

"Yes." Then she laughed. It was like glass breaking. "Of course, while I was running his business for him, I should have suggested a pension plan for over-age employees. I'd have nothing to worry about. I could buy a little cottage, get a cat for companionship, and live the rich, full life every woman looks forward to."

"Who is she?" I asked. "And how do you know it's permanent?"

"Oh, she's quite pretty. Honey-colored and virginal-looking, with a wide-eyed sort of defenselessness about her. Like anthrax, or a striking cobra."

"Come off it," I said. "How the hell could you lose out to a cornball routine like that? She'd never lay a glove on you."

"It's a little trick you do with numbers. She's twenty-three."

"Well, what of it?"

"Oh, you *are* a young man, aren't you? I'd forgotten, men do go through a phase between their first and second passes at the jailbait when they're actually interested in women. But never mind. They're going to be married in January."

"You're getting ahead of me," I said. "He couldn't marry you because he already had a wife. What happened to her?"

"What happened to her, besides the fact they hadn't lived together for the past eight years, is that she died five months ago."

"Well, look—I doubt very seriously anybody could hand you a line six years long, so if he was serious why didn't he get a divorce?"

"He and his wife were both Catholics."

"I see. And now that he *can* remarry—"

"Yes," she said. "You see."

"And I see something more. You'll never get away with it."

"Yes—"

"No. He took everything you could give him for six years, and then when he finally could get married he jilted you for somebody else. If he's killed, the police will figure it out in ten minutes."

"You underestimate me," she broke in. "I'm going to take $175,000 away from him, and kill him. And nobody will ever suspect I did it, for the simple reason they won't even know it was done at all. Does that satisfy you?"

"No," I said. "It can't be done."

She sighed. "You're forgetting something I told you. That I know more about Harris Chapman than anybody else on earth. I'm going to destroy him from the inside."

"Hold it a minute," I said. "If you knew so much about him, why didn't you see this fluff-ball moving in on you?"

"See it? Don't be ridiculous. I saw every stage of it before it even happened, but what do you suggest I should have done about it? Compete with a twenty-three-year-old professional virgin, after he was already tired of me? I saw it, all right; I had a front-row seat. He hired her as a stenographer, and I had the honor and privilege of training her. Sometimes I wake up at night—"

"If it's that kind of thing," I asked, "why the money angle?"

"Money is important to me. I like success. I poured everything I had into making him one, thinking I was doing it for both of us. Do you think I'm going to move aside now and give it up? Let him hand it all to some simpering, featherbrained little bitch who can't even balance a checkbook?"

"Tell me the rest of it," I said.

"First, about the apartment. We had to have a quiet place to work with no chance of being overheard. The motel simply wouldn't do. I was registered there under my right name, and it's imperative that no one ever finds out that I even know you—"

I interrupted her. "What about those detectives you've had following me around?"

"I used another name. The fact they know yours is of no significance at all unless you can be traced to me in some way."

"Okay," I said.

"The apartment is rented under your name. I'm Mrs. J. L. Forbes, and there's nothing to connect me with the Mrs. Forsyth who stayed briefly at the Golden Horn. The people who have the other apartment won't be here until some time in December, so we have it to ourselves. We don't have much time. Today is the fifth, and he'll be here the night of the thirteenth—"

"He's coming to Miami Beach?"

"Yes. Miami Beach, and then Marathon, on a fishing trip. But, as I say, we have only eight days. And in addition, I have to go to Nassau and New York."

"Why?"

"Simply to prove I've been there. When I resigned and left on this trip, Miami Beach, Nassau, and New York were the three places I was going. If I changed my plans, it might look suspicious. So I'll go to both places long enough to send the usual asinine postcards and bring back some souvenir gifts. That means I'll be gone for nearly half of the time we have, but we'll use the tape recorder and you'll have the tapes to study."

"You're sure he's coming?"

"Yes. I made all the reservations for him. He goes on one big-game fishing trip every year. For the past two years he's gone to Acapulco, but this time he's coming to Florida again."

"And after he gets here I'm going to take his place?"

"Yes."

"For how long?"

"I think it can be done in twelve days."

"Describe him," I said.

"Aside from the fact you're both about six feet, you don't resemble each other at all, if that's what you mean."

"What else would I mean? You don't think he's going to be invisible for those twelve days, do you? He may be a voice on the telephone to the people at home, but down here— But never mind. Go ahead and describe him."

"He's thirty-nine. Six feet. One hundred ninety-five pounds. Gray eyes. Somewhat fair complexion, always with a tan. Brown hair, beginning to gray at the temples except that he touches it up."

"That'll do," I said. "I'm twenty-eight. The height is the same within probably an inch, but I'm fifteen pounds lighter. Blue eyes. Darker complexion. And hair that's very close to being black. Q.E.D."

"It's nowhere near that simple," she cut in impatiently. "In the first place, any police officer could write a book on the general unreliability of descriptions. And if you'll take another look, you'll discover that your basic descriptions *overlap* each other on nearly every point except age. And, finally, you're not merely trying to *look like* Harris Chapman—you're assuming the whole character of Harris Chapman. And this same character will be projected quite logically into a strange and finally shattering experience—which is what the witnesses will remember, and not the color of his hair. Incidentally, he wears a hat anyway. You're simply going to make them remember the wrong things."

"Such as?"

"Let me give you a brief sketch for a start. He's quite vain about his appearance, and wears a thin, pencil-line mustache because he thinks his upper lip is too long. He has a tendency toward hypochondria and carries around a miniature drugstore with him, and worries constantly and probably needlessly about two things—cancer and mental illness, the latter because he has an older brother who cracked up in his late teens. When that smoking and lung cancer thing first started several years ago, he not only switched to filter cigarettes, but smokes them in a filter holder.

"He wears glasses—horn rims—and is somewhat hard of hearing in his left ear, the result of a diving accident when he was sixteen, though he refuses to admit the impairment. I'm perhaps making him sound doddering and fatuous, which he isn't at all; he's a hellishly attractive man with a lot of drive, but I'm stressing these quirks and idiosyncrasies for a reason—"

"Sure," I said impatiently. "They're character tags and props. But, look—so I do wear horn-rimmed glasses, grow a mustache, use a cigarette holder, and go around tossing pills into my mouth, what does it buy? I still won't look like him, and I wouldn't fool anybody who's seen him since he was fifteen."

"You won't have to. Jerry, what I'm trying to get across is this: you won't look like him, *but your description will look like his description*. Do you understand now? The point of the whole thing is that *nobody will ever have seen you both*."

"But you're forgetting something. As soon as he disappears, they're sure as hell going to see photographs of him."

"No," she said. "That'll be taken care of."

"How?" I asked.

"To be of any value, they'd have to be good likenesses and taken within the past ten years. There aren't too many. I have most of them, and I know where the others are. He had one made for that saccharine little bitch about two months ago, but we can forget it. It's one of those gooey and dramatic things with a ton of glamor and no resemblance."

"All right," I said. "Tell me the rest of it."

She told me. She talked for a half hour, and when she was through I was glad she didn't hate me. Chapman didn't have a chance. It was brilliant, and it was deadly, and I couldn't see a flaw in it anywhere. They'd never know he was killed. And she'd be a thousand miles away in Thomaston, Louisiana, when he disappeared.

I woke before seven the next morning, but she was already up. She stood in the doorway in blue lounging pajamas, sipping a glass of orange juice.

"The coffee will be ready in five minutes," she said. "And we start to work in ten. When you shave, don't forget the mustache."

She sounded crisp and efficient, and I found out before the day was over I didn't know the half of it. She had a genius for organizing material, and she was a slave driver. By the time I'd showered and dressed, she had my coffee and orange juice ready on the coffee table in the living room and was seated with hers on one of the hassocks at the other end of it. Between us was the tape recorder. The microphone was mounted on a little stand, facing her, and beside it were some boxes of tape and two stenographer's notebooks.

"How many people do I have to talk to?" I asked. "And how often?"

"Two," she said. "Chris Lundgren at the broker's office in New Orleans, nearly every day. And to her, every day. Her name, incidentally, is Coral Blaine."

I drank some of the coffee, and considered it. "It's rough. I've got to know everything about Chapman that these people know, and everything about these people that Chapman knows, plus a thousand business details and dozens of other people. It's almost impossible."

She interrupted. "Of course it's impossible. No mind could absorb all that in eight days. But you don't have to."

"No?"

"Of course not." She waved a slim hand. "All you have to do is carry on two or three short telephone conversations each day without making a really dangerous mistake. Analyze it; what does it take, actually? A quick mind—which you have—some ability in bluffing and improvising, a grasp of most of the salient and obvious facts and a few of the ones that *only Harris Chapman could possibly know*, and there you are—the illusion is complete. And don't forget, you're always in control of the conversation; you're the boss. When you see you're about to get in over your head, change the subject. And in the end, there's nothing connecting you but a piece of wire. Break it. And call back later with the right information. You'll have a prompter."

"You mean the tapes?"

She nodded. "They'll be numbered, and you'll know what's covered in each one."

"Good," I said.

She smiled. "And don't forget, it's only the first week you have to be really careful. After that, it doesn't matter."

I'd forgotten that, and it was one of the really brilliant angles of the whole thing. This girl was clever. And all she wanted out of life was to kill a man. It seemed a senseless waste. The thought startled me, and I shrugged it off. It was her life, wasn't it?

"All right," I said. "Roll one."

"Harris Chapman was born in Thomaston April 14, 1918. Father's name: John W. Chapman. Owned the Ford Agency, and was one of the largest stockholders in the Thomaston State Bank. His mother's maiden name was Mary Burke, and she was the only child of a Thomaston attorney. John W. sold out and retired in 1940, and moved to California. Both still living, in La Jolla.

"Only two children. Keith is two years older than Harris. The summer he was nineteen, after his freshman year at Tulane, he hit a twelve-year-old girl with his car. She wasn't seriously injured, but shortly afterward he began to go to pieces. He quit sleeping, or if he did sleep nobody could figure out when, and lost weight and became withdrawn. It was the onset of schizophrenia, of course, and probably the accident had little or nothing to do with it. At any rate, his condition became hopeless, and he's spent more than half the past twenty-two years in one mental institution or another.

"Harris has always been haunted by this, as I told you, particularly because there had been a prior case of mental illness in the family, a great uncle or something. Fear of a hereditary taint, you see. Foolish, of course, but I told you he has a tendency toward hypochondria.

"He finished high school in 1936. His mother wanted him to go to a Catholic school, so he went to Notre Dame. He graduated in 1941, and Pearl Harbor caught him in his first year at Tulane Law School. He went in the Navy, just barely getting by the physical with the impaired hearing, and was commissioned an ensign. He had a tour of duty on an aircraft carrier...."

She went on talking. She'd pushed the hassock aside now and was sitting on the rug with the stenographic notebook between her knees. I leaned against a chair and watched her, studying the proud and slender face that could have been downright arrogant except for the saving loveliness of the eyes.

"Chapman was a full lieutenant at the end of the war. He went back to Tulane Law School at the beginning of the spring term in 1946, and before the end of it he was married to a New Orleans girl he met at a Mardi Gras ball. Her name was Grace Trahan. She was a slight dark girl with a delicate constitution, very pretty in an ethereal sort of way, and apparently frigid to the point of phobia.

"He never did say much about it," she went on, "but I gather it was pretty horrible on their wedding night, and never did get any better. Psychic trauma of some kind, I suppose; probably something that happened in her childhood.

"They tried to make a go of it, but there were other factors besides her aversion to the bed. She thought they should have more financial help from his parents instead of struggling along on the GI Bill. And she didn't want to leave New Orleans. Less than a year after he'd finished law school and moved to Thomaston to open his office, they separated. She went home to mother. Her health was growing worse. She was anemic, among other things."

Marian stopped the tape again. I looked at my watch and saw with surprise it was after ten. "How are you getting it?" she asked.

"Fine," I said. I lighted a cigarette. "But when do you actually appear on the scene?"

"Very shortly," she replied. "But I want to finish out this roll exclusively with him. It'll be easier to refer to later."

She made some more notes, started the tape, and went on, describing the town, the small country club, and some of his friends. We began to near the end of the roll.

"He has a fast, aggressive way of walking. He won't admit it, but he can't carry liquor very well. Becomes argumentative. Music means nothing to him, and he's a poor dancer. For the past two years on these fishing trips, he's picked up girls, probably very young ones.

"He's totally unafraid of scenes and will argue with anybody, anywhere. Waiters impress him not at all, and I've been through some bad moments when he's sent the same dish back three times, or refused to tip a waiter who gave poor service. I don't mean he's loud-mouthed or uncouth, but he is demanding and perhaps rather insensitive. He always adds up a check before he pays it. He buys a new Cadillac every year because he can charge it off his income tax. He's a poor driver, and drives far too fast. He's self-assured with women, the same as you are. You'll have no trouble playing him. When they describe you afterward, if you learn all this, they're going to be describing Harris Chapman to the last gesture."

She stopped the machine, and stood up. "All right. Re-roll that tape and start playing it back. I'll run out and get us some sandwiches."

"What about the housekeeping arrangements? Do we go out for dinner?"

"Yes," she replied. "It'll be all right if we go around to different places so we won't be remembered."

"You turned the car back?"

"Yes. After all, I'm supposed to be in Nassau. You'll rent one, of course, before he gets here, but in the meantime we can use cabs."

She went into the bedroom. I started the tape, turned up the gain, and walked up and down as I listened to it. The bedroom door was open. I stepped inside. The blue pajamas were tossed casually on the bed and she was beyond it with her back turned, wearing only bra and pants as she stood before the clothes closet. I looked at the long and exquisitely slender legs, ever so faintly tanned below the line of her swim suit and pure ivory above as they flowed into the triangular wisp of undergarment about her hips.

She turned then. I took a step toward her, and she said crisply, "No, you don't! Outside." She took a slip from a hanger, and slid it over her head.

"I'm sorry, teacher, but you're a very exciting girl."

"Yes, yes, I know." She tugged the slip down. "I'm irresistible to twenty-eight-year-old wolves. I'm female, breathing, and within reach."

"Thanks a million," I said. "From both of us."

"You're welcome. Now get out there and get busy."

"You give too many orders," I said, beginning to be a little hacked. I walked on over to her. She stared defiantly. I took her in my arms and kissed her, and it got out of control almost as soon as it started. There was something sweet and wild and wonderful about it, and I was holding her too tightly and bruising her mouth. And for the first time that beautiful control of hers began to crack. She gave a little gasp, and her lips parted under mine. She clung to me for an instant.

Then she pushed back, her face flushed and her eyes confused, and fought free of my arms. "Jerry, stop it!" she lashed at me. I tried to catch her, but she slapped at my arms, and ran over to the bed. She collapsed on the side of it, with her face in her hands. "Jerry, will you leave me alone!"

"What is it, Marian?"

Her hands clenched beside her bowed head. "Nothing! Just leave me alone! Can't you understand? We've got too much to do."

CHAPTER FIVE

I went back to the living room and resumed my study of Harris Chapman. She came out after a while, her composure regained, dressed for the street. "I'm sorry, Jerry," she said.

"It's all right," I replied.

She went to get the sandwiches. When she returned, we didn't even stop while we ate. She asked questions about the things we'd covered so far, and tried to catch me in errors. "Who is Robert Wingard?"

"Robin Wingard," I said. "He's manager of the radio station."

"Good. And Bill McEwen? What does he do?"

"Bill McEwen is a girl."

She shot me an approving glance. "Very good."

"Her real name is Billy Jean, she's twenty-seven years old, unmarried, and she's half the editorial staff of the paper, and sells advertising."

"Correct," she said. "But don't get too cocky. We've only begun to scratch the surface." She finished half her sandwich, threw the rest in the garbage can in the kitchen, and started a fresh roll of tape on the recorder.

"I was born in Cleveland," she began. "And went to school at Stanford. My mother died when I was in my early teens, and my father never remarried. He was a physician. A gynecologist, and a good one. In about thirty-five years of practice he must have made considerably over a million dollars, and when he died a few years ago he left an estate of less than $20,000. Bad investments. Someday, maybe somebody will write a book about the investment habits of doctors. But never mind. It was his money. The point I'm trying to make is that it was probably his horrible example that first interested me in business and investment."

When the war started she enrolled in a business college for a quick course in shorthand and typing, and went to work in a defense plant. And she liked it, from the first. She was alert, interested, and highly competitive, and in less than a year she was the private secretary to one of the top brass of the firm. In the spring of 1944 she met and married Kenneth Forsyth. He was a flier sent home for reassignment as an instructor at an air base near San Antonio, Texas.

They were happy enough, but she couldn't stand the boredom of having nothing to do but police a one-room apartment, so she went back to work, this time for the local office of one of the big nation-wide brokerage outfits. She immediately fell in love with the stock market as if she'd invented it. Here was something you could get your teeth into, and study. She studied it. Money and investment fascinated her. Forsyth remained in the service after the end of the war, but was transferred to another field near Dallas. Keeping house still bored her, so she went to work for the Dallas office of the same brokerage house.

Then in 1949 Forsyth was transferred to the air field near Thomaston, Louisiana, and she was out of a job. She found it unbearably dull. She didn't like small towns and their clique-ridden social life, and for a woman with ambition and a restless mind it was stifling. Then she met Chapman. That changed everything.

He'd just opened his law office, and while he wasn't very busy he did need somebody once in a while to type briefs and answer the phone. She offered to do it, partly out of boredom and partly because he interested her. And before long he interested her even more. Here was a man with drive, business ability, and daring, and he was wasting himself on a piddling law practice. They were attracted to each other from the beginning.

His first venture, in the process of becoming a millionaire in eight years, was a laundromat, and it was she who prodded him into it.

"He defended the owner of the laundromat in a minor damage suit," she went on, "and got him off with a minimum judgment, but the man was in financial trouble and couldn't even pay the legal fee in full. I had an idea, and went out and surveyed the place. His trouble was location; he was in the wrong end of town, where most of the families had washing machines of their own, and he had a bad parking problem. To the south of town there was a large slum section swarming with children. I located a building that could be leased, and told Harris about it. Because of his father's connection with the bank, he had no trouble borrowing the money. He bought the man's machines at a terrific bargain, and moved them. We got the deacon of one of the local churches to run it, and I kept the books. Eight months later he sold it for a net profit of $6,000."

They were on their way. Next came a couple of real-estate speculations that paid off to the tune of better than $14,000. By late 1950 she was working for him full time, and the law practice was only a small part of his operation. He was far overextended and in debt to his ears, but he was growing, right along with the big business boom of the early

1950's. His wife had left Chapman now, and Marian Forsyth and her husband had had several painful and increasingly bitter arguments about her working for him. People were beginning to talk. She refused to quit. The showdown came in less than six months. Forsyth was transferred again.

The choice was up to her. She asked Forsyth for a divorce, and stayed in Thomaston. She was in love with Chapman.

She had no illusions as to what she was letting herself in for. He couldn't marry her as long as his wife was alive, and in a small town no matter how discreet they were, everybody was going to know. I thought of the snubs, and frozen stares. They probably didn't bother her a great deal, I thought—not during the six busy years while she had Chapman and the fascination of the job. But when he jilted her and left her standing alone and naked in the middle of town— That must have been a long, long mile to the city limits.

"Wait a minute," I said. "A point's just occurred to me. You've got to have a legitimate excuse for going back, or it won't look right."

She stopped the tape. "Of course. I still own my house there. It will take some time to sell it and store my furnishings. And don't forget, I won't arrive there until after he's left, which will give it exactly the right touch."

She was right, of course. It all fitted perfectly, like the stones in an Inca wall.

We went on. We finished that roll of tape with a detailed account of how Chapman acquired the rest of his holdings in the next five years and how she'd led him a little at a time into growth stocks in the big bull market from 1950 to 1955, into IBM, and Dow Chemical, and Phillips Petroleum, and Du Pont.

"Always for capital gains," she went on. "Income wasn't any good to him anymore, not in the tax bracket he was in, or approaching. All those years I'd spent studying stocks and the stock market paid off. He rode it up all the way. And last summer, when the market showed signs of running out of steam, we began switching to defensive holdings—utilities, high-grade preferreds, and bonds. And cash. It's safe—except from me."

It was three-thirty when we came to the end of the roll. "Play it back," she said, already making notes for the next session. I ran it. She fired questions at me until I was dizzy. She put on one of the rolls of recorded conversation between him and Chris Lundgren, and played it through. I listened, studying his speech, while she went out in the kitchen and mixed us two martinis.

She lighted a cigarette, took a sip of her drink, and stopped the machine. "Tell me what you heard."

"He's abrupt on the phone," I said, "at least in business matters. No asking how the other party is, or about families. He says *G'bye* just once and hangs up. Your name comes out almost *Mer'n*. He hits the first syllable of Du Pont, and the *u* is *iu*. *Dew-pont*. He slurs hundred a little more than most people. *Hunrd*. He still uses *Roger* once in a while, left over from his service days."

She nodded approvingly. "Good ear. Keep it up."

We knocked off at seven, changed, and took a cab over to Miami to have dinner at the Top o' the Columbus. She was a knockout in a dark dress, so very tall and beautifully groomed and poised. It made me feel good to see men—and women—turn to look at her. We sat by one of the big windows looking out over Biscayne Bay and its perimeter of blazing lights.

"You make all these other women look like peasants," I said.

She smiled. "Honing the old technique, Jerry? Why waste it on me?"

"No. I mean it."

"Of course, dear. Conditioned reflexes are like that." Then she went on. "Now here's a point we have to consider. Lundgren's voice you'll recognize, of course, but you've never heard hers."

I sighed. "That's easy. Until she identifies herself and I'm sure, I can say we have a bad connection and I can't hear very well."

On the way back we ran a test. I got out of the cab at a drugstore not too far away, gave her time to reach the apartment, and called her from the phone booth. She read Lundgren.

"Chris? Chapman," I said. I asked how the market had closed, discussed some stock or another, gave an order or two, and then stepped out of character to ask, "What do you think?"

"Good," she said. "Very good."

I walked back to the apartment in the warm and ocean-scented darkness, thinking of $75,000. When I let myself in she was just coming out of the bedroom. She'd taken off the dress and slip and was pulling the blue robe about her.

She pursed her lips thoughtfully. "Maybe just a *shade* less abrupt. But it's a fine point—"

"Stop worrying," I said. "I can do it." I took hold of her arms. Then I was holding her tightly in mine and kissing her as if women were going to be transferred to some ether planet in the morning.

When she could get her mouth free at last, she murmured, "But I thought we'd work for another hour or so." Then she relented. "All right, Jerry—"

Enlightened management, I thought, never forgets the importance of employee recreation. If the seal balks, toss him another herring. I started to say something angry and sarcastic, but choked it off. I wanted her so badly I'd take her on any terms at all.

Afterward, of course, we did go back to work.

The next day was a repetition of the first. She was relentless. Chapman and Chapman Enterprises and Thomaston ran into my brain until it overflowed. We filled two tapes. I played them back. She questioned me. I played them again. And all the while I was conscious that she herself was taking more and more of my attention. I was thinking about her when I should have been concentrating. I didn't like it, but there it was.

We went out again for dinner, and came back and worked until eleven. I made love to her. She was as gracious about it, and as accomplished, and as completely unreachable as ever. I lay in the darkness thinking of her, and of that one time the façade of coolness and iron self-control had started to crack, and wondered what she was like before she became numb to everything except remembered humiliation and hatred. The next morning, just at dawn, I awoke to find her struggling in my arms, trying to break free.

"Jerry," she snapped, "for heaven's sake, what are you trying to do? Break me in two?"

"Oh," I said stupidly, looking around the room. "I must have been having a bad dream."

It started to come back to me then. I could see it all with a horrible clarity. I'd been running after her across the Golden Gate Bridge, and I'd caught her just before she could leap. I was trying to hold her back.

That day we filled the last roll of tape. She told me everything she knew about Coral Blaine, and she knew a lot—including the fact her name wasn't Coral at all, but Edna Mae. Apparently she was a believer in the old maxim of military science that you could never stop studying the enemy. She described her, psychoanalyzed her, and gave me a complete rundown on the affair from the time Chapman first gave her a job until the engagement was announced.

"I was scared the first time I saw her," she said. "For years I'd done all the hiring and firing of office personnel. He never interfered, hired anybody himself, or cared. I'll admit to being quite unfair a couple of times when I fired girls for no other reason than that they had their eyes on him. But never mind. At any rate, when I saw this Blaine number, I had a premonition. Flawless natural blonde, about five feet three, and of course only twenty-three years old, but it was that dewy and virginal look that frightened me. He's forty—or will be next year.

"He saw the dew, all right; and I could see the cutlass between her teeth as she came over the rail. She was the daughter of an old friend of his, he said; she'd just graduated from some coeducational football factory in Texas and he'd promised her a job. I felt my way very slowly, and I hit resistance right away. I wasn't going to be able to fire this one. Nothing overt on either side, of course, but the resistance was there, and it was firm. So I moved her up to a better job I knew she couldn't handle. And all I accomplished was that I had to do her work myself. She came to work, incidentally, about three weeks after Mrs. Chapman died."

It must have been bloody, I thought. And lonely as hell. A wife in the same position had status and the solid weight of community opinion going for her, but she had nothing. She knew she'd lost, of course, long before the blow actually fell, and in the end Chapman didn't even have the decency to tell her himself. I gathered it wasn't that he was ashamed to, or reluctant to face her; he just didn't bother. Some business came up that was more important.

"You're not coloring this a little?" I asked.

She sighed. "I assure you I wouldn't be that stupid. I'm telling you exactly what happened, because I have to. God knows I don't enjoy it; I'm no masochist. But obviously you have to know the truth, and not some dramatized version. I was informed of the engagement by Coral Blaine herself, in the office, on Monday morning, and if you have any doubts she knew exactly how to do it for the most exquisite effect, forget them. That was quite a day."

Seven thousand years, I thought, from nine to five. With all the eyes watching, and nothing to crawl under and hide. An outstanding day, any way you looked at it. Then a sudden thought occurred to me, something I'd missed completely until now. It was what she had in mind for Coral Blaine.

"Do you think she'll know?" I asked.

She nodded coolly. "Let's say she'll probably always *suspect* I did it—somehow."

As a study in the subtler forms of revenge, I thought, that would be hard to beat. Coral Blaine was having a husband and a million dollars snatched out of her reachy little hands, and she was going to be almost certain it was Marian who'd done it to her. But she not only would never be able to prove it, she would actually help prove it *couldn't* have been Marian.

"If she's only twenty-three," I said, "she has a long and interesting life ahead of her, trying to figure that one out."

"Yes, doesn't she?"

We went back to work. While she was gone to get the sandwiches at noon I suddenly remembered what day it was. This was the 8th. I looked up florists in the phone book, called one, and ordered a dozen roses. It was around four p.m. and we were still busy with Coral Blaine when the doorbell rang. I beat her to it, paid the delivery boy, and brought them in.

She glanced up as I put the long carton on the coffee table before her. "Flowers? Why?"

"Happy birthday," I said.

She shook her head. "Oh, for heaven's sake." Then she opened the box, and exclaimed, "They're beautiful, Jerry. But how did you know it was my birthday?"

"Your driver's license," I replied.

"Snoopy." She filled the vase with water and put them on the phonograph console at the other end of the room. She admired them for a moment, and then came over and put her arms about my neck.

She smiled. "Dear Jerry, the indefatigable chaser of old streetcars he's already caught."

It was no use, I thought. She was impervious; nothing could get through to her anymore, no gesture of any kind. She'd had it.

"Okay," I said. "If you think I've caught the streetcar, that's fine."

"Well, haven't you?" She started to turn away.

I caught her arms, suddenly furious without really knowing why. "Do you think I'm that stupid? And will you ever stop treating me as if I were a kid standing on a street corner whistling at girls? Dear old Jerry, the junior-grade wolf—just tolerate him for a few minutes and he'll go away and leave you alone—"

"Stop it!"

"Do you expect to live the rest of your life with nothing but an obsession? What are you going to do when that's gone?" I couldn't stop. And I knew I was hurting her arms. "You're just ruining yourself. It's nothing but sheer, goddamned waste. You're too fine a woman to be throwing yourself away—"

"I don't have to throw myself away!" She lashed at me. "That's already been done. And nothing's going to stop me! Do you understand? Nothing!"

She tore away from me and ran into the bedroom and slammed the door. I lighted a cigarette and sat down, wondering what was the matter with me. Her coolness enraged me, but when I did succeed in shattering it, we merely had these scenes and that was worse. Why couldn't I just leave her alone? That was all she wanted, wasn't it?

She came out after a while. We both apologized, and went back to work.

CHAPTER SIX

She did some shopping the next morning, and left for Nassau around eleven. The minute she closed the door behind her, the apartment became almost achingly empty.

I assembled everything on the coffee table, and looked at it. Except for his identification, his clothes, and his car, here was Harris Chapman—seven rolls of tape, boxed, numbered, and indexed; horn-rim glasses; cigarette holder; the insipid filter cigarettes he smoked; the map of Thomaston she'd drawn with street names, locations of his businesses and his office, and an appended list of some twenty telephone numbers; three documents containing specimens of his signature, which had come from the old briefcase; and the bottle of guck for lightening the dark shade of my hair and the sprouting mustache.

This latter wasn't really dye, she had said, and if I didn't use too much of it there wouldn't be any noticeable artificial effect, except that of brown hair bleached down a few shades by the sun. I went into the bathroom, combed in a light application of it, and started practicing the signature. When my wrist was tired, I loaded the recorder with the first roll of tape, and turned it on. Her voice issued from the loudspeaker, and when I closed my eyes she seemed to be there in the room. I forced myself to concentrate.

When my brain was numb from memorizing, I went back to the signature again. I found I didn't have as much talent for forgery as I did for mimicry, but after several hundred attempts I could see definite improvement. I kept at it. After a while I tried breaking it down into individual letters and writing each one hundreds of times to correct my errors. Around seven I walked over three or four blocks to a restaurant for dinner, and came back and worked until midnight. When I turned out the light, she was all around me in the darkness.

The next day was Sunday. I worked from seven a.m. till midnight with only brief periods out for food, attacking the job with intense concentration to keep her out of my mind. I was closing in on him. Whole sections of those five hours of recorded data were stamped into my mind intact. I could see him now, and feel him, and there was no longer even any need to practice his speech. The signature was improving. I went on writing it, hour after hour, and listening to the tapes. It was harder than I had ever worked at anything in my life. When I went to bed I was dizzy with fatigue.

She had left me five hundred dollars in cash. On Monday morning I went over to Miami and picked up a rental car, one with a trailer hitch. I drove out US 1 to a sporting goods place that rented boats and motors. Using my right name and my California driver's license, plus the local address on Dover Way, I rented a complete outfit—16-foot fiberglass boat, 25-horse Johnson outboard, and a trailer with a winch. I put up a deposit against the week's rental, bought a spinning rod and some lures, asked the man about bonefishing flats in the Keys, and headed south on the highway.

In a little over an hour I was on Key Largo. I checked my highway map, noted the speedometer reading, and turned off US 1 into the dead-end road going toward the upper end of the Key, watching for launching sites. I found one, made a notation of the mileage, and went on. In a little over a mile there was another, and I noted the speedometer reading at this one also. I needed at least two I could find fast and in the dark, so I'd have an alternate in case the first one was being used or someone was camped near it. There was nobody in sight at either of them now. I practiced maneuvering the car with the trailer behind it. It was awkward at first, but after about fifteen minutes I became fairly adept.

I backed down to the water once more, put on the fishing clothes I'd brought, and launched the boat. There was a moderate southeast breeze, but the water over the flats inside the line of the reefs was smooth. It took about fifteen minutes to run out over the reefs to the edge of the Stream. The boat handled nicely in the moderate sea and groundswell offshore, and would do all right provided the weather was no worse than it was now. I ran back, winched the boat onto the trailer, and drove back to Miami Beach.

There was a driveway along the side of the apartment and a garage in the rear. I backed into it, uncoupled the trailer and locked it in the garage, and I left the car in the drive. When I let myself in the front of the apartment, there was a card from her in the mailbox.

It had been mailed Sunday afternoon in Nassau, and said she was flying to New York Monday night. It was printed in block letters, and was unsigned. "I miss you," she said. I wondered if she did. For a moment she was all around me in the apartment, the remembered gesture of a hand, the swing of a silken ankle, and the smooth dark head it was a joy forever to watch.

I showered, and shaved, using a safety razor to get around the mustache. The latter was beginning to show, and surprisingly it made me look a little older, which was fine. I went to work, practicing the signature. I could forge it well enough now to fool myself at times, but I had to learn to do it faster and more naturally. The next morning I drove over to Miami to a salvage store and bought a second-hand tarpaulin, about eight by eight. On the way back I stopped at a building supply place and bought four concrete blocks, saying I wanted them to patch a wall. At a dime store I picked up a roll of wire and a cheap pair of pliers. I put everything in the trunk, and locked it. I went back in the apartment and worked with furious concentration until midnight.

When I awoke in the morning and realized what day it was, there was a fluttery, sick feeling in my stomach. This was the 13th. He was supposed to be here tonight. I was scared. It was easy to say something was foolproof—but was it, ever? A million things could go wrong. I tried to work some more, but had trouble concentrating. I didn't need any more preparation, anyway; I either had it pat now, or I never would. The only thing it took from here on was nerve. I wasn't at all sure I had that.

The morning passed with no word from her. Maybe he wasn't coming. I began to hope something had happened so he couldn't get away. Then at two-thirty in the afternoon the phone rang. It was a collect call from Mrs. Forbes, in New York, the operator said. Would I accept the charges? I said yes. She came on the line.

"Jerry? Listen, dear, I'm calling from a pay phone because I didn't want this call on my hotel bill. He's on his way."

"Are you sure?" I asked.

"Yes. I just talked to a friend at home. He left late yesterday afternoon, intending to stay in Mobile last night. He should be there between midnight and two a.m. I'm leaving right away, and I'll be in Miami shortly before nine. Don't come to the airport."

"Right," I said.

"Is everything all right there?"

"Yes. Except that I wish you were here."

"I will be, very shortly. Good-by, dear."

The afternoon was interminable. I paced the living room, chain-smoking cigarettes while I thought of a Cadillac and a DC-7 converging on Miami in a sort of cataclysmic and irrevocable vector. I wanted her here worse than I'd ever wanted anything, and I hoped he'd never arrive. He was a fast and reckless driver; maybe he'd have a wreck and kill himself. I went out and tried to eat dinner, and didn't know afterward whether I had or not.

It was nine-thirty when I heard a car pull into the driveway. I opened the front door. She was coming up the walk with the cab driver behind her carrying the small overnight case. The rest of her luggage would still be in New York, in her hotel room. A very smart-looking hat was slanted across the side of her head, and she wore gloves and carried a light coat on her arm.

She smiled, brushed my lips lightly with hers, and started to fumble at her bag. I gave the driver some money. I didn't know how much, but it appeared to satisfy him. He turned and went down the walk. Then we were inside, and I pushed the door shut with my shoulder, and put down the bag.

She broke it up finally, and gasped. "Jerry! After all—"

"Let me look at you," I said. I held her at arm's length. I'd smeared her lipstick quite badly and tilted the hat a little out of position, but there was no doubt of it. She was the smartest-looking and the loveliest woman on earth.

I told her so. Or started to.

"Are you drunk?" she asked.

"No," I said. "I haven't even had a drink. God, how I've missed you. I can't keep my hands off you."

She smiled. "You *must* have been working long hours. No girls at all?"

"Look," I said. "I'm not getting through to you. It's not girls. It's you—"

"Jerry, you're talking gibberish," she said. "And could we sit down?"

"I'm sorry," I said. I led her to the sofa, and sat down beside her. I took her in my arms again.

She tried to fend me off, shaking her head protestingly. "I think I must be getting too old to cope with the under-thirty type of wolf."

"Listen, Marian," I said. "Damn it, will you listen to me?" I removed the hat and dropped it on the coffee table, and put my hand against her cheek, turning her face and looking at the smooth dark line of her hair and the incredible blue eyes. I was overcome again with that crazy yearning to imprison and possess every last bit of her. I kissed her again, and it was the wildest and most wonderful thing I'd ever known.

She stirred. "Jerry, what on earth is the matter with you?"

"I love you," I said. "I should think that would be obvious to a fourteen-year-old girl—"

"Don't be ridiculous." She tried to pull back. I held her more tightly. "Jerry," she protested, "this is hardly the time—"

"Will you, for the love of God, listen to me a minute?" I said. "And try not to kick my teeth out, for once? I'm in love with you. I'm absolutely crazy about you. God knows I missed you while you were gone, but I didn't realize until I saw you coming up that walk just how much you did mean to me—"

She tried to break in.

"Don't interrupt," I said. "I'm going to get through to you some way, if it takes the rest of the night. I've tried to tell you before how wonderful I think you are, but you seem to think it's just some sort of conditioned reflex because I noticed you weren't wearing a beard. There must be some way I can make you understand. Listen. You're what I came back for, when I ran off to New York. I know that now. All I want out of this business is you, and I don't want to spend the rest of my life looking over my shoulder for the police—"

She stiffened in my arms. "What are you saying?"

"That we're going to call this thing off. It's too dangerous. And it's crazy. I want you, and I don't want to be running and hiding all the time like an animal. I realize I'm not one of the soldier types of prospect for the vine-coveted mortgage and the lawn mower, but I can hold a job when I want to. I want to marry you—"

She broke free and pushed away from me. She laughed, but the sound of it was more like that of a bad skiing accident. "You want us to go steady, is that it? Oh, my God. I wonder how I'd look in crinoline petticoats and bobby sox. Or maybe you could just introduce me as your mother—"

I grabbed her arm and shook her. "Marian! Stop it! For God's sake, I never heard of anybody who could make such a Federal case out of being thirty-four years old. You don't look twenty-eight."

Her face was distorted with contempt or bitterness—I wasn't sure which. "You fool! Don't you even know yet? Didn't you hear me say I'd already graduated from college when we got into the war? I'm referring to the *Second World War*. Or didn't you study that one in school? Do you have any idea how long ago that was? I'm not thirty-four. I'm thirty-eight years old."

She began to laugh again. I caught her, but she turned her face away and went on laughing. "I had one last little shred of dignity left, and you want me to throw that away and start cradle-robbing—"

I caught the turning and twisting face between my hands and held it still so she had to look at me. "I don't give a damn if you're thirty-eight," I said savagely. "Or fifty-eight, or ninety-eight. All I know is what I see and feel. You're the loveliest woman, probably, that I've ever known, and the smoothest, and there's a grace about you that makes me catch my breath when I look at you. I think you begin being feminine where all other women leave off. When you go out of a room, you leave it empty, and when you come back you redecorate it—"

"Will you stop it?" She lashed at me. "Even if I were capable of ever loving anybody again, do you think I'd marry a man ten years younger than I am, and as attractive as you are, and cringe every time people looked at us and wondered what I'd used to buy you with? I'll assure you, laddie boy, I don't look twenty-eight to women. And I can't compete in that division any more. I've just had that demonstrated to me, quite publicly and convincingly."

"Forget that meat-headed Chapman for a minute," I said. "If he's too stupid to know what he had, that's his hard luck, and he'll find it out soon enough—"

"Precisely. In about four hours."

"No! Dammit, no! It's dangerous, and I don't want you to do it. Chapman hasn't got anything you need, or even want—"

She broke in coldly. "I beg to differ with you. He has something I want, and intend to have—a lot of money I helped him make for both of us. That's the only thing left now. I suppose it's utterly impossible for you to understand, being a man and a very young one, but I'm through. Finished. I'm all over. I'm something that's already happened. If I started now and worked at it night and day, by the time I could feel like a woman again, I won't even be one. Not an operating model, anyway, or one that anybody but the utterly desperate would have. I poured the last six years of my life into an ageing adolescent, and all I've got left to show for it is humiliation. There are probably women more philosophical than I am who could adjust to that and absorb it and come out of it healthy again. But I can't. Maybe it's unfortunate, but I don't even intend to try. I have nothing more to lose, and I'm not going to stand in the wreckage of my own life like some placid and uncomprehending cow and see them get away with it."

"I'm not going to let you do it."

"Don't be an idiot!" she said furiously. "There's no risk at all. And doesn't the money mean anything to you?"

"Yes. It does. It means plenty. But I've just discovered you mean more. And if that sounds like something out of a shampoo ad, I'm sorry, but there it is."

"And this is Jerome Lawrence Forbes?" she asked pityingly.

I sighed. "All right, rub it in. This is Jerry Forbes, the angle boy. The guy who discovered before he was twenty that this place is just a nut-hatch for the rest of the universe. And maybe when you stop to think about it, it still is. After all these years I finally go completely overboard for a girl, and I have to pick the one who's decided to throw away her union card in the female sex." I lighted a cigarette, and stood up.

"Then you won't help me?" she asked.

"No," I said. I went in and sat down on the bed. I felt like hell. I stretched out, with the ash tray on my chest, and looked up at the ceiling. There didn't seem to be any answer. I was still lying there ten minutes later when I heard her come into the room. She lay down across the bed with her face very near mine. "I'm sorry, Jerry," she said. "I guess I didn't really grasp what you were saying. When you have nothing left inside but bitterness, a lot of things don't come through very well."

"It's all right," I said.

Her eyes looked into mine from a distance of a few inches. "What if I would go away with you afterward?"

"You would?"

"Yes. God knows why you'd want me, but if you still do, I'll go."

I thought about it for a minute, wavering. "It still scares me. You know what we're fooling with."

"Yes. And you know how we're going to do it. Nothing can go wrong." She smiled faintly, and touched my lips with a finger. "You understand it'll have to be a long time afterward? Maybe a year. And that it'll have to be somewhere a long way off, where there's no chance that anybody who knew him will ever hear your voice."

"Of course."

"All right. I have a little money, too. We'll have well over two hundred thousand. Somewhere in the eastern Mediterranean, or the Aegean. Or if you want to fish, somewhere in the tropics. Ceylon, perhaps. Just the two of us. And no strings attached. When you get tired of me—"

I drew a finger along her cheek. "I'd never get tired of you."

"You will, when you get old enough to need younger women."

"But I wouldn't have to wait a full year?" I asked. "I mean, before I can even see you again?"

"No. We can meet somewhere after I'm sure I'm not being watched. In a month or so. Will you do it, Jerry?"

I thought of that dream I'd had when she was trying to jump off the bridge, and felt cold in the pit of my stomach. Maybe it was a warning that something *could* go wrong. But I knew I was whipped. By this time I was conditioned to taking her on any terms I could get her.

"All right," I said. "Let's get started."

CHAPTER SEVEN

I looked at my watch for the hundredth time, conscious of the increasing tightness of my nerves. The waiting was bad; there was too much time to think. It was forty-five minutes past midnight. I was in the rental car, parked on Collins Avenue across from the entrance to the Dauphine. This was another of those glorified motor hotels of the Gold Coast Strip, about two blocks from the Golden Horn. He had a reservation. She'd made it for him, along with his fishing reservations at Marathon, in the Keys.

I lighted another cigarette, and went on watching the oncoming traffic, which was definitely thinning now. I'd already checked the area for pay phones, to be sure I could get to one when I wanted it. I nervously looked at the time again. I'd been here an hour and a half. Maybe he wouldn't drive all the way through from Mobile in one day. His plans could have changed in the two weeks since their bitter fight and her resignation, and he might be going somewhere else. He could have been in a wreck— I came alert. It was another Cadillac.

Well, I'd seen at least a hundred so far; there was no shortage of them in Miami Beach. But this was one of the big ones, and it was a light gray hardtop. Out-of-state license plate. Then I could see the pelican on it. The car was turning into the driveway of the Dauphine. It was Chapman, all right. And he was alone. I exhaled softly. That was the thing we had to know for sure. If he was going to live it up this trip, he hadn't picked up a girl so far.

The Cadillac stopped in the circular drive before the glass front wall of the lobby, partially screened from the street by the planter boxes of tropical vegetation bearing colored lights. I got out and crossed the street.

Chapman had already gone inside, and a bellman with a luggage cart was removing three large expensive-looking bags from the trunk of the car. I went into the lobby and turned toward the two telephone booths at the left rear, beside the archway that opened into the dining room. Nobody paid any attention to me. Chapman was standing at the desk. He was just as she had described him. We looked nothing alike except that we were the same height and—within the limits of the average description—the same build. He wore a lightweight gabardine suit and a cocoa straw hat, white shirt, and a conservatively striped tie. And the glasses, of course.

"Reservation for Harris Chapman," he said brusquely. It wasn't a question; it was a statement of fact.

I didn't hear the clerk's reply, but he turned away to check. I had reached the telephones now. I went through the motions of looking up a number, and just before I stepped inside I glanced toward the desk again. The clerk had returned. He was smiling as he pushed across the registry card. Then he handed Chapman an envelope. So far, so good. But I had to see what he did with it. If he shoved it in a pocket, he might forget it. He glanced at it curiously, and then set it on the desk while he registered. He'd recognized the handwriting by this time, I thought. It was from Marian. She had written it just before she left for Nassau. I closed the door of the booth and quickly dialed the apartment. She answered on the first ring.

"He's here," I said quietly. "And he got the letter."

"What did he do with it?"

"Nothing, yet. Wait." I turned and glanced toward the desk again. "He's opened it."

"Good," she said. "He'll call when he gets up to the room."

I wasn't so sure. He'd just driven over seven hundred miles, and would be ready to fall in bed. But she knew him inside out and should be able to guess his reaction pretty well. The letter was an implied but very arrogantly worded blackmail threat. She had something to discuss with him relative to his 1955 income tax return, and would be waiting for him to call, not later than tonight.

"He failed to report $55,000," she'd explained. "It's pretty well covered, but he knows how they dig once they're tipped off. And that informers are paid."

I glanced around again. Chapman had shoved the letter in his coat pocket and was striding toward the booths. "Hang up," I said quickly. "He's going to call right now."

The phone clicked and went dead. He stalked into the other booth and banged the door shut. I went on talking, ad libbing a conversation with an imaginary girl. He was dialing.

"Hello, Marian? Harris." I could hear him perfectly. "I thought they said you were in New York. What the hell's this let— Yeah, I just checked in. Look, if this is some kind of gag to get me to come out to your apartment, I thought we'd agreed that was all over. It wouldn't change anything, and I don't see why we have to embarrass ourselves ... What? ... *What's that?*"

There was a longer pause.

"Oh, so that's the way it is?" he said curtly. "By God, I didn't think you'd stoop to a thing like this. I guess Coral was right ... You know damn well that return's been checked and double-checked, and they've never found a thing wrong with it ... Never mind what you think ... If you need money, why didn't you take that six months' pay I offered you? ... No, I'm not coming out there. I'm tired. I've been driving all day ... What proof? ... You haven't got any proof, and you know it."

I heard him hang up and slam out of the booth. I pulled down the hook, dropped in another dime, and dialed her again.

"What do you think?" I asked softly, when she answered.

"He'll come, as soon as he thinks it over. Let me know."

"Right," I said.

When I came out of the booth, Chapman was entering the corridor at the other side of the lobby, followed by the bellman with his bags. I went back to the car, and lighted a cigarette. The Cadillac had been parked in the area off to the left of the main building. Ten minutes went by. Maybe she was wrong. Then an empty cab turned into the driveway. In a minute or two it came out the exit, crossed the traffic to this side of the street, and started south, the way it had come. There was a man in it wearing a hat. It was Chapman.

I looked at my watch. It had taken me fifteen minutes to drive up, but the traffic had lessened considerably by now. Call it ten. I got out and crossed the street again, and walked down about half a block to the bar I'd cased before. It had a booth, and I didn't want to go back to the lobby again unless I had to.

There were only three or four customers in the place, and the booth was empty. I was tight as a violin string now, and couldn't seem to take a deep breath. I ordered a shot of straight whisky, downed it, and went back to the phone. I closed the door, and dialed. She answered immediately.

"He left here five minutes ago, in a cab," I said.

"Good," she replied. "Remember, wait two minutes from the time I hang up. I'll be in the kitchen, getting out the ice cubes."

"Right," I said. The drink had loosened me a little now, but it was very hot in the booth and I was sweating. She went on talking. She seemed perfectly calm. The minutes dragged by.

"I think I hear the cab," she said.

I waited. Then I heard the doorbell, very faintly. The line went dead. Chapman was at the front door.

I checked the time, pulled down the hook, and dropped in another dime to get the dial tone. I looked back out at the bar. No one was near enough to hear any of it through the door. Just before the two minutes were up, I started dialing. It rang twice.

"Hello." It was Chapman, all right. She'd got him to answer.

"Mrs. Marian Forsyth," I said brusquely. "Is she there?"

"Just a minute."

I heard him call her, but not her reply. Then he came on again. "She's busy at the moment. Who's calling?"

"Chapman," I said. "Harris Chapman—"

"What?"

Most people, of course, have no idea how their voices and their speech sound to others, but he did. He was accustomed to using dictating devices and recorders.

"Harris Chapman," I repeated with the same curt impatience. "From Thomaston, Louisiana. She knows me—"

"Are you crazy?"

I cut in on him. "Will you please call Mrs. Forsyth to the phone? I haven't got all night."

"So you're Chapman, are you? Where are you calling from?"

"What the hell is this?" I barked into the phone. "I'm calling from the

Dauphine. I just checked in here. I've driven seven hundred thirty miles today, and I'm tired, and I don't feel like playing games. Maybe *you* want to talk to me about my 1955 income tax return, is that it? Well, it just happens I'm an attorney, my friend, and I know a little about the law, and about shakedowns. Now, put her on, or I'll turn this letter of hers over to the police right now."

"What in the name of God? *Marian—*"

I heard the phonograph come up in the background then, softly at first, and then louder. It was a song that had come out the summer Keith had gone mad—*The Music Goes Round and Round*. Shortly before they'd given up and had him committed for treatment, he'd locked himself in his room one day and played the record for nineteen hours without stopping.

"Listen!" I snapped. "What are you people up to? What's that music—?"

He was still there. I heard him gasp.

Oh, the music goes round and round ... and it comes out here...

"Turn that off!" I said harshly. "Who told you about Keith? She's been coaching you. You even sound like me. What's that woman trying to do to me? I offered her six months' pay ..."

"Marian," he shouted, "for the love of God, who is this man?"

I couldn't hear her reply, of course, but I knew what it was, and the way she said it. "Why, Harris Chapman, obviously."

The shots weren't too loud, mere exclamation points above the level of the music. There were two very close together, and then one more. The phone made a crashing noise, as if it had struck the edge of the table, and I heard him fall.

Oh, you press the middle valve down ...

Something else fell. And then there was nothing but the music, and a rhythmic tapping sound, as if the telephone receiver was swinging gently back and forth, bumping the leg of the table.

Bump ... bump ...

... and the music goes round and round ... yoo-oo-ohoo ...

I made it in a little over ten minutes. As soon as I'd got out in the fresh air I was all right. She'd probably fainted, but she'd come around. I parked a block away. The front door was unlocked. I slipped inside and closed it.

One bridge lamp was burning in a corner, and the lights were on in the kitchen. She wasn't in here. I sighed with relief. The phonograph had been shut off, and the phone was back on its cradle. The apartment was completely silent except for the humming of the air-conditioner. He was lying face down beside the table which held the telephone. I hurried through to the bedroom. She was in the bathroom, standing with her hands braced on the sides of the wash basin, looking at her face in the mirror. Apparently she'd started to brush her teeth, for some reason, for the toothbrush was lying in the basin where she'd dropped it. She was very pale. I took her arm. She turned, stared at me blankly, and then rubbed a hand across her face. Comprehension returned to her eyes. "I'm all right," she said. There was no tremor in her voice.

I led her out and sat her on the bed, and knelt beside her. "Just hold on for a few minutes, and we'll be out of here. You sit right there. Would you like a drink?"

"No," she said. "I'd rather not." She spoke precisely, without raising her voice. I had an impression it was nothing but iron self-control and that she was walking very carefully along the edge of screaming. That part of it, however, I couldn't help her with.

The tarpaulin I'd bought was in a broom closet in the kitchen. I carried it into the living room, spread it on the rug, and rolled him onto it. I didn't like looking at his face, so I threw a fold of the canvas over it. There was blood on his shirt, and some on the rug where he'd lain. I went through his pockets, taking everything out—wallet, traveler's checks, car keys, room key from the Dauphine, small address book, the letter from Marian, cigarette holder, lighter, cigarettes, and a small plastic vial of some kind of pills. I tore up the letter and shoved it back in his coat pocket, along with the pills and the cigarette holder. His glasses had fallen off. I put them in his pocket also. All the other items I placed on the coffee table. He wore no rings. I left his watch on his wrist. The gun, a small .32, was on the rug near the phonograph. I put it in another coat pocket.

I rolled him in the tarpaulin and pulled him out into the kitchen, beside the back door. I cut two strips off the canvas to use for ropes, doubled him into the foetal position, and bound him. I was shaking badly now, and my stomach was acting up again. I leaned against the sink, poured a drink of whisky from the bottle in a cupboard, and downed it. In a minute I felt a little better.

I filled a pan with water, located a sponge, and scrubbed at the blood stain on the living room rug. It took nearly ten minutes and four pans of water. I knew a lot of it had gone through to the pad beneath, and that the rug would show a water stain when it dried, but I could take care of that later. I'd have the whole rug shampooed. I washed the pan, and the sink, and turned out the kitchen light. It was a relief to get away from him.

She was just getting up from the bed. I took her in my arms. "I'm all right now," she said. "I'm sorry I broke up that way."

"Everything's under control," I told her. "He had the room key. That was the only thing I was worried about. What time is your flight?"

"I'm wait-listed at five-fifteen, and confirmed at six-thirty."

I looked at my watch. It was five minutes of two. She'd have a long wait, alone, at the airport, but it couldn't be helped. She couldn't stay here. She seemed to be in full control of herself, and rational. She put on some lipstick, and her hat, and I closed the overnight case and found her coat, gloves, and purse. I dropped the Dauphine room key in my pocket. There was horror in her eyes just for an instant as we went out through the living room.

"The car's about a block away," I said. "I didn't want any more traffic in and out of here than we had to have."

She made no reply. I turned out the lights and locked the door. When we got to the car, I lighted her a cigarette. She remained silent all the way up Collins Avenue. I reached over once and took her hand. It was like ice, even through the mesh of the glove.

I parked about a block from the Dauphine. Turning to her, I took her face between my hands, and asked, "I'll be about ten minutes; are you sure you'll be all right?"

"Yes, of course," she replied, in that same quiet, beautifully controlled sort of way.

I walked up past the Dauphine and entered the driveway at the exit end. There was an extensive parking area here, going back along the side of this wing of the building. About two-thirds of the way back there was a doorway. I entered it, and was in one of the ground-floor corridors. I took the key from my pocket. It was No. 226. At the end of the corridor there was a self-service elevator and a stairway. I took the stairway. In the corridor above, I began checking the numbers—216—214—I was going the wrong way. I went back around the corner. A bellman came past, carrying a tray. I swung the key absently, and nodded. He smiled, and went on. 222—224— Here it was. The corridor was empty now. I unlocked the door, slipped inside, and closed it.

The drapes were drawn over the window at the other end of the room. A light was burning on the night table beside the bed, and the bathroom lights were on. One of the three matching fiberglass suitcases was on the luggage stand, unopened, and the others were on the floor beside it. I didn't like the looks of that. He'd been up here approximately ten minutes without unpacking anything, so maybe he'd been on the phone. He might have called Coral Blaine to tell her he'd arrived. We hadn't believed he would, because of the late hour. But if he had, *had he mentioned the letter from Marian?*

Well, there was nothing I could do about it at the moment, and I had plenty of other armed hand grenades to juggle without worrying about that one. I rumpled the bed, and reached for the phone. The front office should know he'd been out; they'd probably called the cab for him. Play it that way.

The operator answered.

"Desk, please," I said.

"Yes, sir." Then she added quickly, "Oh, Mr. Chapman, would you like me to try that Thomaston call again now?"

I breathed softly in relief. "No. Just cancel. I'll call in the morning."

"Yes, sir."

The night clerk came on. "Desk."

"Chapman," I said. "In 226. There haven't been any messages for me?"

"Uuuuh—let's see. No, sir, not a thing."

"Okay," I said. "I won't want to be disturbed until about noon. Would you notify the switchboard not to put any calls through?"

"Yes, sir. And just hang the sign on the doorknob. The maids won't come in."

"Thank you," I said. I got the *DO NOT DISTURB* sign off the dresser, switched off the lights, and peered out. The corridor was clear. I draped the sign on the knob, made sure the door was locked, and walked around to the stairs. I met no one. When I was on the sidewalk in front I breathed freely again. One more hurdle was past.

I swung the car around, went back down Collins Avenue, and took the North Bay Causeway, headed for the airport. She sat perfectly erect and composed beside me, but she spoke only once during the whole trip.

"I took advantage of you," she said musingly. "God forgive me for that. I'm sorry, Jerry."

"What?" I asked. "What do you mean, you took advantage of me?"

She made no reply.

Just before we reached the terminal, I pulled to the curb and parked. It was ten minutes of three.

"What day is this?" I asked quickly.

"Thursday, November 14th. That isn't necessary; I tell you I'm perfectly all right."

I had to be sure. She was on her own from here on. "Tell me your schedule."

"I leave here at five-fifteen or six-thirty. Either way, I'll be back in my room in New York before noon. I check out of the hotel tomorrow at one p.m. and fly to New Orleans. I'll be in Thomaston Saturday morning. From then on, it's exactly as we have it written down."

"Right," I said.

"You'll make certain about the tapes, won't you? And under no circumstances are you to try to call me."

"Don't worry about the tapes. Or about anything. I can handle it. We'll say good-by here. Then I'll swing in, drop you at the terminal, and run. Okay?"

"Yes." She turned, her face lifted to mine.

I kissed her, holding her very tightly for a moment, and whispered against her cheek, "I'll just be going through the motions until I'm with you again. That's all I'm going to say now. Break. And let's go."

I swung in, stopped in front of the terminal, and helped her out. She lifted a hand, turned, and went inside.

It was three thirty-five when I backed into the driveway beside the apartment. The house beyond the high and shadowy wall was dark, and the streets were deserted. I stopped short of the garage doors, cut the ignition and lights, and got out. I unlocked the trunk, and eased it open. Letting myself in at the front, I went through to the bedroom, and changed into fishing clothes. I went out in the kitchen, without turning on the lights, and poured another drink. I dreaded this part of it.

I wasn't even sure I could do it, except for one thing—I had to. I weighed 180, and he 195. But I was in fairly good condition. I eased the kitchen door open, pulled him through it to the edge of the concrete slab, and bent my knees to get my arms around him. Three minutes later the trunk was closed again and I was draped across it, trembling and sweaty and sick at my stomach. They say madmen don't know their own strength. Neither do desperate ones.

I slipped back into the kitchen, closed and locked the door, turned out the light in the bedroom, and went out the front. I opened the garage door, backed up, and coupled on the trailer. By this time I'd probably waked the people in the house beyond the wall, but it was all right. Florida was full of fishermen waking their neighbors at that hour in the morning. I drove out into the street.

I wanted to stop for some coffee, but didn't dare. I didn't know how soon after five it would start growing light. When I was beyond Homestead and Florida City on the open highway I opened the car up to seventy. It was five-ten and still dark when I crossed onto Key Largo. I checked my speedometer at the junction of the two roads, and swung left. In a few minutes I came to the first launching site. It was dark, and there were no cars in sight. I swung my headlights to get a look at it, pulled up, and backed down to the water's edge. I had to get out once to judge the distance.

In a moment I had the boat off. I pulled it around and beached it, and turned off the car lights. The east was gray now, and I noticed for the first time that it was almost calm. That was good; I could go far out, off soundings. Mosquitoes buzzed around my face. I steeled myself, unlocked the trunk, and was just raising the lid, when I tensed up, listening. A car was coming. I slammed it. Headlights swept over me. The car came on, slowed almost to a stop, and then went on. It was towing a boat.

The sound of it died away. I yanked open the trunk, and pawed blindly at the canvas. Somehow, the hated and brutal weight was in my arms again, and I staggered to the side of the boat. I ran back and brought the concrete blocks, two at a time, and frantically felt around for the wire and the pliers. I drove the car out until the trailer was clear of the launching area, and parked it near the road. I was locking it when headlights burst over me again.

The car stopped. It was towing a boat too. A man got out, said, "Good morning," and switched on a flashlight.

My mouth was dry with fear. I forced it open at last, made some kind of reply, and started moving toward the boat. He was directing the driver of the car, throwing the flashlight beam toward the water. It swept over the boat.

"Nice looking outfit you got there," he said. "Get in the stern, and I'll push you off."

"It's all right," I said. "Thanks just the same."

He was still coming toward me with the flashlight. I caught the bow of the boat, and heaved. It shot outward. I clambered aboard, getting my feet wet. I stayed in the bow, between him and Chapman's body, while I picked up an oar and hurriedly poled my way out another fifty feet. He had turned away now and was directing the driver of the car. I sat down in the stern, shaking all over, and started the motor.

The east was light now, but the visibility was still poor. I headed seaward, running at idling speed and watching for obstructions. Off to my left a light flashed. A westbound tanker went past inside the Stream, still two or three miles ahead of me. It was full daylight by the time I was past the line of reefs. The boat pitched lazily on the long groundswell rolling up from the southeast. I went on. The tanker was far to the westward and I could see nothing of the other two boats. I was in the Stream now, completely alone, and probably near the hundred-fathom curve. Key Largo was down on the horizon, and visible only when I crested a swell. I cut the motor and reached for the wire and the concrete blocks.

The boat heaved upward on the greasy swell, and shipped some water as he went over. The sun was just coming up.

CHAPTER EIGHT

I stopped to turn back the boat and trailer on the way into town, and it was nine-fifteen when I got back to the apartment. I had one more drink, made a pot of coffee, and showered and shaved.

I couldn't remember when I'd had anything to eat, but I wasn't hungry. I was running on nerve now, but I was too tense and keyed up to be tired. The real test was yet to come. I had to call Coral Blaine in about two hours, and if I failed to pass, Marian Forsyth and I were dead. I wondered how she was feeling at the moment, knowing it all depended on me and that we couldn't even communicate anymore.

I dressed in a lightweight flannel suit, white shirt, and a conservative tie on the order of the one Chapman had worn. I put my horn-rimmed glasses in a coat pocket, and then stowed away a pack of the filter cigarettes, the cigarette holder, and Chapman's lighter, which was one of the butane jobs. Then his wallet, the folder of traveler's checks, the little address book, his car keys, and the Dauphine room key. But I had one more act to perform as Jerry Forbes. I had to return the car. I removed the rental deposit slip from my own wallet and put it in a pocket.

The straw hat was slightly too large, so I cut a strip of newspaper and folded it inside the sweat band. I put the seven rolls of tape and the other information in the briefcase she'd bought before leaving for Nassau, closed the recorder, turned off the air-conditioner, and took one last look around. I drove over to Miami, turned in the car, walked up a block, caught a cab, and gave an address on Collins Avenue near the Dauphine.

I got out a block away, and walked back, carrying the recorder and the briefcase. Entering the driveway at the exit end, I went up through the parking area and entered the side door as I had last night. There were a few guests in the corridors now, and I passed one of the maids, and a bellman pushing a room-service cart, but no one paid any attention to me. The corridor before No. 226 was empty except for a furry fat man in swim trunks. I unlocked the door and slipped inside, removing the *DO NOT DISTURB* sign from the knob.

It was 11:10 a.m., and I was now Harris Chapman. I was up there on the tight rope I had to walk for twelve days—provided I got past the first step.

I removed my jacket, shirt, and tie, and hung them in the closet, took off my shoes, and picked up the phone and called room service. I ordered a pot of coffee, orange juice, and a *Miami Herald*.

I rumpled the bed some more, went into the bathroom, washed my face, turned the shower on very hot for a minute or two until the room began to get steamy, rubbed one of the fresh bath towels over the wet tiles until it was damp, and draped it carelessly back on the rack. I got the glasses out of my jacket and put them on. They were mildly corrective reading glasses she'd convinced an optometrist she needed because of headaches, and weren't too hard to put up with. They and the mustache changed my appearance amazingly. I looked some five years older.

I opened the bag that was on the luggage rack. It was the companion bag to a two-suiter, filled with shirts, underwear, socks, handkerchiefs, and so on. I pulled out a pair of pajamas, wadded them, and tossed them across the bed. A full bottle of Scotch was nestled among the clothes, and in one of the end pockets there were four or five packages of contraceptives. I thought of what Marian had called him—an ageing adolescent. It seemed incredible she'd been in love with him, but maybe he'd been different before he looked up and saw middle age and panicked.

There were some papers in the top flap. I pulled them out, and one envelope was exactly what I was looking for. It was a statement from Webster & Adcock, his brokerage firm in New Orleans, itemizing the status of his account as of November first. I ran my eye down it, and whistled. She hadn't been exaggerating. *1,000 shares Columbia Gas ... 500 shares Du Pont 4.50 Preferred ... 100 AT&T bonds ... 500 shares PG&E common ...* It went on. The last item was $22,376.50 in cash. There were three more of the same envelopes containing verifications of later transactions. I shoved them all back in the bag. Checking it over in detail could wait. Coral Blaine was the pitfall I had to get past now.

The other envelope was postmarked Marathon, Florida, over a month ago, and contained a letter from Captain Wilder of the charter-boat *Blue Water III*, confirming Chapman's reservations on November 15, 16, 17, and again on 21, 22, and 23.

Remembering I was in character now, I went over and picked up the phone and asked for room service again.

"Hello? Room service? Chapman, in 226," I said irritably. "That boy hasn't shown up with my order— Oh? Okay. Thanks."

He knocked on the door almost by the time I'd hung up. I let him in with the cart, carefully added up the check, added a tip, and signed it. He departed. I poured a cup of coffee, and went on with my investigation. The second suitcase held two lightweight suits, a sport coat, several pairs of slacks, and some other miscellaneous items of clothing, a half dozen bottles of different kinds of pills, and a small leather kit containing all his toilet articles. The third was mostly fishing clothes. It also contained a Contaflex camera, and a gift of some kind, still wrapped.

It felt like a book. I tore it open. It was a volume on saltwater fishing by Kip Farrington, and the flyleaf was inscribed, *With all my love, Coral*. I started to drop it in the bag. Something fell out of it. It was a plain piece of white paper on which was written the single word, *Isle*. It puzzled me. Apparently she'd stuck it in there between the pages. I held the book up and shook it. Two more slips fell out, along with a four by six photograph of a young blond girl in a bathing suit, standing on tiptoes. She was very pretty, but as standardized—pose and all—as an interchangeable part. She made me think of a composite picture. I looked at the other two slips of paper. Each had one word written on it. *View*, and *of*. I frowned. Then they rearranged themselves in my mind, and I shook my head. *Isle of View*. For this he'd jilted Marian Forsyth. That forty country must be rough.

His wallet held a little over seven hundred dollars, two more photographs of Coral Blaine, driver's license, eight or ten credit cards of various kinds, and his Chapman Enterprises business cards, but nothing with a picture of him. I unsnapped the folder of traveler's checks. There were forty-eight of them, all hundreds. He didn't exactly go around barefoot, for a two weeks' vacation. Well, he was a millionaire, it was probably all deductible if he had an imaginative tax man, and big-game fishing came high—to say nothing of nineteen-year-old call girls.

I was stalling now, and I knew it. I'd been through all his things, and if I kept inventing reasons for putting it off I'd start to lose my nerve, and then I *would* flub it. I broke the seal on the bottle of Scotch, had one fair-sized drink, and reached for the phone. I was tight across the chest.

The operator answered. "Long distance," I said. "Thomaston, Louisiana. The number is 6-2525. Person-to-person to Miss Coral Blaine."

"Yes, sir. One moment, please."

I waited. *Remember, two pet names. Remember, she has a very Southern accent.* No, that didn't matter. This was person-to-person; I didn't have to worry about "recognizing" the wrong girl's voice. *Remember, just got up. Groggy. Hard drive.*

Far off, a feminine voice said, "Chapman Enterprises."

Receptionist. Mrs. English. Widow. 36. Brown hair. Pleasant. Son in high school. Wendell...

"Miss Coral Blaine," an operator said. "Miami Beach is calling."

"One moment, please."

Hates Marian. "Adores" things. Chides me for swearing. Argument about scope and magnitude of wedding, settled now, her favor. Honeymoon definitely Palm Springs, Acapulco out, loathes fishing. Get her talking about bridal showers. Gown. Attendants ...

"Go ahead, please."

"Harris, darling—"

"Angel, how are you?" I said.

"Just fine, darling, but I've been so *worried*. You didn't call last night, and here I've been imaginin' wrecks and hurricanes and deadly females carryin' you off—"

"I tried to call you. When I checked in here at Miami Beach. At one a.m.—that'd be midnight your time. But there was no answer."

"I just *knew* it! I kept trying to tell that crazy Bonnie Sue Wentworth that Miama was ahead of us—"

Bonnie Sue clicked in my mind.

"—Henry's in Chicago, you know, at that engineer's convention or whatever it is, so after the movie we went out to the club, and I kept telling her I had to get back because you'd call, but she said Miama was *behind* us—"

"Bonnie Sue's having a good day when she can tell whether it's daylight or dark," I said. "And I wish you wouldn't ride with her. Any husband that would let a featherweight like that drive a Thunderbird has got a grudge against her, or the human race—"

"Harris, she wasn't drivin' the Bird. Heavens, they traded that in, remember?"

So. Don't get too cocky.

"Well, the hell with Bonnie Sue. I want to know how you—"

"Harris! The very idea!"

"I'm sorry, angel," I said. "But how are you? And how's everything at the office?"

"Just fine. And, remember, I said I wasn't going to bother you with old office details on your vacation. The only thing that's come up important is a letter from those lawyers in Washington about the radio station. There's some more forms to fill out."

"Yes. That's the application for an increase in power," I said. "Shoot 'em over to Wingard. If he has any questions, I'll get in touch with him later. But, look, angel, suppose I call you tonight? I just woke up and haven't even dressed yet. And before I drive on down to Marathon there's a real-estate man I want to see."

"That'd be wonderful, darling. I'll be waiting."

"Say about eight, your time. And thanks a million for the book. It's a good one."

"You fibber. I bet you haven't even looked at it."

"I'll just take that bet," I winced. "Isle of View, too."

"Why, you precious. You did open it."

When I'd hung up, I poured one more small drink of the Scotch, and sighed. How could I have been worried about that? Then a very cold hand closed around my insides, and I cursed myself. *Don't get careless.* So she's an idiot. But don't forget, they were engaged; there's a whole area of shared experience nobody could brief you on, not even Marian Forsyth. And just one little slip, one wrong word, can do it.

I looked at my watch. It was still only a few minutes past twelve. It would be better not to check out until at least one p.m.; that would be exactly twelve hours from the time he'd checked in, and there'd be no chance at all any of the same staff would be on duty. The whole switch depended on that. Now would be a good time to hit Chris.

I poured some more coffee, and dug the Webster & Adcock envelopes out of the bag. Spreading out the itemized end-of-the-month statement, I corrected it and brought it up to date with the slips verifying subsequent transactions. Since the first of the month—and that would be about the time Marian had left him—he had sold 500 shares of Consolidated Edison, and in three separate transactions had bought a total of 10,000 shares of some cheap stock called Warwick Petroleum. This was listed on the American Exchange, and had been bought at prices ranging from 3 1/2 to 3 1/8. I just had a hunch Chris had been unhappy about that. Marian had got him to switch over to high-grade preferreds and good solid utilities before prices started to sag, and here he was plunging to the tune of better than $30,000 on some cheap speculation before she'd hardly got out of sight.

I crossed off the Consolidated Edison, added the Warwick, and adjusted the cash. The latter was now $12,741.50. Opening the *Miami Herald* to the financial page, I went down the list, checking it off against yesterday's closing prices on the Stock Exchange. I added it all up. It came to roughly $187,000. I whistled softly. $175,000 of that was ours.

I thought of the places we'd go. Athens, Istanbul, Majorca. And the fishing places—New Zealand, and Cabo Blanco. Passports would be no problem; we wouldn't be fugitives. But it really didn't matter where we went, as long as I was with her.

I snapped out of it. It would be at least a month before I could see her again, and I was in no position to be goofing off, dreaming about her. I reached for the phone.

"Operator, I'd like to make another long distance call. This one's to New

Orleans—"

"Yes, sir. And the number?"

I gave it to her, and added, "Person-to-person to Mr. Chris Lundgren."

"Thank you. One moment, please."

I heard the operator at Webster & Adcock, and then Lundgren's voice.

"Chris?" I said. "Chapman. How's Warwick doing this morning?"

"Oh, good morning, Mr. Chapman. The girl said you're in Miami Beach already—"

"That's right," I said shortly. "But has there been any sign of a rally in Warwick? I see it closed yesterday at 2 7/8."

"No-o—" He sounded far from enthusiastic. "It's about the same, but there's very little activity in it. To tell you the truth, Mr. Chapman, I still can't quite go along with you on it. It carries a lot of risk—"

So I was right. I cut in brusquely. "But, goddammit, Chris, there's risk in anything there's profit in. I got where I am now by taking risks. I'm not some old woman using the dividends from a few shares of AT&T to buy food for her cat. With the tax setup we've got, what good is income to me? I need capital gains."

"Of course, Mr. Chapman. But I just don't see Warwick Petroleum. In a healthy market it might pay off as a speculation, though I'd prefer to see you in a sounder growth situation with better management. But right now the market's going through a period of uncertainty and readjustment, and we ought to give some thought to safety. You're in a very strong defensive position in everything except the Warwick, and I have to agree with Mrs. Forsyth—"

"Mrs. Forsyth's not the only person who's ever heard of the stock market," I said irritably. "And since she's walked out on me, I don't see where she enters into it. But I'll tell you what; I don't believe in nursing losses any more than you do. Let's get rid of it. Get 7/8 if you can, and go as low as 3/4 if you have to."

"Good." He was pleased. "I think that's wise. Mrs. Forsyth—"

"Goddammit, never mind Mrs. Forsyth!" I barked. Then I relented. "Sorry, Chris. What was it you started to say?"

"Oh— I was going to ask if you wanted to put the proceeds from the Warwick in some sound utility, just for the moment?"

"No," I said. "Leave it in cash. As a matter of fact, while I'm over here I'm taking a good look at real estate. This place is booming. But never mind that. Just unload the Warwick. G'by."

I hung up, elated. It was perfect. Neither of them had suspected a thing, and I was already laying the groundwork. I flipped through the paper to the classified section. Real estate. Here we were. Acreage. There were several big listings, some ocean front, and some highway frontage. I tore the section out, and looked at my watch. It was a little after one p.m. now. I dressed, closed the bags, put on the straw hat, and called the desk.

"Would you get my bill ready, please? And send a boy up to 226 for the bags."

"Yes, sir. Right away."

I looked at myself in the bathroom mirror. I was tired; dead tired. But the exhaustion merely made me look a little older. Marian had been right all the time. Chapman and I might not look anything alike actually, but within the limits of the average description we were indistinguishable.

Pretty big man. Above average size, anyway. Six feet, like that. 180, 190. Not old, not young. Thirties, I'd say. Brown hair. Dark, light, reddish? Well, uh, brown, you know. Blue eyes. Gray eyes. Green eyes.

Add a mustache, horn-rimmed glasses, cigarette holder. Add his car, his clothes, his identification. Add the personality traits. Throw in a week or ten days between observation and description. And finally throw in the fact that from beginning to end there was never any reason to doubt that Chapman was Chapman, and what did you have? Chapman.

But only if nobody had ever seen us both. That was vital.

I followed the boy with the luggage cart down to the desk. They were all different—bellman, clerk, cashier. I'd noted them carefully last night when he was checking in.

I scrutinized all the items on the bill, and took out the traveler's checks. "Would you cash an extra one for me?" I asked. "I need some change."

"Yes, sir. We'd be glad to."

I signed them, and as they lay on the desk I compared the signatures with the originals. Good. Very good. I put the change in the wallet, tossed the car keys to the bellman, and said, "Gray Cadillac, Louisiana plates." I stuck one of the filter cigarettes in the holder, lighted it, and followed him. Chapman had come in here, and I had gone out. There was nothing to it.

He stowed the bags and the recorder and briefcase in the trunk. I gave him a dollar, and got in. The car was almost new, and was upholstered in pale blue leather. It was unbearably hot, and I hit the buttons to roll the windows down. I rummaged in the glove compartment for a Florida highway map, and found one, and also came up with a pair of clip-on sunglasses. Fastening them in my frames, I looked at myself in the mirror. It was better all the time. I could *be* Chapman. Then I shuddered. Except that Chapman was lying on the bottom in six hundred feet of water, in the gloom and the everlasting silence, with his chest crushed by pressure. I shook it off.

I took out the classified real-estate ads I'd torn from the *Herald*, and checked some of the listings against the highway map. Several looked promising. One was a block of highway frontage on US 1 between Hollywood and North Miami, listed with the Fitzpatrick Realty Co. of Hollywood at an asking price of $375,000.

I drove up and cruised around the town for about half an hour, looking it over. It appeared to be just about right. There were several motels of the type I was looking for, and it wasn't too far from Miami. It was overflowing with real-estate outfits, of course, and I dropped in at three of them, introduced myself, and explained I was just looking over the local real-estate picture.

It was a little after two-thirty when I looked in on Fitzpatrick. He had a rather small place in a good location on one of the principal streets. Two salesmen and a girl were at work at desks out front. I by-passed the salesman, gave the girl one of Chapman's business cards, and said I'd like to talk to Fitzpatrick if he was in. She disappeared into the inner office. I slipped one of the cigarettes into the holder and was lighting it when she came back out and nodded.

He was a heavy-set and balding man in his fifties with the easy manner of a born salesman and a big nose criss-crossed with tiny purple veins. It was a nose that showed years of loving care, and I reflected that his liver probably looked like a hobnailed boot. We shook hands. I sat down, unclipped the sunglasses, and dropped them in my pocket. It wouldn't do to have people remembering that I had worn them inside.

He leaned back in his chair, glanced at the card, and asked, "What line of business are you in, Mr. Chapman?"

"Oh, several," I said. "Cotton gin, radio station, newspaper— Actually, I'm down here on vacation, for a little fishing. In the Keys, and maybe over to Bimini for a few days. It's been about three years since I was in the Miami area, and I was just wondering what was happening in real-estate values."

"I'd tell you," he said, "but since you're a businessman yourself you'd call me a liar."

He then proceeded to tell me. He did a convincing job. In Florida real estate all the women were beautiful and all the men were brave, he believed it himself, and he possessed the lyricism of the Irish. Fortunes were made right under his nose every day. We decried a tax setup under which it was impossible to make money and keep any of it except in capital gains or oil. He suggested we take a ride around and he'd show me a few of the listings they had. His car was just up the street in a parking lot. Why didn't we take mine? I asked. It was parked out front.

"Nice cars, these Caddies," he remarked, as we got in.

I clipped on the glasses. "I'm not much of a car fan. But, hell, when you can charge them off at least you got something out of the deal. What do you think of highway frontage along US 1 here? Has it priced itself out of the market yet?"

"Turn right," he said, "and I'll show you a block of it that'll double in price in the next two years. Let me tell you what motel sites are bringing—per front foot—right now, within two miles of it."

We drove out and looked at it. I asked a few questions about the taxes, total acreage, highway frontage, and how firm he thought the price was, but remained noncommittal. We stopped at a bar on the way back and had a drink. He wanted to know where I'd be staying the next few days, and I gave him the name of the motel in Marathon. Fitzpatrick was interested. He'd been in the business long enough to know when he smelled a sale.

I dropped him at his office, and headed south. On the way through Miami I stopped at a florist and wired two dozen yellow roses to Coral Blaine at her home address. They were her favorite flower.

He sometimes sent all the girls in the office inexpensive gifts when he was away on vacation, and I had an idea now. I could accomplish two things at once. On the way out of town, going south toward the Keys, I began watching for one of those roadside curio places that sold concrete flamingos. I finally located one, and pulled off.

It was the usual tourist-stopper seen along all the highways of South Florida, cluttered with four-foot clamshells from the Great Barrier Reef, cypress knees, alligator skins, coconut monkey heads, boxed fruit, and postcards. It was run by a cold-eyed man with a Georgia accent and a browbeaten woman I took to be his wife. I poked disdainfully around in the junk for a while and finally settled on the gift boxes of exotic jellies. *Guava, Sea Grape, Tangerine Marmalade—We Pack and Ship.*

"How much off for four?" I asked.

His bleak eyes shifted from me to the seven thousand dollars' worth of car out front, and back again. "Same price, mister. One or a hundred."

"I can see you're a born merchandiser," I said. I opened the briefcase, dug out the list Marian had given me, and wrote down the names and home addresses of the four girls: Bill McEwen at the paper, and Mrs. English, Jean Sessions, and Barbara Cullen at the office.

"One box to each address," I said. I paid him, and added, "Give me a receipt. I've been stung on these deals before."

He gave me one. I carefully stowed it in my wallet, and went out. The concrete flamingos were lined up along the fence at the right of the building. "What the devil are those things?" I asked. "I've been seeing them all along the road."

"Ornamental flamingos," he replied.

"What are they made of?" I asked. "And what good are they?"

"Plaster," he said. "Concrete. These ones are concrete. You stick 'em up on lawns, or in the shrubbery. The ones with bases you set in wadin' pools."

I shook my head. "God, the things you people sell to tourists." He watched coldly as I got back in the car and drove off.

CHAPTER NINE

I arrived at Marathon and checked into the motel with almost an hour to spare before I was supposed to call Coral Blaine. I was practically out on my feet. After a shower and a harsh rubdown, I set up the tape recorder, put on the No. 5 roll, which was devoted almost altogether to her, and listened with the gain turned down. I found I didn't need it anymore. My mind ran ahead of the tape. There were tens of thousands of things I didn't know about her and about Chapman, but everything on those five hours of tape was stamped into my brain.

I called her at exactly nine, and again it was easy. She'd got the roses; that helped. She was going to somebody's house to play bridge. Two of the names she mentioned were familiar, so I made some appropriate comment. I was excited about tomorrow's fishing, and I was getting burned up with Chris Lundgren. If he didn't stop throwing Marian Forsyth's advice at me I was going to switch my account to Merrill Lynch or somebody. Any time I needed that woman's advice about anything—

She sniffed, and agreed with me. It was just too bad about poor Marian, but she guessed when women reached that age they got sort of—well, you know, frustrated and embittered.

"She's in New York, you know. She called Bill McEwen today—"

"What'd she call her for?" I demanded suspiciously. "Bill, I mean."

"She gave her an ad to run in the paper. She's selling her house. Bill said she told her she'd be back here Saturday."

"Yeah. And I suppose she'll be talking about me behind my back to everybody in town. After I offered her six months' pay, when she blew up and quit."

"Well, I certainly wouldn't worry about *her* talking about somebody—"

We exchanged the usual I-love-you's and the I-miss-you's, and rang off. It was beautiful, I thought. And I was becoming about as fond of the catty little witch as Marian was.

I called Captain Wilder of the *Blue Water III*, and told him I was in town and would be at the dock at eight a.m. He told me how to get there. I left a call for seven, took off my clothes, and fell into bed. The moment the light was out, I thought of Marian, and was so lonely for her I ached. I didn't even have a photograph. Then twenty-four hours of tension uncoiled inside me like a breaking spring, and I dropped into blackness....

She was running ahead of me along a sidewalk supported by giant cables in catenary curves, with only emptiness and fog beneath us. She was drawing away, and she ran into the fog and I lost her, and there was nothing but the sound of her footsteps dying away. I awoke and was tangled in the sheet and the phone was ringing.

It all came back, and for a moment I was sick with terror. Then it was gone. I'd expected it, of course; at the precise moment of waking you're defenseless. It was nothing, and would wear off in a few days. I picked up the phone. It was seven o'clock.

Captain Wilder was a chubby and jovial man with an unending supply of chatter and dirty stories, and his mate was a Cuban boy with limited English. To both I was merely another faceless possessor of traveler's checks, to be fished successfully and made happy. I wore the dark glasses, of course, and a long-visored fishing cap. I used Chapman's few words of Spanish on the Cuban boy, and talked a little about fishing at Acapulco.

There was no enjoyment in it. I kept thinking of his body lying down there somewhere, crushed under the tons of water. We didn't catch anything to speak of, which was good. I wouldn't have to fight off the photographers. I explained we'd have to cut the first day short because I had an important business call to make, and we were back at the dock at three.

That was two p.m., New Orleans time. I called from the motel.

"Chris? Chapman. How are you making out with that Warwick?"

"Oh, hello, Mr. Chapman," he replied. "The fishing all right?"

"Lousy," I said shortly. "But about that oil stock—?"

"Hmmm. Let's see. We unloaded 6,000 shares of it yesterday, at 2 7/8. It went to 3/4, and we disposed of two more at that price. It slid off to 5/8 at closing, and has been hanging there and at 1/2 all day. So we still have 2,000."

"Right," I said briskly. "Just let it ride until we can get 3/4." I made a rough calculation. "Now, look. My cash position must be around $30,000 at the moment, or a little better. That right?"

"Ye-es—I think so. I haven't got the exact figures, but it should be in the neighborhood of $34,000."

"Fine. Now here's what I want you to do. I came in from fishing early so I'd catch you in time, since tomorrow's Saturday. Send me a check for $25,000, airmail special delivery, care the Clive Hotel, Miami. That's C-l-i-v-e, Clive. Get it off this afternoon, without fail. I've run into something here that's beginning to look terrific, if I can get it at my price, and I think I can. But I'm going to need some cash to hit 'em with, either for an option or as earnest money when I make the offer."

"Real estate?" he asked. I could sense disapproval. The securities men and the land dealers shared a deep mutual distrust of each other's "investments." Then I realized it ran deeper than that; he didn't have a great deal of faith in my judgment. I'd got where I was in the stock market by riding on Marian Forsyth's back, and now that I'd ditched her there was no telling what would happen. That was fine. What I was doing was right in character. "Excuse me," he went on. "None of my business, of course. I didn't mean to pry."

"Not at all," I said. "As a matter of fact, it is real estate. Highway frontage on US 1. And it's big. If I can get it, I could net a quarter million, after taxes, in eighteen months. It's going to take a sizable chunk of cash, but I'll worry about that after I hit 'em with the offer. And you'll shoot that check out to me right away, huh?"

"Yes, sir. It'll be in the mail tonight. Airmail special."

"Thanks," I said. "G'by."

I hung up, breathed a quiet sigh, and poured a drink of the Scotch. We were rolling.

Next I called the reservations desk at the Clive and asked for a room Sunday night, and added, "I'm expecting a very important letter that'll probably get there before I do. Be sure to hang onto it."

"Yes, sir, Mr. Chapman. We'll hold it."

I took out some stationery and a pen and practiced writing the signature for a solid hour, striving for perfection and at the same time trying to condition myself to signing Harris Chapman so it would be automatic and I couldn't slip and sign Jerry Forbes sometime when I was thinking of something else. It occurred to me that in the short time I'd been in Florida I had been three different people—George Hamilton, Jerry Forbes, and now Chapman, and that in another ten days I'd go back to being Forbes again. A little more of this and I wouldn't really know who I was.

I compared the results of the practice with the originals on the traveler's checks. To my eye, they were indistinguishable; presumably an expert could tell them apart, but there was no reason the question should ever arise. I tore up the sheets and flushed them down the john.

Around six I showered and shaved, and dressed in one of Chapman's suits. The trousers were about two inches too large in the waist, but it didn't show with the jacket buttoned. Wearing his clothes made me feel queasy, but it had to be done. I found a surprisingly good restaurant, and had dinner, after two martinis at the bar. But it was necessary, for strategic purposes, to ruin the steak beyond the semblance of flavor. Chapman always ate them incinerated, so I ordered it well done. When the waiter brought it out, I cut into it just once, beckoned peremptorily, and told him to take it back and tell the chef to cook it.

He returned with it a few minutes later. I cut into it, scrutinized it carefully, and gave him a glacial stare.

"I'm sorry," I said, "but this steak is still raw. Maybe if I wrote the chef a note—"

The place was crowded, and people at near-by tables were turning to stare. I stared back at them, completely unperturbed. The waiter would have liked nothing better than to poison me, but he removed it once more. This time I ate it when he brought it back. It was like charcoal.

I paid with one of the traveler's checks. The cashier glanced at the signature, and as she counted out my change, she said, "I'm sorry about the steak, Mr. Chapman. We'll do better next time."

I called Coral Blaine at eight p.m. She started immediately telling me about some upcoming party, and I let her rattle. I was beginning to feel a little less tense now when I was talking to her, for I was discovering how right Marian had been. She'd said I wouldn't have much trouble with her.

"Dear," she asked, "did you tell Bill McEwen she could start her vacation tomorrow? I don't know why she wants to go off this time of year, but she says you told her it was all right—"

"Yes, it's okay," I said.

"Harris, I think you ought to let her go when you get back. You know I don't like to repeat gossip, but I heard something the other day—"

"What?" I asked.

"You remember last summer when she had to make that emergency trip to El Paso because her brother was about to die? Well, I just found out where she really was. In Dallas, seeing a doctor. One of those, you know— Miss Bill McEwen was pregnant."

"Well, hell, you can't prove a thing like that," I said.

"Oh, the party that told me knew all about it. Except who the man was, of course."

"Well, we'll talk about it when I get back," I said. Bill McEwen's love life didn't interest me. "If you're going to the movies with Bonnie Sue,

I'd better hang up now. You be good, angel. And I miss you."

"I miss you, too." Then she said quickly, "Oh, I almost forgot. Did Judge Kendall wire you, or call?"

"No," I said, puzzled. "I haven't got any wire."

"Well, I'm glad I remembered, then. He called around noon and said something had come up in court and he couldn't get away today. But he said to tell you not to catch them all. He and Mrs. Kendall will be there sometime next week, he's not sure just what day—"

"Oh," I said. The chill spread upward along my back and then down my arms. I opened my mouth again. Nothing came out.

"What did you say, dear?" she asked.

I took a deep breath, and finally got control of my voice. "I—I mean, he doesn't know for sure just what day he'll get here?"

"No. It's a continuance or some legal what-you-call-it, but he's pretty sure he'll be able to make it sometime during the week."

"Okay," I said. "I'll call you tomorrow, angel."

She hung up. I put the phone back on the cradle and lighted a cigarette with shaking fingers. We were dead now. It was like holding a time bomb in your hands without knowing when it was set to go off. But it wouldn't do any good if I *did* know when he was coming, I thought. I couldn't deliberately avoid him; that would look too suspicious afterward. *Kendall?* I tried to think. He was mentioned on one of the tapes. District Judge—

I jumped to my feet. She hadn't left New York yet; I could still get hold of her. But I couldn't call from here. Not through that switchboard out there. I grabbed my hat and ran out to the car. Several blocks away I found a bar with a telephone booth. I got several-dollars worth of change from the bartender and ducked into it and asked for long distance.

"New York," I said. I gave her the name of the hotel. "Mrs. Marian Forsyth."

"One moment, sir."

The fan didn't work, and it was unbearably hot inside the booth. Sweat ran onto the lenses of my glasses. I could hear the hotel operator ringing the room. It went on and on—*five, six, seven*— God, had something happened to her.

"Hello?" Her voice sounded dead, as if she were drugged.

I deposited the money, and the operators got off the line.

"Listen, Marian—"

"What is it?" she asked. She was slightly more alert now. She knew something was wrong, or I wouldn't have called. Even that was risky.

"Are you all right?" I asked.

"Yes. I was just asleep. I took a pill."

"I'll hold on, if you want to go throw some cold water on your face." At least I could let her get fully awake before I hit her with it.

She came back in a minute. "All right," she said quietly.

I told her.

"Oh, no!"

"That's all she told me," I said, "and I didn't dare ask any questions, of course. So I don't know what it's all about, except that they're coming down here and apparently they're going fishing with me. How will it look if I seem to be avoiding them?"

"Bad," she said. "Very suspicious."

"He's important?"

"Yes. And she's even more so. She's one of the Riggs family, who own the new bank, the department store, and the Dodge and Plymouth agency. Both very social, stuffy, and proper, and the head of everything."

"We've got to figure out something, or we're sunk!"

"The first thing we've got to do is keep our heads," she said calmly. She was wonderful under pressure. "In the first place, they may not show up at all. And if they do come, it will be toward the end of the week—say, Friday or later—and it won't matter then how it looks if you've ducked out and they can't find you."

"But that still leaves a full week when they can explode in my face any minute—"

"No. If he couldn't get away today, it means he has something that needs his attention Monday, so the earliest they could possibly get there is Tuesday, even if they fly. So you're in the clear until then. And I'll be back in Thomaston on Saturday. I'll see what I can find out."

"We've got to have some way to communicate."

"I can get word to you. But don't try to call me at home; that's the only thing that's dangerous. So carry right on as if nothing had happened. I'll get in touch with you as soon as I know anything."

"All right," I said. "God, I miss you, and I'll be glad when this is over."

I hung up, and stepped out in the bar and had a double martini. A whole week of it, and it made my knees shaky just thinking of it. A tight rope? This was walking a tight violin string. I couldn't run and hide, and I wouldn't even recognize them. That is, not until they'd looked me in the face and started yelling for the police.

Well, there was no way to turn back now. The only way was straight ahead.

The next day I raised and landed a sail, but told Wilder to release it. It was Saturday, of course, so I didn't have to talk to Chris. I called Coral.

My nerves coiled and uncoiled while I waited for her to say something about the Kendalls, but she didn't even mention them. I finally asked, "Oh, by the way, have you heard when the Judge and Mrs. Kendall are leaving?"

"No," she said, "I haven't heard from him today. But I guess they'll try to get away Monday or Tuesday if they can. They're both looking forward to it."

To *what?* I wanted to yell at her.

I'd hardly hung up when the phone rang. It was Fitzpatrick. "Well, Mr. Chapman, how's the fishing been?"

"Not too bad," I said. "I released a six-foot sail today."

"Fine. I'm glad to hear it. But you want to come down in January sometime and hit 'em off Palm Beach when they're schooled up. Magnificent fishing. But I'll get right to what I called you for. The owner of that piece of highway frontage dropped by today and we talked about it a little. He didn't say so in so many words, but I've got a hunch he might be open to an offer."

"Hmmm," I said thoughtfully. "It'd take a lot of cash to swing a deal like that— What kind of financing did you say it had on it now?"

"One of the Miami banks has a first mortgage for $150,000. But I could almost guarantee that if you wanted to refinance, you could get two."

"And he's asking three seventy-five."

"That's right. But as I say, you can always try with an offer."

"I'll tell you what," I said. "I'm coming back to Miami tomorrow for a few days, and I'll keep it in mind."

"Good. Ah, where'll you be staying, Mr. Chapman?"

"Clive Hotel," I said.

Just after nine p.m. the phone rang again. It was the one I'd been waiting for. When I answered, the operator said, "I have a long-distance call from Brindon, Louisiana."

"Go ahead," I said.

"Hello," she said quietly. "I'm calling from a pay phone here. Judge and Mrs. Kendall left for Miami Beach at three this afternoon—"

"What?" I asked. "I just talked to Coral, and she said—"

"You can't always depend on her information. They're flying from New Orleans, so they'll arrive in Miami sometime tonight. They're going to be at the Eden Roc Hotel. It's just a vacation trip, but they were planning originally to fish with you today if they'd got away on time—"

"But they'll still try to get in touch with me?"

"Yes. I won't try to minimize it. It's a highly dangerous situation now. You simply *have* to remain in touch with the Blaine girl, so they can always find out where you are. They know, of course, that you still have fishing reservations on the 21st, 22nd, and 23rd, so they may want to go on one of those days. Cancel those, and get the word to Coral Blaine as soon as you can. That will help, if she can remember it in case they call her. You were going to cancel them anyway, on account of the real-estate deal, so it doesn't require any change in plan. If the Kendalls merely call you, you're safe. But if they come to the hotel looking for you, you're just going to have to play it by ear, and pray. I'll give you a description of them—"

"Yes, for God's sake."

"He's around fifty-five, almost six feet tall, and very thin. Actually, bony or gaunt would be nearer it. White hair, blue eyes. Rather harsh face. She's almost as thin and has white hair, and the last time I saw her it had a bluish tinge, though there's no telling what it is now. Very glacial manner, and hard gray eyes."

I sighed. "I'll do my best."

"Just don't let them corner you anywhere. And don't lose your nerve."

"Oh, baby," I said. "Keep your fingers crossed."

We fished until shortly after noon the next day and came in. I checked out of the motel around two-thirty and drove to Miami. The Clive was a large hotel on Biscayne Boulevard and very convenient to everything downtown. The doorman called the garage to send a man after the car. I followed the boy in to the desk, and when I asked for my reservation the airmail special from Webster & Adcock was waiting for me. I slit it open and looked at the check for $25,000. This was just the first trickle, to break the dike.

After I'd registered, I stepped over to the cashier's window and cashed three more of the traveler's checks. There was no use letting them go to waste, and I was going to need plenty of cash before I was through. I went up to the room. It was one of the expensive ones, looking out over the waterfront park and the bay. As soon as the boy was gone, I put through the call to Coral Blaine. As Marian had said, I had to keep her informed as to where I was. And it was time, too, to give her the first little nudge.

CHAPTER TEN

"I'm back in Miami, angel," I said. "At least, for the next few days."

She was in a kittenish mood tonight. "I just hope you're behavin' yourself."

"I am," I said. "As a matter of fact, I'm working. That real-estate deal with Fitzpatrick. And by the way; I'm going to cancel those other three days' fishing; I'll be too busy."

"The Judge and Mrs. Kendall are going to be disappointed. Incidentally, they finally got away Saturday, and they're in Miami Beach now. They'll be trying to get in touch with you, and if they call here I'll tell them where you are."

"Yes," I said. "Do that. You don't know where they're staying?"

"No, I didn't hear."

"Well, we'll get together. Oh, say, I saw Marian Forsyth on the street this afternoon. Did you know she was in Miami?"

"You *couldn't* have. Dear, she's right here in Thomaston."

"Well, I know you said she was coming back. But are you sure? I could have sworn this was her. She went past in a car."

She became considerably cooler. "Maybe you just miss her, Harris. Or you're thinking about her."

"Cut it out, Coral. You know better than that. The only thing I'm thinking about her is that I don't trust her. But you're *positive* she's there?"

"Of course, dear. I saw her myself, just this morning."

"Well, you watch out for her. She's probably spreading lies behind my back. By God, what does she want; didn't I offer her half a year's pay?"

"Darling," she said wearily, "you've been more than fair with her. But do we *have* to talk about Mrs. Forsyth?"

"Of course not, honey. And I'm sorry. It was just somebody that looked like her."

After we'd hung up, I got Fitzpatrick's card out of the wallet and called him at his home phone. I caught him in. "Chapman," I said. "You remember—?"

"Oh, yes, Mr. Chapman. How are you?"

"Just fine. I was hoping you could help me out with something. I want to open an account in a local bank, and wondered if you could recommend one. I thought you might have connections."

"I sure have. The Seaboard First National. Go in and see John Dakin. He's the Assistant Cashier, and a good friend of mine. I'll call him as soon as they open in the morning."

"Thanks a million."

"You given any more thought to that piece of frontage we were looking at?"

"Well, yes," I said. "As a matter of fact, I drove up that way this afternoon, when I came up from the Keys."

"You're at the Clive now?"

"That's right."

"I'll be glad to drive down and talk it over with you in a little more detail. Unless you're busy, that is."

"No," I replied. "I'm not doing anything this evening. I might be in the dining room, but I'll leave word at the desk."

"Fine," he said. "I'll see you in about forty-five minutes."

The dining room was just dim enough. He was one of the people they'd be pretty sure to question afterward, or at any rate one of the shrewdest. I couldn't take too many chances with him. The other time I'd been wearing the dark glasses except for the few minutes in his office when I first met him. He wouldn't get much of a look at me here, and this was the last time I'd see him. I took a table for two along the wall, and was just finishing the soup when he came in. I stood up and we shook hands. "I forgot to ask if you'd had dinner."

"Yes, thanks, I've had mine."

"Well, have a drink, anyway." I beckoned the waiter over. He ordered bourbon and water. We talked real estate in general for a few minutes. The waiter brought my entree. I'd ordered roast beef. There was gravy on it.

"No, no," I said. "I don't want all that gravy on it, waiter. Would you change that, please?"

"Yes, sir, of course."

He departed. "I don't know why they ruin meat that way," I said to Fitzpatrick. "All that damned grease to give you indigestion."

"Yes," he said easily. "I know exactly what you mean."

We'd just resumed out conversation when the waiter came back with the new order of roast beef. I looked at it, and then at him, and shook my head. "We don't seem to get together at all. I don't like to create an international incident, but I'm positive I said all outside slices, well done."

"Yes, sir." He was silently raging now, but he took it away again.

I addressed Fitzpatrick. "Sorry to create a fuss, but by God, the prices you pay, the least you can do is get what you order."

He smiled. "That's an attitude more people should have."

I ate some of the dinner, and ordered coffee for myself and another bourbon for Fitzpatrick. While we were waiting for it to come, I took one of Chapman's pill-bottles from my pocket, shook out a pill, and swallowed it with some water. I had no idea what it was, but it probably wouldn't hurt me. Then I stuck a cigarette in the holder and lighted it.

The drinks came. "All right, let's get right to the point," I said. "I want to make an offer on that piece of frontage. $325,000. Will you submit that?"

"Yes."

"Okay," I said. "Here's the deal. I'm on vacation, of course, and all I have with me is traveler's checks. I can't give you a check on my bank at home, but I called my broker in New Orleans on Friday and told him to send me some money. It just came." I took out the Webster & Adcock envelope and dropped it on the table. "As soon as I open that account in the morning, I'll give you a check for $5,000 to submit with the offer. Could you have one of your men pick it up here at the hotel?"

"Of course. We'd be glad to."

"Good. Tell the owner if he's really interested in a deal he'd better let me know tomorrow, because if he accepts I've got to raise the balance of the $170,000 cash to complete the transaction. I don't want to call off my vacation to go home and raise it, but it happens I can swing it by liquidating securities in my account with Webster & Adcock, and I can do that by telephone. It'll take a few days for my deposits to clear New Orleans, of course, but it'll still be the simplest way to handle it."

He nodded. "That would be fine all around."

I stood up. "Okay, then. You can have somebody pick up my check here at the desk around ten-thirty in the morning. And call me right away when you hear from the owner."

I went back up to the room. All this jockeying around with offers was a nuisance, and it was going to cost us $5,000, but for purposes of verisimilitude it was absolutely essential. I mentally went over our timetable. We were right on schedule, and doing beautifully. It was time now to start lining up the girl.

I went out and took a cab, and told the driver I was alone in town and wanted to see some of the night life. He had nothing better to offer than a cheap night club. I had a drink, and departed in another cab. The driver of this one had a more sophisticated outlook, or fewer scruples. He looked over my identification. I voiced some preferences. He drove me back to the hotel, and I gave him my room number.

It was around ten-thirty when she knocked on the door.

She wouldn't do at all; I could see that within the first ten minutes. She was dark and rather pretty, particularly with her clothes off, but she was a good-natured, somewhat unimaginative girl with no particular tensions or any animosity toward anything or anybody. She was lazy, the hours were good, and she earned considerably more than the average nuclear physicist. And she'd lived around Miami for years, and was crazy about it. She was out.

I completed the transaction with her, more as a gesture of conformity than from any particular interest in her, gave her the fifty dollars she asked for, added ten more for no reason that I could think of, and she left. I'd have to try again tomorrow.

I awoke around seven, went through that first terrible instant of remembering that left me sick and shaking, and then tried to appraise it clinically to see if it was any better or worse than on preceding mornings. It appeared to be about the same. Well, it would go away in time.

I had coffee and orange juice sent up, and put in an hour's practice on the signature. From now on, it was dangerous. The traveler's checks didn't mean anything; nobody ever bothered to look at the signatures unless they'd been reported stolen. But this was a bank, and banks were notoriously touchy on the subject of forgery. Then I reminded myself I was being needlessly scared.

As she had pointed out, the only thing I was going to forge, aside from a receipt which would be filed without a glance, was the *endorsement* of a check. And as long as there was no question it was the payee who had cashed it, who would even look at it?

It went off without a hitch: I arrived at the bank shortly after it opened, and inquired for Dakin. He was at one of the desks behind a railing at one end of the main lobby, a nervous, self-consciously hearty, and overworked man who couldn't have described me ten minutes later if I'd been wearing a monocle and a sharpened bone through my nose.

"Oh, yes. Yes. Mr.—" His eyes swept toward the memo pad to verify his old friend's name. "Mr. Fitzpatrick called. Glad to have you as a depositor, Mr. Chapman. And we know you'll like Miami."

I filled out the form, signed two copies of the signature card, endorsed the check, and gave it to him. He carried it off to one of the tellers' windows and returned with my deposit receipt and a checkbook. He assured me it wouldn't take over three or four days for it to clear New Orleans. I went back to the hotel, wrote out a check for $5,000, borrowed an envelope from the cashier, and left it at the desk to be delivered to anybody from Fitzpatrick Realty.

Up in the room again, I got out the list of securities, opened the *Herald* to yesterday's closing stock prices, and made a rough outline of what to sell. It would just about clean out the account; there'd be less than $12,000 left in it. I was just reaching for the phone to put through the call to New Orleans when there was a light knock on the door.

I tensed up. *The Kendalls?* But, God, they wouldn't come up to a hotel room without calling from the lobby, would they? Crossing to the door, I asked, "Who is it?"

"Friend," a feminine voice said. But it was a young voice. I sighed with relief, and opened the door slightly to peer out. It was a big blond girl swinging a white purse. "Oh," she said, and smiled. "Sorry. Wrong room."

"Quite all right," I replied. I went back and put in the call to Chris.

"Hello, Chris? Chapman—"

"Oh, good morning, Mr. Chapman. I see Warwick opened at 2 1/2 again this morning, so we may not—"

"Never mind that," I cut in brusquely. "It's chicken feed. I'm on my way now on that deal I told you about—oh, incidentally, the $25,000 was here when I checked in at the Clive last night. Thanks a million. I opened an account and deposited it this morning. The deal's going through at my price, beyond any shadow of doubt, so I'm going to need $150,000 within the next few days. You got my list handy, and a pencil?"

"Yes, sir. But—"

I paid no attention. "Sell the Columbia Gas, the PG&E, that Du Pont Preferred, Champion Paper Preferred, and the AT&T. That should be pretty close to a hundred thousand. Now, let's see—"

"But, Mr. Chapman, those are all good, sound, defensive issues. I hate to see you sell them."

"What?" I asked absently. Then I did a take, and barked into the phone. "Goddammit, Chris, I'm not interested in being on the defensive. There's no way to stand still in this economy; you keep going ahead, or you're eaten alive by ducks. Let's face it. The bull market's dead, and I'm not interested in making four cents in dividends and giving three of them to the Government. I want to make money; and right now Florida real estate's the place to make it, not in the stock market. When the market starts to move again, I'll get back in, but for now I'm going to put that money to work."

"Yes, sir," he said. He didn't like it, but there was nothing he could do about it. We went on with the list.

"All right," I concluded. "The largest block in there is a thousand shares. You can unload it all in an hour without even a ripple. Get the check off to me as early as you can this afternoon, registered airmail, care the Clive Hotel, so I'll have it by the time the banks open in the morning. It's going to take several days to clear. Got it?"

"Yes. I have it all."

"Fine," I said. "G'by." I hung up, and breathed softly with relief.

That much of it was past now; the Chris phase was complete, and he'd never suspected a thing. It called for a drink, in spite of the hour. I was just pouring it when the phone rang. It was Fitzpatrick.

He was in high spirits. "Well, Mr. Chapman, it looks as if you've got yourself a deal. I talked to the owner a few minutes ago, and I think he's about ready to accept."

"Fine," I said. "I'm raising the money now."

A woman's voice cut in on the line. "Mr. Chapman, I'm sorry to interrupt. This is the hotel switchboard—"

"Yes?" I asked.

"We have a very urgent long-distance call from Thomaston, Louisiana."

"Oh." I didn't like the sound of that at all. "I mean—put it on."

"Harris! Thank God they located you." It was Coral Blaine. "I've been trying for over an hour, but I'd forgotten what hotel you said. This whole place is in an uproar—"

"What is it?" I broke in.

"We've got to have the combination of that old safe, and you're the only one who knows it. Barbara says you've got it written down somewhere in your office, but we can't find it."

I could feel the whole thing caving away beneath us, but I had to try. "Get hold of yourself!" I snapped. "What old safe are you talking about? And what's happened?"

"Harris! That dumb safe that was moved out of here about six months ago when you bought the new one. It was stored in the warehouse, remember? And just before you left you told Mr. Elkins to sell it to the junk yard...."

Someone knocked on the door.

"... Well, yesterday afternoon he and some more men moved it outside onto the loading platform, but the junk man forgot to pick it up. It was unlocked. And this morning about eight-thirty, some first-graders on the way to school—"

I could feel myself growing sick. "Oh, Jesus, not that!"

"No," she interrupted. "Not one of the children. A dog. Judy Weaver's miniature poodle—"

My knees bent, and I sat down. "Well, don't tell me the whole goddamn town—"

There was another knock on the door.

"Harris! Will you *please* stop swearing! That silly girl is practically out of her mind. They've got her under a sedative now, but when she wakes up she'll start all over again. The Humane Society is driving me crazy. Mrs. Weaver says they're going to sue you. Everybody in town is simply furious, and people have been calling up here until I'm ready to scream. Some machine shop has drilled a hole in the safe so the stupid dog can breathe, but they can't get him out. The New Orleans papers are calling up. Barbara says you've got the combination—"

Maybe it would help, I thought bitterly, if she told me that again. Whoever it was in the corridor was banging on the door again. I had to get away from that voice and try to think.

"Hold it," I said. "Somebody's at the door."

I put down the phone and answered it. It was a bellman. "Telegram, sir," he said. I handed him a coin of some kind, and took it.

I closed the door and leaned against it. We'd had it for real now. It wasn't on the tapes; I knew that. I'd been through everything in the wallet and the bags. The little address book! I grabbed it out of my pocket and flipped madly through it. Nothing but addresses.

I looked at the phone lying on the desk. This was the way it ended. You learned everything there was to learn, you took care of every contingency, you memorized, you rehearsed—and then some kid locked a dog in a safe a thousand miles away and you were done.

I still had the telegram in my hand. Through the little glassine window I could see some figures, and the word Brindon.

Brindon!

I slashed it open and stared at the text.

> R32 STOP L2 SLANT 19 STOP R3 SLANT 6 REPEAT R32 ... TAPED BENEATH PENCIL DRAWER.

I sighed, and pushed myself off the door on watery knees. Picking up the phone and holding it a little way from my face, I said, "Sit down, be right with you, as soon as I deal with this crisis."

I spoke into it. "Coral? You there? That combination is taped to the bottom of the pencil drawer in my desk. But, hold on, I'll give it to you. Write this down—right to thirty-two, left two turns to nineteen, and right three turns to six."

"Thank heavens—"

I interrupted crisply. "One of you go see Mrs. Weaver right away and see if you can smooth this over. Mrs. English, maybe; she's good with people. Buy Judy the biggest stuffed toy you can find, one of those thirty-five dollar jobs. And Coral, I hate to be crabby, honey, but I'm working on a real big deal down here—"

"Darling, I am sorry about it."

When I'd hung up I went over and lay down on the bed. I could have used a drink, but I doubted I could pour it. She'd heard about the uproar and driven to Brindon again to send the telegram, probably from a pay phone. I closed my eyes, and I could see her so vividly it hurt. When they made her, I thought, they made only one.

It wasn't only that she'd saved us this time; she'd put the thing on ice once and for all. I could make mistakes by the dozen from now on and it wouldn't matter in the slightest. Only Chapman could have known that combination.

I stayed away from the hotel and sweated out the day. There was no call from the Kendalls.

Her name sounded like something dreamed up by a cheap press-agent. Justine La Ray. Not that it mattered. What did matter was that I was sure I'd found what I was looking for.

She knocked on the door around eleven p.m., and when she came in she sized me up, appraised the luggage and the fat wallet lying on the dresser—all in one glance and without even appearing to—and gave me a bright smile that promised unimaginable ecstasies and almost concealed the contempt she felt for any jerk who couldn't get a woman without buying one.

It would be a hundred dollars, honey. And when I fatuously agreed to this overcharge it merely increased her contempt. I was sweet, and much better-looking than a lot of those fat expense-account creeps—Ugh! Not that she'd ever done much of this of course. She was really in show business. A song stylist.

"That right?" I said heartily. I slapped her on the behind. "We're going to get along fine, sweetie. I always like people with talent. Never had any myself, except for making money. And women."

It might have been a little cruder than usual, but she'd heard the tune. "You don't mind giving me the money now, do you?"

"Hell, no." I waved a hand toward the wallet. "Take it out of there. Why not take two while you're at it, and stay all night? Hell, if you don't get it the Government will, and they don't even kiss me. I'll mix us a little drink, huh?"

I'd been cashing the traveler's checks at a steady rate, and the wallet held close to three thousand dollars now. The rest of the checks were lying beside it.

"You know, I just might do that," she said archly. She took four fifties from the wallet.

She was around twenty-five, a rather slender girl with nice teeth, short dark hair, and eyes that were almost black. There was nothing of the Latin about her, however. Her skin was dead white, and the eyes were cold. I put ice and Scotch in two glasses and set them on the dresser.

"Come on, sweetie, get out of those hot, sticky clothes and into a cold highball. You still got to meet the credentials committee."

We went to bed. I'd had more fun in dentists' offices. She probably had, too; but at least she was being paid to endure it. If she drank enough, she might talk about herself.

"You'd never think I was thirty-nine years old, would you?" I said. "Come on, you'd have said thirty-two, wouldn't you? Hit me in the stomach. Hell, go on; hit me ..."

I'd gone to Notre Dame. No, I didn't play football. I didn't have to; my old man had plenty of money. But don't think I was one of those pantywaists that had it all given to 'em. I made it myself. Radio stations, newspapers, real estate. I was going to be around here at least a week, on a real-estate deal. Stick with me, if you can stand the pace, and we'll have a ball. Feel the muscles in that stomach, Marian. Like the old washboard, huh?

She drank; she had to, to stand me. She began to get a little tight.

Miami, hah! And Miami Beach. Brother, you could have 'em. Vegas was for her. Or L.A. She could go to work tomorrow. Did I know she was a song stylist? The breaks she'd had in this place. That agent of hers—Hah! this was an agent? He couldn't book Crosby. And that roommate running off with three of her best dresses. Imagine, stealing from another working girl ...

Hey, where you get this Marian routine? My name's Justine. I already tolja that three times already. Sure, you called me Marian. Three times, for Chrissakes. Whatta you carryin' a torch, or something? Look, don't call me Marian, Sweetie, or Hey You. I got a name just like anybody else. And you use it, buster. You think I'm some cheap tramp that you just grunt or point or something and hand me ten bucks and I fall over ...

In the morning she gave me her telephone number so we could eliminate the middleman. I gave her an extra fifty.

"You call me, honey," she said, putting on lipstick and giving me an arch glance. I was a crude, repulsive, egocentric blow-hard who couldn't even remember her name, and she detested me, but oddly enough I seemed to have nearly as much money as I boasted I had, and I threw it around.

The registered airmail from Webster & Adcock arrived at nine-thirty. I slit it open, and looked at the check for $150,000. Five minutes after the bank opened, I endorsed it, wrote out a deposit slip, and added it to the account. Now I could get out of Miami and off this live bomb for two days anyway.

Back at the hotel, I called Fitzpatrick. He'd already notified me yesterday afternoon that the owner had accepted the offer.

"Chapman," I said now. "I just received the money from my broker, and deposited it. I'll be able to give you a check for $170,000 by Friday. Or Monday, at the latest. I'll be out of town for a couple of days, but I'll be back before the end of the week."

I called Chris next and told him the check had arrived and that I'd deposited it. He was cool, but polite. I was still a client, if a rather shrunken one. Then I put through a call to Captain Wilder in Marathon and canceled the balance of the fishing reservations.

Coral Blaine was next. She started to tell me of some trouble at the radio station. There'd been an FCC violation. I cut her off. I was in the saddle now.

"Tell Wingard to take care of it," I said shortly. "Authorize him to order anything he needs. I'm up to my ears in this real-estate deal. And I'm on my way to Naples right now to look into a proposition over there."

"But you'll call and let me know where you are?"

"Sure, angel. So aside from the FCC, everything's serene there? No more dogs locked in safes?"

She laughed sheepishly. "I am sorry about that. Wasn't it the silliest thing?"

"It could have been serious as hell. And I'm not so sure it was an accident, either." The dog thing had been a break we hadn't counted on, but it was too good to waste.

"Harris, what do you mean? Of course it was an accident."

"Maybe. But, look— Suppose somebody was trying to cut my throat? Give me a bad name, and make me lose advertisers? A thing like that could ruin me—people going around saying Chapman's a sonofabitch that'd leave an unlocked safe around where kids can play in it. And suppose she'd locked one of the *kids* in it—I mean, instead of just a dog."

"Harris, what on earth are you talking about?"

"Oh, I guess it's silly," I said, abruptly changing tone. "Well, angel, I'll call you later."

"Oh—before I forget, Judge Kendall called from Miami Beach this morning wanting to know where you were staying. They're at the Eden Roc. You can get in touch with him there."

"I'll call him," I said. I hung up, and sighed.

I hurriedly finished packing and called the cashier's office to get my bill ready, and asked to have the car brought around and the bags picked up. Down in the lobby the public stenographer addressed an envelope for me, and I signed the two receipts for Webster & Adcock and enclosed them.

The cashier's window adjoined the main desk. I went over and bought a stamp, and asked for my bill. "And would you cash an extra traveler's check for me?" I asked the girl.

She smiled. "Yes, sir. We'd be glad to."

I unsnapped the folder and was signing them when someone said, "Mr. Chapman?" I glanced up, about to reply, and then went limp all over with fear.

It was the desk clerk, but he wasn't speaking to me. He was addressing Judge and Mrs. Kendall, who were standing about three feet to my left.

Even in the slow congealing of horror, I knew there was no mistake. They were both tall, spare, white-haired, and austere, and dressed in expensive resort clothes.

"Just a moment, sir," the clerk said. "I'll see if he's in." He checked his key rack, and picked up the phone.

I couldn't run, even if my muscles would work. The cashier might call after me, thinking I had forgotten my change. I couldn't give her some excuse and leave; the Kendalls would hear my voice. I stood rooted. The girl went on running up my bill on the machine.

"I'm sorry, sir," the clerk said. "Mr. Chapman doesn't appear to be in."

God, maybe they would go away now—

"I'd like to leave a message," the Judge said.

The clerk put a pad before him, and he leaned over it to write. Mrs. Kendall turned then, and glanced incuriously at me. She saw the traveler's checks, still on the ledge in front of me. Each of them was signed Harris Chapman in two places. Somehow I got my hand on them and pushed them through the window.

"Oh, Horace, I forgot to cash that check before we left the hotel," she said. "I'll do it now, while you're writing the note." She stepped over beside me, and opened her purse. I moved to one side of the window, praying the cashier would take care of her before finishing the bill. But she still had to sign it.

I wondered if I weren't beginning to go slightly crazy now. A jumble of disconnected and idiotic thoughts ran through my mind. Always address the guest by name. Especially when you've got it right in front of you. It feeds his self-esteem. And he'll be sure to come back again. Only if that cashier called me Mr. Chapman, this was one time they were wrong.

Mrs. Kendall spread open her traveler's checks and started signing one, right at my elbow.

The cashier looked up and smiled at me. "Were there any charges this morning? Breakfast, or anything?"

The crazy thoughts went on. Go ahead, answer the girl.

I shook my head at her. It seemed unfair of them, somehow, to expect me to go to the electric chair just so they'd be paid for a couple of long-distance telephone calls.

Mrs. Kendall finished signing her check and stood waiting.

The cashier pushed my receipted bill and the change across to me. She smiled. "Here you are. We hope you'll come back. And thank you very much—"

I wondered if people under the guillotine listened for the blade.

"—sir."

CHAPTER ELEVEN

There was a big parking lot at the end of Biscayne Boulevard, only a few blocks from the hotel. I made it that far, pulled into a space, lighted a cigarette, and slowly uncoiled. I was too limp to drive, and I had to kill time somewhere until they got back to the Eden Roc. By the grace of God I'd got out from under the gun this time, but leaving town now without calling them would look suspicious as hell afterward.

I could phone and leave a message, but that wouldn't be the same thing. They had to *know* it was Harris Chapman who'd called. Then if I were lucky enough to avoid them for the rest of the week it could still look all right.

If— I thought of standing there with the old dragon breathing on the side of my face while she endorsed her check, and shuddered. I couldn't ever go through that again; my nerves would crack and they'd have to put me in a strait jacket.

After about a half hour I started slowly out of town on the Tamiami Trail. Just before I got out of the city limits I parked near a drugstore and hunted up the phone booth. It was almost noon. I called the Clive first, and picked up the message. The Kendalls were looking forward to seeing me, and still hoped we could go fishing one day if I could get free. We could have dinner together one night. Give them a call at the Eden Roc.

They were up in their room. The Judge answered. "Judge? This is Harris Chapman. I just got your note a while ago, and I'm sorry as the devil I missed you."

"Yes, we were quite disappointed." He had a cool, precise voice, with only a trace of Southern accent. "We were hoping to take you to lunch, and remind you of that fishing trip you owe us, young man."

I told him I was on my way to Naples to look at some property, but that I'd be back, I hoped, by Thursday. Maybe we could get together then.

We certainly would. They were going to take me to dinner.

When I arrived in Naples I checked in at a motel, and then visited a few real-estate offices, introducing myself and making inquiries but not staying long. I plugged in the recorder, and began erasing the tapes, since I knew I didn't need them anymore, running them through the machine on *RECORD* with the gain turned down. It was a slow process. I finished three of them.

Around ten that night I was sitting at the bar in a very dimly lighted cocktail lounge. Among the eight or ten customers at the tables behind me was a dark-haired girl in her late twenties. She was sitting at a table with a big man in a Shetland sport coat. I watched them from time to time in the mirror. After a while her escort excused himself and went to the men's room. I stuck a cigarette in the holder, lighted it, and got off the stool as if to go out. Then I saw her, and stopped. I walked over to her table.

"What are you doing here?" I said angrily. "Why don't you leave me alone?"

She was too amazed even to speak. People nearby turned and stared.

"Look, Marian!" I went on, beginning to shout. "I know the lies you're spreading behind my back, but you're wasting your time! Everybody knows I was fair. I was more than fair—"

She had recovered now. "What's the matter with you?" she asked coldly. "I never saw you before in my life."

The bartender was on his way; and so was her escort, just emerging from the john. I straightened and looked blankly around, and then at her. "Oh," I said in confusion. "I—uh—I'm sorry. I thought you were somebody else."

Her escort wanted to swing at me, but the bartender broke it up. He put his hand on my shoulder in friendly fashion and we walked to the door. "Easy does it, Jack." Just as the door was closing, I heard him say to someone at the end of the bar. "Mother dear. You never know. I'd have sworn he was cold sober."

I killed the next day in Fort Myers, still looking forward with dread to Miami. But I had to go back, Kendalls or no Kendalls. I erased the rest of the tapes so I could dispose of them. Even if they were ever found, they'd be harmless.

I called Coral Blaine, and told her I'd probably be home a little ahead of schedule. "The minute I clean up that real-estate deal on Monday, I'm going to start back."

"That's wonderful, darling."

"I wonder if I ought to hire detectives to watch her?" I asked.

"Watch who?" she asked, puzzled.

"Marian Forsyth, of course!" I said angrily. "Don't you know she's up to something? She's dreamed up some kind of wrong she thinks I've done her, and there's no telling what she'll do."

"Dear," she broke in wearily. "Could we stop talking about Marian Forsyth? I'm sick of her."

Late that night I threw the blank tapes and the recorder into the Caloosahatchee River. Shortly after noon on Thursday I was back in Miami, and as soon as I had registered at the Clive I called Justine La

Ray. It had finally occurred to me how to protect myself from the Kendalls.

She was glad to hear from me, and came right over, shortly after three p.m. Chumps of my caliber didn't come along every day, and she was beginning to get bigger ideas. She didn't ask for the money in advance this time, and she did a better job of hiding her contempt and being professionally gay in the face of my crudities and oafish bragging about money, sexual prowess, and stomach muscles.

It now appeared that this crummy roommate had stolen all her clothes.

"I could go back to work in night clubs tomorrow if I had the wardrobe," she said, lying naked in bed with the highball glass and a cigarette. "But, God, you got no idea, honey, what those gowns cost—"

"Where's the strain?" I asked. "Hell, at a hundred bucks a jump—"

She was very brave about it. She never told anybody, as a rule, but I was so, well, understanding— There was her little boy, see. Oh, yes, she'd been married. And this lousy bas— Her husband had died, that is, after a long and expensive illness ...

The Carthaginian B-girls had probably used more or less the same version during the Punic wars. "Gee, that's rough," I said. "And he doesn't even know? I mean, all the money you send him at that school, he thinks you're a big-shot singer. Well, how about that?"

"So if I can just get back on my feet—"

"You stick with me, Marian," I said expansively. "Maybe we'll do something about that gown business. Maybe tomorrow, huh, if I get a couple of free minutes."

I'd bought a fresh bottle of Scotch, and kept filling her glass. She began to get tight, and climbed me again about calling her Marian. It was a little after five now, and I kept listening for the phone.

It rang at a quarter of six. It was on a stand beside the bed, and I reached out for it without getting up. It was not only the Kendalls, it was *Mrs*. Kendall.

"How fortunate," she said, every inch the small-town social leader. "We were hoping you might have returned."

"I just got back this afternoon," I replied. "And I was about to call and see if you and the Judge would have dinner with me."

"No, you must dine with us, Mr. Chapman. Here at the Eden Roc." It was a command performance.

"Wonderful," I said. "Let's see— Right at the moment I'm in the middle of a whole sea of paper work on that real-estate deal, but I should have that wrapped up in another half hour, so—" I made as if to sit up.

The glass I had in my other hand tilted down and slopped whisky and ice cubes onto Justine's bare stomach.

She squealed. "Chrissakes, watch whatcha doin'! Pourin' your goddam drink all over my belly—!"

"Shhhhh!" I hissed frantically. I swung the drink again, as it trying to cover the phone with that hand, and spilled some more. She cursed again. When I put the receiver back to my ear, the line was dead. I asked the operator to get the Eden Roc for me, and after seven rings she finally picked item.

"Hello," I said. "I think we were cut—"

I looked at the dead instrument, and dropped it back on the cradle. If I ever ran into the Kendalls again it would be nothing but sheer accident.

In the morning I gave Justine three hundred dollars, slapped her on the rear, and winked. "We got to stab Uncle for a little business expense some way, don't we, kid?"

Sure, I still had her phone number. And if I got a chance I'd pick her up and we'd go shopping.

I checked out of the hotel, had the car brought around and the bags loaded, and drove over to Miami Beach. I left it in a parking lot six or eight blocks away, and walked to the apartment. It was hot and intensely still with the air-conditioner turned off. The minute I stepped into the room where we'd spent so many hours, she was all around me, as if the slender elegance, and color, and grace of movement were physical things that could reverberate in an empty room like sound waves and keep echoing long after the person who had set them in motion was gone.

I tried not to look at the water-stained spot on the rug.

Changing into slacks and a sport shirt, I left off the glasses and the hat, picked up my own wallet, walked back to Collins Avenue, and took a cab to Miami. At another car rental agency I rented a pickup truck, using my own name and driver's license, and took off for the Keys. On the way out of town I watched closely for that roadside curio place where I'd stopped before so I'd have its exact location fixed in my mind.

It was a long way down the small keys and interminable bridges of the Overseas Highway. On Sugarloaf Key, some one hundred thirty miles from Miami, there was a back-country road that took off through the mangroves and salt ponds and ran along an outer line of small keys parallel to the highway. It was a wild area with practically no houses and plenty of places a car could be hidden.

Shortly after two p.m. I found just the spot I wanted, and checked the mileage back to the nearest bus stop on the highway. I started back. Just before three, I stopped at a roadside place on Big Pine Key and called the bank. Everything was all right. Both my deposits had been collected.

All I had to do was write a check Monday morning for $170,000. We were ready to wind it up.

It was after dark when I got back to Miami Beach. I put the pickup truck in the garage at the apartment, changed back into Chapman's suit and the glasses and hat, and went over and picked up the Cadillac. I drove to Hollywood and checked in at the Antilles Motel. It was one of those I'd spotted before, an older type built when land was cheaper, with carport spaces between the units. It sat back off the street on US 1 not too far from the center of town.

The woman in the office was a spry and chatty type of about fifty. I signed the registry card, and told her I'd be there three or four days at least. I was working on a real-estate deal, with Fitzpatrick. Oh, yes, she knew the firm. They were quite nice. I paid her for three days, and said I'd like a unit as far back as possible, away from the highway noise. She took me back to the next to the last unit in the right-hand row. It would do nicely, I said. In addition to the front door, there was a side door opening into the carport. The bath was a combination tub-and-shower arrangement, with a curtain rod and plastic curtain. There was a telephone. I asked her what time she closed the switchboard in the office.

"Eleven p.m." she said.

The next morning I stopped at the office on the way out. She was talking to the maid. When the maid left, I asked quietly, after a glance behind me at the door, "Is there a woman registered here who has real blue-black hair, worn in a chignon? A slender woman, in her thirties?"

"Why, no," she said, puzzled. "Why?"

"I just wanted to be sure," I said. "If she checks in, don't tell her I asked, but let me know right away."

"Yes, of course," she said uncertainly. "Could you give me her name?"

"Oh, she wouldn't be using her right name," I said. "She's far too clever for that."

I had some breakfast in town, and drove up to Palm Beach. In a hardware store I bought a two-foot steel wrecking bar. I put it in the trunk, and came back to Fort Lauderdale. I cashed several of the checks in a bank, and one in a bar. I sat in the bar for four hours, nursing three drinks, staring straight ahead at nothing and speaking to no one.

At last the bartender became concerned. "Are you all right, mister?" he asked.

I turned my head slightly and stared at him. "What do you mean, am

I all right?"

"I thought maybe you didn't feel well, you're so quiet."

"Well, I'm all right," I said. "And don't you forget it."

"I'm sorry I bothered you—"

"Maybe I have to have a basal metabolism and a blood count before I can drink in your goddamn bar, is that it? Or you want me to take a Rorschach?"

"Okay, okay, forget it."

I went on muttering after he retreated, and got up and stalked out.

Around eight p.m. I registered in a motel in the outskirts of town, lay on the bed with my clothes on until nearly ten, and then grabbed up the phone and called the office. "Will you, for Christ's sake, stop that stupid phonograph?"

The manager was puzzled. "What phonograph? Where is it?"

"I don't know," I said angrily. "Somewhere back here. If only they'd stop playing that same goddamn record over and over and over— Never mind! I'll go somewhere else."

He was standing in the driveway shaking his head as I shot past him in the Cadillac.

I drove down to Miami and called Coral Blaine from a pay phone at two a.m. She was somewhat piqued—she'd been worried, and I'd got her out of bed.

"You haven't called since Thursday night, and when I tried to reach you at the Clive Hotel they said you'd checked out."

"I've been moving around," I said.

"There've been several things at the office. The bank—"

"Never mind the office," I said. "Do you still see Marian Forsyth around there?"

"Somewhere, practically every day. But, dear, do we have to start on *her* again?"

"Tell me something. Do you ever speak to her?"

"No. She never speaks to me. Why should I?"

"Clever," I said, as if talking to myself. "Oh, she's clever."

"What did you say, darling?"

"Oh," I said. "Nothing. But, look, angel, I'll wind up this real-estate deal Monday morning, and be home sometime Tuesday."

I drove back to the motel in Hollywood and went to bed.

The next morning I drove down to Miami Beach, parked the Cadillac in the business area not too far from Dover Way, left the hat and glasses in it, and walked to the apartment. I changed to khaki fishing clothes and cap, backed the pickup out of the garage, and headed for the

Keys. It was one-thirty p.m. when I reached the turnoff onto the back road on Sugarloaf. Since it was Sunday, fishermen were rather numerous, pulling boats behind their cars or casting from the bridges. Three miles from the highway there was a dim trace of a road leading off to the left through heavy scrub where the water's edge was a tangle of mangroves. The mangroves thinned out after about a mile, giving way to small open areas where boats could be launched. Several cars with empty boat trailers were parked in the vicinity, but there were no people around at the moment. I parked the truck off to one side, locked it, and started walking back.

I came out onto the secondary road, and in a short while a man and his wife stopped and picked me up. They had fishing tackle in the car. I told them the battery was dead in my car and I was going out to the highway to pick up a new one. They dropped me at the filling station and general store. I drank a can of beer and read the Sunday papers until the Key West–Miami bus came through. When I got off at the Greyhound terminal in Miami I ducked into a phone booth and called Justine La Ray.

"Where on earth have you been?" she asked. "I thought you were going to call me Friday."

"I've been out of town," I said. "But, look, do you want to take a little trip? I've got to run up to Palm Beach for a couple of days, and we just might get a chance to look into the gown situation around there."

"I'd love to go."

"Pack an overnight bag, and I'll pick you up as soon as I can get loose here. Where do you live?"

She gave me her address.

"I'll see you," I said.

I took a cab over to Miami Beach to the apartment, and changed back into Chapman's clothes. Next I removed all the identification and the cards from his wallet, dropped them in the pocket of my jacket, and counted the money in it. Nearly all the checks were cashed now, and it came to a little over $3,400, in twenties, fifties, and hundreds. It made an impressive looking roll. I shoved it in my pocket, and then made a bundle of the fishing clothes, canvas shoes, and a flashlight.

I called Justine again.

"Look sweetie, I'm still tied up in this deal, over in Miami Beach. I thought we'd stay in Hollywood at that motel where I've been, and go on up to Palm Beach tomorrow. So why don't you run on up to Hollywood? I'll just go on out the beach and cut across."

"But how am I going to get there? And where do I meet you?"

"Hell, take a cab. I'll pay for it. There's a bar—the Cameo Lounge. Meet me there at, say ten-fifteen."

I locked the apartment and walked over to where I'd left the Cadillac that morning. I put the fishing clothes in the trunk, along with the canvas shoes and flashlight. Going up to a drugstore in the next block, I got a handful of change, went back to the phone, and put in a call to Robin Wingard's home address in Thomaston.

"Oh, hello, Mr. Chapman," he said. "How are you?"

"Listen," I said quietly. "This is strictly between the two of us; don't even mention it to Coral. I don't want to worry her. Is Mrs. Forsyth there in town?"

"Why, yes. She's here."

"Has she been around the station, or the studio?"

"No-o. Not as far as I know."

"But you are positive she's in town?"

"Oh, yes. I saw her on the street just this afternoon."

"All right. Here's what I want you to do. Under no circumstances is she to get into the station, or the studio. If she tries to force her way in, or sneak in, call the police. If necessary, hire Pinkertons."

"But—I don't understand."

"I can't explain now. I'll be there as soon as I can, but *keep her out of there*. Don't let her get near them. G'by."

I drove to Hollywood, found a place to park near the Cameo shortly before ten-fifteen, and waited. Justine arrived in a taxi about ten minutes later, and went inside. I lighted a cigarette and remained where I was for another forty minutes, watching the doorway to be sure she didn't leave. She'd have two or three drinks by now, and she'd be smoldering.

I went in. It was very dimly lighted, a small place with a precious aspect about it and a Hammond organ that fortunately wasn't being played at the moment. There were six or eight customers. She was at a small table about halfway back, grimly watching the door. She had a new permanent, and was wearing a dark blue dress and white mesh gloves, and the overnight case was on the floor beside her.

"Well! You finally got here," she said, as I sat down.

"Sorry I was late, cutie," I said. "Couldn't get away."

The casual manner and the "cutie" didn't improve her feelings any, but she was trying to get them under control.

It would be poor policy to blast the goose just as it was about to produce the golden egg.

"It's all right," she said with an effort.

"Well, I wound up the deal." I stuck a cigarette in the holder and lighted it. "I guess our trip's off, baby."

"*What?*"

"Yeah. I can start home in the morning—"

"*Well!* Of all the stupid—!" The black eyes were venomous. "After I spend a fortune in cab fare, and sit here like a mope for an hour and a half waitin' for you to decide to show up—"

The bartender and several customers turned and stared.

"Hey," I said soothingly, "take it easy, Marian."

She slammed her drink down. "And will you, for Chrissakes, stop calling me Marian! I'm sick of it!"

"All right, all right, I'm sorry, honey." I looked around uneasily. "I didn't mean it. Let's have another drink."

I motioned for the bartender, who hadn't missed a word of it, and ordered two martinis. It took several minutes to cool her off. We had another pair of drinks, and decided to go somewhere else. We drove over to the beach to another bar. I was acting a little drunk now, and tried to paw her in the parking lot. She shoved me away.

"Le's ginna back," I said.

"Oh, shut up!"

We went inside and had two more drinks. I noticed she was leaving most of hers now.

"Why don't we go on to the motel?" she asked. "We can have some drinks there."

I bought a bottle of Scotch from the bartender. He didn't want to sell it to me but I persuaded him with an extra five dollars. We drove to the motel. It was after midnight now, and most of the units were dark. I turned the car and backed it into the carport. I was staggering a little, and as I fumbled the door open I dropped her bag. It clattered on the step.

"Be careful!" she said angrily.

Inside, I switched on a light, put the Scotch and the bag on the dresser, and started to paw her again. "Wait a minute, can't you?" she snapped. She slipped off the dress and put it on a hanger in the closet, and took off her shoes. They were blue, with very high heels. I broke the seal on the bottle, and poured two water tumblers half full.

"I'm goin' to put some water in mine," she said, and went into the bathroom. She closed the door. I quietly unsnapped the overnight case and opened it. She had some more shoes. I grabbed out a pair of her nylons, and a pair of pants, shoved them under the mattress on the bed, and closed the bag. When she came out I could tell by the color of her drink she'd poured most of it out before she added the water.

"'S down the ol' hatch," I said, weaving a little, and gulped part of mine. The shoes were lying on the carpet near the corner of the bed. "How's bout a kiss?" I said, and lurched toward her. I landed on them, and heard one of the heels snap. So did she.

"Now look what you've done, you clumsy idiot!" she lashed out.

I fixed her with a glassy stare, and contemptuously kicked the shoes under the bed. Hauling out the wallet, I fumbled a fifty out of it and threw it toward her. It fell at her feet. "Go buy y'self another pair. But don't heave y' weight around. I could buy you for cat food."

I tried to stuff the wallet back into my pocket. It fell to the floor. I reached down for it, and fell over. She stared at me with contempt. I got up, tossed the wallet on the dresser, and went into the bathroom. I made a retching sound, and washed my face. When I came out, she was smiling.

"I'm sorry, honey," she said. "It was my fault, for leavin' 'em there. Here, let me pour you another little drink."

"'S good idea," I replied. "'Pologize. Din mean word of it." I drank part of the whisky, dropped the glass on the rug, and collapsed on the bed. "Lie down few mince. Feel better."

She stretched out beside me, and stroked my face with her hand. "There, there, homey. Ju-u-ust relax. You just had a little too much."

I closed my eyes. We lay perfectly still for about ten minutes, and then she said, "Honey?"

"Ummmff?" I muttered, and stirred a little.

She waited another twenty minutes before she tried again. I went on breathing heavily, and made no reply. After a few more minutes she moved cautiously away from me, and got up. I heard the rustle of the dress as she put it back on, and the careful unsnapping of the bag to get the other pair of shoes. I had to listen carefully to hear the door open, but there was a faint click as it closed.

I slid off the bed, parted the drapes at the front window just a fraction of an inch, and peered out. There was no one in sight except her. All the units across the way were dark, and the woman who ran the place had long since gone to bed. She reached the entrance, turned left, toward the center of town, and disappeared.

She knew I had her address, and the chances were she wouldn't stop this side of California. With a married man she might tough it out and play the percentages, but she should be pretty sure by now that I was single. I'd cried enough about what the tax people did to me because of it.

I went over to the dresser and looked. She'd left the wallet.

CHAPTER TWELVE

I replaced all the identification and the cards in it, and looked at my watch. It was one forty-five. Taking the two water tumblers out in the bathroom, I rinsed them and rubbed them with a towel to remove prints. Next I set to work on the three suitcases. I wiped them all over very carefully with the towel to remove any prints already there, and then replaced them with numbers of deliberately smeared ones—touching them, particularly around the hardware and handles, with my fingers and hands, but always sliding just a little. I did the same thing with all the doorknobs, bathroom fixtures, and the glass top of the dresser.

I pulled out the nylons and the pair of pants I'd shoved under the mattress, held them under the tap in the wash basin until they were thoroughly wet, squeezed out the excess water, and draped them on a coat hanger from the closet. I hung them from the shower head that projected from the wall above the tub, and then slid the shower curtain about halfway out on its rod so they were hidden from view.

I retrieved the shoes from under the bed. The broken heel was still attached, but dangling. Turning out the lights, I lay down on the bed with a cigarette. After about an hour, I got up without turning on the lights, slipped out the side door into the carport, and unlocked the trunk of the Cadillac. Going back inside, I returned with the whisky bottle and the shoes. Stumbling, I fell heavily against the side of the car, bumped once against the wall of the carport, and dropped to the floor. I remained utterly silent for at least five minutes, and then got up with a great scraping of shoes against concrete, bumped against the car once more, put the shoes and the bottle in the trunk, and closed it. I tiptoed back inside, closed the door, and lay down again.

It was nine when I awoke. My clothes were badly rumpled. I had a slight hangover, but it wasn't bad. I washed my face, but didn't shave, and when I appraised myself in the mirror I looked like a man on the wrong end of a two-day binge. Shoving the empty wallet in my pocket, I put on the hat and glasses and took one last look around. Everything was all right. Except for the pants and nylons drying in the bathroom, there was nothing to indicate a woman had ever been here.

I went out, being careful not to leave any prints on the knob as I closed the door, got in the car, and drove out. The woman who ran the place was in the doorway of the office; she smiled, and I solemnly tipped my hat. It was a few minutes past ten when I reached downtown Miami and finally found a parking place. The briefcase the tapes had been in was on the back seat. I got out with it and walked to the bank.

I wrote out the check for $170,000, and presented it at a window. The teller was a girl. She did a take, looked at me again, raised her eyebrows, and disappeared. I gathered it wasn't every day she cashed checks in that amount for grimy and disheveled characters who'd obviously slept in their clothes and hadn't shaved for a couple of days. Well, I'd expected a certain amount of consternation. I stuck a cigarette in the holder, and lighted it.

Dakin came out. As I'd suspected before, he never remembered what anybody looked like. He glanced uncertainly around at the people at other windows, and when the girl nodded toward me, he said, "Ah, yes. Mr. Chapman." We shook hands.

"Do you really want this in cash?" he asked incredulously.

I stopped whistling *The Music Goes Round and Round*, glanced at him as if I thought the question tiresome, and said, simply, "Yes."

I knew then they'd already checked the signature against the card and knew it was genuine. They suspected a con game of some kind, or that I was in some kind of trouble at home and had worked out this deal for disappearing with a lot of ready cash, but in the end there was nothing they could do about it. I'd put the money in the bank, so who had a better right to take it out? He did ask, since it was made out to cash and the girl hadn't actually seen me sign it, if I'd mind making out another?

"Not at all," I said. I made out another, signed it, and said, "But I'm in rather a hurry, if you don't mind."

He looked at the signature, and shrugged. There was a slight service charge for transferring the funds. They brought the money, packed it into the briefcase for me, I paid the service charge, tipped my hat politely to the girl, and walked out with the briefcase under my arm.

When I reached the car I placed it on the seat beside me, unzipped it, and removed ten fifties from one of the bundles. I placed them in the wallet and started out US 1. In the edge of Coral Gables there was a large sporting goods store I'd already located. I stopped and bought a six-foot aluminum car-top boat. While the men were installing the carrier atop the car and securing the boat and oars to it, I walked impatiently up and down, chain-smoking cigarettes and muttering about the delay. I gave the clerk three fifties, and when he brought my change, I asked, "How far is it to Lake Okeechobee?"

"You're headed the wrong way," he said. "It's north. You go back—"

"Thanks," I said, paying no attention. I was already walking out.

It was only a few miles from there to the roadside curio stand. I began watching for it, and when I saw it ahead I checked the mirror to be sure no one was too close behind me. I was clear. I kept booming right on at fifty until I was slightly past it, and then hit the brakes in a crash stop. Rubber screamed, and the car yawed back and forth across the pavement, finally sliding to a stop on the gravel several hundred yards away. I put it into reverse, and shot backward, and slid to a stop again right before the place.

The cold-eyed proprietor was waiting on a pair of tourists from Michigan. They were looking at seashells on a long table—or had been. They'd stopped everything now to stare at me. I leaped from the car and ran over to the row of ornamental flamingos beside the fence. Grabbing one of them up, I hefted it, as though estimating its weight. It was one of the type normally set in wading pools, with a circular concrete base at the bottom of the thin steel legs.

I turned toward him with an imperious gesture. "I'll take one of these."

He regarded me coldly. It was possible, of course, that he didn't like anybody, but I felt sure he remembered me. "I'm waiting on these people, mister," he said. "What's the hurry?"

"Look," I said, beginning to shout. "I didn't stop here to tell you the story of my life. All I want to do is buy one of your goddamned flamingos—"

I grabbed it up in my arms as if to take it to the car, but lost my grip on it and let it drop. It fell over on the gravel. I lunged for it again. At that moment his wife hurried out of the shop and said anxiously, "I'll take care of these customers, Henry."

The Michigan couple was fascinated with the performance. Henry grabbed the flamingo away from me and stalked to the car. Nodding curtly to the trunk, he asked, "You got the keys?"

"*The keys?*" I was aghast. "No, no, no! Put it in here!" I yanked the rear door open. "On the seat."

He looked at the pale blue leather and then at me. "Mister, it ain't none of my business what you do with your car, but you ort to put it in the trunk."

I removed the cigarette holder from my mouth, and stared at him in sheer outrage. "*In the trunk?* Who the hell ever heard of putting a flamingo in a trunk?"

This broke the tourists up at last. They had to turn away, and I heard strangled sounds of laughter.

"I mean—damn it—" I went on, gesturing wildly. "There's no room. My—my suitcases are in there."

He dropped the flamingo on the seat. I shoved a fifty-dollar bill in his hand and got in and roared away. As soon as I was out of sight, I slowed to forty; there was still a lot of time to put in, and only the remotest chance that Henry would call the police and report me as a menace to navigation. If I were picked up he might have to part with the change from the fifty. I stopped in Homestead and bought a roll of heavy white cord.

It was shortly after two p.m. when I turned off into the large parking area at the Theater of the Sea, located between Tavernier and Islamorada on the Overseas Highway. It was one of the well-known tourist attractions of the Keys, a large souvenir shop and a fenced area containing the aquarium ponds and tanks stocked with marine life. There were two performing porpoises, and a guide who conducted a tour. I went inside, bought a ticket, and waited for the next tour.

When the crowd was large enough, some fifteen or twenty tourists, we started around, staring at the fish and listening to the lecture. I paid scant attention and spoke to no one until the guide was squatted at the end of one of the ponds coaxing a jewfish to come up and gulp the mullet he had in his hand. In a moment it did, and then settled slowly back into the rather murky water.

The guide arose. I pushed my way through the crowd around him, and demanded, "Did you say that was a jewfish?"

"That's right," he replied. "They're one of the grouper family—"

I stared at him suspiciously. "I thought they lived in salt water."

Someone giggled at the rear of the crowd. "They do," the guide explained with weary patience. "These are all saltwater fish."

I pursed my lips and nodded. "Just as I suspected. All I can say is it's a hell of a way to treat fish."

He sighed, opened his mouth to explain that the ponds were filled with sea-water, but turned away with a well-you-run-into-all-kinds expression on his face. The crowd tittered. The tour went on. I remained on the outskirts, aloof and disapproving.

I arrived in Marathon at four-thirty, after stopping several times along the way to get out and look at the water. One hour and twenty minutes to go. I checked my watch against a time announcement on the car radio to be sure it was still reasonably accurate, and hunted up a bar. It was quiet, with hardly anyone in it, and there was a telephone booth in back. There was also one out front on the sidewalk, in case the first happened to be occupied.

I ordered one Scotch and water and nursed it for an hour. The bartender tried once or twice to start a conversation, but I gave no indication I even heard him. At exactly five-fifty, I got up and started out. Then I stopped abruptly. "Oh, my God, I've got to make a phone call—" Getting several dollars worth of change, I went back to the booth and called Coral Blaine.

"Where are you, dear?" she asked. "I've been trying to reach you—"

"I'm at Lake Okeechobee," I replied.

"Then you're on your way home?"

I paid no attention. "It's funny, though. I keep thinking I've been here before. I've never been in Lake Okeechobee, have I?"

"Heavens, dear, I don't know. I've never heard you mention it. But I'm glad you've started back—"

"Tell Wingard it was too late," I said. "But he can forget it now."

"Oh," she said, a little uncomfortably, I thought. I was listening carefully for clues. "That was what I wanted to get in touch with you about. He was in this morning—"

And he'd told her, of course. "It was too late before I figured it out," I went on, ignoring her completely. "It wasn't your fault. You kept telling me Marian was there—"

"Darling," she interrupted, "couldn't we stay off that subject, just once?"

I nodded. There it was. I was sure now.

"You kept telling me she was," I continued, "but I didn't believe you, because I kept seeing her down here. Everywhere I went. What she was doing, of course, was going back and forth. But I don't know why I didn't figure out about the radio station in time. I knew how clever she was—"

"Harris, is this some kind of joke?"

"All she had to do was walk in there and pick up the microphone and spread her lies to everybody in the country, and turn 'em all against me. Make 'em think I didn't treat her fairly. The way they turned against Keith, and it wasn't his fault at all. The girl walked right into his car."

"Harris!"

"People believed her, too. I can tell. I see 'em looking at me on the street, and I can hear 'em whispering ... And you know how she was going back and forth? By radio! *Zip*, she's here. And *zip*, she's there. Oh, she was clever, all right. She used my own radio station to ruin me. But I stopped her, even if it was too late. She's here with me now."

"No! You're mistaken—"

"Oh, no," I said triumphantly. "I'm not mistaken. I caught up with her at last. I've got her out in the car. She broke into my room last night, and when I woke up she was leaning over whispering lies to *me*. I tried to make her shut up, but she wouldn't stop. I got my hands around her throat and she tried to get back on the radio waves and get away, but I held onto her. She won't ever tell any more lies about me—"

Her voice was growing shrill. "Harris, it's utterly impossible!"

She'd been very adept with the knife, there in that same office, but she was getting it back now. While she was sitting there listening to me say

I'd just killed Marian Forsyth, Marian was standing at the next desk, talking to Barbara Cullen.

I dropped my voice to a conspiratorial whisper. "You'll hear from me. I'll be in a foreign country, angel, where they didn't hear the things she told, and I'll send for you."

I hung up. I went back to the bar, ordered another drink, and sat for ten minutes or so staring moodily at the mounted sailfish above the backbar mirror.

"Beautiful fish," I said to the bartender. "You know, they catch a lot of those down in the Keys."

He was so happy at having somebody to talk to again he did a clown routine. He picked up the bottle from which he'd just poured my drink, stared at it unbelievingly, and shook his head. "Pal, you're right square in the middle of the Keys."

"Beautiful country," I said. "Next time you go, take the whole family; they'd love it." I got up and went out.

I went on toward Sugarloaf Key, still driving under forty. All the fuses were burning behind me now, but there was still an adequate time lag before the explosions started, and I didn't want to make that turn off the highway until it was dark. When I reached Big Pine Key I could see it was still too early, so I pulled off the highway, drove up a back road for a mile or two and parked, facing away from the highway. Two or three cars went past. If they noticed me, so much the better. It would take a long time to search Big Pine; it was one of the largest of all the Keys.

When it was completely dark, I turned and went back. There wasn't a great deal of traffic on the highway: As I began closing on the turnoff at Sugarloaf there was only one car behind me. I slowed and let it pass, and then made the turn. I speeded up, hurtling over the bumpy country road. In a few minutes I came to the trace of a road going off to the left, and in only two or three more to the openings through the wall of mangroves where boats could be launched. My headlights splashed against the pickup truck. Aside from it, the place was utterly deserted.

I stopped, unlocked it, and transferred the concrete flamingo and the ball of heavy cord. I got back in the Cadillac and went on. The faint ruts ran on for another two or three hundred yards through heavy brush that scraped the car on both sides, made a sharp turn toward the water, and dead-ended among the mangroves. There was a narrow channel here, going through them to open water, but it was never used for launching boats because the underbrush and mangroves were so heavy on all sides it would be impossible to turn or maneuver. I stopped just above high tide, and cut the lights and engine. Impenetrable darkness closed in around me, and thousands of mosquitoes, and utter silence except for the faint lapping of the water. There was no surf, because of the shallow water and the mangrove islands just offshore.

Getting out, I fumbled the key into the lock, and opened the trunk. When I'd located the flashlight, I turned it on, unfastened the boat, and lifted it down. I dragged it down to the edge of the water, put the oars in it, and my canvas shoes. Taking out the khaki shirt, I wiped the steering wheel, dash, door handles, and trunk handle, and then rubbed and wiped my hands and fingers over them to leave a satisfactory number of unusable prints.

I opened the whisky, took a drink of it, poured the rest into the water, and threw the bottle far over into the mangroves. Lifting out Justine's shoe with the broken and dangling heel, I dropped it beside the rear of the car, under some overhanging brush, and checked it with the flashlight. It couldn't be too obvious. I nudged it further out of sight with my foot. Good. I dropped the other shoe in the boat. Closing the car, I pushed off. The water was quite shallow and I had to wade out several steps before I could get aboard.

I sat down and poled it out of the narrow channel with one of the oars. When I reached open water I threw the other shoe overboard. It would move around with the tide, and might or might not be found, but it made no difference. I turned off the flashlight and began rowing parallel to the shore, watching the dark wall of the mangroves. In a few minutes I could see the break in them, and pulled in to the beach. I switched on the flashlight again, and saw the pickup truck. Pulling the boat up, I squeezed the water out of my trouser legs, took off the wet leather shoes, and put on the canvas ones. They had corrugated crepe-rubber soles.

I put the wet shoes and the oars in the back of the truck. Then I carried the boat up and placed it on top of them. Using the flashlight, I followed the ruts on through the brush to the Cadillac. I walked toward the edge of the water, threw the beam outward, and could see the marks of the boat and my tracks on the soft bottom as I'd waded out. The leather shoes had left some fairly good imprints above high tide, also. I walked down, leaving the distinctive track of the canvas ones on top of them in places.

I opened the trunk and took out the steel wrecking bar I'd bought. Slamming the lid down so it locked, I stuck the flat end of the bar under the edge of it and began prying upward. It was stubborn, and I had a large area of steel bent and chewed before the lock finally gave up and it flew open. Then I closed and locked all the doors, and used the end of the bar to knock in the right front window so I could reach the latch. I rifled the glove compartment, leaving everything strewn on the floor.

Taking out the briefcase and my fishing clothes, I took one last look around with the flashlight to be sure I hadn't overlooked anything, and walked back to the truck.

Standing in darkness, with the mosquitoes chewing me, I took off his suit, shirt, and tie. I dropped the glasses in one coat pocket, bent the hat into a mass of straw, and shoved it in the other. I put on the khaki fishing clothes and the cap, transferred the money from his wallet to my own, put his back, in his trousers, along with the cigarette holder, lighter, and his car keys. Taking the flashlight, I went down to the edge of the water and made a mark by which to gauge the tide.

Placing the light on the seat of the truck, I wrapped his clothes around the long steel legs and curving neck of the flamingo, and tied them with the ball of white cord. There was a hundred yards of it, and I used it all. I looked at my watch. It was only shortly after eight. There were cigarettes and matches in the glove compartment of the truck. I lighted one and sat down, suddenly conscious that I was tired. It had been the day-long tension; and I remembered now I had never eaten anything. At nine I went down and looked at my mark. The tide was coming in. That was all right; I didn't want to go out onto the highway with that boat until at least midnight. There was always the chance somebody might remember it.

At one a.m. the tide was at slack high water as nearly as I could tell. I drove out to the highway. There were very few cars on it now, passing at widely spaced intervals. I waited until there was no one coming from the west before pulling onto it, and drove fast so as not to be overtaken. The oncoming cars, of course, could see nothing but my headlights.

At the approach to the Bahia Honda Bridge a road led down off the highway to a picnic ground at the edge of the channel. I drove down, got out with the flashlight, and threw the beam outward onto the water. The tide was ebbing now, beginning to swirl around the pillars of the bridge.

I carried the boat down, put it in the water, and swamped it. It had flotation compartments, of course, so it didn't sink entirely. I shoved. It disappeared downstream in the darkness, headed seaward on the tide, at least fifteen miles from the car. It might not be found for days, or even weeks. I threw the oars in, and then the steel wrecking bar, heaving it as far as I could into deeper water.

Nothing remained now except the flamingo. I placed it on the seat beside me in its mummy wrappings of clothes. The Bahia Honda channel was the deepest in the Keys, and the bridge the highest, and no fishing was permitted from it. Waiting until no cars were coming, I shot onto the highway and up the incline of the bridge. When I reached the top, at mid-channel, I slammed on the brakes and hopped out. One pair of headlights was coming toward me, still over a mile away. I ran around the truck, yanked the door open, and heaved the flamingo over the rail.

It was a few minutes past five a.m. when I backed into the driveway at the apartment and put the truck in the garage. I went inside, turned on the air-conditioning unit, and poured an enormous drink of whisky. I was wrung out, and empty, and felt dead. I'd been up there on the high wire for just a few hours less than thirteen days.

It was complete now. That was the whole package, and I didn't think they'd ever untie it. I dropped the briefcase on the bed and started to open the zipper. Then I shrugged, pushed it off onto the floor, and lay down. It didn't seem to matter whether it was full of money or wallpaper samples. All I wanted was Marian Forsyth.

This struck me as an odd reaction for Jerome Lawrence Forbes. Maybe I'd been somebody else for so long I'd forgotten my own behavior patterns.

CHAPTER THIRTEEN

I shaved off the mustache the next morning, lay in the sun in the back yard for a few hours to erase the faint difference in the tan on my upper lip, and got a haircut, a short brush job. If the barber even suspected the bleached effect wasn't entirely due to the sun, he merely thought I was queer. I returned the truck to the rental agency that afternoon, and settled down to wait.

The story broke a little more slowly than we'd anticipated, but once it did it gathered momentum like a rocket. On Wednesday morning Harris Chapman was a prominent Louisiana businessman who was reported missing somewhere in the Lake Okeechobee area after an apparently incoherent telephone call to his private secretary—and two days later the headlines were screaming *FLAMINGO KILLER*.

Coral Blaine apparently waited a full twenty-four hours before notifying the Florida Highway Patrol and asking them to make a search. She had no address except that I'd said I was in Lake Okeechobee, and reported I'd talked in a "rambling" fashion. Maybe I'd had a sunstroke. To the police it meant merely another drunk. But it got into the paper Wednesday morning, complete with name, and then the deluge began.

From Thursday on the headlines changed with every edition, and the type grew larger by the hour. By Saturday morning they had it all. I got up a little after eight, made some coffee, and brought in the paper.

FLAMINGO KILLER MAD, the headlines said. A quarter of the front page, and nearly all the second were taken up with a dozen different aspects of the case. The boat had been found near Pigeon Key by two fishermen. Chapman's body hadn't been found, but police admitted it could have become snagged on the coral reefs offshore or lost in the impenetrable tangle of mangroves along the water's edge. They didn't expect to find the girl's, not if it were weighted with that concrete flamingo.

The girl was believed to be a Justine La Ray, occupation unspecified, who had been missing from her apartment since Sunday night. A taxi driver remembered driving a girl answering her description to Hollywood. She had been carrying a small suitcase, and she wore blue shoes. She had a police record in Miami and New York for soliciting, vagrancy, and one conviction for shoplifting.

Henry was there, in an exclusive interview, in which he said there was no doubt I was as crazy as a loon. There were pictures of him, and of his curio stand, and of the row of pink birds with their reinforced-steel legs and sinuous concrete necks. After all, he'd given the story its name.

The police were still searching for the man who'd looted the Cadillac of $170,000, but admitted they had no clue except that he'd worn canvas shoes, which were sold by the millions.

There was an interview with Coral Blaine, in Thomaston. Yes, she'd talked to him every day, except toward the last. Now that she thought back she could see the increasing obsession with Marian Forsyth, but she hadn't known there was anything irrational about it until it was too late.

A lot of space was given to Marian and her former relationship with him, but as far as I could tell, she wasn't under suspicion. After all, nobody had *done* anything to him. And she was a thousand miles away all the time.

I read it all, and then folded the paper and tossed it on the coffee table. Not once, from beginning to end, had anybody ever voiced the slightest doubt that it was really Chapman. As she had pointed out, why should they? He said that was his name. And what earthly reason could he have for lying about it?

I went into the kitchen for another cup of coffee. While I was pouring it, I thought I heard a car pull into the driveway in front. The doorbell chimed. My heart leaped. Maybe it was a special delivery letter from Marian. I hurried through the living room and opened the door.

It was a big blond girl swinging a white purse. She nodded coolly. "Good morning, Mr. Forbes. May I come in?"

Alarms tripped, and began to ring softly somewhere in my mind. "Who are you?"

"Remember? Outside your room at the Clive Hotel?" She smiled. "I'm Bill McEwen."

I didn't say anything. I stood looking out at the street beyond her where a boy was going along the sidewalk in the morning sunlight tossing a football from one hand to the other. For some reason the only thought in my mind was that if it had to fail why it couldn't have been at first? Why did I have to go through all that suspense just as a prelude to disaster?

"Well," she prompted, "aren't you going to ask me in?"

I gestured with a hand. She walked past me into the room and stood looking around. I closed the door. She lowered her purse onto the coffee table by its looping white cords, fished cigarettes from it, and lighted one.

She glanced at the *Herald* with its black headlines, and then at me, and shook her head with a faint smile. "It was a masterpiece. I've always thought she was the most brilliant woman I've ever known."

I reached mechanically for a cigarette. Before I could say anything, she went on, "I think my favorite bit of the whole thing was that touch with the pants and stockings. Now, that had finesse. Nothing crude, like spilling blood around the place." She shook her head. "It's almost a shame to spoil it."

I found my voice at last. "You must have known about the fake before you came up to the room. Your face didn't show anything at all when I opened the door—"

She nodded. "I was just verifying it. I was at the desk, registering, when you left the check there for the Fitzpatrick people."

"You were meeting him at the Clive?"

She smiled. "You might call it that." She sat down on one of the hassocks with her knees pressed together and the heavy thighs swelling against the linen skirt she was wearing. Her hair was taffy blond, and her skin very fair. She had a rather square face, and, shrewd blue eyes. She looked as if she could take care of herself, and was accustomed to doing it.

"How did you find this place?" I asked.

"I followed you when you came over here that Friday. I've been right behind you all the time."

"How did you get over here ahead of the police?"

"I haven't told the police," she said.

I stared at her. "*What?*"

"Of course not. I don't work for the police force."

"Then what do you want?"

She gestured with the cigarette. "What do you think I want? I'm a newspaperwoman. On a tank-town paper where we write flattering little social notes about the advertisers, and a real *big* story is a church wedding. So maybe I won't get any kick at all out of walking into the offices of the *Herald* and saying just give me two-thirds of your front page and a by-line and I'll write you the *real* story of the Flamingo murder case."

"And nobody knows except you?"

"Not so far." She smiled. "But, of course, the *Herald* does have quite a circulation."

I sighed. "And you just walk in here—?"

She laughed. "Oh, don't be childish, Mr. Forbes. Anybody who even watches TV knows you never do that. The whatzit is always left in a safe place so the police will get it if quote anything happens unquote."

"I see," I said. "Then you just came over to have a little fun before you break it?"

"No-o," she replied. "Oh, I'll admit I might enjoy watching *her* squirm, but I don't even know you. Maybe I'm just trying to fill in a couple of blank places. You didn't really kill the girl, did you?"

"No," I said.

"I didn't think so. But how did you get her to disappear on schedule? Without letting her in on it, I mean?"

I told her. Why not? I thought. It didn't make any difference now.

She nodded. "Nice touch. So even if she's ever found she'll just deny she was the one. Then they merely start all over, looking for another missing floater."

I studied her, beginning to wonder a little now. Maybe the big story and the by-line weren't what she was after; she could be just softening me up with a little pressure. I'd already recalled the thing Coral Blaine had said about the abortion and the fact they didn't know who the man was. No doubt it was Chapman, all right; but there was just a suspicion of a sour note somewhere. She hadn't called before she showed up at the hotel.

"Chapman didn't know you were coming down here, did he?" I asked.

She smiled coolly. "No. But what difference could it make?"

"I was just wondering how Marian could have missed you. She knew most of the places he'd been."

"What do you mean?"

"What was it, just a one-night stand? Or maybe he gave you the brush after you got caught? Or refused to pay the doctor?"

"Oh. I see Angel-face told you about it."

"He gave you a bad time, didn't he?"

"What makes you think so?"

"It was apparently one of the best things he did. You probably weren't naive enough to think he was going to marry you, so he must have weaseled out of any responsibility at all and refused to help. That it?"

She grinned coldly. "Oh, come now, Mr. Forbes. You're old enough to know a girl's love life is her own secret."

I was pretty sure now I was right. She'd come to Florida with some idea of putting pressure on Chapman for money. Or maybe even something worse.

"Who killed him?" she asked.

"I did," I said.

She shook her head. "I was just wondering if you'd say that. I don't know how she does it. God, even at forty—"

"She's thirty-eight," I said.

"She's forty if she's a day. But—" She sighed. "That's the reason I hate her, I guess. She always had everything. That damned poise, and smoothness. She could fall in a gutter and come out looking as if she were modeling something. What chance does a country girl have?"

"It was a country girl that ran her out on the limb and sawed it off," I said. "But never mind that; let's get down to cases. What is it you really want?"

She exhaled smoke and looked at it. "The money. What else?"

"How much of it?"

"All of it."

"You won't get it," I said. The money wasn't important anymore, but if I let this taffy-haired Snopes run over me she'd take everything, and then bleed us for the rest of our lives. Or until she got bored and turned us in for laughs. I had to fight her, and scare her if I could.

She gestured airily. "Well, I can always write the story."

"Go ahead," I said. "They might give you five hundred for it. And run it under your by-line for two days. Anybody can see that's better than twenty thousand dollars."

"You don't seem to realize the spot you're in."

"I realize it perfectly. All you have to do is call the police. But that way you get nothing."

"I don't want to be a pig," she said. "I'll settle for a hundred thousand. Where is it? Here?"

"Never mind where it is," I said. "You'll get exactly a third, and that's all. When you consider that if the police ever crack it I'll be charged with murder and you'll probably get off with five years, I'd say that was pretty soft—"

She stared. "What do you mean, I'll get five years."

"You don't think I'm going to give it to you without a receipt, do you?"

"My God, how crazy can you get?"

"A receipt," I said, ignoring her. "I dictate it, you write it. That makes you a partner. An accessory, I think the lawyers call it. So then if you ever feel in an expansive mood and want to talk about it with somebody, you go right along with me."

"I won't do it."

I shrugged. She could still take it all, of course, if she had nerve enough to stick it out, but I was pretty sure by now she was too greedy to risk it. "Go ahead and write your story."

"You can't bluff me."

"Look at it this way," I said. "You may not know it, but you can't hook Marian except as an accessory. She was in New York, and she can prove it. And I can hire an awful lot of high-priced legal talent for $170,000. It might drag on for years. While you're writing up the Women's Club luncheons for some hick newspaper for sixty a week. Make up your mind."

She frowned. "I never heard of such a thing."

"A receipt for blackmail, you mean? Well, you've heard of it now. Nothing's free in this world. And when I'm buying protection, I'm going to be sure I get it."

"All right," she said.

I found a sheet of paper and handed her a pen.

"Let's have the money," she protested.

I went into the bedroom and got it off the shelf in the closet. It was in the attaché case I'd bought for it. I set the case on the coffee table and unlocked it. She stared at it, her eyes shining.

I counted it out for her to the last dollar, relocked the case, and put it away. When I came back she was still fondling the packets of currency.

"Ready?" I asked. "Write this down."

She nodded.

"November 30, 1957. Received of J. L. Forbes $56,666 for withholding from the police vital information relative to the death of Mr. Harris Chapman, of Thomaston, Louisiana. Signed, Billy Jean McEwen."

She handed it to me. I gave her the old briefcase to put the money in.

She stood up. "You don't really think you'll ever see her again, do you?"

"Why not?"

"She doesn't care anything about the money. Or you. Or anything at all."

"All right," I said. "Don't let it worry you. You've got yours."

"Are you staying here all by yourself?"

"Yes," I said.

"I see." The glance was calculated and provocative. "Isn't it lonely?"

"No." I opened the door for her. "Chapman's always around."

"Well, you can have him."

"Yes. I know."

She drove off. I went on waiting for the phone to ring.

It didn't. Another week went by. Other sensations began to crowd the story off the front page, but it didn't die entirely. One thing that kept it alive was the continuing search for the man who had looted the car, and the search for Chapman's body. Then there was the concrete flamingo; that had caught the public fancy.

I was growing to hate the apartment. Being away from her was bad enough, but being reminded of her every minute I was here made it unbearable. And I hadn't been lying about Chapman's being in it. I had the rug shampooed to remove the water stain, and all the time the men were working on it I wondered if I were going as mad as Lady Macbeth.

But I couldn't leave. I could have the mail forwarded, of course, but suppose she telephoned? I waited, hating the place but hating to leave it, even for food. Even when I was sunbathing in the back yard I left the door open so I'd be able to hear the phone. Two hours before the postman was due I was pacing the floor by the front window, watching for him. The third week passed.

Then, on December 18th, it came. It was early in the morning. The boy had thrown the paper up on the walk and I was starting out to get it when a post office truck stopped and the driver got out with an airmail special. It was from Houston, Texas. I ran back inside, forgetting the paper, and tore it open.

> Dear Jerry:
>
> This is a very difficult letter to write, but I've avoided it as long as I can. I lied to you. I suppose you have begun to realize that by now, and I'm not asking for forgiveness, but I do think I should have the courage to face you and admit it. So if you still want to, will you come to see me here at the Rice Hotel?
>
> Sincerely,
> Marian

I stared at it, bewildered. What did she mean, she'd lied to me? And then, suddenly, I remembered the other thing she'd said, that night of the 13th. "I took advantage of you." None of it made any sense. She hadn't lied about anything, as far as I could see.

But I was wasting time like an idiot when I could be on my way to Houston. I grabbed the phone and began calling for reservations. I could get a flight out at one p.m. I hurried into the bedroom, changed clothes, and started packing. The phone rang. The airline, I thought, as I picked it up.

"Mr. Forbes? I have a telegram from Houston, Texas. The text reads as follows: '*Urgent disregard letter see news story.*' There is no signature."

"Thank you," I said. I hung up and ran out in the yard for the paper I'd completely forgotten.

It was on the front page, datelined New Orleans but with the usual eye-catching local headline tag:

FLAMINGO CASE
NONSENSE, SAYS PSYCHIATRIST

I sat down, feeling a chill of apprehension.

> New Orleans, La. Dec. 18. Dr. J. C. Willburn, well-known professor of psychiatry and author of a number of books on mental illness, stated today that in his opinion it was highly improbable that Harris Chapman could have deteriorated from apparent good mental health to a psychotic condition in a short two weeks.
>
> Dr. Willburn, who is on a leave of absence, became interested in the case at its beginning, and for the past three days has been in Thomaston interviewing dozens of Chapman's friends and associates. He says he unearthed no prior instances of hallucination or irrational behavior, and that the picture he has of Chapman is that of a practical, somewhat insensitive, vigorous man in the prime of life, too given to hard work for brooding or introspection....

The whole thing exploded in the papers again. The police said they'd never ruled out the possibility the insanity was faked. I was scared all over again, but what was even worse I didn't dare try to get in touch with her. But at least I could get out of the damned apartment, because I knew now where she was. I canceled the lease by paying an extra month's rent, and moved to the Fontainebleau. I bought some expensive clothes and luggage, spending money like a maharajah, and I drank too much.

The story went on. Another psychiatrist intimated that Willburn's statement was ill-advised. Nobody could form a psychiatric opinion from second-hand evidence gleaned from lay observers; Chapman could have been in a potentially dangerous mental condition for months. A third psychiatrist said the second psychiatrist was ill-advised. The police were still suspicious of the fact his body had never been found. And by now they knew I'd bought the wrecking bar. The man in Palm Beach who'd sold it to me gave them a good description. So was this the act of a madman buying a weapon to defend himself against a woman he'd wronged, or that of a coldly logical schemer buying it to jimmy open his own car and fake the theft along with the rest of the fantastic hoax?

But what object could he have had?

By now it was inevitable. On December 20th, when I grabbed the paper off the breakfast cart in my hotel room and spread it open, the bottom began falling out of everything.

WAS CHAPMAN REALLY CHAPMAN?

The story itself was merely a rehash of all the old evidence with a lot of new conjecture. But now that the question had finally been raised, they'd check those signatures, start pinpointing descriptions. But I had to be sure before I ran, so I could warn her. I waited. It was like walking on eggs. Two hours later the afternoon papers were out.

RIDICULOUS, SAYS CHAPMAN FIANCÉE

The police had questioned her about that a long time ago, she told the reporter in a long-distance interview. Of course she'd talked to Mr. Chapman, as she'd said before. Every day. There was no possibility at all it could have been somebody else.

I grabbed the phone and called the travel desk. "Get me a reservation to Houston on the first flight you can."

I had to change planes at New Orleans. It was seven-thirty p.m. when we came in at Houston International. I hurried into the first telephone booth and called the Rice Hotel.

"Mrs. Forsyth," I said.

"Just a moment ... I'm sorry, sir. She has checked out."

"Well, give me the desk, please."

No, the clerk said, she hadn't left a forwarding address. He had me transferred to the travel desk. Yes, they had made a reservation for Mrs. Forsyth on an American Airlines flight to San Francisco on the 18th. No hotel reservation.

I didn't even leave the airport. I walked up and down, chain-smoking cigarettes and hounding the airlines desks until I got out around midnight on a flight to Los Angeles. From there it was easy. I checked in at the Mark Hopkins in San Francisco at eleven-thirty a.m., and as soon as I was up in my room I started calling hotels. I hit her on the second one, the Sheraton-Palace. She'd been there, but she'd checked out at two-thirty p.m. on the 19th, no forwarding address. I caught a cab and went down there, and finally located the bellman who had taken her bags out. He was sure she had got into her own car, and not a cab. He thought it was a Ford.

I was thinking of the bridge now, and my nerves were screaming. I got a handful of dimes and headed for a phone booth, and started down the list of car-rental agencies. I came up with her in about twenty minutes. She'd rented a car on the 19th. No, it hadn't been returned yet. I sighed.

But where could she have gone? Then I remembered Stanford; she might have gone down to look up somebody she'd known in Palo Alto. I took a cab to the hotel, got hold of a Palo Alto directory, and started in on hotels and motels down there. I found her again, at a motel on El Camino Real, but she'd checked out an hour ago.

I rubbed a hand across my face, feeling the stubble of beard. It had been nearly thirty-six hours since I'd slept, and I couldn't remember when I'd eaten anything. I began calling the car-rental place.

Late in the afternoon the man sighed and said yes. She had returned the car about twenty minutes ago, and one of their men had driven her to a hotel. It was a fairly small one, on Stockton, the Fairlane.

The operator got it for me. "Mrs. Forsyth, please," I said, when the Fairlane operator answered.

"She's in 608. One moment, sir."

The phone buzzed twice. "Hello." It was her voice. I could almost see her.

"Marian!" I said. "Marian, darling—"

She screamed.

CHAPTER FOURTEEN

It was five o'clock and traffic was snarled. When we were within a block of it I tossed the driver a dollar and ran. I didn't even pause at the desk. When I got out of the elevator, I asked the operator, "608?" He pointed to the right.

It was the third door. I rapped. She opened it almost at once. She was a little thinner, and very pale, but as smooth and striking as ever. She was wearing a dark tailored suit. I pushed the door shut. There was the same wonderful, slender feel of her in my arms, I kissed her. She tried. I could feel her trying, but she couldn't quite do anything with it. It was no wonder, I thought, with what had just happened. But it was impossible to let her go. I kissed her eyelids and her throat, and the smooth dark hair.

Finally she whispered, "You did have one very small piece of luck, Jerry; I'm not much given to crying. Otherwise you'd need a shower curtain."

"Why?"

"Your kissing me this way after what I did to you."

"What did you do?"

"I sold you out, I suppose you'd call it, in about the most cynical way it would be possible to do it."

"You're not making any sense," I said.

"I think we'd better sit down," she suggested. "Take the armchair." She sat on the side of the bed. I looked around. It was any small hotel bedroom anywhere—Venetian blinds, glass-topped desk, telephone, grayish carpet, and twin beds with dark green spreads and metal headboards finished to resemble limed oak. She crossed her knees and pulled down her skirt. I looked at the slender, tapering fingers.

"Why did you run away from Houston?" I asked. "I was going to warn you if it became serious."

"I wasn't running from the police," she said. "From you. I lost my nerve again."

"Will you go with me to Reno tonight and marry me?"

She closed her eyes and lowered her face slightly. Then she shook her head. "No, Jerry."

"Will you go away with me without marrying me?"

"Please, Jerry—" She stopped, but then made an effort and went on. "I've already told you I lied to you. About our going away together. Maybe I wasn't consciously lying at the time, I don't know. I might even have thought I could do it. But that isn't the point.

"Listen, Jerry," she went on. "I asked you to do something criminal, for money. As long as you were cynical enough to do it for money, only half the responsibility was mine. Do you understand? But then you said you'd changed your mind. You wouldn't do it. But you were in love with me, you said. So I said, that's fine, Jerry. If you won't commit a crime for money, commit a crime because you're in love with me—"

Her hands were twisted tightly together and shaking, and she stopped for an instant and clenched her teeth to stop the tremor of her chin. It was as if her whole face had already shattered, and she was merely holding it together with an effort of will.

"Let's be efficient. Let's don't waste a nice handy thing like your being in love with me, when it could be put to some practical use, like getting you involved in a capital crime and ruining your life—"

I reached over and caught her arms. "Will you stop it? The whole thing was my fault. If I'd had the guts of an angleworm I could have made you give it up."

She shook her head. "There's no way you could have stopped me, Jerry. You don't stop a blind obsession like that. The only thing I could see was that I'd lost everything after it was already too late to start over, so the thing to do, obviously, was to destroy everybody else too. Including you."

"I'm all right, if you mean Chapman. After what he did to you, he doesn't bother me."

"He will," she said. "Unless you get the fact firmly fixed in your mind that you didn't do it. That I did."

"We both did," I said. "But do you think it will hold up for good? Remember, if they ever put a real expert on those forgeries they're going to look very fishy."

"You're in the clear, even if they find out it was an impersonation. They can't prove you ever met me. You were using the name of Hamilton, remember. And when I came down from New York, I called you as Mrs. Forbes, but I used another name on the plane tickets. Also, enroute from the airport to the apartment, I switched taxis in Miami."

I told her about Bill McEwen, and the receipt. She shook her head. "I'm sorry, Jerry. I never thought of her."

"I don't think there's any danger," I said. "I scared hell out of her with that receipt gag. When can I bring the money over to you?"

"Tomorrow," she said apathetically. "It doesn't matter."

I lighted a cigarette and walked across the room to look out at Stockton Street through the slats of the blind. I came back and stopped before her. "Is it just the voice?" I asked.

She shook her head. "No. That thing when you called just now was only because I was off guard, and didn't know you were anywhere near. I just don't want to do you any more harm."

"Did the other men who've been in love with you have this same trouble getting a message through?" I asked.

Her hands were beginning to twist and shake again. "Jerry, please don't."

"No," I said. I crushed out the cigarette. "If I hadn't given up too easily the other time, I might have won. So this time I'm going to try just once more. And after that I'll shut up for good." I squatted beside the bed, balancing myself on my toes with my forearms across her lap. "I know you don't love me," I said. "Maybe you've been hacked down so thoroughly it'll be years before you can care anything about anybody. But I'll settle for less. I'll try to say this without slopping over or getting too sticky about it. I just want you. I want to be with you. I want to try to help you. Maybe together we can still work this out some way; at least we could try. We'll go anywhere you say, on any terms you want, if you'll just give me a chance. After a while I think you'd associate the voice with me instead of with him. I don't think they ever made anybody else like you, and probably they never will again. I'm crazy about you, and I always will be. But that's enough of that. I think you've quit trying to deny that I'm in love with you. It's just a question of whether you'll go with me. Will you, Marian?"

I looked up at her. She'd turned her face away, and the chin was locked again and she was crying without making any sound at all. She looked at me at last, and shook her head. I stood up. She started to come with me to the door, but stopped with one hand resting on the back of the chair. By this time she could trust herself to speak, and she said, "Good night, Jerry," and held out her hand.

"Good night, Marian." I looked back from the open doorway, and as always she reminded me of something very slender and beautifully made and expensive—and utterly wasted—like a Stradivarius in a world in which the last musician was dead. I closed the door and went on down the hall.

She killed herself that night. She must have taken the capsules shortly after I left, as nearly as I could tell from the medical reports in the news. There was nothing about it in the morning papers, of course, and I still didn't know it until noon when I walked into the El Prado Bar on Union Square with a *Call-Bulletin* under my arm.

I spread it open and took a sip of the martini.

SUICIDE CONFESSES

Mrs. Marian Forsyth, 34 ...

It caught me without any defense at all and kept swamping me and I couldn't get it under control. I pretended to choke on the martini and got the handkerchief out and honked and sputtered and snorted while I was heading for the men's room to spare the dowagers behind the snowy tablecloths and half-acre menus the sight of a grown man crying in the El Prado in broad daylight. Fortunately, there was no one in the john. I was all right by that time, and could wash my face and go back outside. I folded the *Call* and drained the martini and walked all the way back up Nob Hill to the Mark. I sat down on the bed to read it, but it was a long time before I even opened the paper. She was dead; what else mattered? The headline said something about a confession, and it occurred to me that if she had left one they'd be here for me before very long. I really ought to do something about it.

Why hadn't I left her alone? She had that absurd feeling of responsibility for my being mixed up in the thing, and apparently my presence reminded her of it. Maybe if I'd stayed away from her she might have been able to handle the other thing.

And I could have stopped her that night if I'd said no and stuck to it. I rubbed a hand across my face. It was nice to think about it now. And I had a hunch now wasn't the only time I was going to think about it.

I read the story. She'd died of an overdose of sleeping pills. The medical examiner believed she had been dead since before midnight, and that she must have taken them very early in the evening.

I thought of her alone in her agony. She had no one. She had a bleak, miserable, impersonal hotel room and her own courage and that almost unshakable poise, and that was it. She hadn't asked for any help, or cried out. She'd merely held out her hand, and said, "Good night, Jerry," and waited for me to leave so she could take them.

Christ, I thought shakily, I've got to stop this. I'll be walking out the window.

There were two notes. The first was to the local police and contained instructions regarding the burial arrangements. The second read:

> TO WHOM IT MAY CONCERN:
>
> On November 28, 1957, an automobile belonging to Mr. Harris Chapman of Thomaston, Louisiana, was found abandoned on Sugarloaf Key, in the State of Florida. It is believed that Mr. Chapman is dead, but this has never been officially ascertained.
>
> Mr. Chapman is dead. I destroyed him. I am solely responsible for this act, and may God have mercy on me.
>
> In making the above statement, I am aware that I shall be dead within the next few hours.
>
> (Signed) Mrs. Marian Forsyth

I went over to the window and stood looking out. I was free now of even the possibility of suspicion or arrest. Down in the hotel safe was an attaché case containing over $110,000. It was all mine—money, immunity, everything. I was the beneficiary of a tormented girl who had just committed suicide in a hotel room. And I couldn't even go to her funeral.

She'd asked to be buried in a little country churchyard only a few miles from Thomaston. What would I do if somebody spoke to me? Pretend to be mute? All I could do was send flowers.

She took all the blame for this thing we had done, gave me all the money, and I sent flowers to her funeral.

Well. I'd been looking for a free ride all my life, hadn't I? So now I had one.

I went to Mexico—not to Acapulco, but to a little fishing village just up the coast from La Paz, in Baja California, where there were no tourists, practically no accommodations, and no one who spoke English. It seemed that now I had plenty of money, all I wanted to do was live like a beachcomber. I wore dungarees and swimming trunks and lived on tortillas and beans and drank nothing at all.

After a while I quit waking up with the outcry frozen in my throat as she went over the bridge railing and fell downward through the fog, and gradually I quit staring at darkness for hours on end with that thing running through my mind: *why hadn't I stopped her?* She was caught in a blind obsession, not knowing—or perhaps not even caring—that if she killed Chapman it would destroy her. But I'd known it, hadn't I? I'd been warned. And I'd failed her.

For the only time in my glib and cheaply cynical, wise-guy existence I'd really meant something that I said, and I hadn't been able to make her understand it or believe me. I simply hadn't tried hard enough. During those twenty minutes in the apartment that night I'd had the opportunity to stop this obscene and senseless waste of a woman who was worth a thousand of me, and I'd muffed it, and let her go on down the drain, and if I didn't stop lying here at night thinking of how many years of my life I'd give just for one more chance at those twenty minutes I'd go mad. That was the thing I had to whip.

But it was going away. I was slowly whipping it. And even if the Mexicans heard me when I awoke in the night, it didn't matter. They didn't understand English.

She had wanted to confess, there in that last hour, but it was evident that she was driven by an equally strong, or even stronger, compulsion to protect me for the rest of my life. She felt responsible for me. It was a sort of *noblesse oblige*. She was older than I was, and more intelligent, and she felt she had taken advantage of the fact that I had fallen in love with her.

I thought about guilt. That was the theme. She was going to kill Chapman and make it appear he had been killed by his own conscience and his haunting fear of the taint of mental illness. It had worked, and then she'd inevitably been destroyed by *her* overpowering burden of guilt. It went on, like a string of popping firecrackers setting each other off.

Except that here it stopped. I had no feeling of guilt for him, not anymore. In the first place, I had a much more elastic conscience; it had been stretched considerably over the years to fit different shapes of situations. And I hated him, furthermore, for what he had done to her. And in the end, I hadn't actually killed him anyway. Perhaps that was the final irony of it. She'd told me how to save myself.

Always hold onto that, she'd said. *You didn't do it. I did.*

Three months passed, and I knew I was all right. It was all going away. The police couldn't touch me, and I was safe in that epidemic infection of guilt. Marble might shatter, but not rubber.

I went back to San Francisco in the spring, completed transferring the money from the safe-deposit box into three checking accounts, and booked passage on a Grace Line freighter for the Canal Zone. I knew now what I was going to do—go into business as a big-game fishing guide in the Gulf of Panama. I'd liked Panama, and there was a boatyard I knew where I could have a magnificent sports fisherman built for much less than I could in the States, a real sixty-thousand-dollar job with the best of everything.

But in the week before the ship sailed there was one thing I had to do before I left for good. I flew to New Orleans. First, I spent two days in the public library, going back through the newspaper files. There was no further mention of the case after the latter part of February; it was apparently headed for oblivion, unsolved—not *if* she had done it, of course, but how.

The police were almost certain now that she had left her hotel in New York that night of November 13th and flown to Miami under the name of Mrs. Wallace Cameron. Then they'd lost her trail in Miami. The night clerk at the Dauphine remembered he'd given Chapman a letter when he checked in, and that Chapman had asked for a cab and gone out somewhere within a few minutes after arriving, but whether it had been to meet her nobody would ever know. Had she come to kill him? Or to taunt him with something guilty in his past that eventually drove him mad?

Three handwriting experts were convinced that the signatures on the two checks and the receipts were forgeries, while Coral Blaine and Lundgren were just as strongly convinced the man they had talked to could have been no one but Chapman. Police had followed my trail back and forth across Florida, and while they had a dozen different versions as to my age and the color of my hair and eyes, the composite picture was that of Chapman, just as she had said it would be. The only things the witnesses were certain about were the wrong things, the ones I'd deliberately planted.

Chapman Enterprises was being liquidated by his father. Coral Blaine was gone from Thomaston. The whole senseless tragedy was complete, except for *how*, and that was unanswerable. But they did know who had been responsible for it all, because she had admitted it—the rejected and embittered woman who had been his mistress.

I rented a car and drove upstate, buying the flowers at one of the towns along the way. The name of the little community was Bedford Springs, but it wasn't on any of the highway maps, and all I knew about it was that it was some fifteen miles from Thomaston.

I'd puzzled for a long time as to why she'd wanted to be buried in a backwoods churchyard in Louisiana when her family would be in Cleveland. Then I'd finally decided perhaps something good had happened to her in Bedford Springs at some time in the past. I'd understood her coming to San Francisco, where she'd been married to Forsyth, and the trip down to Stanford, and what she was doing in those last few days when she knew it couldn't go on any longer.

It was late afternoon when I found it. It was miles off the highway, and there wasn't any town at all, just a white frame church set under some oaks in gently rolling country of small farms and hardwood and pine. There weren't even any houses near it. It was late April now, and all the trees were fully leaved. I got out of the car in front of the church and walked down to the little cemetery that was fenced and appeared to be well tended. Across the back of it was a row of slender arbor vitae and beyond that a wooded ravine and tall trees, and off to my right about a half mile a man was plowing on the side of a sandhill with a mule. There was no sound at all except that of the birds and the trickling of water somewhere in the ravine.

I found her grave, and put the flowers on it, and looked around, thinking it was one of the most remote and beautiful places I'd ever seen. Then suddenly I knew why she had remembered it in that final hour of her torment in the hotel room in San Francisco, and what it had represented to her. Peace. Just peace. It hit me without any warning, as it had in the El Prado Bar, and I started crying. I couldn't help it.

I sat in the car and stared across the railroad tracks at the cotton gin. On the side of it was a large sign that said *Chapman Enterprises*. The day I ever felt any guilt for him, I thought—that would really be the day. I'd never owned any part of her for an hour, and she'd given him all of herself for six years and then he'd thrown her away as if she were something you merely bought and used like an expendable item of inventory.

The town was as familiar as if I'd lived in it for years. The street names clicked and fell in place in my mind as I drove across it. I found her house and parked in front of it in the lengthening shadows of the elms. It was a two-story white frame with a neat lawn and some nasturtium beds in front, only four blocks from the center of town. When the weather was nice she sometimes walked to work. I got out of the car.

Somehow it wasn't late afternoon now, but early morning, and I could see her ahead of me in the sunlight with that beautiful walk she had and the erect, patrician slenderness and the smartness that must have appeared so out of place in this little farming town, and the sleek dark head, complete with the shallow saucer of a hat slanted across the side of it, the one she'd worn the night she came back from New York. And, somehow, even though I was behind her I could see the fine blue eyes that were almost but not quite violet and their nearly unshakable self-possession and poise, and the cool and ineffably feminine humor in them as she leaned her chin on her laced fingers that afternoon in Key West and asked, *And what other personality problems do you have, Mr. Hamilton, besides shyness?* And the same eyes filled with the sheen of tears as she shook her head there in the hotel room in San Francisco. *No, Jerry. It's too late*. Our fine pink flamingo is made of concrete, and I can't carry it any longer. But you let me have it, and I'll find a place to put it down.

This was the square, in the center of town. I turned right at the corner, and walked along the south side of it, facing the entrance to the courthouse where sparrows fluttered about the eaves. How many thousand times had she stepped along this walk, on Monday mornings and Saturday nights and the white noons of southern Augusts? The doorway was between Barton's Jewelry Store and the Esquire Shop. I went up the stairs where the slender heels had tapped, and turned right in the corridor at the top. The etched glass of the doorway bore the gold-leaf legend: *Chapman Enterprises*. I pushed it open and went in.

The brown-haired woman in the anteroom looked up pleasantly, and asked, "Yes, sir. May I help you?"

The inner door was closed. I crossed to it and pushed it open. Mrs. English was watching me with a puzzled frown. "I beg your pardon," she said. "Were you looking for someone?"

There were the three desks, and the safe, and the water cooler, and all the steel filing cabinets, and to the right the two windows looking out into the square. At the third desk, near the door going into his private office, a brown-eyed girl with a little dusting of freckles across her nose was busy at her typewriter. She looked up questioningly.

The large desk in the center was hers. I crossed to it, and touched it with my hands. Barbara Cullen had quit typing now, and was staring at me, and I was aware that Mrs. English had got up and was standing in the doorway.

"Could I help you?" Barbara Cullen asked.

In the slow unfolding of horror I seemed to be standing outside myself, watching what I was doing but without any power to control or change a movement of it. I might still get away, if I ran now without opening my mouth, but there didn't seem to be anything I could do about it. I stood there, merely feeling the desk with my hands. Then I crossed the room to Chapman's office, and went inside. Opening the center drawer of his desk, I lifted out the pencil drawer and turned it upside down to stare at the little card that was taped to the bottom of it.

Right to thirty-two, left two turns to nineteen—

Both girls were in the doorway behind me. They gasped, and when I turned they looked frightened and started to back away.

"Who are you?" Barbara Cullen asked nervously. "What do you want here?"

I went back to the large desk in the center of the room and stood behind it, looking out at the square. Mrs. English retreated to the anteroom. Barbara stood as far away as she could, staring at me. The silence stretched out and tightened across the room.

I gripped the edge of the desk. *God, there must be something left of her, somewhere.* She'd sat here for six years, with her purse in that lower left-hand drawer, touching this, putting papers in that basket, picking up the phone— She'd sat here, where I was standing now, and when she glanced up she looked out that window at spring sunlight and the slow eddying of traffic in winter rains and high school football rallies and funeral processions and the blue October sky.

I stared down at the whitening knuckles of my hands. "Barbara," I said, "it wasn't her fault. You've got to believe it. Some way, I've got to make them understand—"

She cried out. I looked up then, and her eyes were widening with horror. "How did you know my name?" she asked. But it wasn't that. It was the voice; she'd already recognized it.

"Sit down, Barbara," I said. "I won't hurt you. But I've got to tell somebody. I can't stand it any longer. I can't let her go on lying there taking all the blame, when it was my fault. I could have saved her. She couldn't help herself—"

I heard Mrs. English dialing, out in the anteroom, but I went on talking, faster now, the words becoming a flood. All that time in Mexico hadn't meant a thing; you never whipped it or drove it away. You merely drove it underground, into your subconscious, where it could fester beyond your reach.

When the men came up the stairs and into the room behind me I was still talking, and Barbara was listening, but the look of horror on her face was giving way to something else. Maybe it was pity.

THE END

CHARLES WILLIAMS BIBLIOGRAPHY (1909-1975)

NOVELS

Hill Girl (1951)
Big City Girl (1951)
River Girl (1951; reprinted as *The Catfish Tangle*, UK, 1963)
Hell Hath No Fury (1953; reprinted as *The Hot Spot*, UK, 1965)
Nothing in Her Way (1953)
A Touch of Death (1954; reprinted as *Mix Yourself a Redhead*, UK, 1965)
Go Home, Stranger (1954)
Scorpion Reef (1955; reprinted as *Gulf Coast Girl*, 1956)
The Big Bite (1956)
The Diamond Bikini (1956)
Girl Out Back (1958; reprinted as *Operator*, UK, 1958)
Man on the Run (1958; reprinted as *Man in Motion*, UK, 1959)
Talk of the Town (1958; reprinted as *Stain of Suspicion*, 1973)
All the Way (1958; reprinted as *The Concrete Flamingo*, UK, 1960)
Uncle Sagamore and His Girls (1959)
Aground (1960)
The Sailcloth Shroud (1960)
The Long Saturday Night (1962; reprinted as *Finally Sunday!*, UK; and *Confidentially Yours*, both 1983)
Dead Calm (1963)
The Wrong Venus (1966; reprinted as *Don't Just Stand There*, UK, 1967)
And the Deep Blue Sea (1971)
Man on a Leash (1973)

STORIES

The Strike (*Cosmopolitan*, 1954)
And Share Alike (*Manhunt*, 1954; condensed *Touch of Death*)
Flight to Nowhere (*Manhunt*, 1955)
The Big Bite (*Manhunt*, 1956; condensed version)
Hell Hath No Fury (*Nugget*, 1957, abridged)
Operation (*Cosmopolitan*, 1957; condensed *Girl Out Back*)
Stain of Suspicion (*Cosmopolitan*, 1958; condensed *Talk of the Town*)
The Sailcloth Shroud (*Cosmopolitan*, 1959; condensed version)
Aground (*Cosmopolitan*, 1960; condensed version)
The Long Saturday Night (*Cosmopolitan*, 1961; condensed version)
Pacific Honeymoon (*Cosmopolitan*, 1963; condensed *Dead Calm*)
The Wrong Venus (*Cosmopolitan*, 1966; condensed version)

Made in the USA
Columbia, SC
07 November 2021